LOGIC OF THE BEAST

A Campfire Story

By David Garey

Cover Illustration by Christa McLaughlin

Order this book online at www.trafford.com
or email orders@trafford.com

Most Trafford titles are also available at major online book retailers.

Note for Librarians: A cataloguing record for this book is available from Library and Archives Canada at www.collectionscanada.ca/amicus/index-e.html

Printed in Victoria, BC, Canada.

ISBN: 978-1-4269-2386-9 (sc)
ISBN: 978-1-4269-2387-6 (hc)

Library of Congress Control Number: 2009913758

Our mission is to efficiently provide the world's finest, most comprehensive book publishing service, enabling every author to experience success. To find out how to publish your book, your way, and have it available worldwide, visit us online at www.trafford.com

Trafford rev. 3/24/2010

www.trafford.com

North America & international
toll-free: 1 888 232 4444 (USA & Canada)
phone: 250 383 6864 • fax: 812 355 4082

FORWARD

In May of 1983, a slowing economy in the Texas "Oilpatch" led me to venture from the little town of Kermit, to the tiny resort town of Belden, California, with the hope of some future in mining for placer gold. My first summer in California gold country didn't profit me much, but the next year I was back with a used three inch gold dredge, and I spent the four and one half month dredge season in a stretch of river near Belden that other dredgers had already tried their luck in. Being told it had already been worked to death, I surprised the crowd by finding some nice little jewelry sized nuggets, but I seemed to have had an unfair number of dredge breakdowns, nine to be exact, and the crowd down at Belden was keeping track. I have to say that no matter how much of the real world a miner has to deal with in the light of day, the gold always seems to get heavier after you've had a few beers in the Belden bar, that is in the imagination of your future production, and public sympathy will sometimes get you a few beers. One afternoon I was sitting at a picnic table in Belden town listening to the mining partner of Whitey Mauer talk to some tourists. Whitey owned a serious piece of mining equipment, an eight inch dredge run by a small car engine, and his partner

Joe was answering some questions from the tourists about the dredge's production. One lady asked Joe, "Who is the miner they call 'Hard Luck'?" Joe grinned and pointed at my head. Hell of a way to learn your handle! Well, it was good natured humor, a few giggles and guffaws to be had, but down at the end of the line there ain't nothing funny about being broke. There are many that will back me up on that. There comes a point in time when a man pursuing gold may sit down and think to himself, 'What would it be like to be a lucky man?' Since 1849, there have been many who have asked themselves that one. In December of 1995, my luck improved a little. On page 26 of the November 1996 California Mining Journal, there is a color photo of a large gold-quartz specimen I found with a metal detector in a desert far from the Sierra Nevada Mountains. That specimen bought some groceries, paid vehicle insurance, and allowed a few luxuries, but in the fourteen summers of running the six inch dredge I bought in 1990, I have to admit that there have been more times of lean than plenty.

The story I have written was inspired by that line of thinking, that speculation on what it would be like to be a lucky man. The main character, young Thomas Hendrick, desperately needs to be a lucky man. Don't you know, gold solves all problems. But don't you know, gold comes with a price. The characters in this book and their personalities were invented to make the story work, and are in no way intended represent any real people, living or dead. The towns mentioned are very real. Downieville is one of the best known 49'er mining towns. There is realistic language used in this campfire story, so I must say it is a P.G. rated novel. The book, "Bury my Heart at Wounded Knee" by Dee Brown contains descriptions of a massacre in the chapter "Little Crows War" that inspired a conversation in my book about that massacre. All other historical references are from word of mouth, hearsay, and are not to be taken as text book accurate.

That first summer in I spent in California I heard tell that the only sensible way to mine for gold was to find some wealthy investors and mine the investors. I guess I was just one of those fools who thought they could jump into a California river, roll boulders around underwater, and dredge up a living. Another clever little saying in gold country: "believe ten percent of what you hear and fifty percent of what you see". Keeping that in consideration, you should appreciate that the word "fiction" gives a fella a lot of leeway when it comes to contriving a campfire story.

"Hard Luck Dave"

ONE

"Damn it. Every damn time. You were talking my ear off." The man's heart jumped a little as he corrected the skid off the pavement that teased the couple with a view of the drop to the river. The woman was calmer, holding back a laugh, substituting a pretty smirk.

"We'll be the talk of Downieville, and I was not talking your ear off. Poor Tommy and Darcy, 'Dead Man's Curve' gets another. Poor lost souls to lay to rest in the canyon." She was enjoying it.

"Were already the talk," he grinned. "This one horse town has to get around to us on a regular basis. They need to expand and take in some of Alleghany's gossip."

"Don't be cynical Tommy; you know that most of these people like you."

"They like Darcy; I'm just a tag along." It was a kidding cynicism. They were both calming down from the little bought of fear as he slowed down to final grade of California highway 49 that introduces every new motorist to the little town at the confluence of the Downie and the North Yuba rivers, nestled in it's almost alpine looking Sierra Valley.

"You'll miss it every time," she changed the subject back. "And I warn you every trip that you'll miss it, guaranteed."

"I'll be missing that curve when we're ninety, girl. It's going to be one of those little rituals old couples go through."

"No, you'll put us in the river before then." No smile, too serious. "I don't want to live to be ninety."

"I'll never put you in the river, lover. I'd put myself in first." He tried to catch a glance, but she avoided him to yell "Hey" to someone she knew.

"Let's drop the subject," she pleaded. "Let's not talk about the river, ok?" He'd planned on being back working underwater on the 'morrow. It had been two seasons since he'd dived. He had to talk her back into letting him. "Just keep a lookout for Agnes," she teased as he pulled their '49 Chevy Styleline Coupe into the dirt drive. Agnes was on another drunk.

"You go first!"

"I'll hold the door for you, scardy cat. Dave called and said he was coming up, remember? She took him out to lunch, I'll bet." The man pondered on their mutual distrust of her mother. It was common knowledge in the little town that Agnes had caused Darcy some humiliation and misery over the years. He believed that Darcy's personality had developed mostly from the influence of her father, who had died before Tom had met Darcy. He had promised himself the two years they lived together he would get her out of Agnes' house. Some form of cruel fate held them still, he believed, nickeled and dimed them into submission. Or, perhaps, he would sometimes admit to himself, it was the gold.

Darcy's ex-boyfriend, Dave Morrow, had called the day before to say he would drop by on one of his real estate business trips to the area. He visited out of politeness as the friend he tried to make himself to them both, though he had come to be wary of Agnes. Dave now had a wife in Oroville. That would not faze Agnes, who loved to harp on how much more she admired Dave that Tom. Agnes was becoming very manic depressive, and at times downright maniacal. After one of the couples shopping trips to Grass Valley, the month before, a drunken Agnes met Tom at the back door carrying groceries and stuck a loaded little break-down five shot 32 pistol in his face. "You waltz in my back door anytime you feel like it, and that is going to stop." Liquor always made her mean, but he had never seen her like this. "You're dishonoring my daughter in this town, and I am tired of it." The neighbors could easily hear; Darcy had just passed through a minute before. Tom lived with Darcy, and Darcy lived with her mother, everyone knew. Dave had also lived a short time with Darcy, but Dave was the son of a wealthy real estate salesman. "You ring the doorbell, or better yet…" she lost track. He could smell the vodka. The doorbell had been broken forever, and he had his own key, she knew. Usually, a drunken Agnes would sit and stare through the screen door of her 1860's era, two bedroom wooden house that had been the sore thumb of the neighborhood until Tom and Darcy had renovated it. Most of Downieville residents kept up their little original homes that helped promote tourism in the historic mining town. Downieville-ites generally proclaim their community the focal point of that great mass insanity the schoolbooks refer to as the "California Gold Rush".

"Darcy, your mother has a gun on me. I'm serious; she's got a fricken pistol. Come and get this crazy woman off me!" His voice was too shrill, his hands were shaking a little, he was losing it.

"Mother, leave him alone." She wasn't taking it seriously. Maybe she didn't hear the part about the gun. The hammer clicked and the tiny barrel came up almost to his right eye.

"I'm an old fashioned woman; I always handle my problems one way or another, whatever it takes. I guess that you haven't figured that out yet. The next time you think that you can just walk through my back door without knocking..., I shoot trespassers." Getting shot on her property wouldn't be difficult for Sheriff Ramey to prosecute as a murder, and Darcy's friends might enjoy the excuse to lynch Agnes, but that wasn't going to do him any good right now.

Dave Morrow would have been greeted with a hug and a kiss, which he detested. Agnes made as much of an embarrassing spectacle as she could at his visits. "You're always welcome to spend the night. The key is in one of the birdfeeders, just for you." Dave was such a prosperous young man.

"Darcy!" He didn't have the slightest idea of what brought this on. His eyes were stinging, he felt like a humiliated puppy. She pulled back her arm, and Tom mistook the move as a gesture to pass. He turned to far to catch the swing as she brought the weapon down toward his temple, smacking him on the cheek and landing him on his knees, blood dripping into his undershirt. Next moment he was launching towards Darcy at the breezeway, realizing it might come down to blows between mother and daughter. Darcy's glare convinced the cackling old woman to spirit the pistol out through the back door, for fear of what her daughter might be tempted to make use of it. She lacked the nerve to return for two days, leaving the couple to take advantage. At the end of their short reprieve, while lying in each other's arms, the woman confessed "I wanted to kill her. Oh God, we only say these things. She always knows how far she can go."

"Forget it, Foxtail. This is the year we escape. That's a promise!" Foxtail was old miner slang for a trail of powder gold at the bottom of a good pan, the nickname Darcy's father gave her at age three. "We just need to be patient. The third time is always the charm. This is going to be the year."

"How many times have I heard that? You're getting the fever worse that those old timers at the Quartz. That's fine. I got you into it, and you'll get over it. You try one more time, Tommy, but whatever comes out of it, it will be the last time in this river. That's got to be a promise. We can always go live with your mother. You can do something with your life, Tom!"

"If you don't know what you're doing, just ask someone" could be the motto of most small towns. Little goes unnoticed in Downieville, and whether the gossip is malicious or sympathetic, it can always be counted on to be. There was actually little feedback from the pistol incident, but there are always the diehard mouth movers, which in Tom's case were usually orchestrated by Tom's seemingly self appointed antagonist, Vernon Fickett. An Alleghany boy, Vernon sought alliances wherever opportunity presented itself, but even Agnes disassociated herself from the "town weasel". "The key to success comes in knowing everybody else's business," Vernon would joke with his acquaintances, and he lived to prove the effectuation of his bar room advice. "You will never make it from the sweat of your own brow. Men who make it always make it from the sweat of other men's brows." To that credo, Agnes would have heartily agreed, but she despised Vernon.

There were two versions of the pistol incident going around; common sense killed Vernon's version early on, something about a threat to Agnes that Tom never really made. To add grisly humor to the gossip, one of Tom's new acquaintances, Lou Montgomery, also from Alleghany, aggravated things by making threats against Vernon in two bars, hinting that his mouth night get closed by force of fist. "Lou," Tom pleaded one night in the Saint Charles bar after buying him a beer, "do me a favor, man, just let Vernon rant on. I don't take him serious."

"He is going to keep his mouth shut as far as Darcy is concerned. Talk can get a man killed around here. Didn't they ever tell you that?" Lou slapped him on the back and walked away with an almost sinister chuckle.

"Whoa, Wild West!" Tom tried to kid. He never really knew why Vernon targeted him the first year Darcy brought him up from Marysville. Fickett probably thought that Tom fitted a goody-two shoes flatlander stereotype, or wished he would. Jealousy will always make a man enemies. There had been enough local females inclined to flirt with Tom until Darcy made it plain he was taken. He had heard that one night Vernon's girlfriend, Elaine, made a remark complimenting Tom's good looks, and drunken Fickett demanded she stuff her mouth with toilet paper, embarrassing her in front of her friends. Vernon definitely went out of his way to badmouth Tom, and there was always someone willing to repeat the gossip. Tom worried that Lou might lose his temper and beat Vernon up simply for Darcy's sake, and that, he feared, would lower Tom's esteem in the small town. He could not motivate himself to just go out and start something with Fickett. As much as Tom appreciated the advice and alliance Lou offered, he would always be suspicious. Most of his new acquaintances in Downieville had been met through Darcy. From the get go she had made a point of telling him about the two men she had slept with before him, which did not include Lou. Lou had a long time crush on Darcy, though he was six years older; now the infatuation seemed to have evolved into a protective friendship to them both, or so Darcy insisted. But Tom was skeptical. Lou would always be Darcy's great admirer, which made good gossip in both towns. Lou was as respected an Alleghany boy in Downieville as Vernon was despised. To Tom, that seemed quite in line with the competitive relationship between two brother mining communities separated by a mountain range. Both were clannish, intensely proud of their niche in history, and capable of being serious to the point of downright hostility on the subject of local enterprise since the beginning: gold. It was an enigma, but he'd take it as a challenge, tying to figure out how to become one of the ordinary in the little town.

"You need to prove yourself to these people, Tommy," Darcy explained the first time he introduced the subject of marriage. He had anticipated she would welcome the idea of legitimizing their relationship. “I’ve lived here all of my life; we need to wait until we get established. There are people here who look after me, besides my mother. They’ll be watching you until we prove you a good emigrant.” That was somewhat strange and threatening, being referred to as an emigrant from 80 miles away. In the years since he had come to better understand.

TWO

He had met Darcy at a Baptist pot luck dinner in his hometown of Marysville on an April Sunday afternoon in fifty-seven. Church going was not the young man's more enthusiastic pursuit at age nineteen, but he made a point of accompanying his mother, the widow Rene. She seemed to him the epitome of dignity and resolve, sitting with him, her only child, for Sunday sermons. The pew would become a little sanctuary to reflect and meditate through the less exciting sermons. When he wasn't considering his own uncertain future, he would acknowledge the possibility he might acquire a step-dad sometime down the line. He would have a hard time dealing with that. In the four years since they had brought his father back from Korea in a box, there had been several offers of male companionship for his mother. Friendship is exactly the point she had allowed the offers to be taken, with the exception of Max Ingram, whom she dated on and off, but had no plans to marry at present.

The afternoon potluck held both incentive and despair. Despair might be named Emily Honsacker. Freckled, red haired, green eyed, but just plain, she would hound him for minutes on end in such an embarrassing attempt to corral him that he would often end up bolting for a hideout. Incentive was named Carrie Honsacker, Emily's older sister. Three years older that Tom, freckled, red-haired, and unfairly beautiful next to Emily, with green eyes that sometimes teased Tom. He had one date with her, an accidental meeting that turned into an afternoon at the movies, and then she cooled to him.

When Carrie left the potluck with a new 26 year old boyfriend, Tom made some ridiculous excuse to Rene and headed out. He would walk the distance to Ruley's Drive In in about fifteen minutes. He could count on the Anglo and Hispanic crowd that hung out on Sunday afternoons at the Hispanic owned burger hop. Some, the lucky ones, driving their own cars or trucks. Some boys with white t-shirts and a "Lucky Strike" cigarette pack rolled up in their right sleeve, a statement he felt no need to copy. Some with rolled up jeans, girls usually with full length dresses, and some of the less inhibited in tight women's pants. If he was lucky he'd run into the right crowd and get invited to a beach party down on the river bottoms. He'd worry about getting to work on time at the Chevron station on Monday morning when the time came. As he walked past the cinderblock Sunday school wing, he noticed two girls across the street messing with the back wheel hub on a rusted out two door, faded green, "49 Ford. "Jamie Lineman, come by and ask my boss for a job. I can get you on". Jamie's hands were trashed.

"Be sarcastic Tom, don't offer to help."

"I've got it, Jamie." The other woman turned to look and brushed a streak of brake shoe dust on a sweaty cheek.

"Did you pop a return spring, or lose the adjuster?"

"So that's what it is called. We wired it with a coat hanger wire, thank you. I can make it back on three brakes, Jamie."

"Maybe it's you I should get on at work. Are you a born mechanic?"

"It's obvious you ain't or you would have offered to help." But she was still smiling despite herself, a smile that complicated a pretty face and soft, fine black hair.

Tom crouched down beside them. "I guess I got here too late. You grease monkeys need to clean up."

They all stood up and the new girl threw some pliers and a screw driver on the back seat and slammed the door. "Grease monkeys! I came down to go to a dance, Jamie. What are we doing here? Piss on this noise," she said almost under her breath in a little fit.

"Darcy!" Jamie said soothingly.

"He doesn't know how far I drove with that noise."

"That's right, he doesn't." His response was something of an involuntary reaction, reaching over and grabbing the woman's hand. He let go as she turned toward him, and he put on his best smile. She was somewhat short, slim, narrow hips in worn cowgirl jeans, a faded blue and white cowgirl shirt, and cheap shoes. She had dark eyes, fierce for a moment, but they gave in, and she broke away from the staring contest.

"Are you a cowgirl?"

"I'm a country girl, alright."

"Darcy is from Downieville. She came down to see me and I told her about the potluck." Jamie explained.

"Downieville? I know where that is, that's just past Coyoteville, right?" Suddenly, he was regretting pressing the sarcasm. The woman folded her arms and stared at Jamie with what he interpreted as a 'let's lose the clown' inference, so he tried to maneuver with, "I'll get your tire back on before everything gets eaten up inside." He had it back together with the car jack stashed in impressive time, and he held his palms up to show off his chivalry.

"Is your mother still here? I know where you were headed!" Jamie asked as they crossed the street.

"Probably," seemed to answer both questions.

"How about Emily?" She grinned at Darcy, and he didn't answer. The girls went their own way inside, and he was getting antsy about Ruley's, but it was no contest. He had to try and get her phone number. When he caught up with them at the food tables, they were whispering in collusion, and he thought there might be the faintest little smile directed his way when she noticed him staring. Suddenly, it occurred there might be competition around, and sure enough Jamie introduces her to handsome, arrogant Randy Kramer, who notices Tom and moves to block his view. "Tommy, has your mother left?" Emily caught him off guard. He hadn't seen her earlier, and this he knew, was leading to complete aggravation.

"Yeah, she's gone. I was about to leave, maybe I'll see you and Tisha at Ruley's." Emily's fair looking friend Tisha seemed more attentive to the conversation in Randy's direction.

"You know I'm not allowed there. Stick around, Tommy. We're having the youth fellowship at five. Please, you hardly ever come." He wouldn't have minded a friendship, but her predatory tactics were so wanton, she made him the butt of some of the youth group's humor. Grabbing her arm in a gesture of companionship, he said "I might stay, or I might get a ride with you and Tisha. Did she bring her brother's car?" Emily's countenance exuded the pleasure of this much attention even as she had to confess, "We got a ride."

It was getting late and the crowd at Ruley's might be winding down. If he stayed, Emily wouldn't give him a minutes rest. He headed for the twin glass doors at the far end of the hall. "Tom, would you like a ride to your burger hop?" The new girl grabbed a fold of his shirt sleeve just before the glass doors. She had to move with some purpose to catch up to him; he was in his Emily evasion stride. He stared back with such an intense smile that he forced hers into a blush, and she grabbed his hand and walked him through the door simply as a means of diverting the tension.

Jamie caught up with them, almost running, just as Darcy let go. "So, you two are holding hands already," she teased, but a look from Darcy removed the grin. "I'll tell you what, I can afford some malts." Tom said. "There is usually something happening down at the river. If I get us invited, would you two like to go?" He realized in afterthought that they were more likely to get invited than him. He might end up seeing them leave without him.

"I've got a long drive back, Tom. But, thank you. Do you know where there is a country and western dance this evening? Jamie was sure on the phone, but now she's evading the subject now that she has got me down here." If she had come with a dance in mind, she was surely destitute judging by the clothes.

"I'll find out at Ruley's." He situated himself in the backseat and leaned a little over the front seat between them, careful not to get too pushy.

"We won't go out drinking, Tom," Jamie warned. "Someone always brings beer down to the river."

"You're right, they do. Sometimes." He could go for a beer. "Pull in by that piece of junk." The new girl obeyed and parked beside a "42 rust bucket, Ford truck.

"Hey Jamie, Tom. I saved you a spot!" the heavy young man greeted them.

"Hey yourself, Matt. This is Darcy McEarl, my roommate from Chico State last year. Darcy, Matthew was one of our football heroes. He was one of the Mechanics I was telling you about."

"Hello, Matt," Darcy said with a polite smile.

Tom figured Matt didn't pose much competition with his slight pot belly under a football sweater and his scraggly, curly black hair. Easy going Matt made the rounds every Sunday afternoon in the junky, but sure running truck that was his trademark. Matt put his burger back on the metal door tray and slammed his weight against a jammed right door three times to get it open.

"He was top senior lineman," Tom explained, as Matt leaned his two hundred and fifty pound rear end against his truck's left front fender, folded his arms, and began with "How'd you manage this, Tommy?"

"We invited Tom. I'm always having to give him a ride somewhere," Jamie explained as she glanced at Tom with an expression that implied he best not throw out any smart remarks, about the same time Suzy Hernandez made it to the driver's side to take their order. Sunday afternoon flirting's with sixteen year old Suzy were just part of the incentives for Tom at Ruley's. The Martinez family, the new owners, had just recently painted the trim with some donated off pink to try to match the hop girls' pink dresses. "Sad," Suzy had warned them, pretty well reflecting general opinion, but the mistake cost them no customers.

Across town, a more modern burger hop did its share of business, but Ruley's, formerly Danny's Place, was the place. The Martinez family had simply bought into success and still did not fathom why it did so well. Apology's for holes in the vinyl booths or chips in the linoleum got an "Are you serious?" response. The food was only fair, but the owners' were making improvements, and the hop girls knew how to make tips. It didn't really matter one way or the other. It would have taken some effort to ever drive away business.

Suzy opened Darcy's door and ordered, "Let me back here."

"Suzy!" Jamie warned as the girl bounced down beside Tom. "Carl Martinez will fire you."

"I'm on break. I have to see my pobrecito," she said with an exaggerated Spanish accent, one that she used only part of the time, and grabbed him for a kiss on the lips, something she had never done before. Tom wasn't as inclined to run as fast from Suzy as he was from Emily. Suzy was a very well developed, exotic looking young senorita, who enjoyed the best tips average at Ruley's. She was teasing the girls as well, but when she realized she was embarrassing Tom, she backed off. Darcy was obviously uncomfortable with the situation, and stared at Jamie with a frown. "Fifteen will get you twenty, Tom," Jamie grinned intensely.

"You don't need to worry, Jamie. I won't get Tommy in trouble. I'll get your order, OK? Tommy?" She put her hand on his shoulder in an almost mothering fashion. Tom was just recovering his grit, grinning back at Jamie.

"I don't believe that I ever met a child molester before," Matt had to add in a slow droll that got Jamie coughing with laughter.

Tom laid his hand on Darcy's shoulder and explained, "We're always clowning around here. What would you like?"

"Vanilla Malts are fine," Darcy answered.

"Oh shit, here comes trouble!" Suzy blurted as she got out, and then "Excuse me" as she walked away.

"Forget it, Suz. I just met a pretty woman who tells me I piss her off. I imagine she cusses too, on occasion." Darcy turned and looked at him with an expression he was used to getting from Emily, but it was profoundly more effective coming from this woman. "It's Hiame Esposito, Matt," Tom said as he recognized the heavyset man ambling along the back fence, trying to avoid a forest of prickly poppy.

"I'm gone, son. I'm not dealing with his shit," Matt said.

"No, don't leave, Matt. I'll just talk to him a little bit." But Matt got back in his truck.

"Hiame isn't welcome with the Martinez's," Jamie explained to Darcy. "He's been 86'd twice. He starts things." The heavy man's stomach bounced as he trudged; he'd gained too much weight since high school. Matt and Hiame never got along at football practice; Tom tried to maintain neutrality.

"Hey 'Mechanic'", Tom called as he slipped out past Darcy's seat.

"Gringo!" Hiame recognized him and attempted a reenactment of his old line drive. Tom knew now he had made a mistake getting out, but it was too late for any dignified retreat, and he found himself slammed into the car body and lifted nearly to the roof.

"Hiame!" Jamie said tersely. "You don't know this lady!"

"I'm sorry. I'm just kidding around. I'm really not here for fun today. Is Mr. Martinez around? I need a job, man. Friday was the hardest day of my life. Did you hear what happened?"

"I heard your father's business burned down," Jamie said sympathetically.

"Oh no!" Darcy reacted.

"God-Damn, Hiame! I never heard," Tom said.

Most whites wouldn't have much to do with Hiame after his high school football fame subsided. He and Matt had been the top offensive lineman in their senior year winning season. A local radio sports-caster had coined the title "Mechanics" for them. They had enjoyed as much notoriety as the quarterback, these two powerful players who opened the opposition's line time after time. But after graduation, Hiame's half brother Al made news getting arrested for dealing heroin in Sacramento, and although Hiame steered the path of Catholic decency, he developed a reputation for going through the few jobs he had been offered because of personality clashes he tended to instigate. One Sunday afternoon Hiame invited Tom down to a Mexican pig roast on the river, and introduced him to kinfolk and friends, and so Tom tried to maintain friendly terms. Tom knew the business Jamie spoke of as a used furniture shop Hiame's father tried to support kids and relatives with. Hiame's married brother Rueben worked steady on a rice farm and helped them some; Tom had been told that Hiame's religious father refused anything that came from the drug dealing brother, Alfonse.

"I don't think Carl could give you anything if he wanted to, Hiame. I've been checking with Connie every weekend. Have you seen him lately? We can catch him at the coffee shop some Saturday morning." Connie the "con man", Marysville's spoiled rich boy, son of the biggest middleman in the rice and produce mainstay economy. Connie's friends coined "the con man" in high school, not for shady dealings, but simply because they said he could talk almost anyone into anything. Tall, blonde, blue-eyed handsome Connie wouldn't have much trouble talking the girls into anything. Head quarterback during a district winning season two years before Tom's senior year, Connie almost had to fight them off with a stick. Now he was moving into his father's shoes, managing and handling P.R. at the warehouse and rice storage facility he would someday inherit. Connie's old man was known as one of the hardest and meanest successes the town had. Connie's mother had a reputation for soothing things over with people who felt they'd been walked on.

'I wonder what it would be like to be that comfortable' Tom would think with a tinge of jealousy, but like most, he couldn't help but like the "con man". Connie had promised Tom a job at the first opening that came up, and he and his mother had made some visits to widow Rene that left her feeling especially cared for after Tom senior's death.

"He hasn't got anything for either of us right now, Tom. You know how tight it is."

"I don't know of anything going on. I'd like to move on to something better myself."

"You hang on to what you've got. As hard as jobs are to come by in this town, you need to take care of your mother. I'll find something. I'm a good Catholic. God will send me something. I just need to get off my fat ass and do a little hustling." A slight snicker from the girls. "I'm falling way behind. I'm not even married yet, and my cousin Jesus already has sixteen kids, and he's only twenty-six. I need to start making some little Mexicans." Jamie was cracking up severely, partially from the expression on Darcy's face. Darcy's frown might be the indication of the calculations going on in her head, but when she caught Tom's eye she had to stifle a laugh.

"You got this one good," Tom informed Hiame. "Hiame doesn't have a cousin Jesus, Darcy." Hiame's laughter seemed good natured enough; all three figured some of his misery had been soothed.

"My dear lady!" his countenance changed dramatically; even Tom was taken back with the put on as Hiame reached for Darcy's hand, snapped to attention, and bowed forward to kiss the hand in a remarkably chivalrous gesture for a fat man.

"You make a heavy Zorro," Tom had to point out as Hiame walked away. "Take it easy, Hiame."

"I'll take it any way I can get it." He grinned at Suzy as she slipped past him with the malts, whispering something under her breath that the girls would have preferred not to have heard.

"What's going on this evening, Suz? Is there a dance somewhere?" Tom asked as he paid for their drinks.

"There's a baille at the VFW Post. You're going to take them dancing? No, you wouldn't like that. They're old fogies. My parents go there. I mean, they're not fogies. You know what I mean. Sunday's not a good day. Maybe there's a square dance somewhere, but I don't know."

"Don't they have a Western dance in this town?" Darcy asked.

"That's usually Fridays and Saturdays. The Homestead Bar has a good crowd and a live band after six."

"That's alright, some other time."

"Soon, I'll take you both dancing, alright?" He didn't really prefer to go dancing. He might run into his mother at the Homestead, and she might embarrass him with another waltz lesson. He preferred to get invited to a barbeque on the river. Down on the river with the new girl would really impress the crowd. He'd have to make some phone calls.

"Are you sorry you ran into us, Tommy?" Jamie was intuitive. "I know you. You're always on the Yuba on a Sunday."

"Whenever I can get a ride. I'm glad I caught a ride here. Maybe you two should plan a trip to the beach. If we run into the right people, you know, we can play some volley ball or something. They're not a bad crowd, usually."

"Oh yeah, you know everyone, Thomas. Tell me something. Are you going to do the bridge? You remember me telling you about Danny Thomson and Rick Schwarz, Darcy? Tommy was there."

"And you were, too, Jamie. With a beer in your hand," Tom accused. "They're idiots. They started something that's going to get someone killed." Two drunken college freshmen on Spring break, jumping off the railroad bridge at dusk into spring high water. An off duty deputy sheriff decided to make an example and arrest them after their rescuers retrieved them downstream, and he asked them quite seriously as they coughed and spat if they still had scrotums. After the charges were dropped they bragged at having started the tradition, but it really could be credited to the original bridge construction crew. It was illegal now. "I don't need to lose my manhood to prove it."

Both girls were giggling. "There are better ways to prove your manhood in the river," Darcy remarked. "The men in my town mine the river, the North Yuba."

"In the river? How do you mine a river? Like the old Yuba River dredge?"

"No, I mean they dive. I have a friend named Ray who's working his claim on the Downie River this summer, and I'll ask him to give you a job. I think he'd do that for me. You'd be working for a percentage, not a salary."

"Sure, thanks." Tom was intrigued at the offer to visit her in her town, but not enthused at the idea of giving up job security for a gamble mining underwater, but he wasn't about to let her know. Now he'd get her number.

"What did you take at Chico State?" Matt had made it back to his strategic fender location.

"Business management and accounting," Darcy answered. "I still want to get my CPA. I had a job waiting for me at the Sixteen-to-One in their accounting department, but I quit and ruined my chances."

"She quit because Dave Morrow left her. She's a sharp cookie, Matt, and she deserves another chance."

"Jamie, please! Let's leave David out of it. That was as much my mother's doing as anything."

"What's the Sixteen-to-One?" Matt continued.

"It's a hard rock gold mine near Alleghany," Jamie explained for her. "They've always paid good wages, right on through the depression. Darcy was making excellent grades, even after they split up, but when she dropped out, well.., if she'd finished the semester, she could have had the job, even without a CPA. That fricken mother of hers, she scared David off, she's such a busybody."

"They don't need to know my life story. The Sixteen-to-One, that's another job I might be able to get you on, Tom, but it's awfully hard work, underground. I have the connections."

"There's no doubt about that. She's got the connections," Jamie added. "Here's your chance, Tom."

"Anytime, Darcy, I appreciate it. I'll try anything once, anything but the bridge."

"I'll put in a word for you too, Matt. Are you looking for work?" she added out of courtesy.

"Thank you. Not underground, Darcy. I'm kind of tied to this town. I own a business," he grinned.

"It's just as well, Matt. They're a tight crowd up there," Jamie explained. "That's the only thing, Tom. They're not fond of outsiders getting their gold. Darcy can straighten that out." In afterthought she realized the match-making implication, and avoided looking at Darcy.

"I've had some offers to help me get into college. My father died in 1953, and I've had loan offers from two of his friends. I don't really know what I want to do right now, but I know I don't like working for the man I work for."

"I feel the same way, Tom. I just don't know what I'm going to do next. I know I've got to get away from my mother. I can't take much more of her meddling bull-shit. This is her car, of course. I depend on her for everything, and that's got to stop. I'm sorry; I don't like to carry on. Let's change the subject."

"Don't be sorry, Darcy. You're with friends. What does she do? Tell Doctor Tom."

"OK, doc." She frowned and smiled at the same time. "She still doesn't give me a change to make my own decisions. She tried to run Dave's life, too, and Dave resented it. I love her, but I have to get away from her."

"She's a hard ass, Tom," Jamie explained. "You'll understand when you meet her."

"I can't imagine. My mother's been my best friend since my Dad died, except, maybe, for one time. I always ask her for advice."

"Then you're lucky," Darcy sounded edgy. "Let's talk about something else."

"How about a movie?" Tom offered. "I know Jamie likes drive-ins."

"Uh, Tommy, loose lips sink ships," Jamie warned.

"Are you going to take me too, Tommy boy?" Matt teased.

"You won't fit in her car."

"I've got to start back before dark, Tom. It's a long drive." Darcy sounded unhappy. It occurred to him that she'd be leaving out much later from a dance.

"Give me your number, Darcy, and come back down Saturday."

"You can reach me through Jamie. I'll be back sometime, but I can't make plans. The gas costs a fortune."

'Typical female,' he thought.

"Have you heard from Barbara? Someone told me she came back for a visit," Jamie asked in obvious indifference to Darcy. She was lying about the visit rumor. Barbara had been Tom's next door neighbor tomboy friend for years. She ran with Tom's elementary kid crowd, and a kid's friendship is exactly what she left Tom remembering four years before when her parents moved her to Florida. He'd gotten one letter from her, and then out of sight, out of mind.

"Naw, she never made it. I've been thinking I'd like to get out of this town. Maybe she'll invite me to Florida for a summer." Matt snickered, and Jamie had to grin.

"Alright, Jamie, don't push me!" It was too obvious. "We'll plan something sometime, Tom. Right now, I don't even have the money to fix the brakes."

"You come down Saturday, and I'll fix the brakes, and pay for the gas."

"You can't turn that down!" Jamie warned.

"We'll see."

"Tom's a good mechanic," Matt joined in the conspiracy. "He apprenticed with one of the best mechanics in Marysville: me."

Ruley's speaker system, silent all afternoon, finally started crackling. The first tune had to be "Teddy Bear". "Shhh," Darcy begged. "I love this." Cars had come and gone, people known and unknown had passed, but now the sight of an off the showroom floor turquoise and white Chevy Bel Air convertible approaching immediately distracted the conversation.

"Here he is, Darcy," Jamie announced. "Come with me," grabbing her by the arm.

"So what? You go talk to him." The tug on her arm turned into a little wrestling match, with Jamie tickling Darcy's ribs for advantage.

"Can I get in on this?" Tom laughed.

"You're embarrassing me!"

"Don't I always? Come and talk to him. You're too shy."

Connie the "con man" and his fiancée, Beatrice, had pulled in just past a Volkswagen, Beatrice wearing her trademark white scarf and white horn rim glasses, looking as aloof as possible. Jamie pushed Darcy out her door and continued pushing past the Volkswagen, and Tom could tell Darcy wasn't enjoying it.

"He's been here a minute and he's already stolen both my females," Tom complained to Matt.

"You haven't staked any claims, son."

"I don't know the first thing about the mining laws."

"You'd better learn, before someone jumps your claim!"

Tom got out and leaned against the driver's side. "It does my heart good to see them aggravate that stuck up girlfriend of his. She hates it when the females stampede on him." Both girls were right at Connie's door, Jamie pressing the conversation, and Connie obviously enjoying the attention. Beatrice had a choice of facing the girls or turning Tom's way. Tom moved forward to try to catch her line of sight, and gave her an exaggerated smile and wave. She tilted her glasses and decided the girls were better viewing.

"She's not bad looking," Tom continued. "I wouldn't mind getting in her panties."

"I wouldn't want to. She's a Nazi. She should chase after his father. That would be a good match."

"Yeah, that's strange. Matters of the heart. It must have something to do with strange fate."

"You'd better stop thinking fate and start thinking line drive."

"I'll get her to visit. Whatever it takes, even if I have to give up Sunday's on the river."

"The world must be coming to an end."

Tom decided to rescue Connie and walked over. "Howdy, Tom. How's your mother?"

"Yes, how is Rene, Tommy? I talked with her at the market the other day. She sounded quite well." Beatrice wouldn't be caught dead at the market. Her mother's maid did all the shopping. She just wanted to divert the conversation away from the two girl onslaught.

"Mom's fine. Darcy here has promised me a mining job. If you see me at Ruley's in a Thunderbird, you'll know what happened."

"Tommy is a Ford man? I thought you told me you wanted a Corvette?" Connie asked.

"I'd drive a Volkswagen if someone would hand me the keys."

"One of my Dad's managers quit to go to work at the Sixteen-to-One last year, but he had experience in the mines. The starting salary for a mucker could make the payments on a new Chevy, but I hear you have to know someone to get on. You know how that goes. I've got nothing going on right now, Tom. As a matter of fact, I've got some on a four day week."

"I just might have me a mine job." Tom smiled at Darcy. Jamie finally ran out of small talk. "You don't have to leave," Tom insisted on the walk back.

"It's getting late, and I've got a long drive back, but I'll get back down as soon as things work out. I'd like to see you again."

The little grin on Jamie's face meant Tommy owed her. "Make it as soon as you can, Darcy. I'm serious about that job." He hadn't been enthused at first, but the idea of making better wages was playing on him. "I'll tell you the truth, I need some dance lessons." He hated country, did a tolerable two step, preferred a sock hop.

"You want a ride home?" Jamie asked.

"No, I like the walk." He hoped he might get invited to Jamie's. There wasn't any point in getting dropped off. It was depressing. Darcy grabbed his hand, pecked him on the cheek, and then jumped into her car and he had to shut the door like a gentleman. Now he wished he'd taken the ride.

"Now Matt, no!" Matt opened Jamie's door, and she had to duck to avoid giving a tribute kiss, but he beamed like he'd triumphed anyway. Darcy seemed to drive off in a hurry. 'They must have something planned' Tom thought.

"I may never see her again. What a screwed up Sunday!"

"You'll see her again. You need a ride?"

"I need a car."

"Same time, same channel," Matt waved.

Tom took a leisurely pace home. Kids were thick on the residential streets, people were watering their lawns on a sweet, calm spring evening in the San Joaquin Valley, one of the last before nature turned on California's summer furnace. He kicked a beer can along, like he used to do as a kid. He took diversionary routes, just to make the walk last. It was too late to get to the river. He wondered what he'd missed. "Nothing," out loud. It reminded him of the long walks he took after his father died. It seemed even sadder now. He was losing youth's enthusiasm. He was an adult now.

When he arrived at his home street from the opposite direction he usually returned on, he noticed a parked car pull a u-turn at the far end and drive around the corner, but thought nothing of it. About six houses away he heard a car behind him slow down, cross over. He could tell by the noise it was creeping up behind him in the wrong lane. 'Probably a cop,' he thought. Why? It occurred that if it was the police it might have something to do with his mother, and he turned in a little panic. It was the old Ford. Did he leave something in the car? Something in his mind was suspicious. "Are you alright Darcy? Do you need some help? Maybe you should spend the night with Jamie, and I can fix your brake tomorrow."

It was obviously an effort to get it out. "Do you want to come up and meet Ray, Tom? I'm sure he'll hire you. We can put you up on the couch."

He just got in and closed the door as silently as possible, hoping Mom wasn't looking out the window. "I was afraid I'd never see you again," he said as she drove him past home. It took some time to get the conversation going, and she wouldn't turn and face him till they got out of town. They talked about having dinner, but couldn't decide where. They gassed up in Grass Valley and drove on hungry, the conversation leading to anything and everything but that which was on their minds.

"What do you think about Hiame?"

"I feel sorry for him," Tom answered. "I hope he gets a job, but I've got white friends out of work, and if my boss was hiring, I'd tell them first. It's hard. You never think about it as a kid."

"I've got friends out of work too." That was a loaded statement he didn't want to pursue. "How did he get that name? It doesn't sound Mexican." She had changed the subject, realizing the implication.

"He says it's from the German Mexicans. His mother really is from Mexico. I told him once that I think he's really a Yaqui Indian, a Mestizo," he snickered. "German, my ass." Hiame would have laughed, taken it as a friends kidding, but Darcy reacted very obviously, a slight blush, a tightening of her features in the dim light, the dark eyes and hair. 'She's a white woman,' he thought. 'A little Indian blood? It doesn't matter; she's a pretty white woman. That's all I see.' Moonlight highlighted the old grove of big Doug fir, ponderosa, and sugar pine on the ridge before the North Yuba canyon. He was remembering drives with Mom and Dad on winding old Highway 49 through the area. The giant trees were too spooky and unreal when he was a kid, but in the cool spring air they now seemed friendlier. Maybe it was your point of view.

"Everything was working against me taking this trip, Tom. The brakes were the least of it. I had to borrow money for the gas. I have the most beautiful cowgirl shirt with mother of pearl buttons and some brand new jeans I intended to go dancing in. My mother got to them last week and put them in a wash with bleach, and the colors faded. They're ruined. She's absent minded, but I don't know. She doesn't like for me to wear jeans."

"You'd look fine sitting on an Appaloosa in that old outfit, like a real cowgirl. Do you ride?"

"Every chance I get, on an old swayback named Slim." The tension had subsided. "I'll call Ray in the morning and get him to meet us at the Quartz café."

"Ray?"

"Ray Shannon."

"Oh yeah. I'll have to make some phone calls in the morning, too. I don't want to burn any bridges at my job till I know for sure."

Past Goodyear creek she didn't slow down one bit as the curves got quicker. She obviously knew the road, but the speed made him nervous, and he braced himself against the dashboard. "I'm in too much of a hurry." She pulled off at an overlook. The moon had topped the ridge and illuminated a deceptively peaceful stretch of river.

"I remember going to Reno with my parents and some of their friends and kids. We went in three cars, and they decided to drive back through Sierra City to see some of the scenery. That turned into a mistake. Remember that big rain in March, 1950? They turned everyone around in Downieville because they were worried about the bridge downriver, and we had to spend the night in Sierraville sleeping on a church sanctuary floor. I remember hearing the rocks grinding."

"That wasn't the worst Downieville flood. I've seen two we had to evacuate, but the water never got in our house. The miners love that weather, so long as it doesn't wash away their cabins. They want to see it knock a bank in the river and put some gold back in."

He attempted a hoarse version of "Darling Clementine". "Are you making fun of miners?" She couldn't be as serious as she tried. "You're not funny, Tom. Try getting that on Ed Sullivan." But there wasn't enough severity in the tone, and the singing got worse. "Stop it. You're not funny." He stopped it with a stolen kiss. "You won't try that in one of our bars, I guarantee it."

They couldn't watch the river, listen to the crickets, and kiss forever. Another half hour and she pulled into the dirt drive of a little run down old house with rotted wood and broken window screens. "We're going in through my window. I don't want to wake Agnes up." It was so amusing, he thought, like something from Tom Sawyer would do with Becky Thatcher. "I think Jamie fed me a line today. She told me over the phone we'd go to a dance, but when I got down there she started talking about you, and then told me we were going to a pot-luck. She used to talk about you in school. We went by your place to offer to give you a ride to the pot-luck, but you had already gone. She knows your life history, I swear. How do you like them apples? She thinks I went home alone. Serves her right."

"Don't be so sure. Jamie's something else."

"I didn't know you were the guy she was talking about when you walked up, Tom." The man didn't have much to talk about for a while. She seemed to have lost some of her shyness in the dark. He was wondering about the "connections" Jamie bragged about. That she lived in poverty was pretty obvious. But after two o'clock he was only concerned with being allowed to sleep late. He'd think over everything in the morning.

About ten forty-five he awoke to the heat of direct sunlight, and got up to open the window. She was snoring slightly with the sheet covering her legs and her bare little fanny showing, so he covered her up and gave her a shake on the back.

"Shove off!"

"She's grumpy in the morning! Darcy! Darcy, we gotta get up and call Ray, remember." When a sympathetic tone didn't work, he tried exercising, or possibly tempting, his new envisioned dominance. "Get your ass up!"

"OK." She didn't move. She wouldn't move.

'What the hell did you do, Tommy?' he thought. 'Is this serious? I don't know.' He could always head back down and just try to stay friends. He was wary of the responsibility, afraid of losing the way of life he took for granted. But he remembered how he felt the day before, thinking about how miserable he would have been if she had avoided him. It seemed that it might be a matter of fate; it also occurred to him that he needed to take control and not allow fate to rule.

A haggard figure in the doorway out of the corner of his eye caused such a start that he almost jumped out of bed. Grabbing the sheet to cover himself bared Darcy. The door had been shut all night, but he remembered her telling him that Agnes had ruined the locking mechanism, one of the reasons Dave Morrow left. Had he been the object of wrath and contempt in front of all his peers by the most intolerant teacher he ever had, he would not have felt as much fear, anger, and humiliation as he was now feeling. He could feel the hair on the back of his neck standing up. "Darcy!" He shook her, but she feigned a comatose condition. He was sure she knew. 'Chicken.' he thought. Every time he turned to look at the gray streak haired, pale gray-blue eyed woman he had to turn back and try to roust Darcy. There was a malice in the eyes he could not deal with. It wouldn't help to force Darcy up; he realized now why it was so hard for Darcy to cope with her, so he made up his mind to turn and face the music. "Could you leave us alone?"

"Tshh. Flatlander," with an almost laugh, almost cough, and she slammed the door with tremendous force. Darcy scrambled out of bed, tripped, and fell against the dresser, but jumped back up to grab a wicker chair to brace the door. She shook her head of soft hair so fiercely in a fit of anger and despair, it worried him she might hurt her neck.

"I forgot the chair."

"Your mother doesn't seem too much like me. Of course, we haven't been formally introduced," he grinned.

"Who cares? I don't mean that for you, Tommy. We'll worry about her later; I don't think we'll catch Ray till after six. I meant to get up and call. I'll take you out to dinner, 'cause I don't want to get involved here this evening. I'd just get into it with her, so let's go visiting. We'll get you back in time to see about your job in Marysville." Silence for a while. "What are you thinking?" she finally asked.

"Nothing special."

"I guess you must think me pretty impetuous, what I did. That's the first time I've ever done something like that.

I was afraid that things would go along, and I wouldn't get back down again."

"That's exactly what I was thinking."

"Everything has been going wrong for me. I almost didn't get to use the car. The job I was offered at the Sixteen-to-One was filled by a friend of mine. And my mother, God, riding me down all the time, just like she used to do my father. I swear, I was getting ready to drive to another state last night. I turned around and came back for you."

"I would have borrowed a car next Saturday and driven up here."

"Tommy, right now I feel..."

"Sad? Good a word as any. You're excused. You said last night everything was going wrong. Same with me. But today is a new day." He shrugged his shoulders to substitute for the words that finished the statement and walked over to hug her, the kind of a hug he always reserved for his mother.

"Sad. Not anymore!" Then she made a return to the more collected character he had first met. "I'm twenty-one, Tom. I want you to know I won't hold you to anything. I'm not that kind of a woman."

"You can't get rid of me that easy." He put an all out effort into the smile he used now, the one he had once broken Emily into a giggling fit with, but she seemed a fair match. She seemed a better match. "You promised me a job!"

"Get dressed. We're going to meet some of my friends." The thought of getting dressed almost brought the day's progress to an impasse, but they managed to get by by not looking at each other.

Downieville was obviously a walking man's town. Houses at the north end could stretch a pedestrian's patience, but a car would be no great advantage. Up the Downie River, up past the cemetery, hidden in some ponderosa and black oak, sat a well kept Victorian two story, a fine candidate for Home and Garden Magazine, except for the back-hoe front end loader, dump truck, and assorted rusted equipment and cable only partially hidden behind. There were two gigantic cur dogs behind a useless little picket fence that Darcy knew by name, and she managed to keep herself between them and the man they suspected of dubious intentions all the way to the porch. They knocked at the front door several times in five minutes; time enough for the guard dogs to make him extremely nervous. "I should have called. It takes a while. They're home." Finally a slightly obese gray haired lady in an old apron and tennis shoes opened and grabbed Darcy off her feet. "Lynn," was all Darcy could get out.

"Bill! Darcy's here. Bill! What a fine looking young man. You're from out of town. Bring him in, girl." Darcy had to go through the whole squeezing process again when Bill got a hold of her. He was a burly old white haired man, about six three, slightly pot bellied, all in khaki work duds, easily the back-hoe operator type. Everything in the house seemed antiquated, a little dusty, and in a small room by the kitchen Tom noticed boxes of paperwork, probably from a business. They sat at an authentic Victorian dining table in the kitchen and small talked about everyone's background until Darcy felt she could edge into the subject of employment possibilities.

"Bill, I'm going to find some work for Tom so he can move up here. Otherwise, I'll have to move down valley with him."

"No, you're not moving." Lynn sounded like a mother admonishing a daughter. "You should both live here."

"I can put him on my operation, if that's what you want. I'll let Lou break him in. Have you ever run a back-hoe? Ain't nothing to it as long as you don't turn it over."

"No I haven't, Bill, but I know I can handle it, and I'm a fair car and truck mechanic."

"Well, you'll learn some Cummins diesel hanging around this crew."

"I think I've got him a job with Ray, but if that doesn't work out…"

"You bring him up anytime, Darcy. I'll be real careful with him. We've never gotten anyone hurt on my time. I should have been up there already. Lou and Tom Henderson are crying they're both broke again. You can find plenty of excuses when you turn sixty-nine," he grinned.

It was difficult for Darcy to finally negotiate an exit from the old couple. As they got up to leave, Bill pulled some cash out of a thick wallet and pressed it in Darcy's hand. She hugged and kissed them both, like a daughter would her parents.

"Rodger Dodger, Gumbo! Cut it out!" Darcy commanded as they walked onto the porch. Rodger was nudging her, gently, and then simply put his head against her groin and pushed her aside.

"Damn you, dog!" Bill grabbed an old golf club from a door urn and waived it in Rodger's face. Rodger's eyes were moving back and forth at imagined apparitions at Tom's feet, and the low growling was getting worse.

"I knew football practice would be good for something," Tom yelled as he bolted toward the fence. He heard nothing till the leap over, and the snapping jaws and barks were terribly close.

"You did the wrong thing, son. Now he'll never leave you alone."

Rodger had retribution coming, and now he was doing the dodging as Darcy ran him down and rapped him on the head with her little fists. 'Be careful, little girl,' Tom thought.

"What was that money all about?" he asked as they started walking back.

"It's a loan, a gift, really. I've never paid them back. They've been doing that since my father was killed in 1952."

"How much? No secrets."

"Two hundred."

"Two hundred? I only make sixty cents an hour. Geeze Louise, can they afford that?"

"They're millionaires, Tom. They could easily live well in the Bay area."

"They're millionaires?"

"Mr. Rutledge is an owner in the Ruby Mine. You've heard of the Ruby?"

"Not really. I've never heard of the Sixteen-to-One."

"You've heard of the Catapillar Company. The engineers at the Ruby developed the first track machine before the Great War, and they started the Catapillar Company. Every year Bill puts someone to work on one of his personal claims just to help them out. My good friend Lou Montgomery works with him every summer. It's just a hobby to Bill; he doesn't need for himself. He was raised here, and he'll die here, no doubt. He has six sons, but no daughters, so I kind of…" She grabbed his arm and steered him down to a house by the river. By the time they made it back to town they had made four more visits, and at one house he noticed her put a twenty in the hand of a thirties looking friend named Linda who had three kids. 'We can't be doing that,' he thought. 'I work too hard for sixty cents. But if it's a gift? It's between her and Bill.' They had to visit almost every shop and store in Downieville. He was thoroughly enjoying being showed off; he hadn't shaken that many hands in one day in his life.

"Dad," he remembered asking as a kid. "Who started the tradition of shaking hands?'

"I have no idea." Tom senior confessed. "Probably men in tribes. Sometimes it's a way of testing your adversary's strength, one of his strengths. I wouldn't have made much of an impression in those days." Tom knew he would be bigger and stronger early on. Tom senior weighed about one-forty; he liked to theorize "I was gifted with the hands of the German intellectuals, like Wille Messerschmitt. He weighed about a hundred and twelve. You know what he did with his hands and his brain? He designed the ME 109. And you know what I did with my hands." Tom senior was credited with seven confirmed kills, mostly ME 109's, from the tail gun of a B 17 over Europe. "Lucky Seven" his buddies called him at the end of his tour of duty. "Lucky to be alive," he would tell Tom. "I'm not proud of it, killing men."

Darcy finally decided she'd honor her promise of dinner at the Quartz café. Even the cook had to come out and check the new boy in town out. When six men entered and consolidated two tables, she recognized Ray. "I thought he'd be up the Downie all day. Let's let them order, and I'll invite him over." But a wiry looking fellow in an Australian bush hat walked over as soon as the others sat down. "Hello, Vernon." Her tone carried the hint of uncomfortability.

"Darcy, Elaine says hi."

"I thought you two were having a tiff."

"Females sure love the gossip."

"Vernon, this is my friend Tom Hendrick. Tom, Vernon Fickett." Tom had been extending his hand so often it came as an involuntary action, and the smile with it, but the offer met with a statue's cold indifference.

"Vernon!" she warned.

"You've brought up another flatlander, Darcy. Is there something wrong with the boys in our town?"

"Which town?"

"You know what I mean. Well, if he's here, he's here. Dave was a pretty tolerable flatlander. I guess we'll have to put up with this guy, too." The grin was humorless. Now it was Vernon obliging the hand shake, which Tom knew he would have taken through directness, if necessary.

'He's wiry, probably fast, but he's not as powerful as me,' Tom thought. 'He does have a grip for a skinny punk. Dad would have been no match.'

Darcy went to whisper in Ray's ear, and the expression directed Tom's way was considerably friendlier as Ray walked over to shake Tom's hand and welcome him. Ray was obviously more powerful than Vernon. The conversation quickly turned to the business at hand, and Ray needed to know "have you ever dived?"

"I never had the chance, but I practically grew up in the Yuba at Marysville. Some of my friends used to call me the "Otter". I didn't like it, but they were right. When I was twelve, my friends and me saved a woman caught on a snag. We held our breath and dived in the current while my neighbor Barbara held the woman's head above the water. Barbara was a heck of a swimmer."

"Oh, she was?" Darcy was humoring him. "I'm an excellent swimmer. I hope I don't ever have to dive and rescue you."

"Alright Tom, I'll let you try it and see what you think. We'll be back up tomorrow morning. We're close enough to town to commute."

"Would it be alright if I work out the week at my old job? I didn't give notice. That reminds me, I gotta call Mr. Conrad."

"That's no problem. I'll see you Sunday afternoon right here. Get yourself a good face mask, not a cheapie. It's your life. We'll get you a wetsuit from someone around here. I've got two men working with me already. You three will split sixty percent. Can you handle that?"

"That sounds fair. I've got to make some calls. Be back in a minute."

"Ray, what's Fickett up to?" Darcy asked.

"He's not working with me, don't worry about it. He's trying to get on the "Boulder Bound" with Thomas and Hanes right above us. We all decided to drive down for a late lunch. I'd like to see them put his skinny ass to work, 'cause all I've ever seen him work is his mouth." Darcy put her hand on his and gave it a little squeeze, and kissed him on the cheek as he made his goodbyes. An observer would have thought a little affection existed.

Tom had to search for change. "Hi, Mr. Conrad, Tom. I'm sorry about today. I should have called you sooner."

"Tom, you need to call your mother. She's hysterical. What the hell happened?"

"Yeah, I'm going to call her right away. All I'm saying is I've landed another job, but I'll work the week out if you need me."

Silence, then "Tom, you don't seem very appreciative, for what's been done for you. Your mother got you this job. You don't seem to realize the responsibility involved in holding a job, son."

"This is the first day I've ever missed. I'll show up in the morning and finish the week."

"If I had someone to replace you, I'd let you go right now. You work till Saturday, and then I'll have to think about it."

"Fine," and he hung up. He'd only work till Friday.

"Mom, I'm sorry, I know I make you worry, sometimes. I owe you an apology."

"God, Thomas, I've had the Sheriff down on the river. How could you do this to me? I thought you might have drowned. You could have called."

"Yes, I should have. I'm on the river, Mom, in Downieville. I met a girl named Darcy, and she got me a better job."

"Oh..., Ok, Thomas." The tone changed considerably, a realization. "Alright, you're in Downieville. Why couldn't you call last night?" The question probably answered itself.

"No excuses. I'm sorry. I'll be back this evening. I could be home late, so don't wait up."

"Alright, Tom. I'd like to meet this young lady. Just... I'm just glad you're OK. Some of your friends are out looking for you. You need to apologize to them. Except Matt had me call Jamie Lineman, and she said not to worry, that you were absolutely safe, but she wouldn't tell me anything. Is she trustworthy? Come home!"

"Home tonight, Mom."

The couple found it difficult to get away from the Quartz. No sooner had the waitress and cook made their second round for small talk than evening customers who knew Darcy began arriving, some doing their best to prevent an exit. The walk to the house involved trying to out maneuver several children who knew her, some who had embarrassingly direct children's questions for them to answer. They both knew there would be a confrontation waiting.

"Mother, I need the keys!" There was always a set of keys left in a kitchen drawer out of courtesy, but they were gone.

Agnes opened her bedroom door and held on with one hand, obviously inebriated. "Honey, we're going to have to get some things straight."

"I'm driving him back down to Marysville."

"And then what? He's not moving back up here, not in this house. If he moves back up, he can live in a tent. I heard about you getting him on with Ray."

"God, this town! Well, we can always live at the Rutledge's." Another slammed door. "Agnes McEarl, open the God-damned door!" she made the door rattle, pounding with both fists. "I should have kept the keys."

"Darcy, if need be, I can get my mother to drive up." He put his arms around her to stop the pounding.

"We can always get you a ride. I'm just sick and tired of being embarrassed like this. Let's go sit down a while. I'm tired." In her room Darcy flung herself back on the bed, arms askew. She was exhausted, too much so to take advantage. He inspected the furniture and the miscellaneous, one item at a time. "My father was killed in a logging accident five years ago. He didn't die right away. We thought, at least the doctors told us he would live. That woman, that hard woman in there, it almost killed her, but she will never show it. That's the way she was brought up. It was hell for me, and she made it so much worse. I know she loved him, but she wouldn't stop riding him, even after the accident. Now I'm the one who gets it, and I'm sick of it. My father was walking away from a free he felled, and a choker setter set the chain wrong on three logs up the hill, and they broke loose. One log killed the choker setter outright, another hit my father as he tried to get into a little opening in the rocks. The rocks kept it from crushing him. He had a broken shoulder and arm, and a giant hematoma on his back, black and blue. He was joking with us, Tommy. They told us when they thought he would be getting out. The hematoma got into the blood, and that was ten hours of hell. They said he was mostly unconscious. Hell for us."

'He joked with her,' Tom thought. 'Someday I'll tell her about Dad's joke.' Bad memories. Tom senior, sitting pretty in a good TV repair job, serving with the National Guard. Tom remembered the day he came home from school, the argument going on. It was all about Korea. Mom was angry, crying, and scared, and she threw a cup at Tom senior.

"I'll never be near any action," he tried to comfort. "I can't possibly get hurt. I'll be on vacation," he joked. He wouldn't really be a soldier, just an electronics technician, testing some new communications equipment. He had volunteered to go back in after being offered a promotion.

"Why?" Tom asked to a man who hated recounting old memories. No answer. One time only, Tom senior had told a story from his Army Air Corps days. "I saw a plane disappear. I mean, Tom, one second it was there, and then there was an orange ball dissolving away, and then there was one plane gone. No debris. We thought they felt no pain, it was so quick. But I saw some other things that were too hard to take." Unpleasant memories Tom did not want to pursue.

And then the day the soldier came to the door to tell them Dad was dead, a next door neighbor had to help Tom get Rene to sit down, she was crying so terribly. He sat down, too, but he wouldn't cry. They were told: Dad was sitting in a bunker away from the lines, having coffee and talking with the guys, and a shell hit. There were so many stories like that, the soldier said. Eleven men died, one lived, but lost a hand. Now it was especially hard to take if he compared it with the story of the orange ball. It was a closed casket funeral. He'd wake up in the morning and think 'I'll ask Dad' about something. It just didn't set in. One terrible day he got up and walked into the kitchen and said "where's Dad? I need to ask...", and when she ran into her room and shut the door he could not apologize enough. Two months later a man with only one hand got out of a car and Tom watched him walk to the door. 'Soliciting, selling?' Tom thought. He realized who he might be as the man knocked, and Tom headed to his room, but his mother made him return and go through the torment. He felt so sorry for the man, Jake, but he hated listening. And Jake felt so sorry for them. Sitting in his room, after two weeks, staring at the ceiling, walls, Tom thought 'why do I sometimes feel like nothing has really happened?' Thinking about car accidents with kids. Wondering what makes men kill each other. Remembering Dad saying "Napoleon said 'men would rather kill each other than make buttons'". Something seemed to move on the ceiling and he had a vision, or maybe he just got dizzy. A terrible feeling of claustrophobia, something coming down at him. He could hardly make it to the bathroom, he was so dizzy and sick, and he finally let go, vomiting and crying out of fear. Mom begged to get in and comfort him, but he refused her as she had refused him. And then, in the weeks to come, the real hell came.

"Darcy, your mother's not really that different. About a month after my Dad died, something happened between me and my mother. I don't remember what started it; I just know she turned cruel. Everything she did was designed to hurt me. I figured she wanted me out, so I ran away to the river bottoms. There're people living there right now that I know. I knew enough people; I figured I could always get enough food. Detective James Long found me, I've known him for a long time, and he talked me into coming home. Mom came out and hugged me, and I knew it was all over.

She had had to spend three days in the house alone. She'll be alone in the house again. We'll be making plenty of trips to Marysville. If I can't make the gold, we'll just move down there."

"Your mother had some kind of breakdown. My mother is crazy like a fox. Every move she makes has an ulterior motive, so don't buy into any of her tricks. My mother believes, like other people around here, that the gold belongs to the few, the fit." She looked him square in the eye, a probing expression. "My father was part Maidu Indian. I never knew how much, maybe one fourth, maybe less. I never wanted to ask him, not after hearing some of the things she said. Did you ever hear the story of the Maidu? They lived up here when the 49'ers came. There was no war, there was very little killing, because they stayed away from each other. The Maidu mostly ate deer, acorns, and sweet peas, whatever. In one year the miners hunted all the deer, and in that year more than half the Maidu starved to death. I don't think it was intended, and some of the miners came to their relief. My mother thinks people should be weeded out just like animals. Gold is only for a few. She's told me more than once it was the Maidu's turn to lose." She sat up on the bed, staring. Her voice had been emotionless, like she had been talking for someone else; he knew she was still in shock, after all the years. "Lazy Indian," she said.

"Words that hurt always come back," he offered. "She must cry for that sometimes."

"Then again, I could have gotten my black eyes from Tony Lavezzola. I'm supposed to have some of his blood, too."

"Tony Lavezzola?"

"He's that nice Italian boy who walked up the creek one day and started picking up nuggets."

"When did this happen?"

"In the spring of 49. They named the creek after him."

"1849. Alright." A little pause, and then he decided "let me tell you my Indian story, my Dad always used to tell. The Hendricks came from Wisconsin, actually from Germany originally. You could never tell from my brown eyes and black hair..."

"Red hair." She got up and pulled a strand out to examine it. "In the sunlight, I can see red." She was leaning against him and it was hard to concentrate.

"That comes from the Irish side. Who knows what else. But my great grand dad Hendrick, he's always been the family conversation piece. My great aunt Patricia did some kind of research and wrote a paper that my dad kept. Jeff Hendrick was an Indian hater. 'The only good Indian is a dead Indian,' was his saying, and he meant all of them, no exceptions. They say he shot a few. That's 'cause his parents, one brother, and two sisters, they had their throats cut in a massacre in Wisconsin in the 1860's. Jeff's throat was cut, too, but not deep, and he lived by playing dead beside them. They were German farmers, and they were killed because of some fraud concerning some money the government sent to honor a treaty that was supposed to feed the Sioux Indians there through the winter. The farmers had been given part of the Indian's original treaty land, so the Indians had to move and take relief. Dad used to tell us 'here is a good example of the systems good intentions gone to hell'. Well, Uncle Sam sent the money, but the Indian traders who had told the Sioux for years that they were the only white men the Indians could trust, they cheated them broke, and the Indians figured out the principle of inflation too late. They were starving, the money was all gone, and they attacked and killed all the whites they could find, mostly the crooked traders, but some of the farmers too. The irony is that Jeff Hendrick ended up hating California farmers. He moved out here and got a job working a monitor on a hydraulicking mine at Dutch Flat near Colfax. He became a foreman and made good money. You see, I have some miners in my family too."

"I know what happened. The farmers had the hydraulickers legally shut down, because they were putting too much silt in the irrigation water. Some people who used to live around here hated those farmers." She reflected a moment. "So, the son of a farmer ended up hating farmers. How sad. They're a lot of people who have those kinds of stories. It's best to just forget, and think about the future. I try to do that concerning my mother. She probably would have adored Jeffery Hendrick. Let's walk up to Janet's house. You remember her, don't you? I gave her some cash today."

"You owed her?"

"Not money, but yes, I owe her. If her husband John can't take you, then we'll ask Bill. I know enough people; we'll get you a ride."

"You sure do." He was pretty tired himself.

Walking up main street Darcy suddenly stopped and pointed. "That's their car. That's Janet's car. Hey!" She walked across and flagged the slow moving vehicle. "Vernon, what are you doing in Janet's car?"

"John owes me some cash, and I needed a car today. I'm headed to Sac to pick up a few things for Mr. Hanes. I'm his new backhoe man, but you don't need to spread it around. I owe a few right now."

"Who doesn't? Congratulations. I hope you get rich, Vernon. Why isn't Elaine with you?"

"You were right; she's pissed off at me." Tom almost snickered, but the expressions cast his way were too severe. "Besides, I'll have some fun down there by myself. She doesn't like that crowd in Sac."

"I'll bet."

"I'll bet Tom here needs a ride back. It's a shame your mother is such a hothead. I can drop him off. I won't even ask for gas money."

"I don't think so…" She was balking.

"Sure, Vernon," Tom remarked. "I'll give you some gas money."

She looked distraught. "Are you going right away? Could you wait an hour?"

"No, I've got to book, Darcy."

"This is perfect." Tom felt uneasy, too, but he felt he needed to meet this guy. "I'll call you tonight, Darcy. Matt can give me a ride back up on Saturday."

"Be careful with my new man, Vernon! I've only known him for a short while." There was an intimidating tone here. Did Vernon almost flinch? His smile was a mask.

"Love you!" She kissed Tom hard, and after he got in she kissed him through the window. He wished to hell he had saved up some money, so he could quit Allen Conrad right now. He must have bought too much beer for the river crowd, or something. It was hard to keep track.

"I can give you a dollar," he offered Fickett as they hit the quick bends out of town. Vernon waived it off.

"It's not that far out of my way. So, you're going to work in the river with Ray? I tried to get on with him. Darcy got you that job. You know about them?"

"No."

"Yea, she'll tell you. They used to be a hot item. But, you know, Ray's from around here. That's the thing about people coming up from the valley and working. Not everyone in this town has a job."

"I realize how lucky I am."

"How long you known her?"

"Awhile."

"God, the things you hear. Got told you only met her yesterday. I used to date Jamie."

'I doubt it,' Tom thought. 'No way in hell.' "I'd prefer to live near my Mom. She's widowed. But the people here are so friendly, and the job I had pays nothing."

"Shit, yeah," Fickett laughed harsh. "The people are so-oo friendly. It took me forever to get in, and I'm from Alleghany."

"Where's that?"

No answer. "The thing is it might be smart to just forget the job and the girl. You know, one of those flings, one time. The people up here aren't that friendly, guaranteed. There's gold up here, and there's always people thinking about our gold. Curiosity killed the cat, and a few people as well, who strayed where they shouldn't have been. I'm just telling you, in a friendly way, those smiles hide what these people really think about flatlanders."

"Well, maybe you can help me talk Darcy into moving down. Thing is, where she goes, I go."

Vernon slammed his hands down on the steering wheel, braked hard, and pulled off under a grove of live oak. 'This is it,' Tom thought, heart pounding. 'This guy is definitely going to get antagonistic.' His mouth was awfully dry.

"You don't seem to be taking what I'm saying seriously. Let me show you serious." He walked back and opened up the trunk, pulling out a rifle case.

'God, he's just trying to intimidate. We're on a main highway. Don't lose it!' Tom thought.

"You see this twelve gauge pump action. Get out of the car!" Tom obliged, staring him hard in the eyes. "Take this, hold it. My Dad gave it to me. You ever shot a gun, boy?"

'If he calls me boy again, I should smack him,' Tom thought. Fickett was probably in his late twenties. Tom took the gun, pointed it at some rocks.

"I used to sleep with that loaded by my side. I lived up Goodyear creek one summer in a tent. Didn't know who would get me first, the animals, the weather, or the people." Tom didn't want him to see how relieved he had suddenly become. "I'll give you some shooting lessons, Tom. Up here everyone needs to know how to shoot." Tom handed him back the shot gun and Vernon stashed it, and began to pace and gesture, the eyes a little wild looking, the forehead intense. Tom wondered if he wasn't dealing with an unbalanced man. "No, you won't need shooting lessons. You'll see. You won't stay. Not everyone is as friendly as me. Get back in the car. I'm late." And then the conversation became casual, as if nothing had happened. Tom realized he was dealing with another outsider, but he wasn't going to make an effort toward friendship. Fickett would like to have counted Darcy's new flame as an ally, he was sure, but something about the man made Tom uneasy. He wouldn't have trusted any man with that wild eyed look out in the woods.

Back home, Mom came out to meet, and offered much thanks to Vernon for the ride. "I have a chocolate cake I just frosted. Could you eat a piece with some milk?"

"Yes ma'am. I hardly ever get deserts." Fickett recounted winning a high school chess championship, as he eyed the furniture in such a way that Tom suspected he was casing the place. Tom wondered what Vernon thought about the wealthy Rutledge's, and how many more like him he might run into in the small town. He would never let himself get like that, no matter how rough the finances got.

Vernon offered him a night on the town, telling him he would introduce him to the people he needed to know, but Tom slapped him on the back and said "some other time, Vernon. I'm awfully tired. Have a good one." Vernon smiled and waved. Perhaps he would be no problem.

THREE

And so, in two days time, the young man's life had changed dramatically. He had fallen in love, he had no doubt, but he had also been infected with a fever. A very dangerous fever. On Tuesday, the fever for Darcy became unbearable, and on the third long distance call she informed him that Bill was taking a trip to Sacramento and would be dropping her off Wednesday afternoon. He asked her not to make it too early, but when he got home it was apparent Mom and Darcy had been conversing awhile. Their expressions and tones relieved him; things were going well. Once when Darcy's attention had been diverted to family picture album Rene winked at him with such a twinkle in her eye Tom knew she really liked her. He dreaded the conversation he knew was coming with Mom, avoided getting caught alone with her, but she finally cornered him after supper. "So, very young man, you've made up your mind you're going to live with this young woman you've just met, even though you're not married. Tom, how do you think that's going to look for her in that small town? I won't have a son in this house who treats women the way Randy Krammer does."

"I love her, Mom, I know. We've got to give it a try, the job and everything. Working with Ray is going to be my big break. I know it is. If I come back with enough to open up my own garage…"

"Tom's Garage. That sounds wonderful. You'd extend your friends too much credit, and you'd be out of business in no time," she teased. "She seems pretty mature; you two might be able to make it work. You have to be hard to run a business. You know I wanted you to go to college, son. You also know I want you to be happy. If I have to put up with a little gossip, I can handle that. Being in this house alone, well, I think I'll just go out and get married as soon as you leave." It didn't sound serious.

"We'll drive down every week, Mom. And when you meet her mother…"

"I've heard all about her mother. You know I've still got a good left hook." She feigned a punch that just touched the tip of his nose, like she'd done so many times with Dad.

"She'd better never say anything to you!"

"Tommy!" Now the fist hand caressed his cheek. "I'll fix the guest room for Darcy." That was all for show, in case a neighbor got too nosey. "There is one thing, my son, and you'd better listen well if you want to be welcome in this house. If it doesn't work out, you chalk it up to experience. You're young; you've got plenty of time. How do I say it? You walk away a gentleman if you have to."

Allen Conrad took an instant liking to Darcy when she arrived at work with Tom Thursday morning, or so it would seem when he took Tom aside after lunch and gave him a twenty dollar bonus. About two thirty Phil Macilroy showed up, a year since Tom had last seen him. "Get out from under that truck and help this girl pump some gas!" Darcy had volunteered to cover the gas pumps.

"Hey Phil, where have you been hiding out?"

"Working rigs in the 'oil patch' down by Bakersfield with my uncle. I'm already a derrickman. I ran into Jamie, or should I say she ran into me. She said I should be sure and meet this older woman Tommy's been hanging out with, just in case you two don't work out." Tom grinned despite himself. "The Martin brothers are throwing a barbeque Saturday on the west beach, and their ugly sister invited me." Phil squinted his eyes. "I got Jamie and you two invited. You can bring some beer if you like, you won't insult anyone." Phil had been a first team offensive end the same year Tommy played defensive second team end. Walking down the river beach on Saturday afternoons, Tommy sometimes ran into Phil's crowd from high school, partying and playing softball or volleyball. What could a guy do? Walk way around? Someone would offer Tom a beer, and Tom would play some ball. A little car mechanics talk, a little gossip, maybe a polite remark from a girl about Tom's part in the winning football season, and then it was time to head on. He felt more comfortable with his own crowd. Tommy was OK, but Tommy wasn't in. Hiame wouldn't even have been OK. The highlight of Tom's football playing had been an intercepted pass that he took for forty yards. He didn't much like to compare with Phil, who everyone thought would go on to college ball. Phil had dropped into the blue collar world to help his kinfolk out.

"I appreciate it Phil, but I'm moving to Downieville tomorrow…"

"No excuses, Jamie said. Darcy said she'd love to go."

"It's up to her."

"He says it's up to you," Phil warned Darcy as they walked out of the garage. "We'll count on seeing you both."

"It's up to Tom," she corrected as Phil got in his truck. "It sounds like fun." She waived, and then to Tom "he's cute!" Tom smiled, hands in his pockets. "Maybe I shouldn't have been so hasty," loud enough for Phil to catch. When Phil was gone, she asked "you don't really want to go, do you Tom?"

"Last week, I would have loved to have gotten invited. But we should head up to Downieville."

"I don't know what I'd wear, anyways. I didn't bring anything down."

"Well, wear that cheap cowgirl outfit. You looked good in it to me." He had gone too far again, ignited a reaction.

"Listen, Daddy-oo, I've had two years of Chico social events, and this girl will look sharp. I've got two years on you, Tommy, so…"

"Darcy, it's me that's uncertain. I don't mean they snob me. They've always been friendly, but that's not my crowd. I want to go if you want to go, but I'll warn you, if Randy Kramer shows up, he'll have his arm over your shoulder up against a tree, drilling you with his twenty question routine."

"I've already been warned about Randy. I know his type. I was raped at a school party in Chico, Tommy."

"Darcy!" he said slowly.

"I don't want to talk about it right now. If we go to the beach party, I'll have to go shopping."

"All you have to wear is a pair of shorts and a shirt. They play volleyball. Darcy, you're the only reason I'm being invited."

"I know."

"Look, I'll call Matt and Jamie, and Tom and Susan Ellis, and a few others I know, and we'll get something going some Sunday afternoon. I'm just not into it right now. I want you to myself awhile before I have to start dealing with Marysville's hit on artists." That was too outspoken, her realized in afterthought, and she smirked at him and giggled with deliberation.

"Yeah, I shouldn't be too hasty. There must be a lot of cute boys in this town. There were plenty in Chico. I need to meet a few more like Phil before I make up my mind."

He had already turned and headed back to the truck. "Older women!" he complained. Her laughter was innocent enough, she was teasing. That was only fair. He needed to do some heavy thinking.

That night Tom demanded she recount the incident at a sophomore campus party when a drunken senior had slipped her a Mickey and taken advantage. "You didn't prosecute the bastard?"

"I came close. My mother was fit to kill. Dave was away, visiting his parents. There were several girls who made it clear how nasty it would get if I tried anything. He was a prominent student, with a career and a future and all that shit. I let it drop. I heard later about his bragging, and then it was too late, I guess."

"I'd take a ski mask and a steel pipe…"

"Tommy, let's drop it! Dave tried to get something done, and it only got him in more trouble than it was worth. He got right in Greg's face, he was so angry he was spitting, tears in his eyes, it was horrible. Greg just smiled at him, he had his buddies with him, and they were practically laughing. One of the campus security told him to leave Greg alone. We had a teacher try and help us prosecute, but the only witness was a friend of Greg's. My mother talked about getting him, about some of her friends getting rough with him. That's one of the few times she's been on my side. It got scary; I talked her out of that."

"Dave sounds like a decent guy. I'd like to meet him."

"You will. He's been very good to me since we broke up. You need to meet Linda, too."

"Let's just head up, and Monday morning I'm going to jump in the river and help Ray find a fortune. I'll be glad to be rid of this job." He had to set her straight about Allen Conrad.

"Tommy," Allen ordered one afternoon, a year before. "We need to talk about your responsibility to this job."

"Did I do something?"

"I'm going to need a little more out of you. It takes a lot to keep this station in the black, and I'm going to ask you to get motivated and help me realize a profit margin." That statement was ridiculous. Tom did most of the mechanic repairs, pumped gas, did almost everything but the books. Tom was an excellent mechanic, Allen admitted, having worked with Matt for years in Matt's parent's back yard garage. Allen was a griper, a whiner, and sometimes a cheat. Rumors of some of the things he pulled on customers drove off some of his business, but Tom pulled in teenage customers for gas.

"What do you need, Allen?" He was working every minute of the full eight hours. He'd asked for six days instead of five, been turned down, and then demanded to work six.

"I need this shop cleaned after closing; I need you to stop telling your friends the cheapest way to get a repair. A business is all about making a profit, and you can make a difference by giving it your 100%. I think it's not too much to ask you to spend some extra time in the shop after closing."

"Allen, are we talking about overtime?"

Allen let out an exasperated, exaggerated long breath, as if he were dealing with a complete incompetent, leaned one arm against a bench, and glared off at some imaginary advisory.

"Allen, I want overtime. It's the law." Tom folded his arms.

"Jobs are hard to come by, aren't they, Tom? Your mother is having some financial troubles right now, as I hear it. She needs your support."

"That's right. Some overtime would really help."

Another long breath. "Well, I don't know. I have several young men in mind. You've been a fair worker, but I need someone willing to give it their best. Your mother got you this job. I was thinking you'd do it on a volunteer basis, no set hours, but something to show a little pride in this shop."

"You're asking me to work for nothing?" No answer. "Mr. Conrad, I can go back to work with Matt landscaping this summer to get my mother by. If you think you need someone else, then hire them. Matt always takes care of his hands."

"Then this afternoon is your last. I think you're going to make you mother very unhappy."

Mom was practically crying when he told her. "Why does this have to happen right now? We need every penny, Tommy. Couldn't you just make him happy till something better comes along?"

"So I work for free. I'll be home late, real late if I know Allen."

"No, you're right. He's a bastard. He'll just take his mile if you give him an inch. Call Matt and tell him you need to go to work."

Allen hired a complete incompetent, his teenage business dropped to nil, and he ended up negotiating with Rene for Tommy's return, with a nickel an hour raise, she made sure.

"You'll never have to worry about Ray cheating you," Darcy assured. "But you have to understand, if Ray falls on his face this summer, well, 20% of nothing is nothing. I live in a town full of risk takers. Tommy, would you really take a steel pipe to Greg, if you had the chance? That's over with; I want you to promise me."

"I'll figure something more subtle than that. Greg doesn't know me. I think maybe Dave and I can think something up."

"Tommy, he's not around anymore. Just forget it."

It was an intriguing idea. Help Dave with the matter, before Greg figured out Tom's interest in it. That had to be the most efficient means of payback, the unknown advisory, except, he realized, it might be too much like war.

It had been years since the one time he had actually used a steel pipe on anyone. That was seventh grader rich boy Connie's doing back in Tom's fifth grade. Those were the days when Tom stood by himself in the schoolyard at lunch time with no money for food. Minding his own business, hoping for no more trouble than he could presently handle. John Keats collected Tom's thirty-five cents every day. John had been bumped back twice; he was much bigger than most of the kids in his grade. He'd discovered the most seemingly riskless means of profiteering in the capitalist system: extortion. One day Connie walked up to Tom with an intense expression. "How come I never see you in the lunchroom, kid? I want you to do something for me. I know what's going on. He took everything in my cousin Terry's pocket, Tommy. Seven dollars."

"God Damn!"

"You like missing lunch? I'll bet you'd like to put a stop to it, too."

"Yeah..." Very insecure yeah.

"Don't look like that, Tom. We're going to help you; you're going to help us. Jack and me, you know Jack, don't you? We've got an appointment with John after school, only he don't know it yet. You're going to bring him to us." Tom's stomach was turning. Connie was bigger than him, too. "Terry's too small to help us, so it's up to you."

"What do you want me to do?"

"Don't look like that! What would your father think if he knew? Do you think he'd take that shit from anyone?"

He was right. Dad would have tried something. "When my German blood get's to boiling," he would say. He would probably get whipped, but it wouldn't be from backing off.

"Hell, I'll help you, but you promise you won't leave me."

"We won't run out on you, Tom. If you knew me, you'd know I don't do that."

Tommy, with the dollar Connie lent him, flashing it in John's face, and then whipping into the lunch room. John followed him in and walked up to him at the lunch line. "You'll see me at three thirty. You got to be sick, to be so crazy. You got the flu?" When Tom would not acknowledge him, he whacked Tom on the elbow for effect.

After school Jack met him in a restroom to chart an ambush. "Connie's got a steel pipe for you. Just don't get scared and run the wrong way." He had to make sure John was at one entrance, then sprint out another, but make sure John saw him. It worked too well, he was running like a quarter horse, but John was making surprising headway for an overweight boy. Tom's lungs hurt, his eyes stung, he was terrified they wouldn't show up. He found the alley, fences on both sides, and it was such a redemption seeing Jack walk the far end, and Connie closing the trap. There was a lot of screaming, threats, kicks, and a few pipe whacks for effect; John was genuinely terrified. Connie urged Tom to get in a few licks, and Tom made a pitch with his pipe, his hands a little too loose, and the pipe slipped and hit John below the belt. He worried he might have really hurt John, gotten himself in trouble, but he was so glad to get an escort home with his new allies.

After that day, he avoided John as much as possible, but it was inevitable they'd pass each other in the hall. John just looked ahead, never bothered him again. One day at lunch Connie, Jack, and two of their friends moved their trays to Tom's table. "Feels a hell of a lot better, doesn't it Tom? You've got food in your stomach, and safety in the hallway," Connie reminded him. "That's how it works, Tommy. You got to stick together. Nobody does anything by themselves, 'cept I did one time. You backed me, and I won't forget it." Tom just nodded. "When I was a fourth grader, I had to deal with a jerk named Stan who wouldn't lay off me. He wouldn't let me forget, I got a girl's name. My mother liked the name Connie, but not my Dad. I love my mother enough, I'll keep the name. She says it's a good Gaelic name for a boy or girl. But in the fourth grade I hated it. 'Hey Connie, hey sweetie.'" Jack was trying not to laugh. "I wouldn't take it anymore. You know what I did?" Tom hoped he would reveal some slick maneuver he could use some day. "I kicked the ever loving dog shit out of him, and he was bigger than me." That wasn't what Tommy wanted to hear. It was pretty ironic; Tom would think back, a young man that had the females after him in his senior year shouldn't mind the inconvenience of having a girl's name.

"Darcy, Vernon told me you used to go with Ray," Tom said as they lay in each other's arms.

"Ray, and then Dave. I had an affair with Ray that started when I was 16 and he was 32. It was wrong, I know; I could have got him in trouble. After two years I realized that he wasn't going to make a commitment. I met Dave at Chico State when I was 19. Mountain women start early, I guess, Tommy. I had known Ray for years; I always had a crush on him. When his conniving mistress left him, I have to admit, I threw myself at him. A lot of people knew."

"I can imagine that happening. He's a handsome enough guy."

"Now…, now I have to know who my competition is."

"You don't have any competition. Certainly not Emily, and Ellen and I haven't seen each other in years. Jamie was teasing about Barbara."

"What's this I hear about you and Fran Smith, from Jamie?"

"Jamie needs to write a newspaper column. I didn't really date Fran, technically. Fran goes through a lot of guys. That's just her way; she's in demand. I still don't think she has just one boyfriend right now. I'm not saying she's loose, sexually, but she just can't make up her mind. I'd call her up and plan something, and she'd call me up at the last minute and say 'something has come up here, Tommy, and I'll have to take a rain check'. Something was usually someone. About the time I'd get smart and leave her alone, she'd call me. So what am I going to do, say no? I tried to once, but she is pretty."

"Prettier than me?"

"You'll never get me to open that can of worms." She was still smiling. "I went steady with Ellen Travis. She was sweet, but we weren't right."

"How many, Tom?" She seemed to have gained the tone of a more mature, worldly woman than a twenty one year old. He resented this line of questioning, and was surprised at its directness.

"Only one, Darcy, That's no one you need to worry about."

"I told you, now you tell me."

"She's an older woman. It was just one night, and I haven't seen her since."

Seventeen year old Tommy, a little drunk from beer, down on the south beach by Linda town. He'd swam across with his shirt and shoes in his hands after a friend called him over, and Ellen was there with a crowd of about thirty people. They finally got a break from the crowd and talked for an hour by the fire, and in the dusk light she got up for some excuse to talk to someone. Next thing he knew he saw her headed downriver alone, and she glanced back and smiled right at him. She had had too many beers too, but she managed to disappear in the short willows before he could catch up. He could hear her at times, but as fast as he was she managed to outflank him, and when he gave up and headed back it was no surprise to see her sitting with some girlfriends in the sand, chatting away as if nothing had happened. She gave him one long look, a smile that he interpreted as 'I like you, Tommy. I'd like to, Tommy. But no, I won't.' Lanis Hinten sat down beside him and said "I know you like Ellen, but stop and think, Tom. Are you ready for the serious life?"

"What's it to you?"

"She's my cousin, Tom."

"Sorry, I didn't mean anything…"

"Forget it. You're not thinking anything the rest of us haven't thought. Just stop and think. That's all I'm saying." Lanis put a powerful hand on Tom's shoulder. "I think I'm going to introduce you to someone, and I'm going to lend you ten dollars. Come with me. Hey Lawrence, John…" Tom felt real uneasy.

"I'm heading home in a little while."

"No, you ain't, you're coming with us. You'll be home late tonight."

What does this have to do with anything? He thought of running, but he couldn't logically think of any real threat. They drove him to the Skirmish Bar; a joint he heard was pretty cowboy redneck. "You know I can't go in there. I'm under age."

"You're already legally drunk, Tom. I'll buy you a Coke. I can get you in. You're going to meet someone you need to meet. She has two kids, and she's a widow. She needs a little cash to get by right now." Tom felt the hair on the back of his neck stand up. A hooker with kids! He should have run. Inside, Lanis had a little talk with the bartender who frowned severely. Lanis had to argue a few minutes. Finally the bar man turned away to clean some glasses, and Lanis motioned Tom over. Second bar stool from the end sat a fair figured middle aged brunette tending a drink who had not turned once since they came in, but when she finally glanced around Tom could tell she had once been very attractive. She recognized Lanis and smiled, and gave Tom a smiling glance, and when she turned away Lanis slipped him a ten. There was no way out of it. Tom's legs felt weak as he walked over and sat down.

"Hello, honey." He resented the tone, adult to child. "You're a friend of Lanis?"

"Yeah." Someone sat a Coke in front of him, but he didn't notice who did it. "Yeah, we were down on the river. Lanis was going to take me home, and we just dropped by." That was a lie; it was way out of the way. He hoped she wouldn't ask where he lived. "Yea, uh, can I buy you a Coke?"

"Oh, no, thank you honey, not right now." She stared at him, and the smile made him a little jumpy. He almost had to turn away, but she turned off the strange, aggressive smile and toyed with her drink. "Did Lanis…, did he say something to you?"

"He said I should lend you some money." He was gaining a little more control, sounding a little more mature. "It's none of my business, but I'd like to help you out, seeing as you might be having some hard times."

"A lady never has hard times, but I could use a little cash, I have to admit." There was just a little smile directed at her glass. "Why don't we run over to my place and watch some TV? I'm getting bored to tears here tonight." She turned to finish the drink, and then grabbed Tom's arm for the walk out. Hand in hand, and now he was getting knowing grins from several patrons.

She really did have two kids, and the babysitter had to be sent home. He felt very strange about it as she put her two little girls to bed. He had to call a friend to get to lie to Mom in case she called, and then he called Mom and lied that he was spending the night with the friend. The next day he turned down the ride she offered, kissed her on the cheek, and walked to Matt's. He didn't want to face Mom for a while; he had the suspicion she could look right in his face and tell.

Lanis caught up with him eventually and had to rub it in. "You know the mark of a real gentleman? A gentleman knows better than to call a good woman a whore, even if she is one." If there had been a little resentment over Lanis's meddling, some long, hard thinking made him appreciate the reason for it. There would always be that little niche in his memory that reminded him how incredible it might have been to make love to Ellen on the beach and fall asleep with her drunk, like some other couples did occasionally in the willows.

"So, Tom, you're refusing to tell me about this one woman. I'll find out sooner or later."

"Who was that that said we need to forget the past and concentrate on the future? There's one little chore we need to do Saturday before we head up."

"Huh?"

"You'll see."

Matt drove them to the Chevy dealership around eleven, after they bought him breakfast. "I can't stand to see this. I'm a Ford man. See you in a little while."

Tom introduced Darcy to a salesman named Mark, who said "you two need to be looking at a coupe, something for a young couple."

"We can't even afford a used car right now." Darcy was uncomfortable even looking.

"We can always dream. I need to get motivated." Mark handed Tom a clean rag to wipe any fingerprints. "Get in the driver's side, Darcy."

"Tommy, not this car!" But she obliged and slipped in the red and white Corvette. "It's alright to dream, but we need to be practical." She tried not to let herself get enthused, but it was enticing.

"I know a hell of a lot about this car. I bought the Chilton's manual, but I need a Chevy manual. It's amazing; they still haven't sold this 56. This is going to be a very enjoyable car to work on, the first time someone brings one to my garage." She couldn't help but smile.

Agnes allowed them to move in Saturday without a word said; they were both relieved at her indifference. Monday found Tom ready with a new diving face mask and a used tight fitting wetsuit that Ray had dropped off and Darcy had spent a Sunday afternoon patching. Ray was late at the Quartz for breakfast, and they managed to get upriver by eleven. He introduced Tom to Whitey, a local, and Leroy, from Calaveras. Whitey was friendly enough, but Leroy seemed backwoods, neither smiled nor glared, and said very little. His clothes had been patched more than the average person would have bothered. He said, simply, "How do" as Tom shook his hand.

"I'll be back for Tom at six," Darcy said as she got ready to drive away. "Mother says she's fixing us dinner, Tom." They were close enough to town that she could shuttle him to work and back. Leroy camped in a tent with two watch dogs and guarded claim, but he would often get brought breakfast by the crew.

Tom wasn't impressed when he saw Ray's dredge sitting in a pool below some mild rapids, floating on two logs instead of pontoons. It was obviously a homemade rig, right down to the jet Ray had welded himself, and the plywood sluice box. The sixteen horse power cast iron engine was old, as was the Berkley water pump, but the Navy surplus HUKA compressor for divers air seemed new. Tom already had a fair idea of what the work involved. Details and trivia filtered into his consciousness as procedure and equipment were explained, but he knew before he arrived that they would be basically excavating the river bed, the bigger the better, he figured. If the dredge looked like junk, it served its purpose, and it had impressive power pulling up gravel.

Down in the underwater pit they had already started sat a large steel basket fitted with two cables, one to a double drum winch sitting on the bank, and one to a 'Dead Man' pulley chained on a strategic tree across the river and back to the winch. The set up was simple enough: pile rocks into the basket and winch them up to the bank, or winch rocks too big to move by hand with a cable, and dredge up the gravel to be run through the sluice box in which all the gold would hopefully be caught in gravity traps. "All summer long, six days a week," remarked Ray. "Or until we become too rich to get motivated. It get's painfully cold in November, but if the weather holds I keep going. Get a better wetsuit, Tom, as soon as you can afford it." It was painfully cold on this April day, and Ray allowed every diver to set his own time limit. There were usually two divers down at once, for safety sake, but Tom's first dive found his underwater partner gone after ten minutes. He was stinging with cold, but excited with the prospect of seeing gold. After an hour, he'd still seen no gold, and suddenly he wasn't getting enough air. Out of the water he got a strange response from Ray as he yelled his concern. Ray just waved him off, told him to "get back down there, you need the practice," and went back to talking with Whitey. He stood looking for a minute, and walked back underwater. It was ridiculous; there was less air than before. He came back out, dropped his weight belt in the shallows, and tramped up to them.

"Something wrong?" Casual expressions.

"You know there is!"

"Yes, I guess I do." Ray's grin was a little too serious. "You were having too much fun for your fist day, Tom. You needed to feel what it's like to be without air down there, so I opened the release valve up a little on the compressor. Some guys get the jitters diving, but you were too confident, and that can be dangerous too. I'm real serious about safety on my rig. If you had just kept trying to dive, I would have probably let you go. And one more thing, if anyone gets in trouble down there, I expect everyone who works here to get to it, no matter what it takes to get the man out. That's why the second air regulator is so important, and I have a third if need be."

"I was having too much fun, except I didn't see any gold. Do you think there might be something in the sluice?"

"Could be, but I doubt it. Almost all the gold in the gut is course, and we find most of it on or in the bedrock, down in the cracks and crevices. There's a bar downriver that has some fine gold in a clay layer, and we're going to move downriver tomorrow to work it for a week and pick up some operating money. We'll never get rich down there, but we can count on getting some gold. Let's walk down and take a look."

Downriver was an opportune spot for a private talk. "How often do we split gold?" Tom asked.

"Once every two weeks. Don't worry about it. We'll always get enough out of this bar to keep everyone going. I take out gas money, but if the equipment brakes down, I take care of that. The score I'm hoping to make this summer might not come for some time. It'll come off of bedrock down deep. Down at the end of my claim I suspect there's some serious gold down deep, too deep for my six. I need a ten inch dredge down there." He pointed. "Right next to the rapids."

"What size engine would run a ten?"

"A Chevy straight six. I have the engine and pump, but I still need pontoons for this dredge. I ruined my old ones on the rocks last year. If we hit something real good, I'll bring a ten in here, but don't hold your breath. I told these guys I'd get the ten going last year. If things get tight, I'll help you and Darcy out."

Tom studied the sand and gravel bar across the small river. "Looks like you've taken out about a fifth of the bar," he speculated.

"That's all about fine gold over there. You're going to learn about black sand and gold. It takes a whole day to process the black sand. You'll love it."

"Work is work. It all pays the same."

"Yeah, it does, over there. But I like to think the old timers left me a little something out of courtesy. A little spot they missed, that's all we need. I know the history of this stretch of the Downie, and it was filthy rich. There's an ancient river channel crossing just above the curve on the 'Boulder Bound', and again across mine. I know they were sloppy, cause they left one little virgin spot in the gut that we found last September." Ray was grinning severely as he reached in his pocket to produce a flat slug of gold to hand to Tom. "Don't drop it. I don't want any dings in it."

"Good Lord, Ray! This is the kind of gold they get around here?" Now he was enthused.

"Used to get, a hundred years ago. That's a fourteen ounce piece I took out of a pothole in the bedrock. That really turned some heads at the St. Charles. Biggest piece I ever got."

"There are people in Marysville who would hit you over the head for it. Should you be carrying it around?"

"There are people here who would too, but I need to show it off a little to sell it. You know you can't legally sell gold to anyone but Uncle Sam. The only gold you can sell privately is a collector's specimen piece, and Uncle has to know about it."

"How much did you get out of the pothole?"

"About five pounds, three ounces. I should have gotten the ten going, but first one thing, then another. It doesn't last as long as you think it will."

"Not in the St. Charles, Ray," Tom kidded.

"I admit we drank a little gold up."

"I saw Bill Rutledge hand Darcy two hundred dollars last week like it was nothing. I know you guys have to work hard for your money."

"Bill has been doing that since Bob died. He has a soft spot for Darcy, and Darcy turns around and lends a lot of it to her friends. Too many people hit on Darcy for money."

"I've been thinking about that. I hate to get dependent, maybe we can pay Bill back some day."

"I wanted to talk to you, Tom, to get some things straight between us right away." The tone was serious now, but not malicious. "I guess Darcy has told you we used to be together. I'm certainly glad to help the both of you out. She was good to me, and I hope no hard feelings ever come up over it." Very serious tone.

"I don't have any hard feelings, Ray, considering the opportunity you're giving me. If I had any hard feelings concerning Darcy, it would be over something that happened to her in college. Did you hear about that?"

Ray nodded yes. "I'm not proud of what I did with Darcy. This whole town knows that. I was married seven years ago to a very good woman, which I really learned to regret losing. I left my wife for another woman, and that woman ended up giving me a royal screwing. That's when Darcy came along. I'll never get back with my ex-wife, and I'm still thinking about the bitch that got me away from my wife."

"Ray, it's really none of my business."

"Yes it is. You need to hear an explanation. Darcy came along at the right time, make that the wrong time. I never really intended to marry her, and I just let it keep going."

"And now you're wondering what kind of a guy she's getting herself involved with."

"She seems to be doing alright." Ray's features reminded Tom of some of the Roman statues and pictures, a very Roman nose and curly black hair. Had to be some Italian blood despite the Irish name. There was a frown on his face as he leaned his six foot three frame up against a rock and surveyed the creek. The long arms were powerful enough; he could move bigger rock than Tom, no doubt.

"Ray, I'm starting with a clean sheet. And so is Darcy. I'll do right by her even if we ever break up."

"If you two decide to get married, you won't just be marrying Darcy. You'll be marrying this town."

"I'm going to get her away from Downieville. I'm going to have my own business someday in Marysville, a garage."

"And you're going to get the seed money right here, this summer?" That was the perfect description for it: seed money. "Tom, a lot of men have bet on seed money from gold in the past hundred years. There aren't that many success stories, I guarantee you. No one ever said life was fair. I've had seed money twice in my life, but I didn't have a fucking clue how to invest it. I think a man with his priorities set deserves a chance at some seed money. We'll kick it in the ass this summer and see what we come up with. And by the way, take a look in Bill's fish tank the next time you get over there if you want to see some real gold."

It was getting time for Darcy to show up, and the two men walked casually back to camp. "This has been a kind of whirlwind tour for me, Ray. I might have been loafing on the Yuba beach again this weekend, but now I know what I need to be doing. Darcy needs to be rescued."

"That's an interesting way to put it." Ray lit up a cigarette. "Want one?"

"I don't smoke. Thanks."

"Good habit, not smoking. I'm told I need to quit if I keep diving. I've got early emphysema. Working in the Sixteen-to-One didn't help my lungs any, either. I'm getting old now, I can't handle mucking anymore."

"Darcy tells me it's rougher than diving."

"Sometimes, right after they shoot the rock, but it always pays. I'm going to say one more thing. You need to know that if something happens and I can't run this operation, Whitey will take over, and unless you screw up, you'll have the job all summer."

"Are you getting lung problems already?"

"It's not that. I might be sitting in jail before summers out. I have a problem alright, two of them." Almost a smile, but not quite. "I've got two underage females after me right now, and frankly, there's not much chance I'm going to give that up. What I need to do is fall in love again with a woman my age, but unless that happens…, it's too easy for me. I won't be young forever, I keep telling myself, but I just can't seem to stop." That could have been the most arrogant statement a man could make, Tom thought. The matter of factness about it. A lot of men would have resented hearing it, but there was no arrogance intended, and perhaps there was remorse. It inspired all kinds of thoughts about imagined secret meetings, suspicious parents, and the law.

"That's definitely your business, Ray. Darcy is my business, and I'm just down here to make a living."

"I envy you, Tom. My shot at happiness is over, and I just don't care anymore."

"Not necessarily. You miners put so much into luck. Your luck could change."

"What do you mean, 'you miners'? When you jump into the river tomorrow and come up bitching about sore muscles, it won't be 'you miners'."

Leroy walked up with the first grin Tom had seen on him. "How would you like to be in charge of the black sand, young fella? I think we should make him our black sand specialist."

"Am I volunteering?"

"I think you are," Ray remarked.

"Work is work. It all pays the same. Let me see that big nugget again."

Ray waived his head no. "You're going to have to dig up one of your own down there." He dropped his cigarette and crushed it with a boot heel, and the honk of a horn in the trees up the hill announced Darcy on the switchback road leading to camp. Ray studied some rocks near his feet, and with a seemingly unconcerned expression he explained "she didn't leave me. She just gave up on me. She had to."

The couple was asked in for a cup of tea at Whitey's place in town, and introduced to his wife and kids. Whitey did some furniture building on the side, in his own shop. He owned his inherited house and property outright, and made much of his winter income off of made to order furniture of local hardwood and fir. Like many in the area he had worked in either the logging or mining industry most of his life, and at age 45 confessed himself too old to go down in a hard rock mine anymore. A tiny house, and a small yard, but an enviable amount of security and happiness, Tom thought. To be an integral part of the little community and live the rustic life, that wasn't so bad. Whitey's wife Jan kept Darcy going in a long winded conversation about the despicable attitude of some well known local spouse abuser, and Darcy's end of the conversation seemed to center around the phrase "I don't know why she keeps going back to him?" After a second and more thorough tour of the woodworking tools Tom and Whitey found the gossip at an end. Darcy offered her apologies for having to leave by reminding that Agnes was fixing them a dinner. As she got up she produced some folded sheets of paper that had obviously been in her purse for some time, and spread them on the coffee table for Whitey's inspection. They contained pencil sketches of a dining table and chairs that Darcy was certain she would finally be able to purchase from Whitey in the fall.

"I'll have some good black oak when I drop those trees on the Reeds property, but I won't get to it till winter," White explained.

"How much would you charge us for it?" Tom asked, realizing the design had probably been inspired by both her and Dave.

"Half of what I'd charge Bill Rutledge," Whitey grinned.

Darcy drove much slower than usual through town, and finally pulled over to talk. "There's something going on. I know her so well, Tom. Why don't we just go have a beer at the St. Charles?"

"We're going to have to put up with her for a while. She's going to have to get used to the situation."

"You don't know what she's capable of."

"We'll just sit down and be as gracious as possible."

"That doesn't usually work with her type, Tommy. My father used to get up from the dining room table and leave for a bar, and no decent person in this town blamed him."

"I think I handled her fairly well the day we met. She won't faze me again."

"Alright. I'm ready if you're ready." But as the house came into view it was "Oh God, no!"

"What's the matter?"

"That's Dave's truck. I can't believe she'd do something like this!"

"Calm down. I've been wanting to meet Dave, and his girlfriend. Now's a good time."

"Now's not a good time, and I only hope Linda is here. Christ, I need a drink."

"So do I. Now let's go in."

"Love you, babe," as she kissed him on the cheek. "You're so brave."

Dave was slightly shorter than Tom, skinny, with sandy blond hair and blue eyes, and as in the case of Ray, a potential ladies man. Tom could tell as they shook hands and sat down to chat that he was the personable, outgoing type, just the man to excel in promoting real estate, but from the handshake Tom knew he would make a poor miner. Pencil and paper only, and Tom could just picture Dave being intimidated by the now heinously imagined Greg.

"I thought we should all get together for a nice dinner and evening," Agnes explained. The comment might as well have been some dire insult, from the expression on Darcy's face.

"Where's Linda, Dave? Didn't she come up with you?" Darcy asked.

"No, she had some, uh, flu symptoms. She sends her best."

"I'm fixing a traditional Scottish dinner. It's been so long..." Agnes seemed absent minded. "I don't think I've made this since Robert passed on."

"You made that fish recipe several times for us, don't you remember?" Dave corrected.

"You're quite right. I don't know what I was thinking." That may have been a very accurate statement, from the mournful little sigh the woman tried to stifle as she led the way to the dining table. Darcy caught up with her and wrapped her arms around her from behind, gave several little hugs, and sat down while giving Tom a puzzled look. Perhaps if some devious intent had been planned for the evening it had been waylaid by the sting of painful memory, and all four sat down, gave grave, and got started with several minutes of bland conversation. But gradually the woman focused her thoughts, and some motive was definitely brewing. "I believe our town has so much potential. It's so beautiful in this canyon. Someday I know there will be fortunes to be made building glorious, fine homes for those retiring wealthy Bay area entrepreneurs."

"Mother, we've had this conversation several times before. I'm sure Dave doesn't want to talk real estate on his leisure time."

"That's why I'm holding on to this property tooth and claw, if I have to." As if Darcy hadn't spoken. "It doesn't look like much, but I'm going to make sure my grandchildren have some land to secure their future."

"No glorious, fine home for those rich flatlanders would fit on this little plot of dirt!" Darcy was red faced by now, and both men had lost the hope of a non-partisan evening. Tom had already been enlightened in detail how a girl's early affair with an older man could make for the dread of an unwanted pregnancy. Dread gave way to the longing for children by the time she met Dave, and she had become concerned with the fears of sterility, but possibly because she was an unmarried woman in a church going community she put off the doctors visit. She had told Tom that she would have children one way or the other, by adoption if necessary.

"I believe grandchildren were the new topic at hand, young lady." Dave was blushing, frowning. "Of course the subject of children and land go hand in hand. Only the riff raff and trash of society let lust interfere with the need for a planned responsibility to children."

"You're quite right, mother. There are too many people around who let lust rule their sense of responsibility, but

I doubt that any present would qualify in that category." Darcy was gaining the upper hand, but Dave had his hands together, finger to finger, against the bridge of his nose to hide his discomfort. There was an elegance in the woman's caustic attack. Was it acquired, or hereditary, this talent for arrogance? More importantly, when and over what does she plan to stab at Tom?

"How my daughter can turn things around. I think handsome Dave here would make a very responsible parent, and perhaps Tom as well." Perhaps? He could almost snicker at that. That was no attack, just a feign. "Well, what I was trying to lead to was the subject of commerce, and the future of this town. The gold is through, the real gold was done years ago, and while I believe it is admirable that so many manage to scratch out some grocery money…, well, we all know that we need a new source of economy. Anyone with any insight will agree that Downieville's future depends on its development and promotion of the canyon's beauty, a beauty that will be augmented by some of those exquisite two story dream homes we see in Home and Garden."

"Absolutely." Dave had it back under control. "I just hope I can manage to get in the market at just the right time."

"That's why I invited you up tonight, David. You have so much insight into this, and so much privileged information at your disposal. I know young Tom has good intentions, but he must learn from experience the futility of these foolish gold expeditions, and with no real training in anything that can amount to any kind of a future for my daughter…" Darcy was redder than ever, but a smile from Tom soothed her fears that he would succumb to the insults. "I was hoping you might consider using a little of your influence sometime in the future..., perhaps there might be some little..., how can I say it? You know, it's not what you know, it's who you know."

"Absolutely. You know, Mrs. McEarl, I will always be a friend to Darcy and Tom, and I would be glad to recommend Tom to my father's firm if he decides to get a realtors license."

"Oh Dave!" A sigh of temporary defeat. "You know that irritates me. Call me Agnes. You know better."

"The fish is delicious, mother." Darcy could have been stifling a laugh, Dave was downright cheerful, but Tom continued in a serious direction.

"You may be right, Agnes. I may need some new line of work by fall, but summer hasn't even started, and I have to say that I have really enjoyed my first day on the Downie. I think that if I have to give up playing in the river, which I used to love to do when I was a kid, I can set my mind on a very reasonable line of work for me to support Darcy. I'm a mechanic, Agnes, and that's going to be our future, no matter what becomes of the gold."

"You have a job you can go right back to? Am I correct in assuming this?" Agnes was so serious, he was beginning to feel that vulnerability again, and he was intimidated. She was one of those people who could turn so quickly, and make you feel it.

"I can get a job with my reputation. I quit to come up here; I wasn't fired, and I actually have a clientele..., people my age." That was a long shot.

"Fine. We shall see." So terse.

"How is Linda, Dave, aside from the flu? I want so badly for us all to get together. Tom's planning a barbeque in Marysville. I don't know how soon, but I've got to meet his friends, and you have to be there, in volleyball shorts he tells me."

"Volleyball wasn't the subject. The subject was..., real estate, of course. And my daughter's future, and I have to say..."

"Mother, you're spoiling your own dinner with these serious topics. Can't we just sit down and relax and enjoy this meal without something always coming up?"

"I have to agree, Agnes. We can find some other time to discuss real estate," Dave added. "I've just met Tom, and I know we have a lot to talk about."

"Alright!" She picked up her napkin and threw it down for effect. "Why do I go to so much trouble? Excuse me." And she got up and left for her bedroom.

"She'll be back in a minute and act like nothing has happened," Darcy remarked.

"Yeah, she does this, Tom. I thought of making up some excuse to not come, but I decided to placate her. When she's having one of her anxiety attacks, and begs for companionship..."

"David, that attack was just another of her little tricks. You know that."

"I wish I'd brought Linda up. That woman got me to leave her behind, and she wanted to come. You're right, I should have known better." There were little looks going on between them. First lovers, engaged to marry, now just friends?

"Dave, I need to have a talk with you sometime. Darcy told me about a guy named Greg when she was in college."

Dave looked extremely uncomfortable, and Darcy demanded "could we please just drop all unpleasant subjects tonight? OK? That subject is history, Tom. Alright?"

"Yeah, Tom. There's not much that can be done about that now."

"That kind of a guy needs to be dealt with the same way he deals with other people."

"You're right about that. He wouldn't know you."

"Dave, please! And you, Thomas, you're getting ready to see me get angry."

"I apologize. When she gets back, we'll get the conversation going about her grandiose plan for Downieville's economic development." Sympathetic chuckles. "And I'll explain to her that after I buy my first car at the end of summer with my gold money, with our gold money, mind you, it'll probably be a used car, I'll get around to reconstructing her old Ford, top notch. Matt and I can make the rust disappear."

"Just don't talk mining tonight, Tom." The loving tone had returned. "That's not going to be a good subject in this house. My father used to mine with a partner after logging season, and she had some nasty fights with him over it. Father and his partner owned a backhoe and wash plant, and they worked their claim for years. All they ever made out of it was a living. To my mother, just making a living is just another shade of failure."

"So I'd better really hit it this summer?"

"So we'd better plan on moving to Marysville in the fall."

"I think that would be the best thing for the both of you. We're just down the road in Oroville, and we'll expect you to drop by when you have a chance."

"When we move to Marysville, it'll be to buy a house, and a repair garage."

"Tommy!" She was smiling, but perhaps she thought the same thing her mother believed, that he was just going to learn a lesson with gold. Agnes did indeed return, and they were able to finish the evening with more pleasant subjects. About eleven, Dave had to protest that he would be home too late. Tom and Darcy assured him that they would attend his September planned wedding.

Walking him to his car, Tom reminded "if that guy Greg shows up, I expect you to give me a call."

"I hear he moved to Phoenix, but if I ever see him, yeah, I will."

"Good riddance," Darcy said, and Tom put his arm around her waist and pulled her close. It was a strange situation. Tomorrow he would be working for her fist lover; tonight she made her goodbyes to the second. There were looks between them, but Tom told himself that was over for good. And the business about a payback to Greg, he had set his resolve that it would not be laid to rest, depressing as the subject made him. He had had previous experience trying to set the world right; he knew well fate played no favorites.

That had been a black time in his life that he remembered seemed to begin with a little conspiracy, borne in the minds of kids. Older kids, not kids much longer, 14 to 16, and getting too big to be meeting on the river island they'd kept a clubhouse on for many years. Younger kids had claimed the junk board house, but these almost not kids had some serious business to discuss, and the looming adult world may have influenced their retreat to the island. "Kids talk, kids don't do!" That was the instigation; Barbara was the instigator. For Tom, it had much to do with his loyalty to her as a friend, and his realization that she was becoming a woman. At 15, Barbara had a thing for a guy name Ted O'Neil, and Ted was in a world of trouble. Barbara had asked Tom, Matt who didn't show up, 'Red' Moore, Ron Carey, and Tom Audrey, who didn't show up either, to attend the meeting. None of the guys, including Tom, were enthused, but all were sympathetic.

A year before, Ted had been just another kid in the system, fair grades, and plenty of friends. Tom knew him from PE to be one of the better athletes, a little bigger and tougher than average, but not mean. A well liked kid. During the summer Ted's father died unexpectedly of a blood infection, and by August Ted's mother had remarried. And practically everyone in school knew the rest. Ted started back to school a week late, and when he arrived he still carried the bruises on his face from the last beating Chuck, his stepdad, had given him. His whole attitude had changed. He avoided talking with people, got angry when confronted, developed an attitude with his teachers. School seemed to have become purgatory for Ted, but home was hell. The students knew, the teachers knew, his mother was getting the worst of it. She was working, supporting them all, and coming home to a man that rewarded her and her son with the cuff of a hand. Fortunately, the sister had been spared, so far. Most kids Tom talked to couldn't understand why Ted's mom wasn't able to rid herself of the mistake, why she and her kids remained prisoners, but some seemed to think it was the man's right to do as he pleased with his family. Mom had a talk with Tom and explained that there were too many legal complications involving the woman's property that were making it difficult for her to get a divorce. And she had heard that there was some intimidation involved, but that was already known. The stepdad had supposedly conned Ted's mom into believing he had financial security in several local properties, and that he had ties with a construction project in Sacramento that would make them comfortable. The ownership of the properties turned out to be in legal dispute, and the characters he was involved with were into shady dealings. It was apparent he had no intention of trying to get some work to help support them.

It was just more juicy gossip to a lot of people, but not to Tom, who had to hear about it from Barbara more than he cared to. The year before had been the year of Barbara's first friendship with a boy other than Tom. Ted often walked Barbara home from school, and saw her on weekends. But now Ted saw her very little. He had asked his mother to let him drop out of school and go to work, but she begged him into staying, with help from Barbara. It was all Barbara would talk about to Tom. He needed Dad's advice, but Dad was in Korea.

The clubhouse meeting turned angry. Ron and Red threatened to leave unless Barbara calmed down and stopped arguing. No one seemed to have any idea of what could be done to help. "Why don't we just kill Chuck? We're kids. They're not going to execute us," Red taunted.

"You see. You won't do anything. Nobody's going to do a God-damned thing. Have you seen Ted's mom? Have you seen her face? Right now she has a black eye. Why doesn't the law do something?"

"What can we do? It's not like we won't do something," Ron pleaded.

"We aren't going to kill anyone," Tom pointed out. "No one here has what it takes to kill, not if we all swore a blood oath. But I know something we could do. I'll do it, if someone backs me up. We could break his shin. I used a steel pipe on John Keats in the fifth grade, and I've still got the pipe."

"Where can we catch him?" Barbara pleaded.

"You aren't coming!" Tom warned.

"The hell I ain't. I God-damned well…"

"Shut up, you boney little red-head, you're staying home," Red demanded. "We can get him when he leaves the 'Conquistador'. He's there almost every night, falling down drunk. At least, that's what Pop told me. Pop despises him, says he's an arrogant SOB. But he also says he's dangerous."

"Do you know what he looks like? I've seen him three times," Tom asked.

"Yeah, I know him. My baby brother collects Halloween masks. It's either that or ski masks."

"We should each get a steel pipe." Ron actually sounded enthused.

"No, I'll do it. Just back me up," Tom said. All had thoughts of the righteousness that could be rendered. He wouldn't be permanently injured, but he would have a hard time getting at Ted's family in a leg cast. Tom already had a sinking feeling in his stomach. Dealing with a man as hard as this wasn't going to be as easy as talk would get it, and it could land them all in juvenile hall.

"When? What day?" Barbara begged.

"Right now. We'll get him tonight, if we can," Tom assured.

"You just go home, and we'll tell you when it's over, Barbara," Red said.

"Well, get going! It's going to take an hour just to get home." And she grabbed each one for a hug and a kiss on the cheek. She was really growing up fast, Tom thought.

It took a good hour that Saturday afternoon for Red and Tom to bed, coerce, and finally bribe three Halloween masks from Red's little brother. Fate would have it there was a vacant lot several buildings from the 'Conquistador', and fate would have it that the stepdad was known to walk past the lot coming and going. Red went in the bar door just fast enough to confirm that Chuck was inside, and the three boys set up their ambush from behind a small berm at the back of the lot. By nine, they were getting bored and edgy. Around eleven, Red said "that son of a bitch must have fallen asleep."

"I'm not giving up. I'd just have to come back next week. If you guys want to leave, I don't blame you," Tom answered.

"Something will screw up with you here alone," Red advised.

"I have to admit, I'd hate to have to shit and get by myself."

"Do you believe in guardian angels," Ron pointed out.

"If he's got a guardian, it's a demon," Red answered. "I'm going back in, just to check." He walked back so casually from the bar; they all knew Chuck was gone.

"God, we should have checked every hour," Ron griped.

"He must have walked out the other way, or someone picked him up," Red said.

"I'll tell Barbara, and I'll be back here next Saturday. He won't get away. His time is coming," Tom assured.

Fate can be a hard diviner, harder than Tom could have anticipated. No one believes the horrors of the world can touch you personally. He invited Barbara over Sunday to explain what had happened, and to reaffirm his commitment to the task. He wouldn't leave her with the slightest hint of how relieved he had been to be reprieved one more week before he would have to start worrying about the consequences.

Wednesday after school she came banging at the front door, pushing right past Mom in tears, and grabbing Tom's arm to pull him to his room. "We're moving, Tommy. My Dad's company is moving him to Florida." Rene gave them their privacy. She already knew. "They just told me today, but they've been talking about it for over a year. I think I love Ted; I can't stand this. They've given me two weeks to get ready. I don't want to lose Ted." Time for a long cry. Tom assured her it changed nothing for Saturday's plans.

Something was gnawing at him, something was wrong. He had weighed all the possibilities, and made up his mind, he could face any of the consequences to come. But he hadn't conceived of that which fate could deliver. Late Friday afternoon the soldier came to their front door. The messenger of death had saved Ted's stepdad, for a while. Time slowed down, and it was a slow and insidious process for the hurt to take hold. The rest of the world voided around Rene and Tom, and all manner of human endeavor became inconsequential. Barbara's parents allowed her to stay just long enough for her to attend the funeral. And on the day after Barbara and her folks drove away, Ted blew pieces of his stepdad's skull into the plaster of the living room wall with the 44 revolver a friend gave him.

"Thomas, I have some incredible news for you," Darcy said as they watched Dave drive away. She stood in the porch light, hands on hips, with a teasing grin. "We're going to have a baby!"

Tom caught himself from a severe frown, folded his arms, and squinted at her. "Don't look like that, Tommy," she laughed.

"You couldn't possibly know in this short a time!"

"Oh, but Tommy, I got it from an irrefutable source. Cathy Minten called this afternoon to give me the good news. Mr. Vernon Fickett has taken it upon himself to make sure that all the right people in this town are informed. It seems that you got me pregnant in Marysville, and you decided to take responsibility for your acts of passion and move up here to prevent me from being disgraced." She rocked an imaginary baby in her arms and chuckled.

"I thought the honorable trade of behind the back gossip was solely the ambition of the female."

"Thanks, Thomas!"

"Someone should remind him that he needs to get his shawl and break in his porch rocker before he starts his career as a gossip."

"Unfortunately, when men gossip in this town, it usually starts real trouble, and more men gossip than you'd think. People get into fist fights, and quit being friends. Vernon has already made enough enemies, he can't hurt us any."

"He'd better shut his trap about you. As far as I'm concerned, he's on the same list as Greg."

"Don't even kid around here about ambushing someone. I wouldn't put it past him, but he doesn't care. People expect men to duke it out, fair and square."

"If he wants to start something, he knows where to find me."

"His girlfriend has been my good friend for years, Tom. I'll never know why Elaine stays with him, but you know, they say love is strange. They live together at her parent's house, and they're not married, either. That's when he's not visiting his kinfolk in Alleghany, or staying up at the Smith Ranch."

"What's he got going at this Smith Ranch?"

"Not much of anything, really. It's one of those places where men go when they're down on their luck and they've run out of money. I hear Vernon tries to run the place."

"So he's kind of king of the bums," Tom grinned.

"It's alright to say that to me, Tom. But don't talk around town about the Smith Ranch. Nice guys can end up there, too. But I'll never let you head that way, baby." There were several Smith ranches in the northern Sierra, true ranches, but the locals knew the Smith Ranch for its true priority. Edger Smith started rooming miners in his barn in the 1880's, taking all manner of barter as rent payment, and by the depression his grandson had built two bunk houses with the labor of tenants. The Smith's were Mormons, and all local men who would say Christian grace before a meal and who made some effort toward the maintenance and upkeep, and some contribution to the bean pot that was always kept, and who behaved themselves in accordance with the unwritten rules, were welcome. Outsiders were allowed by invitation only. It was not a proud thing to admit attendance at the ranch. Women and children were welcome only during the day to visit, as it was assumed they would always have some better offer of retreat. If a man's wife had the grit to kick him out, the locals might tease him with "headed to the Smith Ranch".

"Vernon was eighty-sixed once, and he really doesn't need to be there. He just seems to be one of those guys that think he was put on earth to keep everyone else in line. Whenever he gets some scheme going he always manages to get a few from the ranch involved. You mark my words; he'll get 'em all thrown in the calaboose. I'll give him credit for one thing, he is intelligent enough to have gone to college, and it's a shame he didn't have the chance to go. It might have changed his attitude. Lord, does he hate flatlanders. He was beaten in a state high school chess championship by a flatlander."

"That's a petty hate. I hope there are enough people around here to judge me the way I judge people, one at a time."

Darcy wrapped her arms around his waist and squeezed. "You don't know how many people have taken to you!"

'And you're the only reason I'm up here,' he thought as they headed for bed.

FOUR

He was sound asleep, early in the morning, and something was grabbing at his face, his nose. It wasn't a dream; he had to rub his eyes open. 'What the hell was that?' he thought. 'A rat?' He lay back down for a second. 'No, probably a cat.' But he wasn't sure. This time he was wide awake, and some small paws pushed at his ear and temple. He reacted so involuntarily that he swatted it with enough force for it to hit the wall, and he heard the unmistakable whine of a cat in distress.

"Joe Joe!" she was up "What the hell is going on? Did you hurt my cat? Did you throw my cat against the wall?"

"You have a cat? You never told me."

"Joe Joe. Come here baby." The lights went on, and Darcy grabbed up a skinny black Egyptian tom cat that sat crouched, whining in the corner. "I can't believe you hurt my cat!"

"I'm sorry. I thought it was a rat." He knew better.

"A rat? How could you think Joe Joe was a rat? You're going to pay the vet bills if you've hurt my cat."

"I didn't know you had a cat."

"Yeah, I forgot to tell you. But listen, buddy, you'll get kicked out of this bed before this cat ever will. Are you alright Joey? Did the bad man hurt you?" Now there was just a little humor in her tone.

"Tell Joe Joe I'm sorry. I was asleep."

"You tell him." The cat wasn't enthused at another introduction to Tom, but he allowed him to scratch behind the ears as Darcy held him.

"How did he get in here? The door is shut, so is the window screen."

"He has a hole in the closet floor. I haven't seen him for two weeks, but he does that a lot. He is really Joe Joe the second. My first Joey was his father, and his mother belonged to the Parker's. Old Joey died about the same time as my father. Go back to sleep, Tom. Tomorrow is a workday, and I expect to be supported in a comfortable lifestyle." She was teasing now, and Joey was purring. No big deal.

"How's your man going to support you if your cat keeps him awake at night?"

"Deal with it, sweet. And remember, we can put you in another room."

"Yeah, but then I wouldn't be worth a shit at work."

"Tom, what do you think of my name?"

"What do I think of your name? What happened to go back to sleep? I think you should change it to Sophie, maybe Gertrude. What's wrong with it?"

"You don't think it's a little to masculine?"

"You mean like Connie might be a little to feminine? Connie is his real name, not Cornelius. What does it matter? No one is going to mistake you for a boy."

"My mother gave it to me, just to spite my father. When I was born, my father had a bet on a boy, and he lost some bucks. Mother suggested he name me Darcy after Darcy's raiders in the Civil War, because Darcy was one of her favorite dime novel heroes when she was a little girl. Father said if sounded ridiculous, so naturally she went and put it on the birth certificate. She liked to point out he could take me hunting or fishing just like he could do with a boy, because I had the right name for a tomboy."

"So are you a tomboy?"

"Only when I get on a horse. I can outride you."

"Maybe."

"Wait a minute. Get to be friends with my cat. I want to show you our picture album."

"It's two in the morning," he whispered as she slipped off to search in the dark at the hallway closet.

The baby pictures were quickly passed as she searched for a picture of Robert, but he had to stop her at one picture of a bare bottomed baby. "I recognize that fanny." The photo of about a thirty year old looking Bob would have startled Tom's mother. "He looked a little like Elvis. Do folks ever tell you that? He really did."

"He looks like someone else, doesn't he?" She said looks, not looked, he thought sadly. She was smiling intensely, looking for an acknowledgement, and it made him terribly uncomfortable.

'I can never replace your father. Take me for the man I am,' he thought, but he said nothing. On the next page, an even greater surprise. "I didn't know you had a sister. You never told me. What happened to her?" Darcy gave him an uncomfortable look, and let him figure it out on his own. "Oh!" The clothes were out of style, and those pale eyes made the recognition complete. "She was a very pretty woman, Darcy. She looked so much like you, I mean her features, and it's just that your eyes and hair are different."

"She could still be an attractive woman, if she took care of herself, and laid off the booze. But she's given up on that, completely, and I think that makes her even more dangerous. Dangerous to our future."

"Would you like to go back to school?"

"What brought that up?"

"Our future."

"There are a lot of things I'd like to do, Tom, but you have to be practical."

"You need to tell me if you need to finish school."

"Yes, Tom, I wanted to get my CPA."

"When we move to Marysville, you should finish school."

"Thank you, Tom. Good night."

"Good night. You think I look a little like Elvis?"

"Go to sleep. I think you look more like.., that movie star, you know who. He always plays a tough guy."

"Oh yeah. I know who you mean. That movie star that looks like me."

"He's right on the tip of my tongue."

"Elvis is a sissy. Everyone knows that." She gave him a severe look. "I mean, he's alright, don't get me wrong. But he's a blond, and he feels he needs to dye his hair black. You didn't know that, did you?"

"Yes, I know that. But he's awful cute. Do you think Dave's a sissy?"

"I think he's a nice guy, just like Elvis. I used to think Elvis was just another punk in a leather jacket, but now I admire him. I hear he takes real good care of his mother.

But you need a tough guy in your life, just like me." It was an enjoyable teasing.

"Victor Mature."

"Victor Mature? I don't look anything like him. Well, maybe."

"Not all blonds are sissies, Tom. Look at Connie, or Gorgeous George, the wrestler. And as far as Elvis goes, he could have pink polka-dotted hair as far as I'm concerned. Just as long as he dyes it black, I think he'd make a great Teddy Bear."

"You already have a great Teddy Bear!"

"Yes, I do. Now go to sleep!"

"I don't think I can, now. I'm wide awake. I think I'm going to need a little more loving to get to sleep. You can blame your cat for that."

"Good grief, Tom. You're going to be so tired in the morning." But she couldn't deny him.

When the alarm went off, he reset it an hour later. "You won't be doing that tomorrow," she warned him, head buried in her pillow.

"You know Ray. He'll be late at the Quartz."

At the second alarm, she got up and made him get dressed. "It's going to be hard to get motivated today," he protested.

"I wonder why? I'll motivate you!" She threatened him with a hair brush.

"I feel like taking the day off," he said nonchalantly. "I've just met the enchanted Indian princess, and work seems a little out of text." He pulled on her nightgown, and she seemed genuinely annoyed. "The enchanted Indian princess in the enchanted Sierra forest. The hell with work."

As he pulled her back against his chest and wrapped his arms tight.

"This is April, 1957, and this is Downieville, California, where people work to make a living. Work, as in showing up every day, on time, and putting in a good effort, as in impressing the boss, so that money can be earned, and bills paid…"

"No, no." He was snuggling too close, and she was squirming, but without antagonism, at least not yet. "How can this be the real world?"

"Where did you get this Indian princess idea?"

"If you had been a Maidu, you would have been a princess."

"Did my mother say something?"

"About an Indian princess? Is there a princess?"

"Yes there is. But you won't get to meet her until Halloween. She's an Aztec princess."

"This must be a costume party, right?"

"Every year. The Downieville Halloween dance. So my mother hasn't said anything about the Aztecs yet?"

"Aztecs?"

"You'll get an earful, sooner or later. They're the only Indians she has any admiration for. She's a genuine Aztec worshipper."

"The Aztecs were ruthless and cruel." A moment of silence for them to reflect on the inference. "I guess that's what got them to the top of the heap."

"I saw a documentary on the Aztecs a few years ago, made in Mexico. It was so incredibly beautiful, Tom, the legend of the prince and princess. The Aztecs believed that life in this world was so hard and bitter, even for their royalty, so the priests demanded that the royal couple be sacrificed. That would insure that the gods send them to an eternity in heaven together."

"Darcy, that's sick. How can you see that as beautiful?"

"Because they're right. Life is too hard and bitter."

He grabbed her again, and hugged her so tenderly. "Life is to be lived. My mother says that."

"They took the prince up to the temple and cut his heart out…"

"Jesus Christ!" he interrupted.

"… and then the princess drank a cup of poison so she could join him. You wouldn't do that for me, to join me in heaven?"

"How do I know you'll join me, if I get it first?" He was trying to tease. "You might run off with one of the priests, after I get it!"

"I wouldn't do that to you. I'd kill myself, too." She was dead serious.

'Who are you thinking about right now?' he thought. 'Ray, Dave, your father?' "Darcy, the Aztecs sacrificed their enemies, usually the men. They did it to terrorize their opposition. Thank God we don't live in that kind of a world. I think I'm ready for work now. I should appreciate this life."

"You're mother says you are a very responsible young man."

"I'm going to work today for one reason: I love you!" That got a hug and a kiss. "You know the prince and princess would better serve the people alive."

"In reality, the people serve the royalty, in any culture."

"Is that your mother talking? You don't think the royal couple could make a difference in the lives of the people?"

"Not really. They're really powerless. The priests run everything."

"Then your mother must be a priestess."

"Must be."

"Oh shoot, I almost forget. I thought about this all day yesterday, what would be a good time." He had something stashed under clothes in a suitcase. "It was my grandmother's. I inherited it."

She was almost panicking; the expression on her face, but it was panic and joy mixed when he opened the ancient ring case. "This is not the time. Oh Tom, it's beautiful." She was fighting tears. "I said we should get to know each other, and you should get to know this town, and I mean that, but…, how exquisite. Have you got a picture of your grandmother?"

"It's an engagement ring. That's what I intend it to be. It was her wedding ring, and it's a full carat."

"Yes, yes, I accept it. But let's not make any date yet."

"No, not yet. Let Fickett say something about this. Anything he wants."

"I love you, Thomas."

"You set a date with Dave, didn't you?"

"Yes, but we kept putting it off. First it was me, then my mother advised us to give it some time, then Dave backed off. I should have known an old girlfriend showed up. Maybe it was supposed to be that way."

"And he lived here for a little while, when you weren't in college."

"Yes."

"Let's get down valley as soon as we can."

"Let's get to work as soon as we can."

FIVE

Dredging would soon enough become routine. The rigors of the cold spring water dictated short work runs; working Saturdays made up for the short work days. After two months the water was getting comfortable, but they just weren't running into the significant gold Ray had been hoping for. It looked like Agnes might get the satisfaction of saying "I told you so". But Tom wasn't really worried.

Sundays were for church, noontime meals, sometimes with Agnes, and afternoon outings. Darcy knew so many places to retreat, when they weren't invited to friends, that they could spend their time exploring, and one hideaway on the river became an instant favorite with Tom. A giant, slow water pool with sandy beach followed by a narrow, steep sided chute with several little pools, and pinnacles of rock on both sides that he could dive from. They'd set their towels out on the sand with a wicker basket full of snacks Agnes had actually prepared for them, along with some wine or beer, and if no one was around, they'd skinny dip for the afternoon. Darcy swam fairly well in the shallow side of the pool, but on the first outing there when Tom tried coaxing her downriver to witness his diving skills, it was apparent she was having a problem. He made a couple of ten foot dives into the first little pool, but when he asked her to follow downriver, she was obviously distressed.

"That's excellent, Thomas."

'Uh, Oh,' he thought. 'She's using Thomas instead of Tommy.' "Am I scaring you? I check the bottom very carefully. I won't try any higher dives, even though I am so-oo good. You can hold onto the sides and float down. Come on, Darcy. I won't let you get into trouble." She wasn't about to follow. He walked back to where she was sitting on a flat slab of bedrock, staring listfully at the water, knees drawn up to chin and arms around legs. "You better get back in the water. You know you blush if a jay sees you naked. I think I saw some kids upriver." He needed to see her handle the current, and show him that she was the 'excellent' swimmer she had boasted. "It's a little cold," he rationalized.

"Yeah, it's cold," she eagerly agreed. It was aggravating him, but he wouldn't push it. Getting into that cold water would frighten her, he knew now.

Several days later he mentioned it to Agnes. "Darcy tells me she's an excellent swimmer, but I think I'm going to have to keep an eye on her."

"You need to stay right with her. To Darcy, the term excellent represents the achievement of two summers of swimming lessons. She is very proud of how much she progressed. Tom, there was a time when she would not go anywhere near the river, or a swimming pool, or even a little child's pool." The woman sat and cleared her throat, and took a few moments to compose her conversation. Tom studied the woman at a time when she did not seem so much an adversary. Even with the disheveled gray-brown hair and wrinkles there was attractiveness yet in the features of the woman. "I drink; you know that. I've always been a social drinker. My husband…" she had to compose again, "my husband rarely drank, but when he did, watch out! He drank out of depression. He drank himself into the hospital twice with alcohol poisoning. Darcy…, something happened on the river. He would never forgive himself for it, Tom. He took Darcy fishing with him, when she was six. She loved to go out with him, until this happened. He was drinking, this one time, because we had had a fight." She was fighting tears, this hard woman. "I would never have wished this on any man. He fell asleep, drunk, and she slipped and fell into the spring high water. You won't believe how she was saved. A dog! That's what Bob and Darcy both told me. He said he heard her screaming, and she had her arms around a dog's neck, a huge dog, as big as one of those bastards Bill Rutledge owns. Bob grabbed her and raced our old Ford truck back, and she was alright. She just swallowed a little water…, no, she wasn't alright. She wouldn't go out with him anymore. I had to talk her into giving in and going on a picnic with him a year later. It was horrible; she loved him, but she would not forgive him that." Silence for a full minute. "I've never cared much for animals. Darcy loves horses, and we've got a horse down the road that would die of a broken heart without her. I have to say, I would love to have found that dog. He would have lived the life of comfort with us."

"Did you husband ever find out about the dog? No one was there?"

"Dogs run everywhere around here for miles. You know it was some miner's dog, just out running. Bob said it jumped out, wrung itself off, and ran away. It was a beautiful dog, shiny jet black, maybe a mastiff. I'll warn you, Darcy is touchy about this subject. She took an awful lot of ribbing on that story."

He had to mention it. "What happened with the dog on the river, when you were a little girl?"

"Who..., what brought that up? I guess she's going to tell you every little thing." She was angry, and it surprised him.

"Yeah, it makes a good story."

"So that's what you think. If you don't believe it, it's no big deal. No one else does, either. Its Darcy's little girl story. Just drop the subject," she said with sarcastic anger.

"I believe it. I didn't know it was such a sore memory."

"It's a subject I don't want to hear about again! I almost drowned, alright? I almost died. And everyone thinks it's such a good story. Black dogs are supposed to be supernatural, either demons, or messengers sent to warn you. Everyone thinks we made it up."

"Screw everyone," he grinned back at her anger.

"Yes, screw everyone, and kindly don't remark about that dog again. I would love to have kept that dog. I am in the water screaming, and my father is drunk asleep. And all of a sudden there is a big dog beside me. It looked at me, and I grabbed it and hung on, and that's all the strength I had left. You don't know what that feels like, and you never want to know. It almost couldn't pull itself out, because I wouldn't let go, but it pulled us both out. FINALLY, finally my father wakes up! And then the dog runs, shit, like it was running to a fire."

"I believe that if the water still scares you, we should take it easy and stay away from the current."

"The water doesn't scare me!" Angry again. "I almost died." And then in bitterness "I almost hated my father, Tom."

"I've run into trouble in the big Yuba, by myself, with no one around. I've swallowed water more than once. You just have to get over it, Darcy. Of course, I have a reputation to maintain. I'm the 'Otter'."

"Well, hallelujah, Otter!" She could almost laugh. "I can take care of myself. You don't have to worry about me."

"Yes, I do." And that called for a kiss.

SIX

June brought dry Mojave heat, earlier than usual. All the divers enjoyed the reprieve from the "liquid ice" that would return in the fall. Whitey convinced Ray to give up the hole in the gut to concentrate on making some sure money for a while out of Ray's "River Bank". Everyone had bills to pay, and the bank wages were steady, but they were low. The second week in July everyone had caught up enough to risk some gambling in the gut. The first day Tom found a two pennyweight nugget in the gravel, but Ray advised that the gold they were looking for would all be on or in bedrock. Ray started digging deep trenches looking for some sign. A wine bottle on bedrock brought some laughs. In late July the crew ran into a huge boulder where the bedrock was dropping and the pit was getting deep and dangerous. Big boulders were supposed to drop gold in a flood, but the results behind the boulder were meager, as it had apparently been worked as late as the depression days.

"Tom, find us an Irish pot hole!" Ray commanded one day.

"Right, boss. Under a rainbow, right?" Tom took his turn on the hose nozzle, and looked in a new direction, deciding to follow an underwater shelf towards the bank.

It dropped back into another trench, and the consistency of the gravel changed. There were no more broken, jagged rocks; every rock was smooth and rounded, with patterned stains on the gravel, almost like it had been painted. Brown, dull yellow, black, maroon, and on the bedrock there was a consistent thin layer of black sand, dotted with gold dust. "Look in the sluice box," Tom demanded after a two hour dive.

"Yeah, this is the place!" Ray snapped his fingers.

The crevice got deeper downriver, and every rock in it was sitting on gold chips and little nuggets in a gray clay or black stained gravel. Under a two hundred pound blue rock that was incredibly heavy for its size, Whitey found a six ounce gold-quartz piece, and came up to show it off just as some miners from upriver arrived to share some beer, and within two days the rumor in Downieville was that Ray's crew had struck it.

Gold does not glitter, it glows, and in the end it weighs. The men were not getting rich, but they were finally getting ahead, and the spirit of the quest was back. This wasn't real work, this was adventure. And it became a little side show as well, with all the people dropping by, curious to find out if the rumor was true. People who were welcome friends, and people who really shouldn't have been so nosey, but Ray welcomed them all with courtesy, careful to warn the crew never to leave the sluice box unattended.

"Have you ever heard of 'Poor Man's' creek, Tom?" Ray asked me one day as they sat keeping an eye on Leroy and Whitey.

"It sounds like the wrong place to look for gold."

"It was anything but poor. It's over on Nelson creek on the Middle Feather river, and it's famous for the 'Poor Man's Massacres'. It was so rich that when the small time miners got wealthy and gave up, the Bonnie Mae mining company bought it all up and flumed the creek for the deep gold. I think that was in the 1860's and 70's. Bonnie Mae made millions off that creek, but they had to shoot their way to the bank. There were so many people trying to high-grade the sluices that they put up the famous signs 'sluice robbers will be shot on sight'. And they shot more than one some days. That was one neck of the woods you didn't want to accidentally stray into. Some of the high-graders shot first, and they were asking for it, but some of the poor bastards just wandered in by accident. They had mass graves. There are still some places you don't want to hike in these woods, Tom."

"Vernon mentioned that, the first time we became acquainted." Both men grinned. "Darcy says never go back country without someone that's known around here."

"Well, you can probably get away with it if you carry a fishing pole, but I'd be packing a weapon, too."

"She says I'm more likely to run into a still than a crazy miner."

"Did she tell you..., about Agnes?" Very severe grin now on Ray.

"Yeah, Agnes seems almost proud of it. We were watching a gangster movie one night on TV, and out of the blue Darcy says 'you know my mother was a gun moll'. I didn't really want to hear something like that, I mean, there's still a lot I don't know about the both of them. I figured she was exaggerating..."

Ray broke into laughter. "No, she was telling the truth. She did six months, but it was just shine. A lot of people did shine in the depression. Someone always has to get caught."

Darcy had continued that evening with "my mother the gangster", trying to aggravate Agnes.

"Let's just watch the movie. Movies are fun. If you really want this young man to know, fine, I'll tell him. Movies are fun, real life is not."

"Oh, mother, can't you take some kidding? A lot of people used to make shine during the depression. Shine is fine, they used to say. There were hard times, and everyone has to make a living, so people made shine to get through the hard times. It was a little game, with unwritten rules…"

"And you weren't even born, young lady. I made good money, and I kept my kinfolk from starving. The only thing I'm not proud of was getting caught."

"Downie-Dew." Darcy wanted to tell it. "Some of the best came from our woods. Now there was better that came from the mountains north of Phoenix, but we were closer than Arizona." Darcy was telling it like she had heard it a few times.

"And I had a 26 Cleveland Roadster rigged with a false gas tank. Now let me tell this!" Darcy was ecstatic at forcing this confession. "I ran shine to Modesto for four years. This canyon had some of the best sipping liquor in California, bar none. You just ask around. I met some of the most prestigious and prosperous people you can imagine at the 'Speak Easy' I delivered to…"

"Underworld characters, mobsters!" Darcy delighted at prodding.

"Shut up! Do I need to put you in the other room?"

Darcy giggled and got up. "I'll get us some 7-UPs."

"I met all kinds of people besides the Mob. It was a social thing."

"And cutting a little off Uncle Sam's share made everyone feel better about the hard times," Tom theorized.

"Exactly. But it wasn't always a game. It's sad that people occasionally got killed over a social thing. Our Federal Government had to take the whole thing too seriously. I was shocked when Sheriff Dean nabbed me, I mean, I assumed he knew. I thought he'd just look the other way. I always took a secret route to Modesto, and he knew right where to find me on the mountain. We have a little saying around here, and it still applies. 'Never betray a still'. I still don't trust those Alleghany distillers."

"And never double cross a partner," Darcy added from the kitchen.

"Conway Dean was very civil about it, and I ended up getting six months. One of my correction officers is still one of my dearest friends, Tom. Bellamy comes up almost every summer to pick and jar blackberries. She's retired." Tom smiled in sympathy.

"Not everyone in Modesto was as charming as she makes them out, Tom." Darcy returned with the drinks.

"No," angry that Darcy had dared to make it serious again. "Not everyone."

"Some of them were into things a little meaner than selling shine." Now Darcy was too serious.

"Some of them were. I didn't have much to do with that crowd." Tom wondered how accurate that was.

"Let's forget about it," he tried to get it over with.

"She's lucky she didn't get a concealed weapons charge, too. Pistol packing Mamma." Darcy smirked.

"I wasn't a mother yet, and yes, I would have shot someone, to defend myself, of course. There was some nasty competition." That was depressing enough for Tom to hear.

The men sat in silence for a while, watching the underwater workers through crystal clear water, until Tom said "pistol packing Mamma", and laughed.

"Don't kid her too much about that. She still has that little 32."

"Ray, if you see a good deal on a car or truck, we need some wheels."

"Why don't you wait till I get that business done in September, so you can get something that will last? You don't need a junker."

"I've got to get a car, man. This asking Agnes every time we go to a movie or something, it gets old."

Whitey came out of the water to show off a three quarter ounce nugget that would be put in the strong box Ray carried. Ray took the smaller gold to Sacramento every two weeks to sell the Federal buyers, and everyone's share came in cash after expenses. But Ray was not being completely up and up with Uncle, and all four men were willing accomplices whenever gold was stashed. The law stated that all gold produced in the U.S. must be sold to the government. Ray had an appointment with an overseas buyer in September who would pay up to twice the government's rate of twenty-nine dollars an ounce. The men knew they could do jail time, but as in the case of the shine makers, not all small time miners rendered unto Caesar. So when a few people were around, Ray allowed a cleanup in front of witnesses. But with a lookout posted, other cleanups took place late, usually along with some minor dredge repair, whether necessary, or simply as a front.

Tom had learned from the men the dilemma of Federal gold price laws, the fixed price here, verses a higher market value in other parts of the world. Ray and Leroy definitely enjoyed arguing over the law, Roy accusing the government of dictatorial methods, and Ray arguing that the price fixing had some justification, but agreeing that the price needed to be raised at regular intervals to keep up with inflation of miner's operating costs, both placer and hard rock.

"We used to have a gold standard in this country, Tom." Leroy explained at one lunch break. "The entire world respected our currency with gold to back it. A gold standard would open up a lot of old mines and put people back to work, and make our money sound. When we've lost our gold mining industry altogether one of these days, it'll be God-Damned too late."

"That's absolutely true," Ray agreed. "We need to mint some American gold coins again, but let's do it the way South Africa does it. If we went to the gold standard right now, we wouldn't have enough gold to back our currency." Tom had never given thought to the economy and money supply, but now he could relate it directly to his own well being. Ray continued "Our currency is valued around the world, and its value is based on the productivity of this country. We've gone well beyond the gold standard days, and our currency is still sound. What we need is a miner's lobby. We need to let the price find a worldwide set value, and we need to mint a gold coin valued by its weight, with no face dollar value. I'll be Tom never heard what Ulysses Grant did to the silver industry to promote a dollar value."

"Yea, well I've heard it." Leroy walked away.

"Ulysses Grant, the Civil War general?" Tom asked.

"Grant the President. He took a train to Cripple Creek, Colorado, one fine day, headed for a little paper signing ceremony. Some greedy factions wanted him to change the currency standard from silver to gold, and that was when people demanded we back the paper with metal. Both industries were doing just fine, and a lot of people wondered why the U.S. couldn't just set its standard with both metals. The silver boys took all the cobbles out of the street leading to his hotel, and replaced them with high grade silver ore, but the gold miners got one up and managed to get hold of the brass head posts from his hotel bed, and they electroplated them with gold and put them back before he arrived."

"Influence peddling! Those guys were acting like a bunch of kids."

"It could have been a fine little comedy, but a lot of people weren't laughing. His advisers got him to change the standard to gold, and the next day the price of silver dropped by almost half, and it practically killed the silver mining industry through the 1870's. By the end of the week thousands were out of work, wondering why the hell he had to do it."

"That's ridiculous. Why did that cause the price to drop?"

"You've got to understand, the value of silver and gold is all psychological. In order for silver and gold to have some value, they have more than a collector's value, they have some use. The price of silver is definitely influenced by the photo industry. A sharp rise in price would hurt that business."

"I hear the price of diamonds is controlled by the South Africans."

"Exactly, but who determines the price of gold? Right here, Uncle Sam does. The jewelry market uses a lot of gold, and industry uses some, but what's its real value? It's real value? It's all in your head."

"Yea, like when I think about what it would be like to buy a new car without having to finance, right after Ray hits his big pocket!"

"Dream on. Gold's real value is in the jobs the mines create, and the prestige its production gives to a state or nation. I think our law makers set the price because they are concerned with the history of violence associated with this particular commodity. Gold has maimed and killed a lot of people in these hills, and I'm not talking about mining accidents. Uncle thinks he can put a handle on the greed, but he's got to wake up and realize he might be killing the industry."

A sound industry, producing prosperity out of the ground, paying wages that bought goods in the consumers market. Gold was a very useful commodity in itself, Tom realized, a raw product that could serve directly as money. A fuel to keep other industries in full swing. And as for those historical myths concerning the evil inspired by gold, they did not concern Tom.

As September approached the crew found an end to the gold producing crevice, and production played out. Each man got to pick as a share of the gold cut several specimen pieces. At the last gold selling of August Tom had gotten so far ahead of the wages he would have made at his old job that it did not immediately concern him when the gold ran out. With money in his pocket Tom finally got to organize a Yuba beach barbeque the first Saturday in September with the help of Rene and Agnes, a week before Dave and Linda's wedding. Dave and Linda showed up with friends from Oroville, and there were questions from both Tom's friends and the new crowd as to whether Darcy and Tom had set a date for their wedding. Darcy carefully evaded the pressure some people could put on with remarks about having plenty of time to plan it, and though it was just a technicality in Tom's mind now, it did concern him a little.

All the times Tom had beach bummed on weekends, he decided he would welcome anyone he knew who happened by, but he wasn't really expecting Hiame. The crowd was intense on a game of volleyball, and Hiame was making a point of avoiding them, trekking barefoot upriver by the water's edge, dressed in filthy shorts and tee shirt, but Tom noticed him and tried to be cordial. "Have a beer with us, 'Mechanic'," Tom yelled.

Matt looked peeved, and Arnold Hanley gave Tom a severe frown and demanded "let's keep the game going."

"I'm going to talk with him a minute."

Hiame slowed and turned when he realized Tom was walking after him. "Hey, Tom. I didn't know you were in town. I'm not dressed to visit your friends." Hiame looked rough, tired, and unhappy.

"You can grab a beer and head out."

"No, I'm too angry right now, I can't handle it. My brother's getting me so pissed off, I'm afraid I might kill him, if I have to listen to any more of his crap. He and his friends are rebuilding Papa's house, and I'm supposed to be helping them."

"That's great. I'm glad you won't have to move."

"Yeah, that's great. Great to have a roof over your head. That's for sure. The money is coming from Al's heroin deals, Tom. My father wouldn't have anything to do with him, until after the fire, and I think he and his friends may have set it. Now he's so welcome again."

"Maybe he's trying to make amends."

Darcy interrupted with "have a Coke, Hiame."

"Thanks."

"There's food."

"No thanks. I'm headed somewhere."

Darcy smiled and walked back, and when she was out of earshot, Hiame said "I'm liable to beat Alfonse's head in. I'm going to lose my temper, and then my life is going to be over." Tom could sense the tension in the big man. Hiame was not a man to be taken lightly. "I'm going to tell you something, as a friend, that you will never repeat." Tom nodded in compliance. "I went to a party at one of Al's friends last Saturday, and that was a big mistake. You remember that cute Mexican cheerleader named Marie?"

"Muy bonita, senior. I haven't seen her in a long time." Everyone on the team knew Hiame had a thing for her, but it would never go anywhere. With long hair down to her waist and a cameo face, she got looks from all the guys.

"She was at the party. My loving brother knows how I used to feel about her in school. So what does he do? He tries to set us up."

"Hey, maybe he's not such a bad guy."

"He's got her hooked, Tom. She told me we could spend the night in a bedroom if I brought her a hit. She had the needle and the tourniquet, and I, just..., just walked out. I couldn't believe it."

"Jesus Christ!" Tom shook his head and took two steps back. "Doesn't he ever give it a rest? Fuck him, Hiame. He's not worth ruining your life over. Just worry about getting the house built, and learn to be practical, man. Make the best of what you can take advantage of."

"I can't control my temper. You know what's going to happen to her. In five years you won't recognize her. She'll be a prostitute in West Sac, and, Christ, I would rather see her married to a nice Mexican boy. And he thinks I should have taken advantage of her, that son of a ...," Hiame had to look across the river, and slam a fist against the palm of the other hand. "Cain slew Able, the Bible says."

'But which are you?' Tom thought. 'Cain, or Able?' "Hiame, remember those hankies. Think of all those handkerchiefs, man. Hiames's hankies." Tom grinned, and Hiame had to smile. Second winning game, the first game Hiame and Matt heard the crowd chant "Mechanics, Mechanics!" Something about coming back from those first two miserable games to a winning streak gave them such an enthusiasm, they felt invincible. Coach had taken out the quarterback, a senior who was a real prima-donna that was always arguing, and given a junior second team quarterback a couple of plays. Something just worked right, so when the senior came back in and fumbled, coach removed him from the game, and made him second team. Then quarterback Bill Timmons asked Coach Phil Metzer to give him second team fullback Hiame to match Matt on the offensive line, and the Mechanics began to tear apart the opposition, opening up an advantage for Bill time after time. The tiny, unenthused crowds from Marysville soon grew to an intimidating full stadium. Second winning game Hiame slipped, fell on his face, and let Bill get nailed. After a few seconds of silence, the Spanish Marysville girls began whistling and taunting "Pobrecito" and "Pendeho", and waiving handkerchiefs. Hiame got up, walked past the ref towards them, and bowed so stately that all the girls clapped, and even the ref had to chuckle. After that, almost every Marysville girl, Spanish or Anglo, carried a "Hiame's hankie", and at the end of each game Hiame would walk the bleacher front for the fluttering of the hankies, this time as a tribute to a winning game.

"Those days are gone forever, Tom. But you're right. Papa's house is getting rebuilt, that's all that matters. I'm going to let the Sheriff worry about Al. So how's your job going?"

"We just ran out of gold." Tom neglected to mention how far ahead he had gotten with a new bank account and seven ounces of specimen gold hidden away. He was a true miner now. Never let on to what you are really getting. "But I love the work, and I know there's more gold."

"Well, you take it easy, Tom. You seem to be on top of it." And he turned and headed out.

"That man needs to lose a lot of weight," Darcy said, walking up. "I brought him another Coke. Too late."

"There goes a righteous man, Darcy. I'll tell you later," as they walked back.

Arnold Hanley greeted them with "how's he doing? I feel bad about the way we treated him. That guy doesn't even look the same. Christ, we had some great games, but man, he looks like a bum now. Some people really go downhill." He shook his head.

"I think he's a slob," Betty Cambell sneered.

"Betty!" Darcy warned in a friendly tone.

"He's gone downhill," Susan Ellis said. "You never saw Hiame play. He helped us get into the district playoffs, and we should have offered him something to eat."

"Speaking of..." Darcy pointed out. "We need to start some charcoal, and Tom says we should let the boys have some games to themselves."

"Yeah," Arnold demanded. "I finally get to spike, for real. The girls have to go."

The beach along the Marysville Yuba flood plain comes in tiers, with higher benches, and plenty of sand in many places, ideal for picnicking. Sandy roads make traveling difficult for cars, and the barbeque crowd was not expecting a newly painted, well waxed 48 Chevy convertible down the rough road past the flat they had all parked on. The car was so obviously well kept; the owner meticulously cared right down to the whitewalls. He finally stopped at a dip that would have bottomed him out, about two hundred feet from the crowd.

"I don't believe it! Two of them in one afternoon." Tom Ellis remarked.

"He's probably looking for Hiame," Tom realized.

A very black haired, fair skinned Spaniard of about five foot four, slim, and definitely dressed in a style that had something to say, Alfonse started walking toward them, and then turned and waved at the Spanish girl accompanying him. She shook her head and leaned on an elbow.

"I'll bet you're looking for Hiame," Tom greeted him. "You want a beer?" Tom thought that what he should really do is quit being so polite with some people. Al wore a velvet black vest over a silk dark purple shirt, and jet black slacks and square toed boots, the boots obviously expensive.

"No thanks, uh, you're Tom, right?" Tom nodded. "Yes, Hiame, he's very lazy. He has some chores to help us with today, but any excuse, and he runs away. We're building Papa Esposito a new house, and Hiame should be more respectful."

'Not in those clothes, you're not working!' Tom thought. "He was headed upriver about an hour ago," Tom pointed, feeling like he had betrayed Hiame simply by being polite.

"He can't escape," Al chuckled. "We call him Hiame-cito, the petite one." No one but Betty seemed to find this amusing, Tom noticed, and there was definitely a cold stare from more than one. "I know where he's going." And he headed back.

"I think he just wants some time to himself," Tom remarked loud enough for Al to hear, and Al turned briefly and gave him a look that chilled him right to the bone. 'A known drug dealer,' Tom thought, 'who's done time'. But had an alien landed, lacking more detailed information, Al would have definitely made a better first impression than Hiame.

"Is that the drug man?" Darcy asked Tom under her breath.

"Yea, he sure dresses to impress," Tom answered.

"I think he's divine." Betty had overheard. "He can't be the brother of that slob!"

"Shut up, Betty!" Her boyfriend John McCary demanded.

"You shut up. Don't tell me how to think!"

"Betty, he sells drugs." John's voice was getting angry.

"Kids, let's change the subject," Arnold ordered.

"He sells heroin to Marie." Tom had to reveal, remembering too late his promise to secrecy.

"Oh Shit!" Arnold said. "Hiame will kill him."

"What's this about?" Darcy asked.

Betty demanded "all right, tell me everything. This sounds juicy."

"It's very simple, Betty. Everyone knows Hiame liked a cheerleader named Marie. Al sells drugs." Arnold explained.

And then Betty finally realized. "Oh, that's no good!"

"Yeah, Betty, it's downright cruel," John added.

"Then Al should go to jail!" She seemed to have made a revelation.

"It's his home away from home," Tom grinned at her.

After the late drive back to Downieville, a weary Darcy asked "so, did you enjoy it? Did you make an impression?"

"You made the impression. Hiame once invited me to take a trip with him to his mother's home town in central Mexico, a place called Selada. Maybe we can get him to take us both down there."

"Oh, wouldn't that be fun! Is she dead now?"

"Yeah, Hiame used to sit on the bench and tell about that place, about how much he missed it. He spent a summer there when he was nine, helping his uncle grow melons and squash. He could talk for minutes about the fantastic melons, and then he'd mention that they use human waste for fertilizer."

"Uuh! No thank you."

"He could make the place sound like Shangri-La. The people have such a good attitude, you see. There's a mine, too, that belongs to the whole village, and only one family mines it. It used to belong to the Spanish Crown three hundred years ago, and it was given to the villagers before the Crown lost Mexico. There was a fault in the ground, and the ore disappeared at the fault, so the state gave up, but a villager asked permission to look for a continuance above ground. He found it, and the Viceroy gave the mine to the village, with the condition that 10% go to the church, and 40% go to the state."

"An honest Viceroy. How rare, honesty in the mining industry!"

"Now 10% goes to the church, and the rest is shared by the village."

"How long do you think that will last, before some big company takes it away from them?"

"Probably they'll keep it. The mine is cursed, but they didn't know why until the 1950's. No one who works in the mine any time lives past forty. The ore is radioactive. It's got gold, silver, copper, zinc, and some uranium and radium."

"Cancer? I've heard about mines like that in America."

"I used to kid Hiame, 'radioactive Mexican coins, man'."

"You'll never work in any cancer ground. Are Hiame and Matt still at odds?"

"They had a hell of a fight that year one afternoon after school at practice. Matt says Hiame accused him of saying something against him as a Mexican, and I know Matt wouldn't do that. Those two guys are so powerful, no one could get them apart, and Coach Metzer screamed at them and got sick over it. He had a heart attack later in the season, and that fight probably helped bring it on. He didn't get to finish the winning season, it was sad. Matt knocked Hiame against a chain link fence, and the points gouged a big hole in Hiame's side, and he had to have stitches. Somebody got a water hose on them and finally stopped it. The whole thing got swept under the carpet, but the whole school knew. No one wanted to lose the 'Mechanics'."

"I'd like Hiame to show us the Aztec pyramids. I mean, an Aztec princess should definitely get to see her pyramids."

"Tell me, what, princess?" He tried to tickle her sides, but she could be as fast as her cat, and she bounced off the bed, warning with a finger not to push it.

"You'll have to wait a few weeks, and then you'll see. Me and the Halloween kitty."

"How do you know Joe Joe will be in town for Halloween? He may have a pressing engagement."

"He'll make it. He always has. Tom, I don't want to be too nosey, but I want to know about this fight…, after your father died, that your mom says you and she had. I know you ran away for three days, you told me that. What really happened?"

"She doesn't really remember everything herself, I'm sure. My Dad died, and we should have taken care of each other, but everything just went wrong. It was hell, what can

I say? One night she dated a real low-life, someone she had nothing but contempt for when Dad was alive. She quit going to church for a while. But that's all over, and that's all I can remember." Silence for several minutes gave Tom the time to remember. A week of strange attitude; maybe he was going crazy too, it was hard to say. People were coming by, trying to cheer them up. The second week she skipped church, and started telling people over the phone she was too busy to have them visit. Then Ronald Smith, a divorced member of their church, came to the door one evening and talked her out for the night. Tom could not stand the guy, and believed she thought the same, but she just gave in and went out with him. One o'clock in the morning he's sitting on the couch and they come in drunk, falling all over each other. It was a nightmare, Ronny gave a gruff hello, and Tom got up and walked to his room without answering. At six in the morning he was woken by crashing sounds in the kitchen, pots and pans being slammed.

"I can't bring anyone into my own house without being embarrassed. Who needs it? Why is he living here? He should find his own place to live." He couldn't believe his own ears. Was she going to kick out an underage kid? It was too early for her to date respectfully, and certainly not that bastard. She was having some kind of a breakdown. "I don't need this shit! I'm not going to put up with it. I'm going to sell this house, and he can get the hell out!" She left in the car, and he packed up a tent and backpack, made two calls, and left for the river. He was out of school for three days; he knew they would look for him. When he was brought back, she apologized, made some promises, and told him she never wanted to lose him. And then she started seeing

Max Ingram. If he had to pick someone to replace Dad, if he absolutely had to choose, Max would be at the top of the list. He just couldn't stand to think about it, but he treated Max with respect, and Max was being very tactful.

"Your Mom says you both went in for counseling." Darcy said just as he almost fell asleep. They had both been too tired to make love.

"Yeah, I went to see an ex-deputy sheriff who does social work, just to make her happy. We got it all worked out. She was just worried about me."

"She says you made some kind of a statement that got her upset."

"I shot off my mouth one night, and said I was going to get a pistol for our protection, now that Dad was gone, and she took it the wrong way. I only meant I wanted to protect her. So I went to see this guy, Marlin, somebody, I forget his last name. I told him I was just blowing off steam; I didn't mean to scare her. He turned out to be a pretty cool guy. He knew a hell of a lot about Ted's case, after he got arrested. I guess you've heard about him?"

"All about him. Jamie says he got a hell of a bad deal. I guess when you kill someone, you have to pay something."

"Let's change the subject. Think about our trip to sunny Mexico, and your pyramids."

"Don't get my hopes up for nothing, Tom. I'd love to take a trip, for about six months. A year. FOREVER!"

"You'd miss Downieville the first week."

The visit to counseling with Marlin had been done under protest, but Marlin immediately made Tom feel at ease. Tom promised he'd put off getting a weapon until he was out on his own. Marlin guessed very accurately some of the thoughts and problems Tom was dealing with at the time, and then brought up Ted's case. Marlin had done some of the questioning for the state prosecutor, and helped work out Ted's plea bargain. "You can never take back a bullet, Tom. You don't know how many young men I've had to cuff in my career, but very few of them for something like what Ted did. You should take a safety training course before you get a weapon. Can I schedule you for one?"

"Yeah, sure. That would make her feel better. Did someone get in trouble for slipping Ted that pistol?"

"They would have been charged with complicity, if we could have figured out who it was. Ted swears he had it all along, but his mother disagrees." Marlin folded his thick, powerful fingers on two massive hands. It wasn't hard to imagine Marlin grabbing a suspect, slamming him against a wall, and cuffing him. He just had that look to him. "There was more than one law officer involved in that case that has stated to me they wish to hell someone could have gotten something done before it ended in homicide. Everyone liked Ted and his mother. But civilization has to be run with a set of rules. When people kill people, it is the duty of others to demand retribution. That is what keeps a society from chaos. Ted was given six years for second degree murder, even though he was minor. He lost his temper, Tom, and look what it did to his life! Look what it did to his mother! He says he tried to walk away from Chuck. Chuck was drunk, and dared him to shoot. Ted should have kept on walking. Chuck called him some unrepeatable adjectives. I've heard similar stories, but this was the only time the step-dad's brains ended up on the wall. I saw that, Tom. Would you care to see the photos?"

"No."

"I personally think Chuck had a death wish."

"Ted never asked Chuck into his life."

"There is no absolute justice, Tom. Once a bullet has left a gun, it is too late. Any time you take a weapon, you need to take the responsibility that goes with it. If you ever shoot someone, Tom, we will come after you. You will be arrested and tried, or you will spend the rest of your life like William Bonney. Your mother was telling me you've collected several books about Billy the Kid. Now think about that. Was that a romantic life? I doubt it. Never again being able to walk amongst your fellow men, always looking over your shoulder."

"That was a war. They called it a range war. I have no intention of shooting anyone, Marlin." Tom tried to grin. "My mother gets things blown all out of proportion. I don't know anyone I would even vaguely want to shoot." The grin turned sour.

"You frightened your mother when you said you thought Billy the Kid was justified in stabbing a drunk that tried to molest his mother. Talk to someone, whenever you feel the need, Tom. I'm always here, and your preacher is concerned about you as well. And take the gun safety course. No one wants to keep you from owning a pistol. It's your right, but it comes with responsibility." Tom walked away from the session with a great deal of respect for Marlin.

'History seems to show reason the all time loser when it comes to human disputes,' he thought sadly as he walked out. And 'I sure would hate to have him coming after me'.

A little cold chill running down his spine, to think about ending up where Ted did.

"Tom."

"I'm sleepy."

"Tell me how you and Ellen broke up."

"All right." He was laughing, and sat up in bed. "I guess I'm not sleepy. I just realized one day that I didn't want to marry her. We dated, we palled around, and I just wanted to stay friends, but she was thinking about marriage. We just quit seeing each other."

"You never went to bed together?"

"Never. Now I'm sleepy again."

"All right. You have to go to work tomorrow, so go to sleep. And I'm real sleepy, so don't even think about..." He threw his pillow at her, and she threw it back. She went to sleep quickly, and he took an hour. Fran had been such a tease, he wouldn't have missed it. He was seeing Ellen, junior year, but he wasn't thinking anything serious. Fran calls him up one Saturday afternoon, she's having some problems in algebra again, and he has to go over. Fran was the cheesecake pinup girl, in the world of young male imagination. She flirted with so many, but she wasn't a bitch, in any form. Fran was spoiled, but she was sweet. It's a wonder she got along with so many of the girls. Fran's slightly wealthy parents are gone, and they end up doing homework on her queen size bed in her second story bedroom. Fran considered Tom "Extra Cute". He was one of her favorite flirts, and he enjoyed it, but he was a little surprised to end up there. He was wondering..., sex with Fran? In his imagination, that was a very private place in his mind, but in the real world, that was something else. She was facing him, her lower legs folded over her dress, her soft brunette tresses on her shoulders looking so tempting, but she seemed serious about the homework. He could move closer on the bedspread, and risk getting 86'd. Naw! Better not to take the chance. There were lots of other guys she could invite over.

"Tommy, I could use a Coke." Down the stairs, into the fridge. He could have cased the place, if he'd been that kind. They just ended up finishing homework, and watching TV.

And then, he had to mention it to Matt the next Saturday at Matt's parent's backyard garage. Matt just barely fit under the 50 Studebaker he was rebuilding. "You're telling me you were both on Fran's bed, and you didn't try anything? Son, I could ruin you. I hold your future in my hands. Didn't try anything; if that gets out!" Matt had more to say about the Catholic Church's view on sex than any human Tom had ever met. Catholic righteousness was the dominant theme in any discussion with any other males on the subject. "Cheap sex makes for cheap human life, Tom. It's a universal equation. Nothing but misery comes to those that do not respect the covenant that is demanded, the covenant that separates us from the animals. A few moments of pleasure are never worth a lifetime of despair." But now Matt was rubbing it in. "I'd better not tell Pop. He thought you liked girls."

"It's a crying shame."

"What?" After a spell.

Tom moved closer to the garage door. "It should have been you there, Matt. It would have been a sure bet." Matt never got invited to Fran's house. "All you would have to do is let her get on the bed first." Matt looked out from under the Studee. "And then you do a belly flop, and she rolls right to you. Gravity triumphs." He ducked just in time to avoid the ratchet extension that flew past where his head had just been. "You're going to break a tool."

"Something else is more likely to get broken. What color was the bedspread?"

"You'll never know. I don't kiss and tell."

"Yeah. If you'd gotten a kiss, I'd have heard about it within minutes. Good luck next time."

It was all so harmless, or so it seemed for about two weeks, until Ellen called him up on a Saturday morning for a little homework. Ellen's parents were downright poor, and Ellen's bedroom was very small and modest. She had a collection of dolls she'd started years ago, several photos of Sinatra, and an ancient vanity chest that she swore was colonial. All the times he'd entered the inner sanctum, it has always been as the friend. For some reason, he could not imagine himself taking advantage of her there. At that Yuba beach outing several months before, when he'd chased her through the willows, both of them inebriated, he would have tried. But not here. She wanted to do some homework, and they could relax on the bed. Tom wondered if someone told her. Fran could have just mentioned it to someone. She wouldn't have meant anything by it, and there had probably been other guys for homework on her bed, but he hoped it hadn't gotten back to Ellen. And when he heard her parents leaving through the front door, slamming the car doors, and driving away, he asked "where are they off to?"

"Groceries. If we're lucky, they'll be gone two hours." She smiled a nervous smile, and then moved closer until she was right beside him, moving her English book to where they could both view it. This wasn't about homework, and he almost had to swallow. Ellen was slim, flat chested, and neither pretty nor plain. She was your average girl, nice blue eyes, and he'd never heard her say anything mean about anyone. Too many thoughts were going through his head. Ellen was going to want someone to marry her one of these days, and take care of her for the rest of her life. She wasn't looking for a broken heart. None of them were. Tom wasn't going to marry her, he realized now. She wasn't really having problems with English; she made better grades than him, whereas Fran had always had a hard time with algebra, for real. He could have gotten aroused at Fran's, but now he was cautious. She moved against him and giggled a little, and then put her left hand under his shirt and started caressing his back. She knew, he was sure. All about that day at Fran's. 'What are you going to do, Tom? Go all the way, and then tell her it didn't mean anything? God, I'm going to have to tell her. You'd better grow up, and make the decision,' he thought, and then said "I need a Coke. You want one?" 'Same ploy Fran used', he mused. "Ellen, I'm getting dizzy lying to long. How about we take a bike ride?"

"Alright. I'll get us a Coke." Was there anger in the tone of her voice? They walked her bike to his house to get his, and then rode to the park, hardly saying anything. He could think of nothing to say, nothing that could express what he was feeling. He could see baby diapers and bills changing his life, and he just wasn't ready for it. The hint of anger was gone from her voice when he left her at her porch step, and she suggested they see a movie next week. He wasn't surprised when she turned down his invitation to the movies a week later, and he found out she went with a guy named Joe instead.

This was going to be hard to explain to Matt for one cruel reason. Matt was infatuated with Ellen. The friendship Tom took so casually, Matt craved so obviously. Ellen had always given Matt a big hug when they dropped by to visit, and Matt couldn't tell Tom enough how lucky he was to have such a good woman in his life. But Matt was pretty mature. "You did what you should have done, if that's the way you feel, Tom. You wouldn't have anything to give her, anyway. Not right now." That hurt a little, and maybe it made them both even. Matt would have loved a date with her, and he would have something to offer her, more than the average male junior could imagine. Matt was already a successful young man with a landscape business that had started three years before with a mower, and that now fueled a bank account that provoked rumors and jealousy. He actually employed other guys his age through the summer, including Tom, and Matt was ambitious. He knocked on doors and got openings, largely on account of his personality, and he was a hard, meticulous worker. By his junior year he had landed several real business accounts, which included the maintenance and pruning of two orchards, and the upkeep of a multimillionaire's five acre estate. Tom didn't like to even think how far ahead Matt was. Matt liked to boast that righteousness and prosperity go hand in hand, and that was one philosophy Tom differed on, but not to the point of argument. 'If righteousness promotes prosperity, then does poverty and hardship come as punishment for wrong deeds? I don't think so,' Tom would consider. Not that he wanted to see any ill or hardships befall Matt, but he resented that one attitude. Matt sure seemed to make proof of his point.

Two weeks after Tom and Ellen broke up, Matt invited Tom over to help test drive his latest project. He had begun working on a 50 Studebaker Champion Regal sedan four months before, repainting and reupholstering, a contract job for a customer, he told everyone. Was it coincidence that Matt's mother had made some comments back in March of 50, overheard by young Matt, that the Champion Regal they were admiring at the showroom was the most comfortable looking car she had ever seen? There was no way they could have afforded it. They were just looking. Now the used car in the garage was just a reminder. Once, she had mentioned to Matt and Tom that she wished it would be out and gone as soon as possible. It reminded her of life's disappointments. Matt promised. He just needed the money. He had even Tom fooled.

That morning, two weeks before her birthday, Matt and Tom drove, braked, turned, and checked signals. When they returned home, Matt took an envelope out of the glove box, placed it on the dash, left the keys in the ignition, and got out chuckling. "Watch this! Maw! Mom! Could you come out?" through the screen door.

"You know better than to call me in that tone. How dare you yell at me! Do I need to call your father?"

"Please, Mom. I need you to check something. Could you drive it to the end of the block, and then back?"

"Drive it? I'm busy."

"Please, just one time."

"Oh, OK. I'd like to drive it anyway."

"And when you get to the end and turn around, stop and read the instructions in the envelope. It's critical."

She gave him a stern look. "I don't take instructions!"

"Just read it, and then come back."

Tom watched her drive so carefully down the street, turn, stop and park, and then come speeding and careening back, just missing the mailbox as she skidded up the drive. "Oh Lordy! John! John!" she yelled through the screen. "Come here! Oh, come see what your son as done. John, I need you!" Matt was laughing, and Tom's looks made the laughter even worse.

"Matt! What on earth? What have you done to upset your mother?" John was short, skinny, totally unlike his son. "I can still take a belt to you, son!" Matt was doubling up, holding his stomach.

"Take me for a drive, John. It's for my birthday!" And she ran and hugged Matt.

"My God! You did this? The whole time, you son of a gun. Boy, who gives you these ideas?"

That sure didn't do Matt's business any harm. It got around quick, and that was just an example of the attitude that always seemed to get Matt through doorways. It depressed Tom that he could think of no present for his own mother that could come anywhere near matching that, none that he could afford.

Thinking about that car now reminded Tom of Darcy's April birthday. There was plenty of time to think of something. Maybe a trip to Mexico. Wouldn't that be fun! That might cheer Hiame up, too. Maybe things will work out perfect. Maybe they'll run into some gold in the morning.

SEVEN

But they didn't run into more gold in the morning. Day after day, week after week of looking. Days of risk, near accidents, under ten feet or more of water, working with a couple of men whose age was beginning to show. One afternoon Leroy and Whitey took over the nozzle after Tom and Ray had started excavating a huge boulder, one that looked unstable. Ray had been removing gravel on one side of the rock, and when he came up he remarked to Tom that they would make sure the rock was safe with a "dead man", a chain around the rock that would be cabled to a large tree upriver. Apparently Roy decided to start digging directly downstream from the boulder, and Whitey came up and yelled for Ray. "He moved, Ray! I think that sucker is sitting on some loose rock, and I think it might go. He waived me off."

"Where is he? Below it?" Whitey nodded the answer. "Tom, go get me that 15 foot chain. Let's take care of it right now."

As he started walking upstream, Tom noticed a swirl of muddy water surface, the sign of a cave in underwater. "Ray! Ray! Mud!" Ray was still wearing his wetsuit, and he grabbed Whitey's regulator as Whitey unhooked his weight belt and swung its 50 pounds of lead to him. Tom acted so quickly, it was more instinct than anything else. He was in swim shorts and tennis shoes, and he left Ray way behind, swimming straight to the spot. One big breath and he dived nine feet in murky water to see Leroy tugging on a leg, his leather steel toed boot caught beneath a 200 pound boulder, something Tom or Ray could have gotten out of on their own. Up for another breath, and Tom was down, grabbing a pry bar and moving the rock enough for Roy to pull free. Tom had swallowed a little water, and he gasped for a few seconds as he floated down to get out by Whitey. "He's OK. It wasn't the big one."

"Yeah, well Ray will shut it down. Leroy thinks like the old-timers, Tom. He won't stop till quit'n time. He's getting old, and so am I. I can feel it."

When they both came up, Ray was obviously pissed. "Don't change holes on me, Leroy! You know better. Not under a God-Damned widow maker."

"You're right, Ray. It was a mistake, but there's no reason to quit early."

"No, we're done. We'll take the rest of the day off. I don't like tempting fate."

"Thank you, son." Leroy said to Tom simply, matter of factly.

"You cover my back, I cover yours," Tom answered.

"Do you like Cajun food? My wife is from Louisiana."

"I've never had any. I'm sure I would."

Tom didn't think anything of it until two days later when Darcy informed him they were going to Leroy's for dinner Sunday evening. "Now Thomas, Leroy is a very poor man, and I don't want you making any remarks, not even by accident, when you see his place."

"It's a real dump, uh?"

"It's a dug out cabin, one of the 49'ers originals, down by Calaveras. Roy owns his own property, and he's always wanted to build a proper house on it."

"He's got more than I've got."

Roy's place had been dug into the south face of a hill, to get winter sunshine for warmth where the miners had to winter through a snowpack. An earthen roof that connected directly to the ground, rotting old wood walls, but a good brick chimney. The insides were cramped and meager looking.

Leroy's wife was probably a cutie in her youth, and her personality was the antithesis of his, joking with them, full of enthusiasm at having visitors to talk to. After a delicious rice and chicken meal, she asked "Do you like country music?"

"Country Western? Yeah." Tom answered with little enthusiasm. He thought she might play a record or turn on the radio.

"Sierra Hillbilly, I like to call it. Mountain music, Tom. We're going to a fiddle pick'n tonight."

"Oh, Tom's got to get up…" Darcy protested.

"No, Ray's going to let you both sleep late. I asked him to," Roy said. "I want my friends to meet the man who saved my life."

In private Tom remarked to Darcy "He's making too much of this. Ray would have gotten to him if I hadn't. It was no big deal."

"It obviously was to him, and her. Let's be nice to them, Tom. They don't get to see many people out here." It turned out to be more fun than they could have imagined. There were over thirty people at the neighbor's barn, and apparently they almost always had Sunday sessions there, local talent always welcome. Tom and Darcy clapped and danced to the talent of the old base fiddle, one proper violin and two fiddles, one clarinet, one trumpet, and one old piano.

"These people are good enough to play at the Homestead," Tom commented. "How do folks get by around here? What do they do for a living?"

"One doesn't ask those kinds of questions. These people scratch out a living raising livestock, some of them get work down valley, some of them barter, and some actually get gold. There's deer in the woods."

"Shine?" he whispered, grinning at her.

"Shh," she whispered back. "You'd have to ask my mother."

"Don't dance with too many of these young men!" he warned. With a smirk she walked across the dirt floor and grabbed the arm of a skinny fifteen year old. Nothing was ever mentioned about Leroy and the incident, but from the friendly looks he was getting, he suspected they all knew. He wondered what he could have done for Roy, had it been the other way around.

"Were all these new folks to you?" he asked on the late drive back.

"Almost all. I know more Indians in Reno than white folks down there."

"Injuns? Now what are you doing hanging out with the Aborigines?"

"I have a good friend in Reno named Claire Whitehorse who is full blooded Piute. Several years ago she invited me to a cowboy-Indian rodeo in Kingman, Arizona, and I had such a good time, I can't tell you. A lot of the Reno Paiutes, you know, they have reservation land right in Reno, they helped put on a rodeo and pageant, and there were some Maidu there, too, that I got to meet."

"Do you know of any relations?"

"None at all. Claire tried to get me to do some asking around, but I told her it would get my mother angry. She asked me if I was ashamed of my Maidu blood, and I told her 'of course not'. Anyways, we took a bus to Kingman, and I had a ball. The only fly in the ointment…,"

"Let me guess. You're mother did something."

"I got to meet Andy Divine, and he got me scheduled for a movie audition in Hollywood, Burbank actually. He called up some of the bigwigs, and had it all set up. He thought I would be perfect for the part of a pretty Apache girl in a movie he was helping produce. I would have made my college tuition, at least, if I'd got the part, but I never went in for audition."

"Auh, crud. I can guess. Your mother didn't want you to play the part of an Injun."

"I'm too spoiled as it is. I don't let those little letdowns get to me. Have you ever heard of the Mojave Indians?"

"I'm sure I have. Who did they attack?"

"It's ironic you ask that. According to Claire, there weren't any Mojave's around when the white man got there. They had all disappeared, all at once."

"What, a disease?"

"What do you think? How does a whole race of people, you know, genocide?"

"Before the white man? It must have been Indians."

"Claire says the Paiutes and Mojave's were traditional enemies, and she thinks her ancestors may have had something to do with it, but Indians will never admit something like that. The Mojave's were Indian miners, Tom. They mined and traded turquoise, the rock of the gods."

"Well, there's a reason. Who took over the mines?"

"They were abandoned."

"I don't even like to think about those things, but you know it was greed." Annihilation. It was un-imaginable, something the average American could probably not envision. To be killed in your own territory, to lie dying, just hoping your wife and kids would be spared. "That do you think happened to the women and children?"

"I know I would have killed myself."

"I would want you to live. You wouldn't want to miss the next Halloween dance."

"Aha. Yes, I have to admit, there's something to live for. And I could meet someone to replace you."

"Ooooh!"

EIGHT

Ray gave everyone a three day holiday for Halloween. He may have had some heavy celebrating planned for himself, and everyone was so tired of endless weeks with little or no gold. Halloween was the first day off, and shopping in Grass Valley for deals on candy was fun in itself. Tom bought himself two pairs of slacks, and asked Darcy to pick out a nice dress for the dance. "That's all been taken care of."

"You're keeping something from me."

"Just be patient."

There were two huge jack-o-lantern pumpkins in front of the porch, and one smaller one just inside the door when they got home, and Joe Joe was perched on top of the inside jack. "What's going on Joe-buddy?" Tom asked.

"He turned up about two hours ago, crying for his treats," Agnes explained.

"I don't believe it. He's been gone five days."

"He saw the pumpkins." Darcy said as she handed him a treat, a tiny piece of fresh fish.

"At sundown, the witch appears," Agnes said, with such obvious enjoyment of the moment.

"Yes, the witch is coming."

"Witch? I thought we were talking princess?" Darcy smiled with no answer. "I guess I'm the candy man," Tom said.

Kids started showing up just before sundown. "We're going to have a lot of second and third timers, Tom. This is a small town, and we don't say anything about it," Agnes explained.

Darcy was gone half an hour, and when she returned, Tom said "they've all been asking for the witch. That's not Darcy! Wait a minute." Agnes was laughing good naturedly. "Is that really you?" he asked. "How in the..., did you do that?"

"Secrets of the trade."

"Well, I'd have to be rip roaring drunk to go to the dance with the witch, much less go home with her." She stuck out her tongue at him. She had a huge, Middle-Eastern looking nose, and warts, blotches, dark spots under the eyes, and a shaggy gray wig.

"Just a few more years, and I'll be there," Agnes joked.

"No, Agnes, never." Tom offered, and she now was capable of such a warm smile.

"Joe Joe, Halloween!" Darcy ordered, and the skinny black cat arched his back, hair straight out, just to get his next treat. He guarded his pumpkin top domain for minutes on end, and when he left, she could always get him back with a treat. The witch gave out candy for an hour, and then disappeared again.

"God!" Tom just stood there, when she returned, staring, watching as she moved from the standing smile she first offered to start handing out more candy. "Unreal!" he said. Agnes was beaming.

"You're making me nervous, Tom!"

"I can't help it. You are beautiful!"

"Yes, she is." Agnes smiled, so proud.

"You're both making me nervous." She was dressed in a tight fitting homemade buckskin blue dyed Indian girl outfit, decked with a beaded belt made with real turquoise and silver, and tassels of both leather and beads, obviously the product of many hours of meticulous work, probably from when she was a sophomore in high school, one size smaller. Her face was slightly powdered, less lipstick, her soft black hair filling form more in the white girl style than in pigtails as he had imagined. A beaded headband sported three blue dyed turkey feathers and six blue jay feathers. It might have been just a pretty costume, innovative, but Darcy was stunning in it. A little too stunning. Several taller, older boys were showing up now for candy, a little too old for Halloween, Tom thought.

"There's a guy, I swear, he's back, and he's changed outfits."

"Yes, he did. That's Billy Joe Turner. He used to write letters to Darcy. He's only thirteen; he's just big for his age. Get used to it," Agnes warned. And then in a whisper "it'll get worse at the dance."

He headed for the bathroom, re-soaked himself with some Old-Spice, put on a dab more of Brylcream through the hair, then changed his mind and toweled it back out. Listerine again, then a breath mint. "What the hell. This is supposed to be fun. I need a Rolaids." It was all for naught, they had an hour to go, and later he had to go through the whole process again. As they got ready to leave, Tom had to boast "my Maidu princess".

"Understand me!" Serious, for the first time that evening, Agnes demanded "that's an Aztec princess's outfit. I don't ever want her introduced as a Maidu!"

"Alright. She's an Aztec. I just hope she doesn't order my heart cut out." The attempt at humor made no impression. It was like trying to mix hot and cold water in bad plumbing, he thought. It either ran hot or cold. No in between. Agnes drove them to the Community Center, and said "I'll be asleep. Come in quiet."

"How do we get back?" Tom asked.

"We'll get back. I always do. Now remember, Tom, I have a lot of regulars I dance with. It doesn't mean anything."

"That's alright. I'll have a lot of regulars before the night is out." Through the doors he could hear a live band put'n out 'Tennessee Waltz', fairly well, but not professionals. The band was dressed all cowboy with a lady cowgirl singer, strategically located opposite the three fold down tables that supported five large punch bowls and snacks. Darcy deposited a dollar bill in the donations container, right next to the "No Liquor Allowed" sign. The room was fairly crowded, the dance area a little too small, perhaps.

"Lou!" Darcy yelled across the room as she headed toward a cluster of five people. "Lou," as she approached them. "First dance."

"I had better be!" Lou Montgomery replied with a slight smile. The taller man beside him, a 6'5" skinny older man, stared with a downright hostile glare, and Tom felt instantly out of place.

"Lou, this is Tom Hendrick, my fiancé. Tom, this is a very dear friend, Lou Montgomery, and I always give him the first dance."

"Howdy." Tom offered a handshake.

"Welcome to Downieville, Tom. Bill tells me we may have to find you a job at the 'Cinnamon Bear'." He seemed friendly enough, but the taller man turned and walked away quite rudely. Lou was 6'2", quite obviously a powerful man, even more so than Ray. His pale gray-blue eyes reminded Tom of Agnes's eyes.

"Don't mind Greg. This is Sissy June, Ardell, and Erick." Erick and Lou were both dressed in jeans and dress shirts, but both women were in costume. Sissy June, Lou's cousin, a woman old enough to be Tom's mother, was another witch, and Ardell was some kind of a "Lady in Red", perhaps a saloon girl. Red feather tassel, tight red dress with sequins, and red shoes made the pretty green-eyed red head a stand out, and Tom had to grab her hand and ask "first dance?"

She simply smiled a yes as Erick took Sissy June's hand and told Tom "just remember, she's already been corralled". Tom hadn't even noticed the wedding ring. Darcy wasn't wearing her engagement ring, being that it was "a little too loose", and she worried that it might get lost after she had a little too many. Tom had asked earlier where the drinks would come from, since no liquor was allowed at the dance, and Darcy had simply replied "you'll see".

"You're even prettier than Carrie Honsacker," he had to offer, as he struggled with a polka, trying not to stumble over her feet. 'How can she do a polka in that dress?' Tom wondered. "But Erick looks like a big boy, and I guess I'd better keep that in mind."

"Erick is a sweetheart, Tom. He lets me dance with all my old boyfriends." Erick Swartz was handsome enough not to worry, sandy blond hair and blue eyes.

"He's a lucky man."

"Darcy is a lucky woman. I was waiting just to meet you." The eyes were just a little mischievous, and Tom believed the compliment more than just politeness. "We already know Tom likes redheads."

"Boy, it's a small world."

"And Lou like brunettes, Tom. You're from the valley," she said as the dance ended, and she took his hand and led him to one side of the band. "Tom, don't take it wrong if Lou dances a little too much with her. I'm trying to get him to spend some time with Nancy O'Day. As a matter of fact," she said with a frown, "I've just about guaranteed Nancy that she'll get a date with him."

"Lou works with Bill Rutledge, doesn't he? I may be working with him next year."

"Lou is like a favorite son of Downieville, even though he's from Alleghany. He's 27, and it's hard for us to get him to date anyone…, else, uh, you know. We're running interference for Darcy, several of us girls, Tom, so don't worry about it."

"I didn't know anything about it," Tom said with a severe look. "Darcy never said anything about dating Lou."

"She should have, Tom. They didn't date that much, but, well, everyone knows. Everyone but you, I guess," she said, trying to smile. "Lou is a good man, don't get me wrong. That jerk, Greg, that was just talking with us, him, you'd better watch out. He's definitely a backwoods boy.

But don't worry. Lou doesn't let any of his friends get out of hand."

"I don't care if Darcy dances with every guy here, Ardell. She's looked forward to this all summer, and I know she's enjoying herself. I hope she can make it to the Downieville Halloween dance every year till she's ninety. She's my Aztec Princess."

"You are a sweetheart."

"Hey," Erick said, walking up swiftly. "Bring back my lady!"

"He likes redheads," Ardell teased.

"Hey, I like Indian Princesses."

"I intend to marry the chief's daughter, and she's not a redhead," Tom said.

"Where's your costume?" Erick asked.

"Where's yours?"

Erick pinched a fold of his Levis, and pulled up a fairly new gray and tan cowboy boot, standing on one leg. "I came as a Sierra Hillbilly."

"Very funny. I can't get him to wear a costume," Ardell said.

The perfect couple, Tom thought. Earlier in the day, at a main street bookstore in Grass Valley, Darcy had introduced Tom to two elderly ladies out shopping from Downieville, Emma and Tracy. They seemed friendly enough, but when they moved to another aisle, Tom could hear their conversation too clearly. "He's not her brother, how could you think that, Emma? You're getting senile. Agnes had one child, don't you remember?"

"He looks just like her. They might be twins."

"He does not look just like her. He's from Marysville. He's her fiancé." Darcy's face was wrinkling up, trying not to break out laughing, but Tom was a little embarrassed.

"I think it's scandalous. They are definitely related, it's so obvious. I think he's from down south, maybe Calaveras, or Auburn. You're not supposed to marry your relatives. You know that's bad. That Mackin clan, they did that a lot, and their kids are half retarded."

"Shh! Not so loud!"

When they left, Tom had to point out "that was so rude. Do we really look that much alike?" It was such a revelation; Darcy frowned and evaded the question. 'Opposites attract, but so do those who match,' he thought. 'We just look right'.

"Tom, those ladies are a couple of town characters, and they do that with everyone."

"What's their story? Are they widowed, or old maids?"

"One is widowed, and one had a husband that beat her. Emma is a little deaf."

"Does Agnes like them?"

"No."

"Then I do." She frowned severely at that.

The dance band played five more pieces, and Tom danced with Sissy June, Ardell again, a downright ugly thirty year old who told fairly good dirty jokes, and finally with Darcy, twice. "It's time for intermission," the singer Sonia announced after a fair rendition of Patty Page's 'All My Love'. "Now everyone should know that I have an interest in the St. Charles. Hoss and I are distantly related, so..." Chuckles from the audience. "I want you all to walk down and buy a drink." Laughter now. "Because we all know I'm not making any money here, and I may need to borrow from Hoss to get out of town." Much laughter.

"How did you get related to Hoss?"

"It was a distant marriage, twice removed. You know, one of those things. Don't hassle me, or I may need a drink myself."

"What would you like?" the same man asked.

"Gin and tonic."

"Watch this," Darcy said. "We'll stay here. You don't need a drink right now, do you?" In five minutes all but a few had walked to the St. Charles or The Narrows for a beer, or perhaps a martini. In ten more minutes the band started a short, loud tune, and when most had returned Sonia explained "now don't anyone worry about having too much to drink tonight. Sheriff Ramey always keeps a couple of doors open, and we all know the accommodations are quite comfortable." And through the laughter she started playing a fiddle, leading the band in a Hank Williams tune. When she started 'Tennessee Waltz' for the second time, Tom grabbed Darcy from the hands of an eighteen year old and explained "next song, please. I need her for this one." He wouldn't stop staring, as he attempted a waltz, while she deftly managed to make his mistakes look good, and she returned a dreamy look. "My best friend will never take you away."

"Are you through with redheads?" she demanded.

"Forever."

"Lou is dancing a lot with Nancy O'Day. God, I'm so happy tonight. He wouldn't leave me alone last year, God bless him."

Tom felt a little twinge, like a cold wave spreading though the nerves of his body. "You haven't said anything about this."

"Later. It's no big deal. Well, yes it is, or, I mean, it used to be, but I know Lou is getting over it."

"Let's drive to Reno, and get a quickie marriage."

"Tom, you would." She took no offense.

"As a matter of fact, I think we should drive to Mexico tonight, and not tell anyone, not a thing. Well, maybe except for my mother."

"Alright, Tom. I'll get Agnes to lend me some suitcases. Whose car do we borrow?" She leaned forward, and they touched foreheads as the song ended. With his arms around her and hands on her shoulders, he took a long slow kiss as they stood on the dance floor. No one was noticing, too many were into similar maneuvers.

"Hey, I get this song," the eighteen year old finally reminded him.

"Yea, you do." And he turned and went looking for Ardell. About twelve thirty, the crowd thinning a little, he noticed a man pouring a small bottle of unmarked liquor in the fullest punchbowl, and then consolidate two almost empty bowls of punch into it. About ten minutes, another man did similar. Deputy Sheriff Engel had been in and out all evening, testing the punch, but apparently he had gone home for the night. Darcy danced less now, talking more with friends, and turning down invitations.

"Are we ready to leave?" Tom asked after a dance with one of the five witches present.

"Are we ready to leave? What's your hurry, babe... babee!" Darcy was slurring too many words.

"Darcy, you know about the punch!"

"I shore do, honey." She sounded so much like Agnes. "OK, Tom. I'm just kidding. That's 'cause I'm an Injun." She really was getting drunk. "Not yet, Tommy. Not yet, because..."

"She needs to go home, Tom," Ardell said behind him.

Tom turned, as Erick advised "It's time to get her home."

"We didn't bring a car."

"Neither did we. Most of us walk, that live in town. You know, because of the booze. You should get her walking now. Darcy, it's time to head home," Ardell said softly.

"No." Now she sounded like a little girl. "No, not yet. My daddy used to dance with Agnes on Halloween. Did you know him?"

"It's not Halloween anymore, honey."

"Ardell, you look like a French whore!" Darcy said, and let out an exhale under her tongue that was almost a raspberry.

"Yes, I do." Ardell giggled.

"And I look like a drunk Injun."

"You look like a princess. A Maidu princess," Tom said firmly.

"No, it's got to be an Aztec. No, I want some punch."

"No, no, no, no!" Ardell sounded like a school teacher.

"OK, OK. I give up. Point me to the door." The shine, and whatever, was really taking effect. Tom noticed himself hit just a little. It came on sneaky.

Ardell walked Darcy to the door, and said to Tom "she knows the way very well, even drunk."

"I am not drunk, and you look like a French whore!" Ardell laughed outright. Darcy was doing her mother's voice quite well.

"Some of these boys must be trying to make some time. We females need to watch the punch bowl a little more carefully." Ardell winked at Tom. "I remember Erick trying that one on me."

"She can hold her liquor," Erick advised.

Darcy started walking quick little steps, swaying a little, and then stopped. "I don't feel good."

"Neither do I. Are you going to be alright?"

"Yeah, I can make it." But after several hundred feet, she confessed "I might not make it. Oh! If I can get it up, I might be able to make it."

"Oh, no, Darcy, sit down, maybe put your head down. You barf, and I will too."

"That was some rot gut they put in there. It's worse than last year. Oh, I'm glad she stopped me. Ohh! Why do I do this?"

"Darcy, sit down, take a rest."

"No, I've got to keep moving. That was some God-awful booze. Someone should be shot." Several more feet and it was "Oh, no, here it comes", and she ran across the street and threw herself against a large boulder at the edge of the drop off to the river, to let go over it.

"Rats." Tom caught up and tried to grab her, but she pushed him off and went at it again, and he had to upchuck too, down on his knees.

"Hey, baby." She tried to laugh, breathing hard. "We do this fairly well together." She turned and rested her back against the rock, slowly sinking down to her seat, and Tom crawled over to sit beside her. "Let's rest here a while."

"That was pretty bad liquor. I've never gotten this sick before, not even when Sammy James challenged me to drink twelve beers."

"Twelve. How quick?" She asked with closed eyes.

"Half an hour." He wasn't getting any better. They sat for some time, getting very cold. The air was chilly and dank from the first good rain of the wet season, four days before, but the frogs and crickets were still in chorus.

"Are you two still alive?" Ardell's voice woke him. "I was right to call Agnes. You'll freeze."

"Thanks," Tom said as Erick and another man helped them on to a blanket in the bed of an old pickup, and soon they were being delivered to an irate Agnes, who protested "she did it again. She always gets me up." Tom fell asleep on the couch, waking several times to the noise of Darcy getting sick at the commode. He wondered if he should get up and check on her, until he heard Agnes's voice. He was so sick himself, he didn't want to move.

Some time mid-morning he awoke to the TV, turned down low. "Ahh!" He closed his eyes back, and heard Agnes walk up to place a cold wash cloth on his forehead. "Thank you." Agnes removed the cloth and used it to wipe his face, ears, and neck, and asked "would you like some orange juice?"

"Maybe later. How is she?"

"Hah. Paying her penance. You know…" then loudly "them Injuns can't hold their liquor."

"I heard that! Oh God! Oh!"

"She's OK," he chuckled. "I feel like shit. I'll never do that again. No wonder there's a 'No Liquor' sign."

"Ohh! Ahhgh!" Bam, Bam, Bam, Bam, Thud, Thud, Thud, Thud, Thud, Thud. The noise of Darcy slamming her feet on the two types of wood flooring made two distinctly different harmonics. At the bathroom it was "I need to get a bed in here. Oh God, please, just let me pass out!"

"Nope," loudly, with the grin of the Cheshire Cat, "them Injuns can't hold their liquor." Agnes was enjoying this. "This makes us even for waking me up."

"I heard that. Ahhh!" Thud, Thud, Thud, Thud, Thud, Bam, Bam, Bam, Thud, Thud, Thud, Thud, Thud, and then over the toilet again.

"Didn't even make it to the bed!" Agnes laughed as she wiped Tom's face again and pushed a pillow under his head. He was snickering now, too.

"Thank you, Agnes. I ain't worth a damn, not for helping her." He closed his eyes and lay still, thinking that if he could just get back to sleep, he'd feel better. But Darcy's agony went on for a good two hours, until she finally passed out in bed. Come sundown, he awoke to hear them both up, watching TV, Darcy sitting in the recliner across the room.

"Don't even come near me!"

"I won't."

"Don't even touch me! I am so sick, Tom. I'm getting some orange juice down. You're going to have to sleep on the couch tonight."

"I will. No wonder Ray gave us extra days off. I wonder how he's feeling. We never saw him."

"He called and asked if you two would live, and I told him he'd see you day after tomorrow," Agnes said, and came over to wipe Tom's face and arrange his pillow.

Darcy shortly went to bed, and about midnight when he got up to relieve himself, he had to peek in her bedroom. There was enough light from the open door to see her curled up in a ketchup stained nightgown, the blanket on the floor, some of her fine hair caught in her mouth, snoring away. "You're a lucky man," he said out loud, and then covered her up with the blanket. 'Just another crazy, mixed up kid,' he thought.

NINE

The November water was getting very cold, even with the garden hose set up that delivered a steady supply of engine exhaust heated water into both divers' wetsuits. Tom had bought a brand new wetsuit in August, but it was already getting holes that Darcy mended with patches of his old suit. And they weren't getting much gold. One morning at the Quartz Café over coffee Ray told Tom that he would shortly let Roy and Whitey go for the season. The cold water was too dangerous for men of their age. "Would you like to keep working till winter sets in, Tom? I'm going to need one hand, and I don't quit till it's over."

"Sure, Ray. I'll stay, just to catch up. The sooner we stop, the sooner the money's over."

"Starting in November, I set my share of the gold aside for my two daughters."

"Where do they live?"

"Cincinnati. I want Monica to set up a trust fund for college. She's good at that sort of thing. The more we make now, the more I can do for them."

'Trying to make up for the divorce,' Tom thought. "When we do quit, uh, what is your last day?"

"I don't put a limit on it." That didn't set well with Tom, but he said nothing further.

Mid November saw a dry, mild Indian summer that lasted Thanksgiving through mid December, but the water was getting dangerously cold, and Tom found himself getting serious cold headaches from the gap between his mask and neoprene diving hood. He wore heavy rubber gloves now that were awkward, but definitely warmer than bare hands. Darcy often came down early to watch over things, now that only one diver at a time dived. They had moved the dredge to an area upriver where they had found another huge boulder, one that was sitting on a bedrock shelf, part of the rock sticking out over the hole they were opening up. They looked the boulder over and decided it was probably safe, but neither was really sure. Ray worked under it with no hesitation, and so Tom took his turn, trying not to think about it. After about an hour, he saw a small rock dropping through the water in front of him, and came up to find Darcy in tears, sitting on one of the chairs they had brought down to the river. Ray was up in camp, apparently. Tom shut off the dredge and swam over to her, asking "Princess, what's wrong?"

"I threw ten rocks at you. You weren't paying attention. I don't want you working under that rock!"

"You can see it from here?" She nodded yes. "Ray started the hole, and he thinks it's OK. I have to admit, it makes me nervous. I'm getting sick of the cold water, and we're not finding any gold at all, but I think I should stick it out with Ray. You know, in case I want to work with him again."

"Ray is usually very safe. It just made me so nervous to see you under it. But if Ray looked it over..."

"I don't think we'll stay there long."

"Ray has never said anything about his brother, has he, Tom?"

"I didn't know he had a brother."

"Ray and Will were both in the Merchant Marine in World War II. Will was killed. That's why Ray is usually a very safety conscious man. Don't ever bring this up! Ray told me every damn detail, and I wish I'd never heard it. Ray is funny on this, Tom. He has problems, sometimes, dealing with the memory, and he gets real pissed if someone mentions it."

"I'll just forget it."

"I wish I could. Twenty six ships were in his convoy to England, and only nine made it. Ray told me about a night where everywhere you looked the ocean was on fire. Men were screaming in the water, and the fire was catching up with some of them. He lost Will that night. Will was on another ship. He can't handle it."

"I'll never say anything. I'm beginning to wish I'd never volunteered to stay. I can't handle this cold much longer. I wish he'd just quit. He wants to find something for his daughters, and it just isn't there."

That night, Darcy poured a hot bath for an aching Tom, and scrubbed him down as he lay in silent agony. He was desperately tired, and mentally down. He dreaded going to work every day, now; he hoped for rain to shut them down. Ray was hurting, too. But Ray was doing penance, and Tom feared Ray would keep pushing himself, making Tom suffer with him. Sundays off were so welcome now, and one mild Sunday evening they took a walk across town. Darcy stopped to visit a friend, and Tom decided to walk a while by himself, until an old Dodge sedan slowed down beside him, four men inside. "Hello, Pilgrim," Vernon said from the front passenger seat.

"Hello, Vernon. Howdy," to the men, who all seemed younger than Vernon.

"Getting rich?" one of the men said.

"Gett'n cold." One of the men chuckled.

"Take a ride with us, meet the boys."

"Alright." Tom got in the back.

"This is Noal, Timothy, and Phil, down from the Smith Ranch. We've been getting some odd jobs around town."

"How'd that work out, up at that claim?"

"That man was a crook," Vernon said harshly. "Noal, let's drive up to the cemetery. Give him a little history lesson."

Phil snickered at Vernon's remark, but Timothy sounded friendlier when he complained "it's getting late".

"Naw, Tom needs a history lesson," Phil said.

They parked and walked to the cemetery fence, and Vernon turned and addressed them all. "Boys, it's getting hard to find any work around this little town. Maybe we should hike on down valley and see what these flatlanders have to offer."

Tom felt ill at ease now, but he would ride it out. "There ain't much work in Marysville, now that the rice has been harvested."

"Aw, you mean you're taking all that Downieville gold, flatlander, and you can't offer us some hope of honest employment." Phil was severely sarcastic.

"Phil!" Timothy said. "He's Bill Rutledge's friend. Leave him alone. I don't want to get on Bill's shit list."

"I wish I had a steady job, right now. Darcy and I are wondering how we are going to get through the winter, cause we ran out of gold three months ago." He wasn't lying; he just wasn't mentioning his bank account.

"Yeah, well welcome to gold country." Phil sounded less severe. "That's what a lot of us wonder this time of year. Folks with kids, and what not." Now the tone was almost friendly. "I cut eight cords of firewood, and no one has money to buy."

"Yeah, Agnes is telling me I've got to cut her some firewood. She can't afford to buy."

"You've never done it?"

"Can't be that bad," Tom said.

"Tom." Vernon motioned. "Let's take a little walk." The other three men stood talking to themselves, as Tom and Vernon walked along the fence line. "A lot of history lies here. I've got kinfolk in the ground. Almost everyone buried was a local, but every once in a while a flatlander makes it in. Usually with some special invitation, like, say, a rope, or a bullet."

Tom grinned in the dim light. "Yeah, I guess a lot of flatlanders aren't as well mannered as me."

"You see those boys over there? Every one of them wonders how they are going to make it, year by year. That's why they stick by me. I was born to lead men. I'm going to get them something better. You remember your Roman history? Remember an Emperor named Tiberius who was famous for fighting gladiators in the arena, and always winning? There was a reason he always won, and that's the same reason I will win. I'm going to be a senator some day. I'm meeting the right people now, who will make the difference when the time comes. You should have come with me to Sacramento when you had the chance, 'cause you are the kind that would have made an impression on my friends, and you would have done yourself an advantage." Vernon paused, scanning the gravestones. "But you might end up getting on Downieville's bad side, if you're not careful. That Emperor, he was sharp. He knew he had the crowds' admiration, and the man picked to fight him was always carefully chosen. It was a death sentence, sure enough, to fight the Emperor. It was all psychological. The fool selected to fight the Emperor didn't have a chance in hell, 'cause they were all against him. That's the way the world really works. Some people don't even realize that they are already defeated, and that smiling faces really have ill works in store for them. You've got to get in with the winners, man. That's all that really counts. I spent one summer on Goodyear Creek, running a sluice box with a claim owner's permission, pick and shovel. That's the last time I choose to be a fool, and it made me decide for once and all what I needed to do. I almost starved to death that summer." Anger now. "No one, not even my kinfolk, came to check on me. It was just my tough luck."

"Hell, I ran away from home for three days, down on the river, when I was fifteen. Scared the shit out of me." Tom put in.

"Really?" Vernon sounded friendlier. "Well, Tom, you need to do some serious thinking about your future. You see those fools standing there?" Silence for effect. "They think I'm reading you a Downieville version of the riot act.

Wonder what they would think if they knew I said the three of them couldn't outsmart me, and you're a peg above them too, I can see that. They'd quit me for a while, then get anxious, and I'd mention some little money maker I was stirring up, and they'd all be back. I was born to lead men. Not to say you're being outright stupid, but you should have come to Sac and met some people."

"Maybe I'll take a trip with you down sometime." Tom was placating again, just figuring he could always get out of it. Apparently, Vernon realized it.

"You're not taking me seriously. Go to the library, Tom, next chance you get, and read a book by Fred Reinfield, 1953, on chess. Read page 141, the section that describes maneuvering against weak pawns." Vernon turned to yell "hey guys, it's getting cold."

"It sure is," Timothy yelled back.

When they delivered Tom back they found Darcy and her friend standing in the front yard. Tom got out and said casually "I'll keep my ears open, if anyone needs some wood. I've got to cut Agnes's wood, you know…"

"Take it easy," Phil said, downright congenial, as they drove away.

"What in the hell…, I called Bill, Tom. Mrs. Mahoney saw you get in the car with Vernon, and called us. What's going on? You weren't going to walk me home?"

"Oh, now, me and the boys just went up to the cemetery for a little chat." He couldn't help but play on it. "Vernon wanted to show me how considerate people are around here, being that they reserve a special section for flatlanders at the cemetery." He was chuckling now. "But, Phil, Timothy, and Noal, they seem like 'good ole boys'."

"That's not funny. Bill wouldn't think it was funny, either, being that he is ready to call up a posse."

"Oh, good grief. I'm sorry, Darcy. I just thought it polite to have a little talk with some of the locals. I guess I'd better call Bill."

"I guess you'd better."

Tom called and explained on her friend's phone, but Bill demanded he see them in person, and drove to pick them up. Lynn fixed up a pecan pie and ice cream treat, and after they finished she pulled Darcy off to the kitchen to let them talk. "I can pretty much read Vernon, Bill. I would never have got in that car if I thought I might not come back."

"You're probably right. I don't know what Vernon is capable of, but I doubt you were in any danger. But, you see, just being associated with him is not going to set well with some people around here. You know what happened with his job at the Boulder Bound, don't you. He got caught hygrading the sluice, out and out, and he almost got arrested."

"How stupid can you get?"

"He's lucky he didn't get shot. He's from Alleghany, and so is Lou, and you talk about two different horses from the same pasture. I wouldn't give a dime for Vernon's opinion on anything, and I intend to make Lou the manager of my river claims, including the Cinnamon Bear. Come here and look at this." They walked through a hall to a far storeroom, and Bill stopped beside a huge lithograph on the wall. "That's about my uncle, believe it or not." The picture was printed in 1879, and the caption read 'Much concern over the lost soul of young John Rutledge. The Sheriff of Alleghany meets the Sheriff of Downieville that fearful night of 1873, and together they thwart a potential war between the two brother mining towns. Liquor spawned anger is diffused by the two determined lawmen.' The scene depicted a crowd of men holding torches, met by a smaller crowd on some Sierra road, and the artist had done a remarkable job in conveying the expressions of anger on the men. It had been a fearful looking night, indeed. A crescent moon, torches blown by the night wind, the moonlight showing distant mountain crags, and gnarled, twisted high country trees. "I was born in 88, and the uncle I never met disappeared in 73, right before his wedding date. He was betrothed to a pretty redheaded girl named Emma Dessault, from Alleghany. Both families had approved of the marriage, and then he just up and vanished from the face of the earth. There has always been some distrust between the two crowds, and a lot of the people here think he was killed to keep her from marrying him. Those boys were going to tear Alleghany apart, board by board, looking for him. That's ancient history…" he chuckled a little, "kind of like me. But I bring it up to help explain something. I wouldn't put it past Vernon to get himself in on something that mean, and I can tell you're not that kind, Tom. You're a very likeable young man, with a good future, if you play your cards right, but you must understand one thing. There's only so much gold around here, and about a hundred years ago we began getting very protective of our gold reserves. I have to admit, I don't like the idea of flatlanders getting any of our gold myself, but I think maybe in your case…, well, Vernon is out, as far as I'm concerned. You can take his place." Bill smiled.

"He thinks I already have. Did that young woman, did she get over it?"

"She never married."

"How can people do shit like that, Bill?"

"You don't want to know what people are really capable of. They don't tell the half of it, about the Indian wars."

"Ray told me to look in your fish tank, to see some gold, just to change the subject."

"Hah. That's right. You never saw my fish tank decoration." He seemed ecstatic as they walked through the living room. "I love to watch first time viewers."

Tom peered in the 25 gallon tank filled with colorful varieties of fish, waterweeds, and a bubbling mermaid whose lower body swayed as the air was released. She was sitting on a large, sort of butter- pumpkin colored flat rock that looked almost plastic, and the rest of the tank looked pretty standard. "I don't see any gold," Tom protested.

Bill was laughing as Lynn walked out of the hall and said "take another look, Tom!"

"Oh, man. That's huge!" Tom was skeptical. Bill pulled up his sleeve, reached in and removed the 'rock'. Now it looked more serious.

Bill said "both hands" as he handed it to Tom.

"Fourteen pounds. Can you believe it?" Darcy said, walking up. "It's been cleaned with nitric acid, and then vinegar. Big nuggets are usually dull from mineral stains."

"My father picked that off the bedrock of the Ruby Mine in 1897."

"You shouldn't have it out here," Tom warned.

"Yeah, everybody tells me that. I guess I'd be real angry if it turned up missing, but you know what they say, 'life is a gamble'. I wouldn't be hurting if it got stolen, just angry."

Tom thought it a little arrogant to display it like that. That was too much temptation, and there were too many hungry people out there. He didn't doubt Bill was the kind to shoot an intruder. "If Ray finds one of these tomorrow, I'll never get out of that cold water." They could all laugh at that.

TEN

More dreadful days of clammy, ice water. Tom's fingers began to ache, and he feared he might be getting arthritis. No gold, just bust-ass work, and his resentment was beginning to show. Few friendly words were spoken now between the men, and Ray himself seemed a different man. From mentor to tormentor, Tom thought. Why couldn't he just take out a portion of his earlier profits for the kids, Tom wondered. It was some kind of insanity, truly, to keep working in that dangerously cold water. Tom would ask about the weather report, even though he already knew, and Ray would answer that nothing serious was headed their way, and comment on how lucky they were to have such a late winter. After such a remark Tom would try not to say anything to Ray for the day, except to answer him, hoping he would take the hint. Then one day, a week before Christmas, Ray said to Tom after a morning run, simply "get dressed". Tom could not get out of the wetsuit quick enough, and he warmed his hands by the fire Ray had built, drinking hot coffee in gulps. Ray had situated the camp chairs a little different, and Tom was told to seat himself across from Ray, his back to the hillside. Ray sat a fifteen inch long wooden box on the chair next to him. The box looked a little worn, but well made, perhaps for jewelry or gold, but instead it held a large caliber long barreled pistol that Ray took out and held in an admiring manner. "It was my first three-fifty-seven, Tom."

"It looks well made."

"Smith and Wesson, nickel plated. I have some serious talking to do now, Tom."

Tom did not like the tone of Ray's voice. They were not the friends they had been earlier in the summer, it was obvious, and Darcy's remarks about Ray's mental health did not make Tom feel any easier. Ray almost caressed the gun, then pulled the hammer back, and pointed straight at Tom's eyes. Tom's heart was suddenly out of control, his eyes stinging with tears, but he managed a "what's wrong, Ray?" This was not the Ray he had grown to know. This man must be insane. Ray had an almost lifeless expression, like he was looking at nothing in particular, and then the barrel moved slightly, and the discharge sent sparks and smoke close to Tom's face. He almost lost control of his bowels, and he stood up and tried to yell "God-Damn it, Ray. What did I do?" but it came out weakly.

"Sit down!" Tom sat, worrying he would have to crap. "Pretty horrible getting shot like that. My Dad did that to me when I was fifteen. I offer no apologies for what I just did, Tom. I did it for a good reason." Tom wiped tears from his eyes. "I did it as a friend. There are some people back in these woods, hell, anywhere, for that matter, that will kill for gold. I want you to always remember that if you have the hint of trouble you will come to me. Me or Bill, or both. Now take this, and step over here. You don't ever want to get where you were just at with someone who would really kill you." Tom stood up, still feeling sick, and walked numb legged to stand beside Ray. There were five bottles lined up on a board behind where Tom had been sitting that he hadn't noticed before, and one shattered one. "Show me how you use a six-shooter." Tom still felt numb, but he held the pistol steady with right hand and pulled the double action trigger evenly on each shot, leaving five more shattered bottles. "You'll have to get your own holster, but the box comes with it."

Tom could think of nothing to say. He knew it was intended as an extra valuable gift, from Ray's point of view. Finally, "thanks. Thanks for both the pistol..., and your concern, Ray." He almost wanted to say how sorry he was about Will, but he knew better.

"I have something special for Darcy, too, for her 'wish can'." And he held up one of the prettier gold-quartz pieces from his share of the take.

"Wish can?"

"Heck, she hasn't told you about the 'wish can'? I can't believe it. Everyone knows about the 'wish can'. Oh, by the way, we're done for the season. If it doesn't work out with Bill next year, see me right here." Tom could almost smile, almost.

Ray delivered Darcy's nugget at the dinner he bought for the whole crew at the Quartz Café. Leroy and Whitey had been invited the day before; Tom and Darcy had to be surprised, and the dinner was really for them, they knew. And as if nature had taken a cue, the clear, cool afternoon sky turned gray at dusk, and a steady rain set in. Darcy wrapped her nugget in a paper napkin and carefully placed it in her hand purse, and at home she slid under the bed to retrieve a sixteen ounce coffee can to put it in, already heavy enough. Tom stood watching, leaning against the door.

"All summer long, right under my nose. Well, if she'd given me the boot, I could have used the traveling money."

Darcy got up and wrapped her arms around him. "You can have it all, right now, if you want. It's not really gold. It's something else. There are twenty three nuggets in the can, eleven ounces, and every one of them was a gift after my father died. The biggest is from Bill, of course. Actually, three are. When we went to my father's funeral, an old miner named Zack walked up to me on the street. His breath was terrible, bad teeth..., I was a little afraid of him. He just walked up and put a nugget in my hand and said 'make a wish', and then walked away. A lot of people saw it, I guess. For several years, this went on. Someone would walk up and put one in my hand. I never knew who to expect next, or if I expected one and didn't get it, well, I wouldn't hold that against someone."

"I guess it beats a tooth under the pillow. You and Bill, both, are just inviting a thief."

"If it happens, it happens. It's not gold, Tom. Well, yes it is, if we really need it, it could become gold."

"We don't need it. You're right, it's not gold."

"What did Ray give you, in the box?"

He opened it, and she almost shuddered. If she had known what happened, she would have scolded Ray, but Tom would never tell. "I never want to have to use it, but it will always be a cherished gift. It will be hid better than the 'wish can', I guarantee you. No kids will find it. We didn't get his daughters one little nugget. All those rotten, stinking days of work for nothing."

"That's what it's all about, Tom. You don't want to get gold fever. It's ruined so many lives."

ELEVEN

Christmas in the little house was cheery enough, what with a dinner Christmas Eve in Downieville, followed by a Christmas day dinner in Marysville. Rene and Agnes finally got to meet, and seemed to get along quite amicable. Tom gave Darcy a special, ornate carved wooden box for jewelry he purchased from an antique shop, a fairly nice gold watch, two brand new pair of cowgirl shirts with mother-of-pearl buttons, and two ladies Levis. Darcy refused to move the nuggets to the box, protesting it might take the 'magic' away, and filled it with all her other jewelry instead. She gave Tom an expensive holster and belt for the pistol, clothes, and a set of Proto ratchets and sockets. They gave Agnes a set of kitchen plates, saucers, and utensils, and the promise of getting in all the wood she needed. They gave Rene a small crystal chandelier that had been sitting in a local's storeroom for years, until Darcy talked them into parting with it. It was the best Christmas Tom remembered in years.

There were still two cord of split wood in Agnes's wood pile that would last a while, luckily, as the weather decided to make up for a dry fall. Sixteen inches of rain fell in the week up to New Years, and then it began to snow.

Not the dry, powdery snow of the high country, but the heavy, dangerous 'Sierra Cement' that can crush roofs, and an alarm was set at night just to get them up to check on the roof. Three feet of packed, wet snow sat on the ground January tenth, and then it began to rain again, a warm rain. The rivers were roaring, and the Highway Patrol closed 49 from Sierra City to the last Yuba bridge past Downieville. But the weather broke before it reached flood stage, and temperatures stayed in the fifties, allowing the snow to melt. Come February, it was time to cut firewood.

Agnes borrowed a huge McCullough chainsaw that was obviously a logger's, and with a borrowed two ton Dodge Powerwagon they headed out one sunny morning. "Where are we going?" Darcy asked, as Agnes drove. "Up to get those Doug firs we saw last year? Those would be easy to get, Tom. They're about a foot thick."

"I have a project. I want to get something before someone else claims it, if it's still there. So, you never cut wood, Tom?"

"No, but I catch on quick."

Through several muddy, slippery turnoffs they headed backwoods, and Tom considered how easily he could get lost there. "There it is", Agnes advised.

"Mother, no!" Darcy demanded. "This is crazy. You brought us up here?" Just up the high bank of the rutted dirt road stood a dead sugar pine, five feet at the base, and a good eighty feet tall.

"I would guess about five, maybe seven cord in that one tree. We're lucky no one has got it."

"Oh, Agnes." Darcy was practically in tears. "Sugar pine is too pitchy, anyway, this is ridiculous."

Tom did not like this at all, knowing what Agnes was capable of, but managed to say "We'll get it."

"No, Tom! Good God, this is a good way to get killed. We could get those Doug firs so easy."

Agnes had an old, dirty dress on that billowed out from the several bustles she was wearing for warmth, and when they stopped up road from the tree, she was actually able to lift the saw out before Tom could get to it. "You stay in the truck, Darcy. That way you won't see it when it comes to get you," Agnes said, laughing.

"Agnes, if you want this tree cut, let me have the saw!" Tom demanded.

"No, I'll make the first cut. That's critical. I watched Bob do this so many times, I'm almost as good as he was."

"I know that if you hit a knot, the saw might buck", Tom offered.

"Yes, and Sugar pine is known for knots."

Darcy sat in the truck, and Agnes actually managed to start the drop side cut. Then with her instructions and three refuelings, Tom got most of the rest done in about twenty-five minutes. The tree was just barely standing, and Tom's stomach was turning. "If it falls on the road, we might as well set up a tent for the night."

"It won't. I need this wood. It will last me through spring."

Darcy continued to stay in the truck, even as it went down, and it hit just where Agnes had predicted, but almost slid down the hillside. Five more hours, and they had a cord of three foot rounds pulled into the truck bed with a chain drive hand winch and a ramp. "That was nifty. You are a good woodman, Agnes", Tom teased.

"I tried this once with Dave. Poor young man, he couldn't take it, and we were just cutting twigs."

That evening in her room, Darcy threw a fit. "Are you going to always give in to her bull-shit? That was outrageous, and you just gave in to it."

"No", he said, trying to corner her for a hug. "I outdid her. That was better than arguing."

"Yeah, well the next project she will make even worse. You can count on it." But she allowed a kiss.

TWELVE

Nature allowed them to gather the rest of the tree, but not split much. The weather the canyon is known for set in. Days of howling wind with driving rain, as the temperature often stood at 29 degrees. How anything could survive in the forest, Tom could not imagine, including the transient miners reported to live in little homemade shelters. Day after day of pots and pans to catch the leaks, even though Tom had used a five gallon bucket of roof tar in September. He really missed Marysville's milder weather, but cuddling with Darcy at night kept him going. The bank account from summers dredging was getting smaller, and there were things he needed to help his own mother with. And there was always some little diversion. "Tom, I have something to tell you, and you need to take care not to over react", Darcy said one afternoon.

"You're pregnant?"

"I wish. No, I remember a time we were discussing the subject, according to you know who."

"Vernon, what now?" Tom was unconcerned.

"According to my source, you had a conversation with him, remember?"

"Yes", Tom chuckled. "He was going to reserve me a spot at the cemetery."

"Tom, he accused you of hygrading Ray."

"Accused me! He's the one that got caught stealing. What's wrong with that fart?"

"He has told some people that you admitted to him that you also, and I repeat also, did some hygrading. I guess he thought he could cover himself, you know. Heck, if Tom does it, it must not be any big thing."

"I'd better call Ray." Tom was shadow-boxing now.

"I already did. He says he would trust you any day of the year."

"Thank you. God, what's wrong with people?" Tom was battering the closet door, just hard enough to make some noise. "I know its psychological warfare. All I have to do is kiss his boot in front of his friends, and then I'm in."

"If it were someone else, it could be serious, but Vernon, no."

"I know what we can do. We can head over to Grass Valley for a movie, and hit the library. I need to look up a book by Reinfield on chess."

"Mother has a book by Reinfield, but let's see a movie anyway, if it stops raining." And she retrieved the book. Page 141, 'the weakness of pawns moved in a foolish manner'.

"Well, well, well. So Vernon lost a chess tournament to a flatlander. I know one move I'm never going to make. I'll never fight him with his advantage. Let him lose his temper, and I've seen he has a temper. The man who loses his temper loses the fight."

"Not always. Beverly Hatfield beat me up after school when I was fourteen, and it was her temper that did it. Of course, she's a lot bigger than me. She's big boned."

"Is she still around?"

"She lives in Nevada City. I'm still afraid of her, but she's afraid of Agnes."

"I'd have to grab her by the hair, and pull her off."

"No, you wouldn't. You don't touch a woman, even if one is fighting me. Then some men would come after you."

"Rules, rules! I'd pull her off, and then worry about it later. Look, I'll make a deal. You don't get in any fights, and I promise not to box that skinny farts head in."

"It's a deal. I don't want to risk getting my teddy bear hurt."

"Not a chance! Not a chance! I could smoke him any day of the year." Tom boxed an imaginary foe, danced and dipped, and then attempted a high kick that almost lost him his balance.

"OK, tiger. Let's just go see a movie. Preferably one where the Indians beat the white guys."

THIRTEEN

Darcy's birthday was coming up in April, and a trip to Mexico could be the perfect gift. He got Darcy to drive them down to Rene's for a few days on some excuse, and with Rene running a diversion, he drove to Ruley's, bought a cherry Coke from Suz, and got her to promise to connect him with Hiame. When Rene answered Hiame's call the next afternoon, she said "Tom's friend" and pulled Darcy to the front yard for some early gardening. Darcy left looking a little suspicious, as Tom answered "Mechanic, what are you up to?" He hoped she thought it was Matt.

"Tom, what's happening? It's good hearing from you." He sounded like he'd been drinking a little, and Tom could hear Papa Esposito's full house in the background. Hiame didn't sound much enthused about anything.

"I want to ask a big favor from a big man."

"Yeah, I figured. No one calls 'El Gordo' anymore unless they want something."

"Yeah, well see, I'm worried you're not exercising enough, and so I'd like to get you on a program, kind of like Coach would have done." It was going over like a lead balloon. Just silence. "Hiame, Darcy's birthday is coming up in April, and she wants to see the Aztec pyramids, she's told me, and I figure if we can get you to take us down there, we can get you back in shape running those steps."

"What are you talking about, man?"

"A surprise for Darcy. I'm taking you up on that boast about inviting me to visit your relatives in Mexico."

"You can't be serious. I'm broke, man. I'm just bumming in Papa's house, as always." He still didn't sound enthused.

"We can only afford two tickets, but I can get a friend of Darcy's to buy her a ticket, and she'd give it to you, just to get you to give us a tour."

"Hey, man." Now there was a hint of cheer. "Don't bull-shit me, man. I'm down, man, down."

"Then get off your duff, and get with the team."

"Oh, man, see my uncle, my village. God, I want to get out of this place."

"I want to surprise Darcy, even though we talked about it earlier."

"I'm in, man. You want the pyramids? I'm your tour guide. Special low rates, gringo boy. You'll need passports."

"We're getting them tomorrow. I'll call you when we're ready."

In the morning, Rene told Darcy "I'm going downtown on some business. Would you like to come along?"

"No thank you, Rene." She sounded unconcerned.

"Come on." Tom grabbed her arm. "Let's get out and see Marysville."

Darcy looked perplexed, and gave in. Rene went in to a drugstore after parking right by a small photo shop whose door sign advertised ‘Passports’. Tom got out casually and said “we should get a portrait sometime”.

“What on earth for?” She sounded almost irritated as she accompanied him in.

“Hey Billy, we’re ready.” Tom said to the man behind the counter.

“What’s going on?”

“All you need is the photo, and your birth certificate,” Billy said.

“They should be ready by the twelfth. We should leave before your birthday, Darcy. I mean, that makes sense, right? Hiame’s going to be our tour guide to the pyramids. We got the poor man’s package deal.”

“You were serious! I’d love to take a trip. Does Agnes know?”

“You’ll have to tell her. Bill is buying an extra ticket we can give Hiame.”

“Get ready for some friction with Agnes. I knew your mother was up to something.”

It ended up in a short argument with Agnes, who demanded “what purpose does this trip serve? You’re taking my only daughter into a foreign country. If I had more daughters, it wouldn’t concern me so much. I could afford to lose one or two.”

“You see, Tom, I told you she has a sense of humor. You got to go to Modesto and party all the time, mother. You were spoiled rotten. Now I’m going to Mexico, and Tom and I have been talking about other trips, too. Maybe Europe some day.”

A local tour agency got the three of them round trip bus tickets to Mexico City, with an allowance to stop along the way for the diversion to Hiame's little town, Selada. Tom had never seen Hiame so enthused, dressed like he was going to Mass the day they boarded. He thanked Darcy three times for the bus ticket. Two days of cramped and uncomfortable traveling, with fairly decent hotel stops, got them to the turn off point, and they boarded a bus that looked like it wouldn't make it around the corner. Hiame had been warning them all along what to do or not do, and now the natives looked somewhat unfriendly, hard stares from poor Mestizos who undoubtedly felt some jealousy, but one cheery, chubby woman asked something in Spanish, and Hiame interpreted: "she asked if you are newlyweds".

"Tell her yes," Tom said, and Darcy smiled a little 'I know what you are thinking' smile. "These people must have hard lives."

"Hard lives make hard people", Darcy said. "It's no different than in the Sierra."

"No", Hiame corrected. "These people are happier than you think, as long as they get enough to eat. Drought killed half our village in the 1700's, but if you were to come here at harvest time, you would see people who really know how to appreciate God's favors. You would see some happy people."

Conditions in Selada were even more meager than they had expected. Hiame called ahead, and they were met at the bus stop with a burro team that they had to ride for two miserable hours, but Darcy never complained. No one in the village spoke English, and Hiame's uncle put them up in a small, stark room. They were beginning to wonder if it would be a miserable vacation, until the first meal. They were directed to a set of heavy wooden tables brought outside by some of the younger men, and served a feast they could have not imagined come from so poor a village. Mexican dishes they were familiar with, some they had never seen, so many, so much, obviously to impress the guests. Melons and squash seemed to be the specialty, and local beer and wine served, cooled by the village ice machine.

"I wish we could talk to these people", Tom said.

"They are enjoying your company more than you can imagine. The last American here was a mining geologist in 1952, and this gives them a chance to show off."

Tom wondered who the village miners might be, those men who knew they lived under a sentence of death. A skinny young woman came up after the meal and hugged Hiame. "This is my cousin, Carlota. Carlota, son mi amigos, Darcy y Tom."

"They look like brother and sister", she said in Spanish, and when Hiame interpreted, Darcy broke out laughing, shaking her head no. They all attempted to participate in the music and dancing that followed, Darcy catching on to the moves quite better than Tom. Hiame looked like he 'had arrived', obviously a happier man.

"Would you move here, Hiame?" Darcy asked as they walked back to the house.

"If my life does not go anywhere, if I run out of options, I know I am always welcome here. As long as the village survives, I survive. Three hundred years, this village has been here."

The plan had been for them all to see the pyramids, but Hiame suggested they go to Mexico City without him, to let him spend more time with his relatives. He gave them the name of an honest cab driver, and with a note in Spanish, they were able to connect after a day. His English was very poor, but he was able to get them to the pyramids via a tour bus. Finally getting to stand on top of the stone structure, Darcy stood for minutes facing the light wind that moved her fine hair, and looked out over pageants of the ghosts. "Your mother is right. You could have been an Aztec princess. There are no women around here that can compete with you."

"I'm just an ordinary half-breed, fella. Don't know how you could be so confused."

"I can see you with every color macaw feather on a beautiful head-dress, in the robe of a royal lady."

"What beautiful pageantry they had. It's such a shame it's all been lost."

"No, it's not. They were too cruel. All the other Indians hated them. They got what they deserved."

"Don't let my mother hear you say that!"

They danced at a different nightclub every night and shopped the markets of Mexico City for two weeks until their resources ran low, and they had to fetch Hiame for the return. He was practically crying as he said his goodbyes to the villagers. One old man had some lengthy advice for Hiame, and then handed Darcy a very ornate wooden little cross. "Gracias, mi amigo", she said.

"He says to use it to ward off 'El Bestio', the Beast. 'El Bestio' is very jealous, and wants all the pretty young senoritas for himself. If he is very jealous, he can destroy a young couple's future."

Darcy frowned, and said "I wish he hasn't said that". She went to deposit it in a suitcase, and when she came back, she handed Hiame a one once nugget. “For you, Hiame, for luck.”

When interpreted, the man who gave her the cross said something again. “He says you made the Beast very angry, but you helped ward him off. He doesn’t want people to know there are ways to outsmart him.”

“Tell him the Beast gave my fiancé a very dangerous fever, gold fever.” Which, when interpreted, brought laughter from many.

FOURTEEN

Tom started his second season of gold fever learning from Bill, Lou, and a worker named Tom Henderson how to run a tractor with a backhoe and front loader attachments. The same basic piece of equipment farmers use to pull blades had been adopted to dig and move earth. The backhoe side was used to make two piles, one of rock too big to go through Bill's small trommel, and the other of pay dirt. Bill's Cinnamon Bear placer mine was patented, private land, but he still had rules of land management to follow, and being close to the Yuba River, he was obligated to dig a recovery pond to catch run off from the wash plant. They were basically mining a dry ancient river bed, which meant they would be in the hot sun all day, sometimes in hundred degree temperatures, but Tom found a way to cool off at the end of the day, after Darcy picked him up. They had a secret spot to take a dip in, and Darcy seemed to be doing better, day by day.

Bill had had a mining geologist evaluate what might be on the property, and where, and speculation in camp was enthusiastic. Another similar operation a mile down river had hit a fifty thousand dollar pocket one season. They were running much more material than Ray could run through his dredge, and soon Tom was in awe of his share of the take. He was steadily making up to three times as much as he had when Ray had been in the good stuff. Within a month of starting, he had put an expensive set of tires on Agnes's Ford, as well as his mother's Dodge, and into the second month he put a rebuilt engine into Agnes's car on a two day weekend Bill allowed him. In July, Tom and Darcy bought their fist car, a 49 Chevy Styleline Coupe, from a friend of Darcy's. She had been told it had been fairly well kept, with only 80,000 miles, but Tom looked it over and speculated it was more like 180,000 miles. "Never mind", he assured Darcy. "Matt and I can fix any problem." Any problem soon turned into every problem, and within a month it was sitting in Matt's parent's back yard garage, awaiting a rebuilt engine and tranny. "Heck, might as well give it a paint job and new upholstery. We won't get a better deal anywhere." By the time that was done, they had four times the original cost into it, but they had a good vehicle.

"How are you and Lou getting along?" Darcy asked on a regular basis.

"He treats me like kinfolk", Tom answered one day.

"Of course he does. He wouldn't want to make me angry."

"Will you tell me about it?"

"I'll tell you that there are women in this town trying to match-make him. I won't tell you about him until the end of season. Then, I promise. He's a good man, Tom. One of the best to come out of these woods, and he's respected everywhere. But you tell me if he says anything to you, under any circumstances. I want to know."

Several days later Tom found himself working the hillside with the tractor at an angle, and he was finding it hard to place one of the two stabilizer bars that were used to keep the unit from slipping. The more Tom tried angling the bar and moving with the tractor wheels, the more of an angle it seemed to skid to. He was getting too near a drop off. "A good captain goes down with his ship", Lou said, walking up with a grin of enjoyment. "If you drop Bill's backhoe on its top, he's going to be just a little pissed, I'd say."

"Naw, can't happen. I can figure this out. Don't need no advice, now." Tom tried using the backhoe bucket to pull the tractor up, and when that didn't work, he tried driving and pulling at the same time, a dangerous move, he was sure.

"There you go", Lou advised. The tires were spinning and the tractor was rocking back and forth, but he got it to move about a foot up, and then he replanted the bucket. Eventually, this got him to safety. "Take a break. I say so."

The two men sat in the shade of a live oak and drank a couple of cold sodas. "I'm making the best money I ever made in my life", Tom said.

"Be careful with it. You never know, from day to day. Bill and I have been speculating that we might be getting near the gut of the old river channel, and that might be like answering the 'Sixty Four Thousand Dollar Question', but I never count my chickens before they hatch. I've learned. Say, I heard some things awhile back, about a lie Vernon Fickett told about you. I want you to know I had a little talk with him the other night, and he's promised to lay off you."

"Thanks, but it's no big deal. I'm not going to let anything he says or does get to me, and if he wants a fight, he'll have to instigate it."

"The only people you have to worry about are that crowd at the Smith Ranch. They're all out of work up there, and it's easy for them to swallow a Vernon Fickett story, if it's about a flatlander. I heard Ray gave you a three-fifty-seven pistol last year, and I think it's time to incorporate you into our volunteer posse team, Tom. That would make a good impression on a lot of people. Hell, it seems every time Sheriff Ramey calls up a posse, I'm the first to get a badge. Can I count on you next time?"

Tom could just visualize some backwoods boy seeing Tom, the flatlander, help arrest a relative. It wasn't a pleasant image. He could get on someone's bad side. "Of course." Tom sounded very unenthused, and tried to make "call me the next time" sound a little stronger.

"I will. You serve on a posse, and you'll be in. I've been on so many calls in the past six years, I think Clarence is trying to get me to apply for Deputy, but I'd never take it. It seems every time something serious comes up in this town, Lou is expected to volunteer. I had a grandfather that left me a little heirloom I keep as a reminder of certain responsibilities in this world, a brown hood. As good and determined a Sheriff as Clarence is, well, there are times when a western lawman needs the righteous men of his community to back him up. There are times a Sheriff can get outgunned, even today. Now you walk into church on a Sunday and see all those men of good intentions, good Christians, and you think that's all it takes. But I tell you what; it takes a little more to be a true Christian. A man has to stand up and be ready to fight for decency. There are some men with good hearts who are just too terrified to face evil, and while I won't hold it against them, I have to reserve my respect for those who will stand up against evil. It takes a strong arm to stop a strong arm. There are so many instances in the old West of corruption and injustice being finally stopped by a strong arm, when all else failed. Sometimes, even, by a former outlaw, one who knew his new opponents so well. People were practical in those days; the Sheriff's were chosen for grit more than anything. My grandfather used to put on the brown hood, being that he believed in its necessity at times. He was a vigilante, on occasion, and I'm downright proud of that. In the middle ages, men of absolute evil wore the black hood, but the brown hood is the antithesis of that hood, Tom. Men who put on the brown hood did it to protect themselves and their families from men of evil."

"I can see that. If the outlaws knew who they were, they could retaliate."

"Exactly. I'll tell you a story that happened several years ago to a young friend of mine. Won't tell you his name, but he and his wife got an invite to go to work in the oilfield in the Bakersfield area. They got down there to meet a friend named Ed at a little bar in town, but Ed was late to show, and my friend got conned into going out to work with a local paint contractor, a real low life. The contractor checked them into a motel, took him out and left him on a job with no transportation, and, well, to make a long story short, he came back and tried to talk her into believing she needed to give him sex in order for her husband to keep the job. He had her shirt off, she ran crying from the motel, and that son of a bitch tried to pull her back. Ed drove by about that time and rescued her, and got the bastard to tell where he had left her husband. They were so shook up they drove right back here and never went back for the other job. Now, some friends of mine and me, we got to thinking." Tom did not really want to hear this. "We drove all the way back down there and met with Ed for a little late night rendezvous with this contractor. Someone he didn't know suckered him out of the bar, and we took him on a drive out to the pump jack he had my friend painting that day. He was still drunk and belligerent; being the kind he was..." Lou stopped for effect, Tom caught the drift of was instead of is, and felt queasy, "and told us we were all a flock of pussy's. Ed put a noose around his drunken neck, tied the other end to the horse head, and told him to say his prayers. The rope had been fixed to separate, but he didn't know that. When we turned on the pump jack, the rope didn't separate till he was six feet off the ground, and he screamed and shit his pants. He was gett'n religion mighty quick, now that he was sobered up."

"That's funny. I'll bet he changed his ways", Tom said. 'If it's funny, why does it make your stomach so sour', he thought.

"Yeah, well it's hard to stop bad habits, I guess. Ed told me that he started up his practice of using power to get sex again, and someone found him with a bullet in the head about a year later. One of these days, Vernon is going to really piss me off. He's done some things, even before I met you, that I really don't tolerate. And you really don't want to see Lou when he's pissed off!"

'That's so true', Tom thought. 'I don't ever want to see Lou pissed. Ray and I together couldn't take him out.'

"But I'll tell you what. Lou is a righteous man, but Lou is not a happy man. Sometimes I wonder if there is any real reward for righteousness." And the strong arm for righteousness got up and walked away, leaving Tom feeling miserable.

After dinner, after Agnes had retired that night, Tom demanded "tell me about Lou. Now is the time. I need to know!"

"What did he say?"

"He asked me to volunteer for the next posse. He told me he believed true Christians must fight for decency…"

"And?"

"He told me he is not happy. He said there may be no reward for righteousness. Tell me everything. Let's just get it done."

"OK. You asked for it. Let's just get it done. When I was sixteen, I'd known Ray and Lou for years. Lou was 22, and I kind of went out with him, not a date, Tom, just a picnic. And then I started talking more with him, when I saw him, but I was just trying to be a friend. He was seeing a nineteen year old girl, and I didn't think anything of it, till his girlfriend tried to bitch me out in public one day, and told me to stay away from him. I told her I had no intentions on Lou, and that we were just friends, but it got back to Lou, and he had a big verbal fight with her, from what he told me. Then they broke up, and I still…," she wiped the tears that were beginning. "I didn't want to date Lou, I just wanted to be friends, but he didn't understand that. He came to Agnes and made some statements asking how she would react to us marrying when I got older, and she told him and me both she thought he was perfect for me. She adores Lou. She has told me so many times he would be the perfect son-in-law. Well, I told her I didn't love him, and I told him. I didn't know how much that would hurt him; it frightened me to see how much that seemed to hurt him. He told me someday I would change my mind, and see how we were right for each other. Tom, he hasn't dated anyone since..., no one I know of."

"That's wrong. He's wrong. I'll bet there are women chasing after him right now. He's got so much going for him. It's not like he's ugly, or dirt poor."

"It's a nightmare. I think the world of Lou, but I could never marry him. After Ray and I broke up, I heard Sandra Kazinski in the St. Charles one night..., say something..., shit, I had to leave. She was talking where I could hear her, and she knew it. She was telling the crowd how the men on some islands in the Mediterranean rape a woman who denies them, and if the other people approve, but she refuses to marry him, they stone her to death."

"No way! That's worse than the Aztecs!"

"She said Lou should just have his way with me, and then I'd marry him like I should. I could have killed her. And then, a year later, someone told me that Eleanor Smith from Lincoln tried making a pass at Lou in a bar in Nevada City, and Lou just stared her down. She was so embarrassed that she called him a queer in front of everyone, and he said 'I love someone else. I wouldn't go to bed with you if you were the last woman on the face of the earth'. And then he walked out." She was crying now. "Can't he see how I feel? I feel nothing for him. I need to leave this town. It's not just my mother, it's him too. That's why I threw myself at Ray. Can you understand that?"

"Yes."

"I know what I did was wrong. Ray could have been arrested, but my Daddy was dead…"

"Do you know that's only the second time I've heard you call him your Daddy since I met you? Eventually we will move to Marysville. You just have to be patient and let me get up a grubstake."

"Hah, hah." She was laughing through the tears. "He's talking like a miner." She shook her head. "He's beyond hope, but I love him."

"Next year is going to be my season. Don't ask me how I know. I just know."

"But after next year, if we're still broke…?"

"We'll move one way or another. I won't be able to tolerate another year with nothing to show. And as for Lou, Clydesdales don't mate with Shetlands. He should know that."

Several days later the crew found a drop in the bedrock; terraces that led deeper and deeper in the bedrock held placer gold the ancient river had washed in millions of years ago. Some of it they had to sweep out of the cracks with whisk brooms and dust pans. The sluice looked so pretty at the end of each day with all those little yellow metal stones. "Somewhere it will level out, I assume", Bill said viewing the terrain. "And supposedly that's where the pay streak will appear. The deepest channel always held the biggest nuggets, from what my Dad said in the Ruby."

'Count your chickens', Tom told himself. 'What if we make enough, move right now? No, I don't think it will happen here.'

Two days later the other Tom broke into a hollow in the gravel and rock, and called everyone over. "She's a been had, Bill. But what the hell, we're doing good enough in the high bedrock, I ain't disappointed." He was lying, everyone was disappointed.

Lou inspected with a flashlight, careful to not stick his head in far enough that something could fall on him, and reported "It's a drift alright. A big drift! Do you want to open it up, see if they left anything?"

"Let's not go in too far. The shoring will be rotted out. We'll just stay this side of it and head up the mountain. Them old farts, they covered up their entrance. I'll bet they got filthy, stinking, lousy rich!" Bill said with a sour grin.

"We're doing alright. We should be glad they didn't get the rest", Lou said.

'Three times the gold I made with Ray when we were into it. Now is the time to be careful with my, uh, our small fortune', Tom thought. 'Still, I sure would have liked to see some of what those old-timers saw in that mine.'

FIFTEEN

"Thomas, we can afford a few things now", Darcy said one evening, while watching TV.

"Yeah, what?"

"Can I let Janet's husband cut mother's firewood this year? They have kids, and they need every penny."

"Of course. I don't want to cut wood. Your mother would direct everything."

"And..."

"What?"

"Can I let the Simmon's kid mow our yard?"

"What else?"

"The roof. Michael Jenson is going to college."

"Oh my God! My gold! It's slipping between my fingers! I'll be broke by the end of the year. Didn't I say I'd put you in charge of the books in my garage? You told me you were trained for it. Whoever you think we should hire, I agree."

"And?"

"What?"

"Can we start looking at a house in Marysville?"

"Next time we visit. I promise." He had hoped she would say it's time to start planning the wedding. That was the thing the girl was supposed to demand. People had stopped asking. They were common law, as far as he was concerned. In September of their first year, the Downieville Baptist preacher Melvin Lewis had caught Tom alone and scheduled a talk after church.

"Tom, have you discussed a wedding?"

"It's all for Darcy to decide on a time, Reverend. I'm not going to press her."

"That's a beautiful ring you gave her. Rings really mean nothing. It's the covenant that impresses God."

"Yeah, I have a Catholic friend in Marysville that can't stop talking about the covenant, but right now, there's no woman in his life. I just don't want to push Darcy. She's had a lot of anguish in her life…"

"I know. That's true enough. Lynn Rutledge tried to get her to see a mental health counselor several years ago." Silence, Tom could not reply. "Tom, many women get married just for the sake of marriage, and others dread making a permanent mistake. Some couples go through incredibly rough times, and always seem to manage to bounce back. And then there are those like Agnes and Bob were. I'm not saying they were wrong for each other, but, Darcy had to put up with a lot. I should be telling you both to get your butts in here and get it done." Tom laughed outright. "But I know better. Maybe God has a plan. Don't either of you hesitate to knock on my door."

They would be going on a second year next spring, but Tom had made up his mind not to mention it again. It was not a viable possibility that she would change her mind and leave him. It was not possible that he would meet another woman that could get him to leave her. With her heart and soul, she did her best to make him happy. But still, he wondered, was there something, some mental wound, something that motivated her against making rational decisions sometimes? 'What about your mental health, Tom? What about the time when your world fell apart?' he thought. 'Remember what you were going through, and how the world seemed so different from that new perspective.'

The crew continued to produce good gold, working parallel to the old mine shaft, careful of the cave-ins that took place as some of the rotted timber was removed. "Bill, dead man!" Lou yelled one morning. Tom thought he meant the mechanical term, at first, until he heard "dead miner!"

"Don't tell me that! Now we have to call the coroner. Well, that's alright. He deserves a decent burial."

"Can we work around him?" the other Tom asked.

"Hell, no! But we can drink a round to him", Lou laughed.

"Yeah, quit'n time, boys. Back tomorrow", Bill ordered.

Tom looked down through the rubble and saw part of a partially disintegrated shirt and one human rib bone protruding, the rest covered in dirt. "Hey, let's run him through the trommel. Maybe he had some change on him", he joked.

"I second the motion", the other Tom added.

"I know you think he's a good subject for a few jokes, but stop and think, if that had been you lying there", Bill said.

"If it were my bones lying there, I wouldn't much care at that point, now would I. Of course, if I had been murdered..., but he probably wasn't murdered", Tom reasoned.

"He probably was," Lou said. "I don't think they closed the entrance and left him by accident."

"Even if he has a bullet in his skull, the coroner will probably rule it out of date, and they'll just bury him down valley. Well, what say we drink a toast, have a wake for him. Maybe he was Irish", Bill offered.

"Hell, yeah", Lou said. "He's costing us some money. Might as well send him off right."

The four men sauntered into the St. Charles in good spirits, and Mikey, the barkeep, asked "what are you doing off work, Bill? You didn't hit a pocket?"

"Naw, we had to call the coroner. Give us a pitcher, Mikey. We might just all get drunk."

Mikey's face flushed white, and he asked "someone get killed?"

"Yeah, about a hundred years ago", Lou said.

"Shoot, just run him through the wash plant. You're wasting the coroner's gas", Mikey laughed.

The men laughed a good minute before Tom could say "I told them to. They wouldn't listen." Tom sat between Lou and Tom Henderson; it seemed the right time to kick back and shoot the bull. The men spent an hour and four pitchers enjoying the excuse to cut work and talk, speculate, and gossip, until Bill and the other Tom made excuses to leave. Lou seemed to have some things on his mind.

"Makes you wonder, sometimes."

"What?" Tom said a little slurry.

"How many ole' boys ended up out there with a bullet in the head, all over gold. Of course, I'll bet a hell of a lot of them just gave up one day and laid down and died. Couldn't find any gold, couldn't take any more. You're liable to run across a skeleton anywhere. They say that in the Gold Rush less than ten percent found enough to keep going."

"Yeah, and they shot all the deer out pretty quick, Darcy says. She says the Maidu starved."

"Some of the whites did, too."

"I guess it's easier to understand a highgrader risking a bullet, when you think about what it's like to starve to death. What will you do, what will Downieville do when the gold runs out?"

"Hell, we were one of the very first mining towns, and we're still alive long after the rest dried up and blew away. We've got lumber, and tourism, and we've got heritage."

"Agnes says someday you'll get a big housing development, and that'll bring in some money."

"I hope not. Let this place stay just the way it is. We've calmed down a lot from those Wild West days. I'll tell you what, that Bodie over in the eastern Sierra, that was hell on earth while it lasted. They needed the vigilantes in that town. Human life wasn't worth the change in a man's pocket. There was a lot of human degradation associated with some of those mining towns, I hate to admit. Some of it was greed, murder, but over in Leadville, Colorado, hell, it was just negligence."

"What happened there?"

"The pneumatic drill. Automation set in, and two men could do the work of eight with that drill, but the worst of it was the rock dust it created that gave the miners silicosis of the lungs. They killed a lot of miners with rock dust until they figured putting water on the bit would make the bit last longer, and just happened to stop the dust. Hell, they didn't care. There were no laws protecting miners in those days. If you wanted a job, you had better be ready to risk your life."

A lot of things were going through Tom's mind now, mainly concerning Darcy, but he dare not mention her, so he asked "do you think we could still hit a pocket, something they missed?"

"I doubt it. The geologist told Bill that when the mountain faulted as it rose, it cut off part of the old river channel. There's some prime property on the ridge above, but it doesn't belong to Bill, and there's going to be a barren gap in between."

"I won't let that bother me. I told Darcy that our strike won't come till next year. I don't know why, but I just feel it."

Lou looked at Tom with a little off grin and said "don't tell that to too many people around here. There've been people in these hills ended up talking to themselves, talking like that, and most folks just leave them alone. I've heard some miners swear by the people who say they can witch gold, but I've never seen a rich witcher. You haven't tried witching have you?"

"I don't know anything about it, but I'd try it if I thought it would help."

"That's the right attitude. One thing you never do around here. You never cry about hard times. Everyone's had them. There've been a few good strikes around here, but most folks are just trying to get by. Everyone thinks we're all getting rich up here, but the economy of the valley has gone way beyond us."

"Ray was talking about that last year. He says the real gold is in America's productivity, and to go back to a gold standard would kill the goose that laid the golden egg."

"It makes you stop and wonder, what's going to happen when that valley fills up, and there's no more room. Some day something's going to cull the heard. A famine, a plague, or a war. I dread another depression. I hate to think about it, but it's inevitable."

"And here you are telling me to keep trying. I've got to believe tomorrow will always be better than yesterday."

Lou put a powerful hand on Tom's shoulder as he got up to leave and said "It's like I said, the skeletons belong to the quitters. I'll see you tomorrow, Tom, and we won't run out for a while, I'm sure."

Tom sat by himself for a while, drinking the last of the pitcher and talking with Mikey and a man Tom's age from Alleghany named Jeff. He was just about to get up to leave when he heard Mikey say "hello, Vernon, John."

"Hey Mikey, set us up some drafts. Well, look at this! The most heartbroken man in all of Downieville, and the man who stole his woman, working on the same claim! Can you imagine it? And here he sits, this flatlander, acting like he owns the place!"

"Outrageous!" the other man said in a voice full of malice. "Shit like this doesn't get by us in Alleghany!"

"John! And you too, Vernon! You're fix'n to get eighty-sixed!" Mikey said harshly as he pulled out a broken pool cue and slapped it on the bar.

"He's even got the bar-keep catering to him", Vernon said, obviously placating the other man.

"I mean it! If you want beer, sit down and shut up! Otherwise, get the hell out of my bar!"

"Alright, Mikey, Cool down, now. We won't start nothing here."

"Naw, not here", the man named John said as an obvious threat. This new man had Tom's stomach muscles tight. He wished he had left the bar with Lou, but there was no avoiding it now, and he was realizing that Lou's comments about Vernon getting him on some people's bad side were all too true. John was to be taken seriously, malicious black eyes, jet black hair, probably some Indian or Mexican blood, and a bit taller and heavier than scrawny Vernon.

Tom realized a rebuff. "So I'm a highgrader, Vernon. Ray doesn't think so. As a matter of fact, he says he'll have me back on his claim anytime."

"Outrageous!" John said, and walked a little turn around, like he was having to diffuse some intense anger, lest he explode with rage. "He wouldn't open his fucking mouth in Alleghany, this dumb shit. He doesn't know, the son-of-a-bitch, what we would do to him."

"Out, John! Right now, or I'll show you what I can do to you! And don't come back for a while. I'm going to have to have some time to forget this!" Mikey said, slapping the pool cue three times on the bar.

"Yeah, John! You're not exactly the most welcome man in Alleghany", Jeff said from the end of the bar. "You're on Eldridge's shit list, everyone knows. I could tell Tom a few things you might not want him to hear." John started toward Jeff, and Tom saw genuine fear in Jeff's eyes, but Mike ran around the end of the bar with the cue in hand, and John did a quick about face and headed toward the door, only to be stopped dead in his tracks by a shorter, older, white haired man with intense blue eyes who now stood blocking his exit. "Hello, Eldridge", Jeff said enthusiastically, as Mikey stopped short of catching up with John.

"Speak of the devil", Mikey said. "We were just talking about you, Elder. What a good thing. You can help me sweep some trash out my front door."

The white haired man smiled and gripped a frame of the door with a gnarled, knobby hand. "John! Like they say in the movies, long time, no see." And then the grin turned grim.

"Elder, I got no beef with you. Let me through!" 'So. This John was capable of fear, too', Tom thought. 'People like him and Vernon always have someone to fear.' "Let me through, Eldridge! I won't take no shit, now!" Now it was John's turn to suffer all the effects of fear. It was obvious from his expression he knew he was outmatched. Tom looked in awe at the white haired man, so calm, but so intense in the eyes. Tom wouldn't want to cross his path, either.

"Alright, boys. I don't want any brawls, not this afternoon. Let him through, Elder. The pitcher is on me."

"Make it a shot, Mikey."

"You got it." And Elder backed up and waived John through. Vernon started to follow, but Tom decided to try to get some things said while he had the chance.

"Vernon!" Vernon stopped and turned. "I've been doing some reading about your favorite game. Thanks for the advice, about making that foolish move. I don't intend to ever make that move."

Vernon walked back, faced him square, and stuck a finger into Tom's chest muscle, as Tom folded his arms and smiled defiance. "You may have already made it. You've got a few friends around here, but you're making the wrong people angry."

"Look, Vernon, I've got nothing against you. And I'm always looking for good advice. I get advice from Bill, and Ray, Lou, and even Agnes. And then from you. The trouble is, I get conflicting advice, you know, and sometimes I get confused. But..." The finger was digging deeper into Tom's chest muscle, hurting a little, but now Tom knew. He could see it in Vernon's eyes. Vernon wasn't sure, really sure, he could whip Tom, and he was just a little cautious himself. 'Like two dogs in the street', Tom thought. 'Hackles raised, neither wanting to get seriously hurt.' Vernon wasn't a mad dog, but Tom had to wonder about John. Him, Tom would have to fear. Vernon was second dog in that pack, whether he admitted it or not. "But you know, I only have one priority in this world, and that is Darcy. And for her sake, I make my final decisions. Lou needs to find another woman, Vernon. And I know he will, God bless him. Darcy needs me, and..."

"Shhh, yeah", Vernon interrupted. "I've heard flatlander stories before. Some people think Darcy made a foolish decision..."

"Some people are wrong", Tom interrupted back. "So what does it matter to you? Elaine is one of Darcy's good friends. For her sake, I think we should stay friends, Vernon..."

"For her sake? What business is Elaine to you? You're on your way out. You just haven't figured it out. Darcy makes foolish decisions. It's her Indian blood. But in the end, she'll come around. She's one of us."

"Who is us?" Jeff said walking up. "Don't think Vernon runs Alleghany, Tom. Don't judge Alleghany by those two!"

"Fuck you!" Vernon said as he turned and walked out.

"I take it you and John aren't the best of friends", Tom said to Eldridge as he sat back on his stool, and Jeff sat down beside him.

"We were partners in crime, some years ago. I served time for burglary, friend, but that son-of-a-bitch; he walked, under suspicious circumstances. That's a long story, and I don't have the time, but I'll just say that partners don't cheat partners, not those that want to die of old age."

"John gets out of Alleghany every time Elder shows up, Tom. That must give a man high blood pressure, all that running around. You'd think a man would get smart and move somewhere else", Jeff said, chuckling.

"That high blood pressure gets to a man, sooner or later. He's liable to drop dead one of these days." Mikey was pretending he didn't hear Elder's remark, and Jeff's face had become too serious. "And Vernon really believes he's one of the Sierra bad boys. What a joke. I know most of the bad boys in these hills, and he's just a puppy dog, I guarantee you. You could whip him, young fella. You do that, and I'll hand you the key to Alleghany. We'll go on a drunk from Downieville to Grass Valley."

"Yeah, I'd like to see you kick his butt. He's got it coming", Jeff said, full of enthusiasm. It was obvious Jeff wasn't going to try.

'Oh, Lord', Tom thought. 'Everyone wants this fight.' "I ain't looking for a fight, but if he starts it, I'll finish it."

"Not if, when", Eldridge advised. "Mikey, get this young man another. I like his attitude. For a flatlander, he's downright tolerable."

"Yeah, but you know he's threatening to steal Agnes McEarl's daughter away from us", Mikey kidded.

"Ah, now, we can't allow that!" Elder grinned. "We'll have to make him into a mountain boy."

"That's exactly what Bill Rutledge is trying to do to me. Bill and Lynn don't want Darcy to leave, but I'm afraid I have other plans for her."

"Don't look now, Tom, but someone has plans for you. You've been caught!" Mikey said. Darcy was standing at the propped open bar door with folded arms. She seemed to have picked up the folding arm habit from him, lately.

"Are we able to walk, Tommy?" She sounded so much like Agnes, he wondered if she was teasing.

"This is good timing, Darcy. First, Vernon shows up to tell me I'm on my way out, then these guys tell me I'm not allowed to steal you away from their mountain, and now you show up." The men were laughing, and Darcy had the faintest grin. "We were having a wake for a poor, dead miner. Come and have a beer."

"Alright. Lynn told me what happened. I'm not angry or anything."

"I hope not. It's a sad occasion."

"Well, then, let's cheer it up. Can I ask the lady for a dance?" Elder said.

"I know a good tune for you, Eldridge. I didn't bring my purse, Tom. Can I have a nickel?" She asked, walking over.

"To dance with someone else. Well..."

"Gimme!" She demanded with a hand out, and she took the nickel to the Juke Box and played Patti Page singing 'Allegheny Moon'.

Elder took her hand and pulled her into a waltz, and they looked like a couple of pro's out of a movie set. Tom thought now that perhaps he should have allowed Mom a few more of her finishing waltz lessons with him. They slowed and turned to the words 'Shine, Shine, Shine' with such grace, and Darcy's short dress allowed too much of her legs to show. Jeff had to whistle. "Easy!" Tom warned.

"I want a dance, too", Jeff threatened.

"The next one's mine."

Eldridge said "thank you, Darcy", as they finished. "That was the perfect tune to cheer up an old Alleghany boy."

"Now I have a tune for my lazy boyfriend", she said. "Gimme another nickel, baby." And when she dropped the second nickel, she turned and started singing in unison to 'MM, MM, kisses sweeter than wine' as she walked in a stalking manner towards Tom. Tom stood up, folded his arms and took two steps forward as Jeff whistled again.

"Careful, boy!" Elder warned. "You'd better take this woman home before the crowd shows up."

"Yeah, it's time for supper."

"It's time for bed, baby", Darcy teased.

"That does it. We're gone!" And he grabbed her hand and pulled her towards the door.

She was dragging her feet, giggling, and yelled "Bye, bye, boys" to the three men who were all now whistling and making innuendos under their breath.

After dinner, after the love, as they lay together and Darcy caressed Tom's chest, Tom admitted "Vernon finally got to me today. Actually, not Vernon, but someone he seems to have influence over. Shit, I have to admit, that guy John scared me. Here's someone I've never met, and... and I seem to have a real enemy in this guy. I was lucky the bartender wasn't on his side. I can just imagine what it would be like to walk into a bar and have someone like that start something, and find out everyone is against you. Pretty terrifying."

"It's happened to people. You know what to do if you see John Hanes again. Get out and call Bill."

"Or Ray. Ray and I had a little discussion on this."

"What?"

"Nothing. I know John was just doing it because he's that type. Just looking to start something. I was lucky Eldridge showed up."

"John is the type that doesn't play fair. He could hurt you if he got the chance. He's half Mexican, and he probably resents you just because you're white, you're the right type of people, and..., and you're getting all that gold. They're probably a few around here that think that way. John is the one that got Eldridge put in jail, at least, that's what everyone thinks, that knows Eldridge. Elder was a deputy sheriff out of Calaveras a few years ago..."

"Really? I thought there was something that, well, he had that look."

"Elder got shot on the job, and had to retire early, because it messed up his guts. He has a pension, but apparently he got a little greedy, and he got caught burglarizing a house in Sacramento. John got away while Elder was being arrested, but he got picked up later in Alleghany. He had a history of burglary, but he testified against Elder, and they let him walk. I guess they wanted to make an example out of Eldridge. Anyway, you were lucky Elder showed up. There's a fight to be seen."

"I don't think so. I think one of these days John is just going to disappear. But in the mean time…, I wonder how many people think from time to time, what I was thinking today?"

"What?"

"That with someone like John, that it might be smart to kill him, just to quit having to worry about it. That is, if the opportunity arose."

"Tom! I can't believe you said that!"

"I'm not the type. But you know there are plenty that would." Darcy turned away from him, and he lay for some time reflecting on it, then cuddled up against her. 'Safe from the world', he thought with some self mockery. 'Safe when I'm lying next to her.'

SIXTEEN

August saw the gold take slowing, as Lou's predictions that they would run into a barren zone came true. The drift mine came to an end where the mountain faulted, and the crew tried working the other side, which turned out to have much less gold. Everyone's moral had fallen. At one break for a cold pop Lou sat down beside Tom and remarked "I'm beginning to really hate those boys who drifted our gold out." He was trying to sound like he was joking, but there was real despair in his tone. "Yeah, I never count my chickens…; I should have kept my mouth shut."

"Darcy and I have been careful enough. We think we can survive till spring, if we have to quit right now."

"We may be quitting sooner than you think. I had some things I wanted to accomplish this year, but they're going to have to wait another season. I've got some money saved, but, my mother needs a roof, some dental work, property taxes…"

"Where does she live?"

"Sac."

"And your Dad?"

Lou looked at nothing in particular for a moment, and then said "same as yours". After a couple of gulps of soda, he added "we had a fairly rough relationship, my Pop and me. I got hit a lot, not like he was mean or anything, but he was a powerful man, and I gave him his share of tribulation, I admit. Heck, I was a hellion in school, from the mold of my old man, I think. Anyway, when I was sixteen, he told me that on my eighteenth birthday he was going to whip my ass for once and for all, to get the piss and vinegar out of me. I told him that I was looking forward to it, that I was going to whip him, even though I was really scared to death. Instead, on my eighteenth birthday, he gave me a brand new three speed bicycle, something I would loved to have had when I was fourteen. He was dying of cancer, for over a year, and I guess we needed to make amends…" Tom wiped the tear that seemed to appear, forced upon him, out of one eye, and felt, as usual, miserable at having to listen to Lou's stories. "He lasted two more months. Yeah, my mother needs dentures. Dentures, or a roof. It's always a matter of these damned petty little decisions." Tom had come to realize why Lou was such a respected citizen of the community. He was a man ready to back his principles, a man with a sense of fair play, but also a man to be feared when he took up the deputy sheriff's posse badge. And he was a man with a likeable personality, a man Tom would have used as a role model in his youth.

'Why in the hell does life have to be so complicated? Why doesn't he find another woman? Why doesn't another woman find him? He will!' Tom assured himself. 'But what if Lou were to say "the hell with everything"? What if he were to come unglued? Don't think about the negative possibilities. Think about the good that has come about, the good that will come about. I will succeed!' "Lou, we're going to find a little pocket. Nothing fantastic. Just a little bonus to get us off this mountain."

Lou started chuckling. "The Great Swami, right? You can see the future."

"Just give it a week. You'll see." It was a foolish thing to say, he knew. Just wishful thinking.

"Don't tell that to Bill, please. Do me a favor." And Lou walked away laughing, obviously in better spirits.

Six days later, after a dismal run of work, the men found a large bedrock crevice running away from the drift mine, and under a large, ancient boulder pinned in the crevice over those long millenniums they found twenty-three pounds of placer gold. Lou walked up that afternoon on Tom as he stood staring at the sluice full of nuggets, and Tom said "don't ask me how I knew. I have no idea how I knew." After staring with incredulous skepticism at Tom's frowning face, Lou walked away, saying nothing. As it turned out, Lou would be able to get his mother's dentures and her roof, and then some. The gold ran out completely a week later, and Bill shut the operation down the first week in September. The pocket turned out to be the biggest one day find of the summer amongst the local miners. There was time now to take a breather and enjoy life. Darcy seemed to be going overboard finding ways to employ locals on repair jobs, not just out of practicality, but also to make work for some who needed it, and Tom respected her reason for doing it. By the end of September, Agnes had a new roof and her first paint job in a decade, along with some carpentry repair of the rotted wood inside and out, and Tom made sure that Rene's house benefited as well. Tom and Darcy still had over two thousand dollars in savings, which they carefully concealed even from Agnes.

SEVENTEEN

With an early end to the season, Tom took to finding some work through the winter, and in early October Rene showed him a job add in the Marysville Tribune for the lumber mill in Oroville. Tom called Dave Morrow and asked him to do some checking for him. Dave called him back and informed Tom that he had made an appointment with the mill owner, John Burney, for an interview with Tom. John, it seemed, was a personnel friend of Dave's father, and Dave assured Tom that John would be a fair man to work for. Tom didn't absolutely need to work just yet, with that tidy savings account to last them through the winter, but he figured he needed to hedge his bets. He wouldn't tell anyone at the mill he intended to quit in the spring to go mining. He and Darcy drove down on a Friday, thinking that if he were hired, they would have the weekend to look for a studio size apartment to rent in Oroville. It seemed that having connections was, as always, a great benefit. John Burney, when reminded that Dave recommended Tom, said simply "start Monday morning. You'll start in the yard, and you'll work under one of my foremen, Jimmy Mandell. You'll have a kind of second foreman, Billy Winters, but he answers to Jimmy. I'll get Billy to show you around the yard today, and give you a little idea of what the work involves. In a little time, if you work out, we'll move you to assist a saw-man." John made several calls on the yard loudspeaker, and Billy came in covered with grease; clothes, face and hands. "Billy, what-cha doing?"

"Trying to get the carburetor to quit flooding on the old yard flat-bed. I'm about to give up."

"Give Thomas Hendrick a little walk around the yard. I'm going to start him Monday."

"Glad to." Billy was a large man, black eyes under sun glasses, slight pot belly, and tattooed arms, not so stout that it kept him from getting around. "There isn't much to tell you today, Tom, except that you have to start at the bottom in this yard, and you have to bust your ass. You work your way into the saw plant, and you can make some money. I'll put you on a cleanup and scrap job starting Monday, unless Jimmy says otherwise. Where do you live?"

"Downieville."

"Downieville? You planning to drive it?"

"No. Darcy and I will be getting an apartment."

"That might take a while. Listen, I just got divorced, and I'm renting a motel room with Buck Maloney, for a while, and we've got room, if you want to share rent. My brothers all live north of Chico. I've got part of a family ranch out there, and I was driving, but it's just more convenient to live here."

"Yeah, it is. Well, thanks, I'll think about it, but I'm sure we'll find something." He wasn't really enthused about any of this; he definitely wasn't planning a career in the lumber industry. "Where can I find you if we don't find a place by Sunday evening?"

"Come by the Crescent Motel, room sixteen, Sunday evening, and I should be there."

Tom mentioned it to Darcy on the drive to Rene's that evening, and Darcy said "there's something I just don't like about Billy. We'll find something." Tom found himself scratching his left palm with the fingers of his right hand as he drove, a habit that was an indication of his anxiety, but now he noticed Darcy pulling the last two fingers of her right hand with her left as she sat watching the scenery go by. They were in tune on this anxiety. "Oh, look at that place, Tom! Look at all those lovely trees and vines. I'll bet that house is over a hundred years old."

"How much gold do you think they'd take for it?"

"Oh, I wouldn't want it. It just looked so comfortable."

Rene drove them back to Oroville Saturday to help them negotiate a place to rent, but the cards were against them. Three excellent small apartments being advertised were taken before they got there. After church on Sunday afternoon they found their only available option, besides an expensive motel room, was an apartment that might come up in two weeks. Tom decided "I'm going to rent with Billy and Buck, just to get started, and we'll just have to play it as it goes. I'm not really happy with this job. Maybe I'll get some good advice from these guys. Anyways, if we don't have something by next week, I'm going to commute from Marysville. I can't miss you that long."

"Any day you want to quit, Tom, just quit. We're not desperate. I'll see you next Saturday morning."

Tom paid Billy his share of the rent on the spot, as Darcy said her good byes. Buck wasn't around. Tom got the floor in his sleeping bag in the two bed motel room.

Around nine thirty Buck arrived with his girlfriend Betty, a chubby, friendly natured blond, both a little soused, and they invited Tom and Billy out to shoot some pool and have a few. Tom figured he'd enjoy the opportunity to get out and meet some locals, but Billy cautioned him in a whisper "watch this prick, when he gets drunk! You probably won't go out drinking with him again, if he starts his shit." The four of them walked and chatted the several blocks to the red-neck bar Buck preferred, and Billy commented "what a dive" as they walked in.

"Betty, call that gal, what's her name, that you met last month. That skinny one. I'll bet Tom would like to meet her."

"You mean Ann? Buck, I don't even know…"

"Shut up and do it!"

"Buck, I'm engaged to be married. I'll just have a drink or two, and then go." Had he been unattached, he might not have minded a blind date.

"Naw, now, I don't see no woman."

"Here we go! Buck, if you start something…" Billy warned.

"Aw, hush up, you divorce. You can't even get something going."

"Lay off! I'm going to have a shot at the bar. Keep your mouth shut around me!" Billy had a good temper, it was evident.

"Come on now, Tom. I'll bet you'll like this one. She's so shy; I couldn't get her to drink."

"I'll call her up and see if she wants to come down", Betty said.

"So, Tom, what do you do?"

"I worked mining gold all summer, but it played out. Up by Downieville. Now I think I need a real job."

"Don't we all. God-damn, it's Sunday evening, and I don't want to work tomorrow. I want to party."

"Don't we all."

Betty returned and said "she says she's not doing anything, and I kind of described Tom." She smiled at Tom. "She says she might come by. She's got a car."

"Hell, yeah. She'll come by. She's a cute one, Tom. You'll thank me." Buck was real drunk, but not enough that he couldn't get up and order a pitcher.

"Cuter than me?" Betty asked.

"I'll get the next one, Buck", Tom offered.

"You bet you will. This one's a cute one. If I didn't have a girlfriend..." Buck said from across the room.

"What's your fiancée's name, Tom?" Betty asked politely.

"Darcy."

"How long have you been engaged?"

"Too long." Tom frowned. "I want to get married right away, she's being careful, I guess. We live together."

Betty's eyebrows rose. "Foolish woman. She'd better think again."

"Thank you. She wants me to be sure of everything, and when the time is right. Hell, I don't know. Her parents had a rough marriage, I can tell. Mine were pretty stable. I was lucky. I'll let her decide a date, finally, but I'll never change my mine. I shouldn't be here."

"No, don't worry. I'm just trying to get Ann to meet more people. She's very shy around cowboy bars. Buck had better not get too drunk!" She frowned in contempt.

"I won't get drunk", Tom promised.

They all played pool and drank, and just as Billy demanded they call it a night, Ann walked in. Skinny, but cute enough, with big brown innocent eyes and brown hair. Her figure reminded Tom a little of 'Olive Oil'; she seemed kind of mousey. Billy gave her his chair and returned to the bar. Pock marked faced Buck was a better match for Betty, but he was all over Ann, leaning close to ask "would you like a drink, sweetheart?"

"Just a Coke, thanks."

"Oh, no. You're going to have a martini."

"Hello, Ann", Tom offered.

"Hi, ya." She smiled intensely. Without a Darcy in his life, he would have liked to meet this skinny girl, who obviously liked meeting him. How many attached guys had he heard say "they wouldn't give me the time of day, till I got married. Then they got downright predatory." More than one, with some such remark. This one was looking rather predatorily at him, and she was way prettier than Emily Honsacker.

"I got an idea!" Buck said, returning with her martini.

"I wanted a Coke."

"I think we should take this show on the road, back to the motel room. We can take some beer, maybe some wine, and play some pinochle, or maybe poker, and…"

"I just got here", Ann said with some anger.

"Buck, would you just cool it tonight. We haven't really introduced anyone yet and…"

"Hush up!" Buck cut her off.

"Ann, where do you work?" Tom tried to intervene.

"Oh, I'm living with my Grandparents. I want to become a secretary."

"I'm supposed to go to work at the mill tomorrow, where Billy and Buck work."

"Ann just moved here a month ago from L.A., and she's…" Betty started.

"Good God!" Buck cut in, knifing the conversation to silence. "It's Tom's turn to get a pitcher. You did say you'd get a pitcher." Too much harshness in the voice now, some hostility. "Damn, this conversation is getting BORE-ING!" as Tom walked to the bar. "We should leave right now."

"Buck!" Betty pleaded.

"This one's on me", Billy offered, trying to grin. "I told you he was a prick."

Tom shrugged his shoulders. "It's no big deal. You could help us break it up, to get us started home."

"I'll try. I've seen him in action too many times. Betty doesn't deserve his shit."

'Billy seems a decent enough guy', Tom thought. 'I think I'll like working with this guy.'

"Tom!" Buck yelled. There were five elderly people sitting across the room at a table, one a genuine 60 year old cowboy, probably from a local ranch, and several people at the bar, and low key comments from more than one would not deter him. "Tom, you said you'd…"

"It's coming!" Tom yelled back. 'Geese, I've only known this idiot for an hour, and already I hate him', Tom thought.

The bartender brought the pitcher over, and warned "keep it down!"

"Sure, buddy, sure. We'll keep it down, 'cause we're all going to the room…" Buck's eyes narrowed, his face wrinkled in a disgusting, wretched grin. Ann looked desperate, staring at Tom, and crossing her hands in a gesture that implied Tom should call him off.

"Buck, I don't think these ladies really want…"

"I don't think", Buck cut in. "I don't know about you!" He was really soused, no sense of decent behavior, no care of what impression he was making on the crowd. The typical arrogant drunk. "We all want to go back to the room and play some, play some poker…, he, hehh, yeah, we all want to go back…" Ann was outraged, but the angry expressions were directed towards Tom. She was too much of a mouse to face Buck.

"Buck, just HUSH UP yourself!" Betty said severely. Slam. Buck's palm came down hard on the table.

"Hey! I said keep it down!" the bartender yelled.

"We all want…, to go back, but Tom, he doesn't want to meet Ann. How strange!" 'It's obvious', Tom thought. 'Buck thinks he can use me to get him some of Ann. Partner switching, no doubt. Only a drunk can get this ridiculous.' "There's something wrong here!" Buck said, too loudly. "Move, Betty!" And he started pushing the round table against Betty's chest, right past Ann. Betty was now in tears, and Ann got up and bolted to the ladies room. "Get up!" Betty got up and just stood, such a hurt look, as he pushed the table farther, making the glasses rattle, and turned his chair around, straddling it with arms folded over the back, just two feet from Tom.

"Jesus Christ!" Billy yelled from the bar. "Buck, I'll kick you out on your face!" he warned.

"There's something wrong here." Buck could have been a drill sergeant now. "I just don't understand. A good looking young man like Tom. I WANT TO KNOW!" Everyone in the bar stopped talking, and Buck's eyes disappeared in an ugly squint. "I want to know how many women he's had! There's something WRONG!"

Tom leaned forward, hands on knees, and stared hard. "More than you'll know in a lifetime, PRICK!" Then he straightened up and folded his arms, tense, awaiting the attack. Instead of an attack, the drunk leaned back and started bobbing his head in a sort of drunken yes gesture. Apparently, Tom's turn to an aggressive posture had impressed the drunk enough to accept the answer. He was so drunk, Tom doubted he could have done much to him, but when he sobered up later, that was a different matter. Buck looked tough.

Now Betty was cracking up in a contemptuous laugh as Ann emerged from the restroom, and Tom caught up with her to offer "I'm sorry."

"Maybe some other time." The smile was so sweet as she opened her purse and pulled out a folded paper to hand him. "My Grandparents address and phone. Call me when he's not around, Tom. Tell me how you're job is going. I want to see you again."

'I should have told her about Darcy. I didn't get the chance', Tom thought as she walked out. 'I wouldn't have met her if I were looking, I'll bet. What do I do with the number?' Tom crumpled it up and threw it in a cigarette urn. "Billy, let's go. Betty, are you going to be…"

"I'll be just fine. He can get home alone tonight." And they left Buck sitting in a chair, staring at the wall.

Buck never got back to the motel room that night, and Tom caught a ride with Billy to work the next morning. By afternoon he was thoroughly despising the yard. Basically, his work consisted of running around, looking for any work to do, trying to look like he was of some value. Pick up scrap; assist some guy, run over here, then over there. The poor piss-ant who has to hustle just to get promoted to the point where he has a real job. About three thirty he ducked into a storage shed by the south fence and sat down for a break of his own making. Hearing some footsteps approaching, he jumped up and started arranging some tools on a shelf. "That's good. Always keep busy. Even when there isn't shit to do, there's always something to do. You're at the right spot, 'cause I've got a little job for you", Billy advised.

"Did Buck show up?"

"Yeah, late." Billy sounded more like a friend than a foreman. "He's inside. Jimmy put him to work on something he really hates. He'll be on time tomorrow." Billy grinned. "Uh, sit down, take a break." As he folded his arms and pulled his bottom lip behind his teeth. "I'm going to let you in on a little inside information, something you'll really appreciate on down the line. The man who owns this mill, John, aah, he's a total idiot, and he's running this mill into the ground?"

"Really?"

"If it keeps going the way it is, the company will go down the drain, and we'll all be out of work. The man has very little experience, he inherited this place, and he's screwing it up big time. He doesn't know how to maintain a profit margin. My two brothers, and several of the yard men, well, we're going to try and save this place. We've got an investor who's going to buy John out, but the mill has to go under before we can get him to see the need to sell. That's unfortunate, but necessary. I know you'll be looking to keep a job here for some time, and we'd sure like to have you on the new crew." This didn't sound right. Tom was antsy now, recalling Darcy's first impression of the man. "Now Buck, he's a prick after work, but here, he's kind of my right hand man. He knows to take the winning side. We kind of make a little money on the side, if you catch my drift. A man never gets anywhere in a stupid little low pay job. That never gets anyone anywhere." Tom knew where this was heading. "At four o'clock, Buck gets his break, and he'll be waiting for you out behind the stacked lumber by the east fence. There's a hole in the fence, and you're going to deliver one of our little bonuses from this operation. If you work with us, I'll assure you a job when the mill is transferred. I'm going to be the manager."

"What are you saying?" Tom felt like walking away, looking to ask Jimmy, but a lot of fear was welling up.

Billy turned a sudden hard glare on him. "You see that old, rusty chain on that shelf?" Tom looked, nodded. "No one ever uses it much. It won't be noticed. Just walk right out through the yard with it, like you're taking it somewhere. That's the best way. And if someone asks, don't mention me. You'll think of something."

"I don't think so."

"Pick up the chain, boy, if you want to stay around here!" It was practically an order, from an assistant yard boss, right? Tom walked over and draped the chain over his shoulder. 'No!' he thought. 'I don't need this job.' "Now just start walking. If he's a little late, you wait for him."

Buck was waiting outside the cut in the chain link fence behind the lumber stack, right on time. “Good man. You’re in, Tom. There are going to be a bunch of shitheads with walking papers when we take over this place, yea, and Jimmy’s going to be the first. Fucking prick! I’m sick of him.” And he walked over to a small live oak and threw the chain down and sprinted away.

‘First day on the job! Why did I let myself get conned? I’m going to quit Friday’, Tom thought.

That evening Billy laid it on the line. “You’re going to get us one bonus a day, Tom. I’ll give you the time as soon as I see where Jimmy puts Buck.”

“Yeah, he’s our biggest problem right now. He watches us like a hawk”, Buck added. “You should see some of the stuff we’ve been able to get past his nose.” Like a boast. Tom felt sick. ‘How do I get out of this? Think, Tom!’

“I was thinking about showing Tom the ranch this weekend. He should come out and pick out something, as his first bonus. We’ve got all kinds of shit. Chainsaws, televisions”, Billy tempted.

“Yeah, Billy got me a motorcycle from Redding, a Norton. It’s a beauty. Of course, I haven’t figured a way to get it licensed, but hell, I love riding it out there. We’re going to paint it, just in case.”

“Can I count on your coming out, Tom?” He sounded like a preacher asking Tom to attend a church gathering.

“I suppose.” He would quit on Friday. Tuesday and Wednesday Tom lifted tools for them. Thursday morning Tom found himself talking to one of the younger yard workers, a half Spaniard named Dick Salcedo.

“How long have you worked here?”

"Almost a year and a half. It's decent enough, not a bad job, just as long as Billy and Buck leave me alone." Tom looked inquisitively. "You seem to be making friends with those two, but I don't trust them. Neither does Jimmy, but John lets Billy give out orders. I think he's going to make Billy a foreman one of these days. If he does, I'll quit."

"I don't like them either, but like you say, Billy gives out orders."

"Billy gives out strange orders, sometimes. He's got something going on, I know it. There was a kid here named Ronny, and Billy got Ron arrested, thrown in jail for two years, last fall. Ronny has no mother, and his Dad wouldn't help him. He's worthless, his Dad. Billy knew this. John didn't really want to prosecute him, man. Billy is supposed to have caught Ronny in the parking lot after work with some tools from the yard, and John just wanted to fire him, but Billy railroaded the whole thing, and went to court with it. Ronny was scared to death of Billy, but I'm not." Tom felt a chill of dread running down his spine. "I wouldn't trust Billy in this yard, not if I owned the place. Something's not right, and you know, Jimmy thinks the same thing. He's told me so."

Tom walked away just as a cold drizzle started, and headed to get a rain slicker. In the gray morning rain the young man felt desperately despondent, arguing back and forth with himself, thinking he should just call Darcy to come and get him. 'She'll be here Saturday morning. We'll just leave like we're going for the weekend.'

That night, with Buck gone to his favorite bar, Billy gave Tom a severe lecture. "I'm counting on you coming out this weekend to the ranch to meet my two brothers Jim and

Ralf, and Ralf's wife, Maggie. We're going to let you pick out a few tools, or maybe a TV. Bring your girlfriend. You can always tell her you're buying the stuff from us. They never figure this stuff out."

"Sounds good. As long as Darcy doesn't have priorities."

"You both come out. We're counting on it. We all are. Jim and Ralf want to meet you, seriously. Let me tell you a little story, about a certain type of guy, the kind who doesn't appreciate the favors some people do for him. My brother Jim was in county lock up about four years ago when he heard a story about a young man, about your age, who got knifed in the Pen. This kid, about 19, was in for five years, and the warden cut him a deal on some time to testify against a three timer who was running some black market in prison. The kid did it, thought he was being smart, but he ended up with a glass shiv in his stomach, and he bled to death. Now that sounds terrible, but I'm going to tell you, no one likes a rat. Even the judges and cops hate a rat. There ain't no lower form of life!" The voice was a practiced maliciousness.

'You're the rat', Tom thought. 'You set Ronny up. I see your plan. Steal as much as possible, get me arrested, and lay low for a while. People like you deserve to get shot. I wish I had what it takes.' "I'm not a rat, Billy. I'd like to keep this job." 'Yeah, lie, Tom. And then talk with Ray, maybe Lou, and Bill Rutledge for sure.' Tom dreaded the coming weekend. He'd be running like a fugitive from Oroville, from the town Dave and Linda called home.

"Good man. Stick with me and Buck. You'll be going places."

Friday morning, around ten, Tom faked a vomiting fit, and Billy escorted him to the locker room, after getting Jimmy's OK. Ten minutes after he lay down on a bench, Tom slipped into John's office. "Are you alright? Jimmy said…"

Tom raised his hand. "I'm better. I have to quit, John. I'm sorry, but I have a personal problem, a terrible problem, back home, and today's my last day. You can mail my check. I can't talk about it, and I can't give notice. Please don't tell anyone in the yard. Please do me that favor."

"You can't talk about it?" John frowned severely. "This wouldn't have something to do with my yard man, Billy?" Tom shook his head no, but his eyes spoke of fear and anger. "I think I'm beginning to see the handwriting on the wall. Son, if you feel the need to get away from Billy, just tell me that. You won't be the first one. I think I'm beginning to realize what a real problem I have in my yard."

"I just have to take care of some personal business, back in Downieville."

John leaned against folded hands and stared probingly, almost angrily. "That's alright, Tom. That's just fine. Let me tell you something, and it's not to get out of this office. Something was stolen out of this office, some money, this week." Tom turned pale. "Something only four men besides myself knew about. Three of those men I trust. I don't need to tell you who the fourth man was. I'm going to give you some advice. Go back to Downieville, and don't visit here for awhile. And if you should run into trouble, call me or Jimmy. Get Jimmy's home phone number. Jimmy's on to him."

'He knows!' Tom thought. 'He's letting me off. Your luck must be changing.' "Thank you, John. Dave said you were a good man to work for."

"Not for Billy and Buck, I'm not." John's grin was downright mean, now. "I don't have anything to prosecute them with, but I didn't get to be a mill owner being a nice guy. I know how to fight fire with fire. Billy's going to be making a trip next Monday, down to Sacramento, for some supplies that aren't really there. My supplier is going to give him the run around of his life." John looked ecstatic. "And Buck will wish he'd gone with him. Jimmy will see to that. Yeah, Billy will get down there in that old flatbed he fixed for me, and he'll be sleeping in it for a few days, or he'll be buying a motel room. He doesn't dare sabotage my truck, 'cause I've got friends down there he's going to meet. They both won't last a week, but they're going to be mad as hornets, Tom."

"Thank you. I'm leaving tomorrow when Darcy get's here."

"See me in a year, Tom. I'll hire you back. I'm going to be doing some talking with the District Attorney next week about getting a young man's sentence reduced. I never felt right about that business."

Tom walked back to the yard feeling so much better. "You alright?" Billy asked.

"I feel great. I feel fantastic."

"Good. You're going to get us a pipe wrench today, and maybe something else. I've got to do some thinking."

Saturday morning Darcy showed up at the motel early. Tom's sleeping bag was old, his clothes and suitcase expendable. He had slipped everything valuable into his pockets, and left the rest sitting like he intended to stay. "Hello, young lady", Billy greeted her at the door. "How would you like to take a trip with us? We're taking Tom out to our ranch over by Chico."

"Oh, OK, uh, right now?" she said. Tom was shaking his head NO behind Billy's back. Buck was still asleep.

"Billy wants us to visit his kinfolk's ranch", still shaking NO, looking almost aghast.

"Sure." Darcy was quick to catch on. "But next week. Agnes has a big dinner planned tonight." Now Tom was nodding YES, looking relieved. "We're celebrating Tom's new job." She tried to smile, even as her heart raced.

"Tom has already promised. You'll be back before dark."

"No, I'm afraid Agnes got me to promise her we'd both help her. You see, there are other guests coming over. We'd love to, next week."

Billy looked peeved, but not worried. "Alright. It changes my schedule, but a week won't matter. This young man has a great future here. I'm going to see to that." Tom wondered if the man didn't believe his own bullshit sometimes. Maybe it was some form of mental illness, but all that should concern Tom now was getting away from him.

"What the hell is going on?" Darcy demanded a block away. "That man scares me."

"I got myself into some trouble. He did, actually. But it's alright. I had a little talk with the owner."

"You left your clothes?" Darcy accused after his explanation. "Oh, shit, that's OK, Tom. I don't know what you should have done. You don't need that job. Oh, no, we don't need to tell Agnes. That's when the real trouble comes in. You know what she's capable of. We should lie to her."

The lie didn't work. "What's going on? I know something's going on. I'm going to call the owner. You're too young to make a decision like this. I know something happened. You're not lazy; at least I think you're not."

"Mother, a man in the yard ordered Tom to steal."

"You didn't do it, did you?"

"He was a kind of yard boss, Agnes. The owner knows, even though I didn't tell him. It's OK. He told me he'd hire me back."

"Yeah, well now you're a rat, no matter what. Just by walking away. That's how it works. I'm going to have to call a couple of men from North San Juan. No one does this to me. I'm going to make the son-of-a-bitch regret…"

"Agnes, John's going to take care of it. I was very lucky."

"He's not going to protect you, watch you every minute. You go back down to work Monday morning, and when my men show up, you finger the bastard. They'll put him in the hospital after work. No one does this to me!"

"Mom, please!" Darcy sounded so afraid, almost like a child. "Mother, this is not the way."

"Agnes, I appreciate your concern, but let's not initiate a war, not just yet. He has kinfolk down there", Tom said, trying to hide his dread.

"Yes, that's possible. That's always possible." The anger was giving in to reason.

"I didn't need that job that bad. Now if they try to make something out of it, then by all means, call your friends."

"I think you're right. You just sit tight, and if they show up around here, they'll regret it. You're too fine a young man to be chucking lumber, anyway."

"Thank you, Agnes." He was thoroughly surprised at the compliment.

"I think you should get into real estate. That would be a smart career move."

"I know you have good intentions, Agnes, but I'm dedicated to the mechanics life. I'm going to drum up some business around here."

"Business you might get. Haven't you learned yet; you've been here a year. Getting paid, that takes time for more than a few around here. A lot of 'em like to barter, Tom, 'cause they're always broke. Alright, we'll see." Tom considered that she may have taken a valium, something he knew she got illegally from a friend, to be giving in without a verbal fight. He'd have to thank the party involved, should he ever meet them.

EIGHTEEN

Tom's second Downieville Halloween dance with Darcy was enjoyable enough, save for the reminders from Lou and Ray that he was now a man under guard. Ray attended the dance, apparently just for Tom's sake. Quite a few of the locals now had a description of Billy and Buck. It was a strange situation for Tom. He appreciated their concern, dreaded ever meeting Billy or Buck again, wished he could get the whole thing past him.

This time he and Darcy were both careful of the punch, reminding each other to stay away. He had to dance a little too much with Ardell again, at least that was Erick's opinion. Second dance with her she offered "do you want to work in the river again, Tom?"

"Definitely. I might go back with Bill, but he's not sure where he'll be working."

"Erick got promised a diving job with Dan MacKenzie. He's the one that took eighty thousand off his claim in two seasons, and Erick is really excited. I'll give you his number. I can't promise you anything, but Erick will put in a word for you. I'll see to that."

Dan MacKenzie sounded surprised when Tom introduced himself by name over the phone. "Never heard of you. Do I know you?"

"No, I'm from Marysville. I'm Darcy McEarl's fiancé. Ardell gave me your number."

"Oh, Darcy's boyfriend. I know who you are!" Tom hated when people did that. "Yeah, Tom, I've got a full crew right now. That depends on what we get into. If we hit something I could hire more…Let's see, I'll write you down. I've got two on hold, you'll go before them. Bob was a good friend, Tom. You'll get first chance, if something changes."

"Thank you. I'll call again in the spring." And then Tom forgot about it. He was halfway thinking of calling Allen Conrad back up, hoping he was having trouble with his mechanic. No, he'd have to be desperate. They could be careful with the money, and make it to the summer. And they could be happy, happy at least until three weeks after Halloween, when the Halloween Kitty turned up run over on the other side of town. Funny thing about a small town, everyone knows even everyone else's pets. There was a little burial ceremony with kids Darcy knew, and Darcy couldn't handle it. For two days she couldn't handle it. Funerals were rough on them both, and three days after, Tom got her out to do two hours of stable work at the Monroe property on Goodyear Creek. In return for a stable clean up, Darcy got riding privileges on the Monroe's slightly swayback gelding, Slim, practically her horse for the past five years. Slim would always run the fence line when Darcy showed up, and she'd have to calm him down before the chores. This day Tom helped with the chores, and then sat by the barn for two hours while she rode the mountain trails.

With firewood aplenty and roof in good condition, Darcy and Tom looked forward to a more secure winter than the previous one, and there was a little money coming in from the occasional vehicle repair in Matt's parent's garage that Matt would split 60-40 with Tom. Sometimes it only paid for the gas down valley, but they needed to get away from Agnes, on occasion. Agnes seemed to be getting more moody by the day, sometimes demanding Tom agree to start real estate school. The few repair jobs he was getting didn't impress her, and she could spoil their day with a liquor inspired tirade concerning her daughter's future. Darcy would assure her that if the next summer was not more productive, they would move down valley, to which Agnes often replied "oh, you don't need to do that! Not both of you!"

Many a time Tom considered bringing up the subject of marriage with Darcy, but he just couldn't think of the words to start with. Preacher Melvin dropped hints to Darcy every chance he got, but she always seemed to have some polite evasion. The weather in March allowed a picnic potluck for the Downieville Baptist congregation down by the Downie, at which Darcy wore her engagement ring, a great relief to Tom.

These days he was having his own thoughts of concern over his self admitted gambling mentality. That was the best description for his gold fever. He really had no definite plans for a future to offer her, other than moving back to Marysville and looking for work. But for now he just couldn't see himself walking away from a chance for some more gold. And what if the summer turned out to be a bust? 'She might leave you, Tom' he would think. 'No, she can't live without me. She'll move with me to Marysville. I know her so well now.'

And then in April came the pistol whipping incident, the revelations and descriptions of such would provide so much gossip around the hills, but it could not diminish Tom's enthusiasm. He didn't know whether he would be working with Ray, Bill, or someone else; it didn't matter. Spring was here, and he was ready. He could see the gold in his mind.

Two nights after Agnes's little assault on Tom, Darcy felt the need to expose a few closet skeletons. "Did I ever tell you about my father's father? He was still alive when Bob died, but he didn't last much longer. My grandmothers both died early, and Agnes's father remarried once. Bob senior was such a riot, Tom. I used to look forward to him visiting. He told great jokes; all my girlfriends loved him. He had more jokes, he'd never run out."

"Was he very Indian looking?"

"No more than my father. Maidu, but mostly Scotch, a direct descendant of a 49'er, Tom."

"Is that like being a registered member of the Daughters of the Pilgrims, or something, when you're a direct descendant?"

"Around here, yeah. I miss him. He could handle Agnes; he never let her talk him down. But Agnes's father, Burt Dunlevy, I have to tell you about him, Tom."

"Why? He's gone. Let the dead bury the dead."

"Just this once. Burt was Scotch and English, and he was a mean man, Tom. No other way to put it. Maybe there was some reason, maybe there's always some reason. Life is sometimes too hard, and I think it's true, only the tough survive."

"Tough, not mean."

"It's hard to tell the difference, sometimes. I never liked Burt. He used to demand I sit on his lap, and I couldn't stand it. I wouldn't want any of my girlfriends to…, I wouldn't trust him. He would talk about how so many women wanted him, all his life, right in front of Agnes, and she thought that was just fine, like being a braggart was a virtue. But that's not important…,"

"No, it's not. Darcy, does it matter?"

"Tom, when I was seven I heard a conversation between Mom, Burt, his sister Evelyn, and two friends from their inner circle, if you know what I mean. They didn't know I was listening. Oh, shit, I hate this…" She pulled a drip from her nose, like a little hay fever, and managed not to let it get worse. "Burt had a partner back in the hills, somewhere, and they had a secret project going on, concerning gold. I thought this would be a good story, something I could tell my friends…, well, when he told it, it made me sick, literally, Tom. I had to go to the bathroom. He shot his partner in the head."

"Jesus Christ!"

"He said the man was a cheat. He made him dig his own grave, and then he shot him. They were laughing at this, like it served the man right. I can still hear their laughter." Tom could see the whole thing, visualize being helpless at Burt's mercy. "Tom, Burt would have cheated anyone, anytime. Now Bob senior, he would have told a cheat to take a hike. That's all he would have done. He was the type that would never back off, but he was a fair man, like my father. Burt was a cold blooded killer, and a coward, as far as I'm concerned."

"And Agnes was laughing, too?"

"No, not actually. That's a good point. Agnes didn't laugh, but she did say 'a man's got to do what a man's got to do'. I don't think she liked the story, either, to tell you the truth. I'll give her that."

"Darcy…"

"Is this an Injun story?" She was sort of laughing, but it was an unpleasant laugh.

"Jeffrey Hendrick shot an Indian dead at a railway station. They don't even know what tribe. Just a drunken Indian, asleep, against the station house. This was in 1889, I think, way after the Indian wars…, he saw an Indian asleep, and he pulled out a Derringer, and shot him thought a railcar window, like shooting a crow. And, so…"

"You're right; let the dead bury the dead."

"Passengers drew pistols on him; they thought he might be a robber, or who knows what. The conductor told him to get off the train, and he threatened to shoot the conductor, and then a deputy sheriff. He had them all intimidated, he was so insane, and they let him walk away. I guess he found some other ride. You can never get even, not in this world."

"How did we get on this morbid subject?"

"I think it was a little inspired by a little gun play in the foyer, excuse me, the kitchen. A certain gun moll decided to embellish on her pistol expertise."

"Go to sleep, Tom!" And she kissed him on his cheek wound.

Four days later Dan MacKenzie called and hired Tom to dive on his operation down the North Yuba. And so this, it seemed, was the man's last chance for some seed money.

He knew that if his third summer in Downieville didn't produce, he would lose interest and enthusiasm. Perhaps both he and Darcy would both start college, with help from Rene and Bill Rutledge. More likely he would try and find some work in Marysville, and move in with Rene. He had a lot still going for him, he had to admit, but he knew that a summer without success would be a terrible letdown.

Darcy was not happy to hear about the job offer. "You were supposed to go to work with Bill. Bill thinks you're still with him. Why don't you call Dan and tell him you're not sure yet."

"I am sure. Bill says he doesn't know where he's going to put his trommel, and that sounds to me like he's not sure where to find some gold."

"He's got five claims. He'll find something."

"Why don't you admit that the water scares you? I'll be alright. I can take care of myself."

"Alright, I hate the river, OK? You don't need to risk drowning, not when you can work on land."

"Just this last time, princess. The handsome young prince has to show the beautiful princess that he is worthy..."

"Oh, shut up! The beautiful princess may run off with a priest, if her lover gets drowned. Yes, I hate seeing you underwater. It's not necessary. You don't think anything of it because you love water so much. Otter!"

"Water, cars, engines, gold. I only love Darcy."

"Oh God, I'm going to dread every day. I guess it could be worse."

"Yes, it could be. I could be in the military, with a war going on. Gimme a kiss!" She squirmed a little, and then hugged and kissed him.

NINETEEN

The day before start up, they made a shopping trip to Grass Valley for groceries for the picnic Dan planned on his claim opening day. Tom was talking so enthusiastically on the trip back that he forgot and ran full speed into Dead Man's Curve. Darcy had warned him, as usual. It was always good for a little thrill, provided it didn't kill you. It had killed some people.

He was going to be sleeping weeknights on the claim; it was too far downriver to commute every day, so he would only have weekends to spend with Darcy. He had to joke more than once that they needed to steal Agnes's pistol, lest she forget in five days of absence who he was.

The route to Dan's claim, south of the river, followed a rough dirt road past the last Highway 49 bridge, till a point high above brought a single lane, winding road down the canyon into view, one with several severe drop offs too close for comfort. Dan's Dodge two ton flatbed truck and three cars brought the group down for their first tour of the claim. There was a fairly large, flat camping area next to a wide river pool below some wide, tiered rapids, a place favored by fishermen seeking routes downstream in a no road zone of the river. And there was evidence of previous mining activity, a concrete platform that had held some equipment a good forty feet from the pool, several piles of cobbles and rock near this platform, and one large pile of boulders farther downriver. The cobbles and rock were recent, but the boulders were obviously ancient, overgrown, like so many of the rock piles along the river. There were five wooden picnic tables around a large fire pit, and an old outhouse up the hill. Most striking in the canyon was the evidence of hydraulic mining on the hill upstream, across the river above the rapids. A very bare hillside with some clinging, scrubby live oaks and much exposed bedrock and manmade rock piles made a stark bare spot in the forest, along with the vertical shale rock cliffs rising up just across the pool. There was one huge Douglas fir in camp, a good seventy feet high, and looking back up the mountain road from camp one huge sugar pine stood out on the ridge, a reference point from many angles, with one unnaturally long branch growing out near the flat crown, pointing almost due east. Such is the characteristic of old sugar pines; long branches that remind one of long arms. Perhaps this one pointed the way home. The place was definitely deep in the back country, with a forty five minute drive just to get to Highway 49 on the rough dirt road.

"I don't like that road", Darcy said from the backseat of Erick's Chevy sedan as they pulled into the parking area.

"Neither do I!" Ardell added. "It's just too dangerous."

"Well, once a week." Tom said.

"I won't mind the road with my pockets lined with gold", Erick rationalized. "I've heard some good things about this stretch of the river."

"I heard they got all the gold", Ardell argued. "I want him back to work with the Forest Service."

"Tell me about it", Darcy demanded.

"He's going to jump school; he's already a firefighter. Jump school in August, no matter what!"

"You hear that, Tom!" Darcy grinned.

"I don't like heights", he pleaded. "Talk about dangerous!"

"But he likes water. I tried to get him on at the Sixteen-to-One this winter, but you know, I'm just as glad there wasn't an opening. I have enough trouble with water; underground, even worse. I'd sit up nights worrying. Hey, look at this. It's the 'Pony Boy'." Darcy opened the car door slightly as Erick rolled to a stop. "Hey, PONY BOY!" she yelled as Erick pulled in reverse to a parking space. Dave Johnston was just getting out of Carl Gleason's car and had to acknowledge her greeting with "the one and only. How are you doing, you little horsewoman?" He sported a sheepish grin.

"What does 'pony boy' mean?" Tom asked.

"He'll tell you." Jim Sanborn, Carl, and his wife Jan all got out and began unpacking a trunk load of food, and Dan jumped from the cab of his flatbed to grab an ice chest and head for the tables. "What happens if you meet someone coming down that one lane road?" Darcy asked as they walked to the tables. "There aren't that many pullouts."

"I'll take Dan's flatbed and push them over the side, if they weren't invited", Erick teased.

"Erick, behave!" Ardell warned.

"Only if it's Vernon Fickett", Tom had to say.

"What-a-you got against Vernon?" Jim had overheard.

"He's a fuckup, Jim", Erick said. "I wouldn't work with him."

"Watch your mouth, honey!" Ardell said, and Jim turned with a dirty little look and walked away.

"Uh oh", Tom whispered to Darcy, and she replied by shaking her head no.

"Alright!" Dan announced after the picnic had been unpacked and delivered to the tables. "Alright, let me have my little talk, and then we can eat and enjoy. I want you to get familiar with that road coming out today. Let's not get anyone lost. I think I'm going to try to mark the intersections. The ladies are welcome to come down here any day to visit or bring a meal, provided they don't get near the equipment. Now, in two days, we're going to set up five canvas tents, some cots, and two good stoves. It won't be just like home, but it will be comfortable. It's going to take several trips down to bring in my twelve inch dredge and the two winches. Let me tell you boys the deal. It's real simple. I'll guarantee you a hundred dollars a week and meals, or ten percent of the gold, whichever is more, and for a while I know it will pay all of you better than a hundred dollars a week. Let me tell you what I'm after." Dan turned and pointed to the bare hydraulicking site across the river. "Those old miners up that mountain put many thousands of dollars back in the river over the years as they washed down the mountainside. They ground sluiced and monitored that hillside up until about 1881, and they washed a lot of gold through their sluices and into the river. I was able to make a tidy little profit on their losses by running a two yard bucket through those rapids. We pretty well cleaned up those rapids and the upper pool with the bucket and a six inch dredge, and the gold played out as we headed down pool. That was in '54."

"We heard you retired on it", Erick cut in.

"Yeah", Jim said. "You must have some reason for coming back."

Dan pointed straight at Jim. "Good reason. We found a huge trench in the bedrock, right about there. The trench is an intrusion of crumbly dolomite that wears faster than the shale, and it's a huge catch in this pool." Dan pointed to a spot about seventy feet down from the rapids. The pool was one of the largest Tom had seen on the North Yuba, a hundred and ninety feet long and a hundred and twenty feet wide at mid pool. "That trench has obviously been worked before, at least where we opened it up. It was too far down to catch the flood gold we were getting, but…" Dan said with an ecstatic smile, "They didn't finish the bottom of the trench or go into the bank. We found gold in every crack in the trench. Now we're going to follow the trench into the bank until we can't go any further, and I guarantee we'll make some money there. When that's done…" Dan turned again and gazed out over the pool. "I've been thinking about that trench for five years. If they missed something out there…, we're talking about big gold, if they missed something."

"Hell, yeah!" Erick whistled, and Ardell put her hand over his mouth.

"Damn right!" Jim said. "I need to buy one new vehicle in my life, Dan. Just one. I want a new truck. I want to know what it feels like."

"You got that right", Tom added.

"Alright, boys!" Darcy said. "I can see we won't get them out of the river anytime soon", as Carl and his wife chuckled.

"This is a gamble, but it's my gamble", Dan continued. "I'm willing to put some of my earnings back in this river to find out, but listen, if the hole is a bust, you men are not going to lose. You will always make a hundred a week, and if you stick it out till I say we quit, you'll each get a three hundred dollar bonus. Carl is going to be your foreman. He gets ten percent just like the rest, but he's forty six, so I don't want him to do much of the diving. That's for you younger men. You'll work in shifts, and you'll get to know the dredge and winches by heart. Now listen to me: when I'm not down here, and I won't be most of the time, Carl will have the absolute last word. Let's understand, if you want that bonus at the end of season, you'd better be prepared to take orders. I've worked with Carl before, and I think he's the best foreman you could ask for. Now I'll let Carl talk."

Carl was a little chubby, his wife Jan still good figured, and he was balding and his black hair was whitening. He had the look of an easy going fella until he stood up, and then the eyes intensified as he leaned on knuckles and addressed them. He had been a foreman before. "Boys, we're going to work as a team down here. That's basically all I require. I hate two things above all else: Running someone off and getting someone hurt. I'd rather run someone off than get someone hurt. I want you all to concentrate on the job and keep your petty differences to yourself. Let's work together. I was a sergeant in the Korean War, and I know how to put a stop to infighting real quick, I guarantee you."

"Aw, we'll get along", Jim said.

"Good!" Carl replied. "Just remember that a month or two from now."

"Good", Dan cut in. "I'll be back down to help set up, but after that I've got other priorities. Carl is your boss."

"And first order is, let's eat. Today is for fun. Work starts Thursday. Everyone come back down with a good wetsuit."

"I'll advance anyone enough to get a wetsuit, if they need it", Dan advised.

"That's me", Jim said.

"This sounds almost too good to be true!" Darcy whispered to Tom. "But I hate having you gone for five days."

"I hate it too, Foxtail. It's not like I'm overseas or something. I have a good feeling about this pool." Tom whispered back.

"I heard that!" Erick said. "I think we're going to find some gold."

Darcy frowned severely, and after Erick had gone to help himself to the food, Darcy whispered "I hate this place!"

"Why?" Tom asked.

"I really don't know. It's so far away, I guess. It just doesn't feel right."

"You'll get used to it."

"What will you do without sex for five days, honey?" she grinned.

"Make up for it Friday nights, Foxtail", he grinned back.

"I just hope I don't run into any cute boys during the week", she taunted so casually, such a put on.

"Yeah, well ask them how much gold they've found. I'm the one that's going to move you to a nice house in Marysville. Don't forget that."

"Tommy, you know I'll live with you in a tent. Don't forget that." And she kissed him hard. "David." Darcy got up and walked to the table Dave was sitting at. "How's Christine doing? I haven't seen her around."

"I haven't seen her in awhile, either. She's in town." He looked a little embarrassed.

"I heard you two haven't been seeing each other."

"I'm hoping this gold will get us back together."

"You shouldn't use gold as an excuse, Dave. I'll bet she misses you. Ask her to come down and visit you. You know you two should get back together." Dave nodded a yes.

It took almost a week to get the dredge and winches ready. The twelve inch dredge was practically a barge, sitting on four twelve foot marine pontoons that had originally been part of a floating ocean dock. There were three hand cable winches with enough one quarter steel cable each tied across the pool in three directions that kept the dredge from moving with a current. All the workers had to do was let cable out in one direction and take in another and the barge could be maneuvered to any spot in the pool. The sluice was twelve feet long, with enough riffles to catch even the fine gold. A Chevy V8 ran the huge Berkley water pump; almost too much power, the men would find out. Two HUKA diving compressors, one just for a safety back up, ran off two five HP Briggs engines. The suction hose was thirty feet of stiff black reinforced rubber twelve inch cement hose that was hard to maneuver, and had to be supported at midsection by a 55 gallon steel drum float attached with rope to the hose. When the hose was full of gravel, the extra weight would pull the drum under water, and the hose would pull the nozzle back, along with the diver, as it sank in midsection. This was a machine that looked like it could swallow up Ray's little six inch dredge and spit it out. In reality it could literally grab a diver, and the men had been repeatedly warned to stay clear of the nozzle intake, lest it pull an arm, foot, or worse a head in. Any man who let his fingers get between a rock and the intake risked getting them broken. For safety there was a rev-down lever on the nozzle attached by cable to the engine. The jet had been designed so that a valve could be turned and the pressure directed in the opposite direction to blow out rock clog ups. Hopefully no divers' appendage would have to be blown out.

Tom was in awe at his first dive. The dredge could open up a hole so fast it was intimidating, and he was sometimes diving deeper than he had before. The nozzle operator had to straddle the steel nozzle, holding the two handles and almost riding it like a horse, all the while the gravel, unless tightly packed, would continuously fall in towards the inlet. It was a situation that demanded the operator stay alert at all times, and it played on all the men's nerves.

Rock problems were dealt with by either a sixteen HP driven winch for pulling boulders, or a twenty-two HP double drum winch connected to a steel basket for loading rocks. Only something weighing tons could slow the operation down, and in such case the men would try and work around it.

The men all took turns as camp chef and dishwasher, and after each dinner came a campfire session, for talk about the operation, or anything on anybody's mind. Friday evenings the men headed home, and after the second week, each man headed home every other Friday with his ten percent share of the cash from the gold Dan would sell the week before, and personally deliver Thursday or Friday. Tom wasn't quite making what he had in the better days with Bill Rutledge. The clay in the part of the trench heading into the bank paid steady with powder gold and a few nuggets, but it wasn't impressive. There were several weeks of work left in it before it became impractical to work, and the men would have to head out into the deep.

TWENTY

Everything seemed to be working smoothly, but not everybody. It was apparent to Tom that Jim was the arrogant man in the group. He had more caustic, critical remarks than all the other men put together, and they were usually directed at Dave. Erick was 29, Dave 34, and Jim 27, so Tom was the kid in the group, but Dave more often acted like it. He seemed to be one of those men locked in the mode in which he acted and talked more like a teenager than his age would warrant, and he was the one who most often asked for explanations, and seemed unsure about making decisions. At times he seemed downright intimidated, but he always managed to get done what he was asked to do. Jim took an attitude that Dave was incompetent, and this led to more than one argument, but Carl would usually put an end to it with a warning to them both. One afternoon after work Dave caught up with Tom at camp and asked "did you hear him?"

"Hear who, Jim?"

"Yeah, down at the boat." The crew used a wooden row boat to ferry back and forth to the dredge.

"No, what's wrong?"

"Hell, you didn't hear it." Dave turned to walk away.

"Wait a minute. What did he say?"

"He said..., he said his cousin Louis is coming up to work on this claim, and I asked him when, and who gave him the job. You know, since no one said anything. He said, 'as soon as you leave'. I'll bust his head open if he starts any shit. I'm not leaving. Keep an eye on him, Tom. I don't trust him."

"I will. Maybe you should talk to Carl."

"No, not yet." Tom felt obligated to ally himself with Dave, since Darcy obviously favored the man. He took this time to ask a question he'd forgotten all about.

"How'd you get to be called the 'pony boy'? Does it have something to do with Darcy?"

Dave had been walking away, but turned with an embarrassed smile, and the men walked to one of the picnic tables. "I really don't mind being called 'pony boy'. It's kind of a little joke, and I've been bought more than one beer in more than one bar by someone calling me the 'pony boy'. I can always use a free beer. Alright, when Darcy was about twelve, I guess, she was given the chance to ride a neighbor's Shetland pony, provided she had some supervision. Agnes talked me into being her supervision one Saturday. I must look like a volunteer. Agnes is so persuasive, and I guess I don't always think ahead. So I took Darcy on this little mountain trail out of town for her to ride awhile. I was on foot; no one gave me a horse to ride. Heck, I didn't mind it at first, but Darcy kept riding ahead of me, so we got to this live oak with some shade and I told her to stop and let me rest, and she just kept moving up with the pony, a little at a time. So here I am, sitting under the tree, and she keeps moving up. Clippity clop, clippity clop, and then I said 'Darcy, give me a minute'. She stayed in one spot for three or four minutes, out of my sight, and then she took off up the mountain. Shit, I was pissed, and I was tired, and when I got up I found the trail forked about a hundred feet past the tree. Now I was scared. I ran up the right fork for five minutes, and then I went a little ways up the left, and then I came back to the tree to wait. That was one of the worst God-Damned two hours of my life, sitting under that tree, other than the half hour I spent in the North Pacific off a fishing trawler…"

"You were lost at sea?"

"Yeah, man, I came back from the dead, I tell people. Anyway, it was about a hundred in the shade, and I had to spend two hours thinking how I was going to tell Bob McEarl how I lost his daughter on the mountain; maybe to a lion, maybe over a cliff. It was horrible." Tom was grinning now, and Dave obviously did not appreciate the humor. "You think it's funny?"

"A little," Tom was laughing.

"Alright... Two hours later she comes back down, and I let her have it. I yelled and screamed at her, I threatened her, and still she had this little smile on her face that reminded me of Agnes's smile."

"Don't say that!"

Now it was Dave's turn to laugh. "I told her that if she ever did that again, I'd tan her fanny with a switch, no matter what Agnes said, but she didn't really believe me, and then I realized what a mistake I'd made telling her 'next time'. She promised me and all that, but I decided to tell Agnes that I wouldn't take Darcy riding anymore, you know, get someone else to do it. Hell, Agnes is one of the people you just can't so no to."

"Tell me about it."

"You'll never guess what Agnes said to do."

"She told you to spank her?"

"Yeah, like a grown man is going to spank another man's daughter. I was going to get Grandma Johnston in on this. I wish I had met Christine then. We could have both taken Darcy riding."

"Who is Grandma Johnston, Dave? She's got to be your grandmother."

"She's my grandmother, but everyone here calls her 'Grandma Johnston', even Sheriff Ramey. She has a lot of influence. Most of the time I live in her backyard tool shed. It's been made up with a bedroom and a wood stove. She doesn't get along with Agnes."

"Just get to the point. Nothing personal, but I'm just interested in this name of yours."

"I got lucky. Bob McEarl was working a job in Sac, and he drove up that next Friday to visit home, and I caught him at the St. Charles, and told what was going on. So he told me to meet him at the Quartz the next day at ten, and he'd have it all taken care of. This is why so many people in this town liked Bob. He could always find some reasonable solution; he just had a way with people. It's too bad he couldn't keep Agnes straightened out. Well, the next day I had five kids on five ponies to take up the mountain trail. I was their guide, and I got a quarter from each one of them. Agnes never offered me any money. Bob talked with Darcy and got her to promise to help me keep track of the other kids. So it worked out pretty damn well, and I got a buck every Saturday all summer."

"Don't you mean a buck and two bits?"

"Darcy always got her quarter back. You know, later."

"Darcy always gets her quarter back, PONY BOY! Don't let Jim get to you, Dave. He's liable to screw himself out of this job. He reminds me of Vernon Fickett."

"I brought Darcy back home one Saturday, and ..., they were having one of their knockdown, drag outs. The whole neighborhood could hear. Darcy grabbed my hand at the porch and turned me around, and we walked to the Quartz for a couple of grape drinks in ice. That was Darcy's favorite."

"Are you trying to tell me..., are you telling me that you were Darcy's first date?" Tom was teasing.

"I'm trying to tell you..., Grandma Johnston said it one day: 'it's not a dignified endeavor for a grown man to attend to babysitting chores. That's woman's work'. But hell, I enjoyed being the 'pony boy', and I was glad to help Bob out. He had enough trouble with that woman. Grandma Johnston thought a lot of him."

"How'd you get lost at sea?"

"My black shark story, I was going to tell that story at the campfire."

"Black shark? Is this going to take long? Maybe I shouldn't have asked."

"I don't like the water much anymore. But I can handle this, so don't get me wrong. I need some gold. Four years ago I had a chance to work on a net trawler out of Alaska, 'cause Grandma Johnston decided to front me the money to travel up and look for some work. Well, I got on with one of those trawlers out of Ketchikan, and I was only out three days and it happened. I didn't know what was going on half the time; I hadn't had time to learn anything. It was that captain, Captain Morsely. The crew called him Captain Bligh behind his back."

"He got you hurt?"

"No, he just didn't want to pull in his net and look for me after I got blown overboard. The rest of the crew made him do it."

"Blown overboard?"

"There was a hell of a squall, but I had my life vest on. There are railings all around, and there's only about a foot of space under the railings. That damn water has so much power. A wave came over the deck and blew me, with the vest on, right under the railing. So now I know I'm going to die. The water was colder than you can possibly imagine, and I was shaking in spasms."

"Shit!"

"I knew they'd never find me; I kept thinking 'why do I keep trying to stay up?'. The will to survive is very strong. I was swallowing water, and I was shaking so hard."

"Alright, I've heard enough. I wish I hadn't asked."

"Wait a minute. I knew I was going to die, but I was scared to death of the black sharks. Ain't that crazy?"

"Dave…, what the hell are black sharks?"

"White sharks, you've heard of them?"

"They're huge. I've heard of them."

"Blacks are even bigger. They swallow men whole. I was terrified one was going to come up and swallow me."

"Yeah, I guess when you're floating in the ocean you can imagine anything. There aren't any black sharks in this river, Dave. But there is gold. Get over it!"

"I guess I get a little nervous, sometimes. Let me tell you something, Tom." Erick was in the improvised kitchen peeling potatoes, as Jim walked by saying nothing. "Dan is an honest man, I've always heard that, and I know we'll get paid here, no matter what. Now let me tell you about another claim owner I worked for five years ago. Don't ever go to work for Peter Morrison. That son-of-a-bitch is a total businessman, through and through, and he really gave me and John McCloud and Jimmy Jones the business. We were diving for him in a helmet diving suit. Have you ever seen one on TV? The brass helmet, with those little glass windows? HUKA is so much better; you just have to dive in one to see the difference. Those helmet suits are harder to get around in, and slower to get out of the way of danger. Anyway, we worked all summer on Pete's claim, chaining boulders to his winch cable to get them out of the way for his drag-line bucket. We'd chain the boulder, and signal to a man looking underwater with a mask on, and he'd signal Peter to pull the boulder with the winch. Man, this guy was dangerous as hell; half the time he'd start pulling while you were still fixing the chain. He got my fingers once, that son-of-a-bitch. Time is money!"

"Shithead! You're right; I'd never work for him."

"One day I pulled some nuggets from the clay behind a boulder they had just pulled, and I brought them up and showed them to the crew, and then gave them to Peter, and man, he threw a fit, and said that if he ever caught someone with gold in their possession, he'd fire them. Well, I'll tell you, Peter always had a new crew every year, and there is a reason for that. He was never foolish enough to hire a former worker back. I think back, I think now that what he did to me, well, he hexed my luck, that bastard. I think he put the hex on me. I had just started seeing Christine, and Peter was paying us in hourly wages, no percentage, and not a very good wage, but I promised Christine that we'd take a trip somewhere after season on the bonus money I knew we were going to get when the job was over. Christine told me to be careful and start saving, but hell, I was spending most of it on her. Come time to quit that day…," Dave was angry. "Shit, we made that bastard a lot of money. We pulled up a lot of gold that summer. He couldn't hide that from us. The day we were done, he gave us a little talk, said 'thanks boys', and that was that. Nothing about a bonus. We just stood there with our mouths open. We couldn't believe it. Two years later someone put sand in his trommel engine. I wish it had been me."

"I guess I'd have been pissed, too."

"We risked our lives all summer for the prick. You don't do that to people around here, not your own kind. If you do good on gold, you give your hands a little bonus. I ran out of money to spend on Christine. Of course we never took that trip. We were talking about marriage, about kids. So Grandma Johnston decided to help me out, and I drove to Alaska. After the fishing boat fiasco, I got some work at a cannery. When I got back, Christine confessed to me she had a miscarriage, and she didn't know if it had been mine or Johnny Paxton's. She had a little fling while I was gone, but Johnny wasn't serious about her, she said. And then I lost my 38 Chrysler, it just got beyond repair, and I'm still without a vehicle, living in my Gramma's back yard. That hex he put on me, it lasted right up to Alaska."

"You really believe that, that he hexed you, on purpose."

"Maybe not on purpose, but he did it. That started my bad luck, I guarantee you."

"Are you still seeing Christine?"

"Yeah... Well, last year. She was a little overweight when I started dating her, and she lost weight, just for me, but she's put it back on. And I've been out of work. She knows I forgive her for that affair, but then Donald Bright and Glen Davis and me, we went down to Tijuana for a week, and I guess she forgives me for that, too. I never meant to get even; I just wanted to get away. Donny said that what I needed was to get out of town and see the senoritas down there, and I guess I could have said no. I ended up meeting this beautiful young Mexican, man she was pretty. I don't' know how young she was, but she took me to her parents home after they had gone to sleep. That was kind of strange. She was so sweet, so good to me that night. Next morning Donny came up the alley yelling for me, 'cause Glen got thrown in jail, and we had to bail him out, and I never saw her again."

"She wants to marry an American, Dave. Then she'd have it made, her and her parents."

"She was so pretty, she should have a portrait made. Sometimes I think I'd just like to give up and hitch a freighter to the South Pacific and start a new life. I'm so tired of this one step forward and two steps back bullshit. I'm thirty-four, and I've got nothing to show. I hear they've got some pretty women in Tahiti, part French, part Chinese, and part native. I'd be like the old man in 'Treasure of the Sierra Madre'. All those native women waiting on me, hand and foot."

"Let me tell you what would happen. You'd get on the wrong ship and end up on the wrong island, with a bunch of leathery women with bones in their noses, and they'd be waiting on you alright, getting you ready for dinner."

"Yeah, that's just about my luck."

"Darcy is right. You'd better get back with Christine before she marries someone else. What kind of a car did you and Christine plan on getting?" Dave looked perplexed. "You two talked about a new car, didn't you? Admit it."

"A Chrysler sedan, maybe a used Imperial."

"Forget used. A new Imperial, Dave, a 59."

"Tom, I've been on a five operations on this river, and I've thought just like that before. Now I know better."

"No, now you will get your wish. Right out there in the deep. They left something, I know they did." Tom paused, to let it sink in. "I knew about that pocket Bill Rutledge found last year."

"I heard about that." Dave looked almost grim. "It hurts all the worse if you build yourself up to it."

"Quit thinking like that. Think big. It keeps you going, and it makes the work go by easier. Now, think about that Chrysler Imperial, sitting in the showroom. What color do you want? Think about how great a new car smells."

"Alright, alright, I know better, but I can sure picture it."

"I'm going to have Darcy walk into the showroom and pick her car right off the floor, to drive away right there."

"I'm thinking this may be my last chance to get on my feet. Jim thinks he's going to run me off, but wild horses couldn't drive me off. I know what ten percent of a strike would do for me."

"Now that's what I like to hear."

"Hardball, that's what he called it. Playing hardball. I'm sorry, Tom. I was thinking about something."

"What are you talking about now?"

"Peter Morrison. I remembered what he called his method of running a business, smoothly and efficiently. He calls it playing hardball. Dan won't play hardball with us, Tom. He's a fair man."

"Forget Peter fricking Morrison. Quit thinking negative."

After dinner Jim stoked the fire to an almost roar, as the crew sat with occasional conversation. "I'm thinking of hitting it. I'm tired", Dave complained.

"No stories tonight?" Tom asked.

"The only thing I can think of is my black shark story."

"Naw, give that one a rest", Tom ordered as Dave walked to his tent.

"I'm going beddy-by too, guys", Carl remarked. "Let's get going by ten," as he walked away. "How about you, Jim?" Tom asked, and Jim shook his head no. "Then let me say something, Jim, before I leave. Let me ask you to think about something. Do you think that what you're doing is going to help your cousin get hired on?"

"Ah, so the squealer came running to Tom."

"Just think about what I'm about to say, Jim. Carl hears most of what you have to say to Dave. Now think, what if we get into some pretty good gold? Dan might hire some additional hands, and you might get your cousin on. But if your mouth keeps going…"

"Yeah!" Erick added. "Carl is getting tired of it, James."

"You won't be doing Louis any good if you get yourself run off, and that could happen. Think about it. Carl might replace you. I know I'm a flatlander, and Darcy is the only reason I'm here. But listen to me, there is gold here. Think of how you'd feel if you got run off, and then we ran into gold."

"I got nothing against you, Tom. Let me tell you something about David. He's a Johnston, and the Johnston's always take care of David. He's never hurting for money, I guarantee you. As far as I'm concerned, he should never have been invited here. He's scared, and that makes me nervous. I don't like working with the guy."

"Yeah, that's true", Erick agreed. "He makes me nervous, too. I can tell he's trying to talk himself into it every time he dives. I can read the guys mind. Fear is contagious, Tom."

"Let me tell you something about thinking real serious, Tom. Two years ago I was living in my brother's cabin on Goodyear Creek with him, his wife and her baby, and we had two other kinfolk besides. We were all trying to contribute to keep us going, but we ran short of supplies. With Lou-Ann needing to make milk for her baby, we couldn't afford to run out of food. The last pot of beans went mostly to her. You want to know serious, think about how every bite of food you take makes you feel guilty because a woman in the house has to make milk for her baby. My brother shot a deer, a doe with a fawn inside, but we ate it anyways. We were starving."

"I'm sorry, Jim. Couldn't you get some emergency food, in town, or somewhere?"

"The Sanborn's don't take charity!" Jim said harshly. "Dave won't be here when we find the real gold. My Daddy told me, you don't get anything in this world by waiting for it. You want something, you got to take it!" And he walked to his tent.

"Ah, what a crew we have", Erick complained. "I wouldn't mind if they both got replaced. Jim is a jerk, and Dave is an accident waiting to happen."

"Dave will be alright. Let him get used to it."

"Do you think Dave will handle it when we turn around and head out deep? That pool is why I'm down here. I've got a little inside information on this place, Tom. I know for a fact that this stretch of river was flumed three years in a row, 1853 through 55. All three of those years the winter high water tore up those huge flumes, and a lot of people think they weren't able to finish down deep. That's my gamble. I guess, come August, if we're not into anything, I'll be ready to make Ardell happy and start jump school. I don't mind jumping, but this is a walk in the park compared to fighting a fire. Good night."

"Good night." 'A walk in the park?' Tom thought. 'Not when we get down deep.' That could make Tommy, the 'Otter', a little nervous.

TWENTY ONE

Breakfast always brought jay birds around the camp, opportunists for any crumbs. Erick had been tempting one fresh out of the nest courageous young jay for days with bits of biscuit or bacon, and this day he was finally able to coax the foolish bird close to the hand that offered the food. Carl almost always spent breakfast hiding, somewhat, from the younger men behind some section of the Sacramento Sunday paper, but for this he had to put the paper down and watch. The bird hopped to within inches of Erick's hand, and Erick placed his hand flat down, with a crumb between his fingers. The jay pecked the food out with no hesitation, and then flew away. "Next time, he's mine", Erick boasted.

"You'll only get one shot", Tom reasoned.

Erick placed the crumb at just the right angle past his hand, and the jay turned for the split second he needed to catch him from behind. Not a sound from the bird, eyes wide, beak open; it happened so fast the jay was in instant shock.

"Let me take care of the son-of-a-bitch, camp robber!" Jim demanded, as he walked to grab the hatchet used to split kindling.

"I don't believe this shit!" Erick exaggerated. "A man has only a few things in life to look forward to: the love of a good woman, the loyalty of a good hound dog, and the obedience of his pet jay bird." Carl was snickering, and Dave was grinning ear to ear. "And this man wants to hatchet my jay bird!"

"Alright, let the God-Damned bird go, so he can rob us some more." Jim looked strained.

"I'll do any God-Damned thing I want with my jay." And he tossed the bird into the air. It was still in shock, and almost fell to the ground before taking wing. Finally, resting in a tree branch, it caught its wind and scolded harshly, as if it felt some honored trust had been broken.

"The love of a good woman. That takes gold", Dave observed.

"If it takes gold to hold her, is she really a good woman?" Erick reasoned.

"I can't make up my mind, which good woman to marry", Jim boasted. "I almost wish they'd let a man marry two women. My problem is a couple of sisters that are crazy mad over me, and I'm going to have to disappoint one of them. I just can't make up my mind." Carl was almost choking, trying not to laugh, and hid behind his paper.

"Shit, what I had to go through to nail Ardell! I just can't imagine what it would be like to have women chasing after me", Erick said with derision.

"Now run this past me again", Tom demanded. Jim was not a lady's man. Skinny but wiry, a littler version of Vernon, Tom thought, but with black hair and a very common face. Erick, if any, would be the lady's man in the group. He was the most physically powerful, and the men had already acknowledged him the one to make decisions when Carl was not around. Dave was balding, but with a little more amicable a face than Jim. He was lanky in the arms, not as powerful as Tom in that respect, but Tom had seen the taller Dave move a substantial rock underwater using his back and legs, and there he might outmatch Tom. Five foot four inch Jim was the runt. Perhaps he had the Napoleonic complex. If he would just keep his mouth shut, he might become an accepted member of the group.

"Carly and Vera Schwartz. They're both blond, and so cute, and I wish there was only one of them. They're crazy about me."

"Did they spend their whole lives deep in the woods, or did they live in a convent?" Erick said with a couple of precision laughs. Jim was beginning to look defensive, a little red in the face.

"Carly is older, and definitely more intelligent. She has a good head on her shoulders, and a man has to consider that when he's thinking about having kids. But Vera is prettier, she has such a…,"

"Come on now!" Dave cut him off, seeing his chance to sling a few barbs back at Jim. "I've seen Carly, and she's not that good looking. Vera, maybe, but I know for a fact she likes Andrew Mathews better than you."

"Shut up, Dave. Your girlfriend has a mustache! And you haven't seen her in, how long has it been?" They sounded like a couple of kids.

"Sometimes she has a mustache, that's true, when she's forgetful." Dave was still grinning. "But it's a petite mustache. It's blond. Now run this past all of us again. Vera is wild about James Sanborn? We need some proof."

"Yeah, James. You come down here and make statements you can't verify. We seem to be lacking some credibility here." Erick was gunning now.

"The man talks about being chased after. Have you ever had one of them make love to you, Jim?" Tom prodded.

"What are you talking about?"

"Darcy likes to ambush me when I've got my head in the fridge looking for a late night snack. I tell her I need something to eat to get my energy back up, but she won't let me have my snack. I'm always tired the second time around, but that's what she's looking for." Now three men were chuckling in sympathy. "I kind of like it when she takes over."

"A real man makes love to a woman. I think you've got it backwards, flatlander", Jim said severely.

"Aw, you've never had a woman make love to you, boy?" Dave goaded. "God, you could be dead tomorrow, and never have known what that's like!"

"Dave!" Erick warned. "Not even as a joke, don't talk about death down here."

"Sorry." It didn't kill the momentum. "Sorry for you, too, Jim."

"Shut up! We are talking about the most important decision in a man's life, and you're thinking it's something to laugh off. That's why you're so fucked up, Dave. You try to laugh off everything, don't you? Maybe that's why you and Christine aren't together. She can see you won't take anything serious. You'll never get her anything in life, she can see that." Jim's old caustic tongue was back in action, and Dave's sudden angry, red face proved the cut had hit target.

"Easy!" Carl warned. The humor was over. "It's time to get to work, guys."

"But we will demand a thorough investigation of Jim's questionable remarks at some further time", Erick added.

Another day of real work, and it was paying just with wages. There was something about that that made it seem like less than gold mining. The men yearned to see some concentration, something that would cheer them up. What gold there was showed up in the sluice, and the further the cut into the bank, the poorer it paid. It was just too much like a job.

There was an old animal trap in camp, one with the spring removed, just small enough that a man could easily carry it underwater, and out of boredom Tom was inspired to a little mischief. Erick and Dave were diving; Jim and Carl were tending the sluice box, Carl sitting in a lawn chair. Tom brought the trap via boat to the dredge, and as Jim pulled the boat in to be tied, Tom motioned silence with a finger and pointed at the men underwater. "Black shark!" Jim still did not comprehend. "Wait till Dave comes up." Jim nodded yes. Forty minutes later Jim said "here he comes". Tom walked over to slip into the water on the other side with the trap and hide until he figured Dave was at the dredge side ladder, and then he took a deep breath and swam under the dredge straight at Dave's legs. It was just too tempting. Dave practically came out of the water as Tom closed the trap teeth into his wetsuit leg far enough to get his attention, and then Tom came up beside him. Jim was howling with laughter, as Carl walked over the sluice, putting a shoe in the running water, to see what was going on. He hadn't noticed Tom get in the water.

"What the hell?" Carl looked angry.

"Black shark attack!" Tom said horsely, laughing with Jim, and now Dave was grinning.

"What?"

"I guess I told my black shark story one too many times", Dave said, trying to laugh, but there were some tears in his eyes, and he put his mask back on and dived back down, probably to avoid Jim's exaggerated laughter.

"What the hell? I got my shoe wet for a prank?"

"I'll bet he shit his wetsuit. God, that was funny!" Jim was ecstatic.

"Wait a minute." Tom took the boat and paddled ashore. After several minutes of looking through camp, he was back with a quart of red paint and a small brush. "I'm going to christen the dredge", he explained. On the side of the aluminum sluice he drew a set of red sharks teeth, and lettered 'El Bestio' beside it.

"What does that mean?" Carl had to know.

"The Beast," Tom grinned, "because it gobbles."

Several minutes later Erick and Dave both came up, and dropped their weight belts. "It's getting dark. Let her settle down a while", Erick explained. The men had been having problems with the mud out the sluice swirling back in on them, cutting off visibility. There were too many back currents in the pool, and they seemed to keep changing directions, no matter how they moved the dredge around. Dredging in muddy water was too dangerous.

Come quitt'n time Jim and Dave were the last on the dredge, and as Tom paddled across to pick them up he saw Jim walk up to Dave and say something Tom couldn't hear, and Dave suddenly smacked Jim in the chest with the palms of his hands, knocking him into the river. "Hey!" Carl yelled from the bank. As Jim swam back and pulled himself up the ladder Dave said "take him back first. I won't get in the boat with the son-of-a-bitch." Jim was grinning. In his little game of psychological chess with Dave he figured he had a good move.

"No, both of you get in. I'm not making two trips."

Carl was waiting for them both, but Erick had walked back from near camp to get the first word. "I saw that, Dave. That was uncalled for. That could be assault."

"Look", Carl said, pointing at Dave's face. "One more stunt like that, and you're out of this job. That's it! And you, Jim." Jim's face had suddenly lost the grin. "I'm sick and tired of your mouth. Your mouth will get you fired." Now Jim wasn't so sure it had been a good move. It was Friday, the Friday in between pay days, and the men weren't in very good spirits.

Tom's spirits were always better with Darcy in his arms, and that evening he felt the need to unburden himself from some of his apprehensions. "I'm beginning to wonder if we'll ever get this project done. This is not working out the way I had pictured it would."

"You can always go back with Bill. I have to admit, that three hundred dollar bonus would be nice, but I don't want you down there."

"Has he gotten into anything decent?"

"Not yet."

"Your friend Dave might not stay on when we get down deep. I don't think he can handle it, and Jim and he are at each other's throats all the time. Dave is a nice enough guy, but he's scared, and that gets to all of us. He shouldn't be down there. And I have to admit…"

After a moment of silence, Darcy demanded "what do you have to admit?"

"The Otter is just a little intimidated himself. I've swam out over that pool, and the water gets to be twelve feet deep."

"The Otter! Scared of water? No way! What a revelation! Seriously, Tom, please don't talk about the diving. You made up your mind, and now you're into it, but I don't want to hear about that deep water. I hate it."

"I'll be fine. I sure am learning what it's like working with people, you know, trying to get the team to work together. When I get my own garage going and start employing people, I can see now what it's going to be like dealing with people."

"That sounds ambitious; when Tom gets his garage going. I knew I picked an ambitious man."

"That will be about all this guy can handle, dealing with one or two people. What was it I said one time? The prince and the princess can make a difference in the lives of the people. What a ridiculous boast. I wouldn't have the vaguest idea of what to do to help the people. I'd be so busy with my elegant lady, attending those lavish Aztec dinners, festivals, and spectacles. Everything would look just fine to me, because I'd want it to. That's human nature. The priests would whisper in my ear, and I'd swallow their bull-shit lies hook, line, and sinker."

"What brought this on?" Darcy laughed. "Tom, I don't think you're ever going to have to worry about that much responsibility. Just your responsibility to me. I know I got an ambitious man."

"Yes, you do."

"Tom, what besides a mechanic did you ever want to do? Wasn't there ever something you wanted so badly, like…, everyone has something that drives them."

"A better football player? I don't know. Maybe I'm just a common man."

"I don't think so. I don't associate myself with just a common man; I will not have you saying that." She was doing Agnes's voice.

"A common man with a common plan. Or is it a simple man with a simple plan. That's probably all I'll ever be", he teased back.

"Guess again! You've got a woman who demands a little more than that." After some silence "I once wanted to be a show horse equestrian. Mrs. Monroe gave me practically a year's training, but that fell through when she had to sell the horse she was training me to ride."

"You never mentioned that."

"It's another sore memory. She wasn't happy about having to sell her Geraud, the horse she spent three years training. That hurt her worse than me."

'Another of life's let downs', Tom thought. 'That's going to stop.'

TWENTY TWO

Monday morning after breakfast the men noticed a car coming down the mountain road. "That's the Sheriff Ramey's Buick. What's he doing coming down here without the Sheriff's car?" Carl observed. After parking, a man of about five foot eight inch, slightly stout, with a fisherman's cap and a red and black checkered wool jacket got out, and pulled a bamboo fly rod and small tackle box from his trunk, and then walked upriver towards the rapids without saying anything to the men. "He'll be over in a spell. He must have something on his mind", Carl explained. After about twenty minutes of fishing the man walked down to the picnic tables with his fishing tackle.

"Morning Sheriff", Erick offered. Tom now recognized the Sheriff, and saw the brass badge pinned to the jacket, but no weapon visible.

"Good morning, gentlemen. Thought I'd have a try at that granddaddy German brown that lives in this pool. I've been after him for years."

"Are you just down for some fishing?" Carl asked.

"Yeah, and to have a little talk with you guys. We've got a fugitive on the mountain. Nothing really serious."

"It's a big mountain", Erick said.

"Yeah, it is. That's why I need to spread the word around."

"Who is it?" Jim sat down right beside Clarence. "A God-Damned flatlander, right? Is it something to do with that robbery in town at Mrs. Wyatt's?" Jim was just a little nervous. Maybe he thought Ramey was going to question him about something.

"No, that was a false alarm. It's those Grant brothers again. Bob borrowed John's car and hasn't brought it back, and John says he needs it real bad. He might file grand theft charges, so naturally, I have to do something."

"How do you know Bob is OK? You don't suppose he drove off a mountain?" Erick responded.

"The word just got back to me. He's, uh, staying with some friends that John doesn't know, and I don't know why he's keeping John's car. I'm sure I haven't heard the whole story." Clarence let out a little sigh. "It's not serious, but…" a change in voice. "I can make it serious. It's the same old story. I just want Bob to come in and talk with me. Every Damn time I go looking for somebody, this mountain swallows them up. Here these people elect me to keep the peace, but when it comes time to get some suspects in for questioning, all those same people clam up. That's called aiding and abetting, any way you look at it. It's not serious this time…" But the Sheriff's tone was too serious. "I'll tell you boys what. The next time I go looking for a felony suspect…, I'm going to run some of these aiders and abettors so far up the river they'll wish they'd committed the crime instead." No one was saying anything. They were all waiting for the Sheriff to finish. There was no doubt in Tom's mind that this man could be very tenacious in pursuit of people, very dangerous to argue with. "Well, if any of you happen to see him..., I don't need to know if you've seen him. Just tell him to come in and talk with me, and we'll work it out. I don't want it to get serious."

"Sure will", Erick offered. "I saw that brown. He has to be over two feet, closer to three."

"I had him on my line two years ago, and he wrapped it around something. I'll nail him. He's just another fugitive, and I'll land him sooner or later." This got the men to laugh, and relieved the tension. "Now what's this about flatlanders, Jimbo? It isn't always flatlanders, but James here would like us to believe..., IT'S ALWAYS a flatlander." Jim looked pale, but the rest could continue to laugh. "Tom here seems a pretty decent young man, I've heard, I mean, you know, for a flatlander. I think it's a good thing, getting some fresh blood up in this canyon." Clarence's eyes were narrowing, a grin forming. "Else.., else too many of them...," Erick almost choked, spat, and laughed at the same time, getting up to walk away, coughing with laughter at some revelation. He had guessed the Sheriff's direction of thought. "...turn out like Jimbo, here." It was a mean smile on the Sheriff's face now, and all the men but Jim were laughing. It was almost too mean, even for arrogant Jim, but it made you laugh, you had no choice.

"I don't care how many females they bring up." Jim tried to extricate himself from total humiliation. "But the flatlanders need to stay down valley."

"Oh, Jimbo!" Clarence's laugh was a little less mean now. "We just have to give you trouble. Well, gentlemen, I see you're about to get to work, so I'm going to do a little more fishing. I came all this way down; it'd be a shame not to give it one more try."

At the campfire that night Carl announced "tomorrow we're going to turn the dredge around and start in the pool. You can see we're not doing any good in the bank." No one had anything to say to this. They had all lost their original enthusiasm. Everyone retired but Dave and Tom, and Dave had to reflect "I know where I'll be heading if we shut down."

"We won't shut down for a while. We'd better not."

"I'll be headed to work Carnie, with the Soim's Brother's show. That's my Grandma Johnston's line of work. You didn't know she was Carnie, did you?"

"I don't know much of anything about her."

"She was sold to the carnival when she was sixteen, for two hundred dollars."

"Dave..., alright, I guess I'm going to hear another Dave story. You know what that black shark story got you!" Tom warned.

"Grandma Johnston has the gift. Someone in the Carnival saw that in her when she was a teenager. I don't know the details, but her mother took two hundred dollars to let her work reading palms and crystal ball for the show. They taught her all that, she didn't know anything about it. It's all a bunch of bunk, but she does have the gift, that's the truth. Two hundred dollars was a lot of money in those days."

"Your Grandmother is a palm reader. What do you do?"

"I don't really want to head back to Carnie. As a matter of fact, I hate it. I'm only there because she got me in, I'm not really Carnie. Put'n up, taking down, slinging a sledge hammer and driving in stakes all day, I hate that, but the people are OK. They're just trying to make a living like the rest of us. What I especially hate is playing shill. I shill for Lloyd Carlson, one of the managers. He's a crook, but he has a lot of influence, so there's not much I can do about that. If I don't shill, I spend a lot more time swinging a sledge hammer, so I shill."

"So this guy, he uses you to rook people?"

"It's just him. No one else does it. You can't do that too much, or you'll get a bad reputation. Anyway, Lloyd says I look like the kind of a guy he could sell the Brooklyn Bridge to, and that makes a good shill. It's the bait and switch, and only greedy people take the bait."

"Yeah, David, you called Peter Morrison practically a crook for what he did to you. What do you think this makes you? And yes, I could sell you the Brooklyn Bridge."

Dave frowned severely. "That's why I don't want to go back, only if I have to."

"Why don't you just stand up to the guy and tell him no, you won't do it anymore?"

"I've talked with other Carnie, and they say they're tired of his games, too. I'm liable to get arrested one of these days. But these are Grandma Johnston's people, so I have to be careful. And I get a cut, if someone takes the bait."

"That makes you no better than Peter Morrison. But don't worry about it right now. We're not done yet. I know all about the bait and switch. My Dad told me a nasty version of that story."

"So?"

"Not right now, maybe some other time." And Tom walked to his tent, with old memories of a conversation that he preferred to have forgotten.

"There was a guy in my squadron named Lawrence Mathen; he was an American, but his parents were from England, so we called him a Brit." Dad would begin a war story out nothing, for no reason, but Tom had learned not to bring the subject up. Tom senior just had to get it out of his system. "That son-of-a-bitch, he wouldn't leave me alone. He was always prodding me, accusing me, damn; I came close to taking a brick to his head one day. I was the German American, both parents. I was the one everyone had to watch, I knew that. Lawrence kept accusing me: 'you think Hitler is right, don't you?' I'd tell him that I just do my job. The whole time I thought he doubted my loyalty, but I was wrong. I think he intended to offer me some money, but I think it would have been a bait and switch deal. That's the oldest con game in the world. One day, he wasn't there for revelry, and we were told he went AWOL. Actually, that's what he intended to do, but that's not what happened. After we completed our tour of duty, one of my buddies, Gus Spanick, and I were getting drunk in an English pub, and he told me the real story. He heard it from one of our MP's. They're not supposed to talk about these things, but talk gets around. Lawrence got caught one night inside one of our planes, and how he got out of the barracks without waking anyone up, well, that was slick. He was doing something that could have caused the plane to lose aileron control at any time after takeoff."

"You mean sabotage?"

"Yes. Towards the end of the war the German SS had agents in England offering money for this kind of sabotage, but our side caught on quick, and some of those agents got shot. Supposedly, Lawrence would give the plane's number to his contact, and if the Germans found wreckage of that plane in France or Germany, he would be rewarded with the equivalent of the cost of that plane in gold. That would have been enough to set a man up real tidy somewhere. I guess that's what you call being practical, playing the odds. That's if you don't give a shit in hell about the men you work with." Dad looked strained now. "And there I was, the German, just trying to do my job. Gus said that after two days from being caught, some special intelligence people executed him. You see, our side had to be practical, too. It was a good thing that none of us found him doing it, because we would have probably beat and kicked him to death, and I would have kicked him the hardest, but that would have been bad for morale, I can see that. I think the traitor would have had a hard time collecting his gold. The SS had a reputation by the war's end, about rewarding dirty deeds with gold. They stole a lot of gold, but they didn't much like letting go of it. They preferred the old bait and switch; they liked to substitute another metal."

"Another metal?"

"Lead."

'Dirty gold.' Tom thought now. 'I'm sure there's been dirty gold exchanged in these hills, but I'd never take any.'

TWENTY THREE

Opening up the trench out river revealed a new obstacle, one that would make the work more dangerous. The top layer of rock, gravel, and clay was pretty stable, but it was sitting on a layer composed almost entirely of loose sand, right down to the bedrock. Somehow the river had filled back in with mostly sand after the flume people had worked it, and a later high water had put the clay packed gravel on top. This meant that once a section of the stable layer on top had been dredged, only loose sand held up the perimeter, and as the men opened up the trench there were continuous cave ins that would send rock and gravel sliding down the sand towards the men. It also meant that the men would have to dredge a wider path over the trench, and that would slow them down. As the bedrock dived, the overburden got deeper, until there was four foot of sand and two to three feet of gravel just on the shelf around the trench. What gold showed up was found in the cracks in the dolomite or the shale walls, and after a poor weeks showing, a large slab of cracked shale appeared on the upstream wall that took almost a day to uncover. Erick and Tom used pry bars to pull down the slab, and the clay in the crack helped put the cleanup to 38 ounces of gold, up from the previous 9 ounce cleanup. That helped spirits, but the deep diving and continuous cave-ins had everyone on edge.

The Monday morning trip down, of the third week out river, brought a hitch-hiker into camp. A man of about six foot three, white haired under a felt cap, but still lively looking, carrying an ancient wooden frame backpack, a sleeping bag and pack tent, a small folding shovel, and a pan and tiny sluice. Carl had picked him up on the dirt road and given him the ride, then offered him breakfast. His name was Joe Randolf, and apparently the rest of the crew already knew him. He was one of the canyon snipers that spent summers trying to eke out a living on gold with just a few hand tools and a diving mask. The crew seemed to enjoy his company. "That's an Italian Alps backpack, isn't it, Joe?" Erick observed after breakfast.

"That was my father's. It's dated 1896."

"Geeze!" Tom said. "That's awfully well kept."

"So am I!" The man beamed.

Erick laughed and said "Joe is eighty-two, right Joe?"

"Eighty-four. I won't be spending a long summer down here, not like I used to. But I'd rather be here than in that hot valley." He was still powerful enough, Tom could see, as he put on his backpack and equipment and started to head down river. "Thank you, fellas. I'm going to miss your kitchen."

"Hit us any time between Monday and Thursday, and we'll fix you up a good dinner. We'll even let you do a little cooking", Carl said.

After he got out of earshot, Erick said directly to Tom across the table "that's one man you don't want to cross. He goes on other people's claims, but if they tell him to get off, he leaves it alone. Most people don't mind him; they've known him for so long. But he went on one ole boy's claim upriver a few years ago, and that fool pulled a gun on him. There's something you don't ever want to do if you're not prepared to use it. Joe walked up and took the pistol out of the man's hand, and threw it in the river. He's got more nerve than I have." Erick nodded his head, perhaps out of respect for the man.

The Friday of that week Erick and Tom did an afternoon dive; as Tom steered the huge dredge nozzle, Erick removed rock to the steel basket. There was a small ledge on the upstream side wall lined with rock, some up to ten pounds, and Erick was pulling rock off it, leaving the clay intact, so that Tom could dredge it later for production. Tom would use a 20 foot extension of five inch hose that would be hooked into the nozzle so that it wouldn't be sucked up, and this allowed the men to get into tight crevices. Tom saw Erick reach for one rock with his left hand and move it, then bend back down with another rock tucked in his right arm that was proving too heavy to hold, and he dropped that rock. Lying flat in the water, Erick was probably getting his wind, with his left hand palm down on a boulder, and then Tom saw the rock fall straight for that hand, and he actually heard the noise as the rock hit hand and the boulder. A could chill went through Tom's spine as he saw the man double up, his hand tight against his stomach, and then the expression in Erick's eyes, that would haunt anybody. Inky, dark fluid was spreading through the water away from the hand. Tom grabbed at him, trying to unlock the weight belt, and Erick didn't seem to understand at first, but Tom finally got it off, and then dropped his, and they both shot to the surface, Tom screaming "get him out! Get him out!" The men wore their regulators underneath the weight belts rather than harnessed to their backs as some divers did, thinking that if the long air lines got tangled underwater, they could more quickly get free of them. Erick's regulator had been dropped out of his mouth, and he now needed help to keep his head above water, he was in such pain. Tom, Dave and Jim helped pull him up on a pontoon.

"Oh God, I'm done! Oh God, my finger! I'm going to lose my finger, oh shit, this hurts! Morphine, have you got any morphine? Carl, please!"

"I don't have any, Erick. I'm sorry, Jesus, I'm sorry. A shot of whiskey?"

"Yes, anything. Aw, shit, no more dredging."

"Which finger is it? We need to wrap it, Erick", Carl asked.

"Don't touch it! It's my index finger. I'm going to lose it."

"GOD, DAMN, SON-OF-A-BITCH!" Carl finally had to blow off some steam. "You weren't watching him?" He glared at Tom.

'What could I do? I wasn't there.' Tom thought. 'He's just angry. He knows I couldn't help it.' But it stung, never the less.

"Let's get him in the car, and Jim, you drive the flatbed. We'll take him straight to Grass Valley, and hope to God we see the Highway Patrol, cause I'm going to be speeding, I guarantee you." It was frightening trip, too fast and dangerous, Erick in the back seat sipping on whiskey, his finger wrapped in paper towels. At North San Juan, they flagged a passing Deputy Sheriff who escorted them all the way to the hospital, and Carl had to slow down considerably, much to Tom's relief. It would have been a nightmare to have a second accident. At the hospital Carl called Ardell and Dan, while the other men made their calls. No one answered at Agnes's. About seven in the evening Dan showed up, and the men escorted him to Erick's room. The wound had been cleaned and he had been given a good dose of pain medicine, but he was still awake and miserable.

"What's it doing?" Dan asked.

"It's throbbing. I need to get to sleep, but I can't."

"Let's talk. I'm going to fly you to a specialist in Los Angeles, and try and save this. I'm going to take care of everything. I talked with Dr. Randell over the phone."

"What are the odds, just tell me that."

Dan waited a minute, and then grudgingly confessed, "Only ten percent. That's what he says, but he says a specialist could up that. Don't you worry about anything."

"Thank you Dan, but no! That would take a much longer time, and it's not a sure thing. The quicker I get this finger off, the quicker I can heal up. I can still fight fire, and I write with my right hand."

"It's your choice. I'll do anything I can."

"Thank you so much."

Tom said "guys, let's leave him alone", and he, Dave and Jim headed to the waiting room, but they could hear Ardell at the front before getting there.

"Where is room 56?" she said, running past them, and Jim simply pointed. At the waiting room, Dave slumped down on a sofa and seemed to fall right to sleep. Tom walked out to the parking lot to pace. After five minutes, Tom returned to find Jim reading and Dave soundly asleep, lucky enough to have temporarily escaped reality. From a room down the hall Tom could hear part of the noises of a woman's voice, one talking loudly, only the higher noises reaching that distance, and he headed back. Ardell was giving Erick, Dan and Carl the fifth degree; she was hissing with fury in this argument. "No, no!" as Tom walked in. "Absolutely not. That's it. I won't stand for it. You will try and save it. I don't see how you can even think..., oh, shit!" as she let out a breath. "This isn't going to happen. And you!" She looked Tom straight in the eye. "You were under with him!" That stung deep. Pretty, kind Ardell, now so full of fury, fury and despair. Tears now filled her eyes that she could not fight back. "I'm sorry, Tom. I didn't mean that."

"Listen, Ardell." Tom now tried to talk as gentle and firm as he could master. "You've got to let him make up his own mind."

"Please, Ardell!" Erick said feebly. "Tell them I need some medicine to sleep."

"Oh, Erick!" She was trembling, almost ready to break down, and she sat down beside him crying. Carl, Dan and Tom walked out to give them privacy.

Darcy came in about half an hour later, almost running, and stopped when she saw Tom. "I thought it was you. We weren't sure. We just heard it was one of the divers."

"How do people get these things so screwed up?" Tom observed, as Darcy squeezed him about as tightly as her strength would allow.

"It was Dan's wife, Jesse." Agnes stood at the waiting room entrance, so much calmer than Darcy. "She's a dip. She can't get anything right. Can we see him now?" She had such a calm, kind and motivated expression now, this woman who could be so intense. She would actually be able to cheer them up, Tom had no doubt.

"Give them a little while", Jim warned. "Ardell just got here."

"And then let's go home", Darcy said. "I was sick the whole time down here. I hope this shuts Dan down, and I can get my man back to work with Bill Rutledge." It was going to be a long, argumentative weekend, Tom knew.

Next Monday was overcast, and that fit the mood of the men. Three divers now. Carl promised to take some of the diving duties, but the men told him no. By Thursday they had made some progress, but it was a poor gold showing. And then at lunch break, Dave announced to Carl "I'm quitting, after next clean up. I've already talked to Dan. You could hire two more divers, if he doesn't find any."

"Alright", Carl said simply. No one was surprised that Dave would quit.

"Why?" Tom demanded. "Not now, Dave. You're doing fine. You can handle this."

"Yes, I think I can handle it, and I sure could use that bonus. That's not the reason."

"You'll change your mind at next cleanup. Stick it out till then."

"I almost said 'I hope you're right'," Carl said. "I'd like to see something show up, but I'm afraid Dan is going to be hiring a new foreman, fellas. I've had a job offer I can't pass up. It's been nice working with you guys, and I'd recommend every one of you. Tomorrow is going to be cleanup day."

'Why didn't he say something Monday?' Tom wondered. 'He just didn't want to kill the momentum, I guess. What a rotten run of bad luck. I guess I should go back with Bill. No!' He suddenly felt a panic. 'I'll spend the rest of my life thinking about this hole. Dan will shut down, if we all quit.' "What about you, Jim?" Tom didn't really care if he stayed, but he preferred Jim to no one.

"Yes." What did 'yes' mean? After some silence, "I think Dave is right."

"Alright, I'll just wait for the next crew. You are all going to regret hearing about the gold we find. I'm going to give Erick a cup full of nuggets, just to make him feel better."

After cleanup Friday afternoon, Tom walked up to Dave and extended a hand to shake. "It's been great working with you. I hope the best for you."

"Thanks, Tom." Dave did not look happy, and Tom was not letting go of the hand.

"Tell me something!" Tom got intense, "what was that you were saying about wild horses?"

Dave almost grinned, "They won't drag me, I'll just walk out." Tom still would not let go the hand; his grip was getting harder.

"I just don't understand. You were doing fine."

"I just received a message, a warning. I can't tell you about it till after the season. I talked to Grandma Johnston about it, and she says I need to be very careful if I was given a warning."

"What the hell are you talking about? Did someone threaten you? We can talk to Lou Montgomery and Ray Shannon."

"No, no one threatened me. Grandma knows about these things. She said it was time to leave."

Tom's grip got even tighter, "What the hell are you talking about? Is this some kind of Carnie mumbo jumbo?" Dave's eyes were watering, his face getting red. Tom felt an urge to smack him, just to knock some sense into him. Dave was passing up his last chance to get on his feet. 'This is the shits', Tom thought. 'I'm so mad at him. I'm mad at them all. This is not Jim or Vernon, remember that.' Tom let go of his hand. "Dave, I want you to think about something, if this was a war, well, think about all those men who have no choice but to fight a war." He was thinking about Dad. "What do they do to deserters, Dave? You're deserting, and no one is going to shoot you, but, by God, you're going to regret it. You know what they're going to say; just like Jim says, 'Dave can't handle it'." That hit home. That one obviously hurt. "Don't pass this up, just 'cause they're all quitting. We'll get another crew down here. Think of what you have a chance to walk away with!"

"I'm sorry Tom, I'll tell you after the season." Tom threw his arms up in the air and walked away. 'God, I'm going to have such a fight with Darcy. Shit, this is screwed.'

"Sorry, Tom," Carl caught up with him. "I'm going to make sure Dan doesn't shut it down. He will get you another crew down there pretty quick, don't worry.

"Thank you, Carl. I'm not leaving."

For the first Friday evening since Tom started the job, the couple did not make love. The argument went on for nearly two hours, till Agnes banged on the door and demanded silence. Perhaps, it reminded her of some of her own marital sparring all those years ago. Darcy was able to manage a 'Good night, Tom' and give him a kiss.

There were two things to be taken care of Saturday; a phone call to Dan got him an appointment to meet him at the Quartz in the afternoon. At breakfast, after Darcy left for the restroom, Tom said to Agnes, "Dave always went home with Carl, so I don't know where he lives. Where is Grandma Johnston's place?"

"You don't need to see that woman."

"It is about Dave."

"I can tell you anything that you want to know about that fool. I'll bet he was the most worthless hand you had down there."

"Actually, he was doing pretty fair. I think he learned to master his fear, you know, since he was lost at sea."

Agnes sneered, then said "you know where Darcy's friend Janet lives?" Tom nodded yes. "There's that little road up the hill that starts right across from her house. Just follow it up, and it's the biggest house."

"Tell Darcy that I'll be back in an hour or two."

Grandma Johnston's two story house was very run down. Walking up the hill, Tom caught a glimpse of the 20 by 30 foot shed that Dave called home. Both needed paint and roof work. If Dave would stay on, they could get all that taken care of. "Mrs. Johnston?"

"Yes? You're Tom Hendrick aren't you? Dave's not here. He took my car down valley for me."

"Good. I'm glad. I just wanted to talk to you, Mrs. Johnston." The diminutive, silver haired lady's face now looked stern, but, she opened the door wider to let him in.

"I think I can guess what you want to ask me; and I don't think I have the right to talk about that. Would you like a cup of coffee? How is Darcy? We all think so much of her, you know. Agnes, I could care less about." Tom grinned.

"Darcy is mad at me, and yes, some coffee would be great. Dave is walking away from..."

"Wait a minute. I don't mean to be rude, but let's sit down and have some coffee before we talk business. This is my parrot, Sunny." A large cage at the end of the living room held a yellow, gray, and green parrot, with a beak big enough to take a man's finger off. "Sunny bites. Sunny is nasty, so stay away from the cage. He is a hundred and four years old, and I still don't know for sure if he is a he. What I like best about Sunny is his vulgar vocabulary. He belonged to a sailor, but, then all parrots belonged to a sailor at some time or another, don't' we know." Tom smiled. "I got Sunny when I was eighteen, at the carnival. I traded a snake for him. I've come close to shooting him twice." Tom had to laugh at this. "I read palms, Tom. I have customers that still come up here to see me after forty years. I love my customers, they love me. I'm one of the biggest liars in the universe, and they know that, but this is how I make a living, plus a little that my husband left me. It's entertainment. I'm going to put a new pot on. Excuse me, I got carried away." When she came back, "Sometimes I am forced to lie about the truth; and that's when it quits being entertainment. You see, I have the gift, they call it. I call it a curse. I see death; nothing happy, nothing good, only death. How ironic can a gift be? The very few times I can actually look into a person's future, and can actually predict, I must lie. I must put on a mask, because you would never want to upset these people and ruin their frame of mind. You do understand, I don't say this to too many people; but there is a good side. I sometimes help investigate murders. I can help the law with an unsolved murder, if I am allowed. Most people don't believe that."

The conversation had become too grim; Tom wanted to change the subject. "Did you see…, something with Dave?"

"No, he did. He had a re-occurring dream when he was a boy, and it came back to him one night on the river. That is a very important sign. He does not want this to get out, because some people in these hills are very superstitious, but, I am going to trust you. I'm going to trust you to never tell Dave I told you, because he intends to tell you later. He saw a large, black entity coming at him while he was being held, as if tied down. He would wake up every time, many times as a boy, and then no dreams for years. Then one more time."

This was giving Tom the creeps, but he wouldn't let this hogwash get to him. "It is only natural that he could associate that dream with the big boulders we're dealing with underwater."

"Yes, but he's never had that dream on other diving jobs." That chilled Tom to the bone.

"Dave is walking away from a good chance. I'll tell you what, if we get into gold, I'll come back up and talk to him."

"He will never go back down there."

"Thank you, Mrs. Johnston. I think I'll leave before Dave shows up."

Back home, he confided with Darcy. "Well, Dave is out; that's for sure."

"I don't want to know about it."

"I've got an idea. I'll invite Ray and all of Bill's crew down." He tried to grin her into a smile, and it almost worked.

"That would certainly make me feel better. You know they're all preoccupied. They won't come." He knew that was true, but he was going to make the phone calls anyway.

Dan McKenzie offered to buy Tom a late lunch, but Tom passed on the food. "I guess I have to admit, I just don't have the enthusiasm for this that I had earlier in the season. Erick is going to take a year to recover, and I, uh…, wonder if we shouldn't leave it alone."

"Dan!" Tom felt such a panic, but masked it. "You're going to spend the rest of your life thinking you passed something up, and so am I. You've got thirty feet of trench opened up, and this winter's high water is going to fill it back in. Then some day you will want to come back and have another look and you will have to spend all that time and gas opening it back up!"

"Yeah", Dan was chuckling, "just like those old timers who couldn't finish parts of this river; and spent the rest of their lives wondering what they had missed. Well, I don't think I'm going to have trouble finding another crew; it's just…," another frown and more misgivings.

"Not with a flatlander down there. He's liable to invite more flatlanders down. You will have volunteers in no time." Tom grinned, a dare.

"That's true, no doubt. But, Tom…, I had a little talk with Darcy, and I feel that you shouldn't be there alone."

'I am being talked about like a child behind my back,' thought Tom. 'She is only doing it because she's worried about me.' "Dan, let me claim watch for the week. The same schedule we were using. I'll take the flatbed down Monday, and bring it back Friday, to make sure that no one plays around with the equipment. You know you'll have a crew by Friday, with all the people out of work up here. We can't let the females influence these decisions, Dan. You know they won't let us do anything, that's if they have their own personal fear of what we're doing, and Darcy is afraid of water."

"Half of it is Jesse. She's so excitable, and Darcy talked to her first. You're right." Dan had a hard look now. "I never let Jesse influence my decisions. Alright, you claim watch, and I'll get a new crew down. But don't start up that dredge!"

"Not till they get there!"

"I almost had a crew this morning, but that fell through because of that Carnie Johnston. Can you believe that! Vernon Fickett called me last night and said he had two boys from Alleghany ready to go to work." Tom's stomach turned. "And then he calls up this morning and tells me that both guys changed their minds because..., I just can't believe how ignorant and superstitious some people are up here. He tells me that he has to look for other hands now because Dave Johnston saw death in a dream. Can you believe that Carnie crap? You know his Grandmother reads palms."

"I know. I just talked to her this morning, and I don't buy that hogwash, but I have to say, I hope Vernon doesn't come down there. I don't get along with him very well, Dan." Tom wondered why Dan had not heard about Vernon hygrading the "Boulder Bound". And, how in the hell did Dave's dream story get out? One or the other had to have said something, probably Dave.

"Alright, you've been a good hand Tom. Vernon is out, and I won't tell him why. I'd make you foreman, but you're a little too young."

"I wouldn't want that much responsibility right now, Dan. Thank you, but I just want to get going again."

Darcy and Tom were on better terms Saturday evening. Sunday church found Darcy holding a bible, with Agnes and Tom at both sides, singing out of the hymnal together. Fried chicken and mashed potatoes for dinner, and Tom was stuffed. Then Darcy stopped the casual conversation; "Tom is going to promise me, and Agnes is my witness, that he will not start the dredge up till someone gets down there."

"Of course I will princess, I'm not a fool. Ray taught me well; never dredge alone." Darcy stared him hard. "Dan is working on it, and I'll bet I'll have a crew down there Monday." Agnes was staring too, and was it, perhaps, a little admiration in that smile?

TWENTY FOUR

It was a strange feeling, driving Dan's flatbed truck down that mountain road all alone Monday morning. This was the first time Tom had driven the road, and it really was a challenge to navigate. There were no second chances for mistakes on this road. There at the picnic tables sat Joe Randolf, and Tom was relieved to have some company. "Hello, Joe. Have you had breakfast? I've got eggs, bacon, biscuits already mixed up, all in the ice chest."

"That's what I like to hear. Where is everyone?"

"I lost the entire crew, man. I'm waiting on anther crew." As if it was his dredge. "You want to go to work?"

"Thank you, but I stay shallow. What happened?"

"An accident; then one thing, and another. You want to stay for supper?"

"I was hoping for a ride out even though it is the wrong time of the week. Supper sounds good, but only if someone is leaving out."

"I'm not leaving 'till Friday, Joe. Come up Thursday evening for supper."

"I'll be here. Let me fix some omelets."

After breakfast, Joe said; "I just might move in full time with my grand niece next year. She tells me it's this old man's time. She has been good to me. But, you know if you give up, that's it! Have any of these fellas said anything about me?" That was not a good question.

"They said that you're a good sniper."

"Anymore, everyone has forgotten. Thank goodness, you see, back in the twenties, I was a man people talked about quite a bit, young fella." Why did Tom not want to hear this? "My wife left me, got a divorce, and I guess I went off the deep end a little. I lost my job, and decided to go back to mining, like my dad had taught me. Well, you see, the son of a bitch my wife ran off with turned up missing about the same time I got myself into some pretty decent gold. 'Course, I'll never talk about that gold. Still might be some left down there." Tom sat, hands folded together between his knees, looking at the sand beside the picnic table. "I just thought someone might have said something. You know Sheriff Conway questioned me three times. My ex-wife tried to get back with me that spring, and she tried her best to make me believe she was sorry. Then she slipped up and confessed he told her the only reason he went after her was to get her away from me." 'Why do people tell me these stories?', Tom thought. "I told her to go to hell." The man stood up and put on his pack, then started grabbing what he needed to carry by hand. "One thing you never want to do in these hills is follow someone who is into gold. That is a very foolish thing to do. I kept thinking someone was trying to follow me. The signs were all there. So I started doubling back, and waiting. Yeah, a lot of people used to talk about me. They never found him, the son of a bitch!" Joe adjusted his pack, moved his angle of posture, got himself comfortable with it, and started to walk downriver. "I finally found out who was following me!"

Sitting at the picnic table for three hours was boring as hell. Finally, there came the noise of a vehicle on the mountain road. A panel station wagon came into view, stopped at the first turnout, and four men got out and began chatting and pointing. One was almost tiny, skinny and smaller than Jim. Finally, Tom got exasperated and waived them down, and they drove on in.

"Hello, Thomas Hendrick?" The skinny little black haired man was like Dave Morrow in that he was a personable, intelligent man. "We're your new workers. This is Brother John, Brother Randy, Brother Melvin, and I am a Tom, too."

"Little Tom, we'll have to call him," John said, and the guys chuckled. John, Randy, and Melvin looked like they could handle it, but little Tom was born for paper and pencil, just like Dave Morrow.

"Alright, if I'm little Tom, I guess that makes me the spokesman. Tom, we're from the Nevada City Baptist Men's Group, and we're here on a mission. Our church needs a new Sunday school wing, and we're all going to donate some of the gold to help get that done. We are also all public school teachers, so we have to be finished by September."

'Uh, Oh!' Tom thought. "That's great, guys. Who did Dan send to be foreman?"

"Uh, well for us, that's me," John said. Tom was grinning in disbelief. "We all need some instruction from you. Dan tells us you know just about everything."

'Alright, I'm foreman,' Tom thought. 'That's no problem.' "Guys, how many of you have dived?" Troubled looks now. Then John said, "I'm the best swimmer."

"That's no problem. That's how I got started. We'll just ease all of you into it. And, we'll make little Tom the sluice box tender."

"Why?" The little man looked slightly insulted. "You mean I don't dive?"

"Well, maybe a little. Who brought wetsuits?"

"I borrowed Jim Sanborns", little Tom said. "We have one more suit that we are going to have to share." John added.

It was almost a fiasco at first, but, Tom kept telling himself that Ray had been patient with him, and now it was his turn. The suits did not fit anyone well, but it seemed the bigger men would turn out to be decent hands. Everyone dived right to the bottom when it was his turn, even little Tom. Tom was going to have a hard time convincing little Tom that the sluice was the strategic location for him. At three-thirty, Tom called it a day early, just to give the men some slack on their first run, and Tom's spirits got higher with the news that they had brought steaks and taters for dinner. It was no surprise that there would have to be a bible reading afterwards. Tom hoped that the men would be discrete and not mention anything about him living out of wedlock with Darcy. These men had some excellent campfire stories, nothing dirty, of course, and, he was already enjoying the company of the 'brethren'. Tom slept so well that night, relieved that things would be back to normal.

The next day, he got the men acquainted with the routine of the rock basket, removing rock from the work site, and coordinating with the winch operator on the bank to pull the basket to the far end of the trench and dump rock into an area already worked. He stressed the importance of watching the walls for loose rock above, saying, "Erick will tell you, you can't let your guard down for a second!"

Into the afternoon, things were going just fine. Tom had put a third airline on the air pump so he could keep an eye on things below, and he dived to see Melvin and little Tom at work. Little Tom was removing rock to the best of his ability; slowly. Tom started helping him with the rock, and little Tom seemed to be enjoying it. After half an hour, Tom moved forward to watch Melvin, and he looked back several times, just in case. Suddenly, little Tom was writhing in the water, his regulator out of his mouth. Tom did not wait for an explanation; he simply charged and pulled his weight belt latch, then pulled his own. On the surface, little Tom had swallowed water and was hysterically panicking, taking Tom down with him. John jumped in to help subdue the terrified man and help bring him to the dredge. They lay him on his stomach with his face over the river so that he could cough and spit up the water, and in five minutes time it was obvious he would live. "I'm getting tired of having to bring guys to the surface", Tom observed angrily. "What the hell happened?"

"That little rubber thing that goes in your mouth, it came off."

"You could still have breathed through the inlet. You can't let yourself panic down there. I'm sorry Tom, I know you're new at this, but you've got to learn this stuff. Let's cut for the day, guys."

"Yeah", John looked concerned yet. "That's a good idea."

The men grouped at the picnic tables, all but Tom, who walked upriver just to walk off some consternation. They all seemed to be in discussion for the full half an hour Tom took. John walked up to greet Tom and said, "We've got something to say. We've been talking it over." Tom was hoping that they had demanded little Tom tend sluice box. "Tom, we've decided we're just not cut out for this. We're going to tell Dan to get another crew."

"What? You guys can get little Tom to watch the box, and everything will work out just fine. You just need some time to get into the routine, that's all."

"No, it's not quite that simple. Tom is the one that got us together, he's the motivator, you see. He's the one that gets us together and gets our spirits up. We were all planning to get in on the bible drive, that is, selling our own personal Nevada City Bible door to door, for donations for the church wing. You see, Tom got us up here, instead, and you've seen what he is like. You can't just put him on the side, you can see that."

"Carl Gleason was our foreman, and he tended box."

"That won't work with little Tom. We want to take him back down, because he's going to get himself or one of us hurt up here. I'm sorry, Tom."

"That's true. He'll get someone hurt." Tom felt horrible. Was this going to go on all summer? "Well, do me a favor and call Dan as soon as you get out. I need a crew down here, and I'm not coming out till Friday." Tom sounded angry, and so he tried to joke, “I guess the good Lord didn’t intend you guys to get the gambling fever!”

“I am sorry, Tom.”

“Are you staying for supper?”

“No, that road is something that we don’t want to be on at night.”

Down on the river, by himself for supper; he had such a despondent, grim feeling now. Darcy was right, this place was cursed. But, cursed places always held the gold, right? Such humor would not work here, not now. Pork and beans out of a can with some bread for supper, and it would be hard to get to sleep.

About eleven, pitch dark, Tom was still tossing and turning, and somewhere in the distance came the low rumble of some kind of engine. There it was again. Someone on this road, at this time of night? Off and on, but just a little louder each time. Tom got out of the tent and looked up the mountain. Sure enough, the flicker of a headlight through the trees, across the canyon, then back this way. ‘This is not good’ thought Tom. ‘Not this time of night.’ Would a new crew be coming down? No, not alone. Maybe Sheriff Ramey? Then he heard some voices, loud, and laughter across the canyon. Then again, drunk, no doubt, it sounded. ‘This is not good. Jesus, my church crew just left me, and this has to happen. God, what timing. I don’t need to be dealing with some drunken mountain boys this time of night.’ And then, “Vernon, Vernon, look!” Just as plain as it could be, as the car almost reached the parking landing. Tom’s stomach seemed to tie up in a knot.

“Oh hell!” He said out loud. ‘Keep calm, Tom. A lot of people know you’re down here, and he wouldn’t dare start some shit. But, he is drunk. God, why did they have to leave? If they'd just stayed till morning.' He had to admit, he was scared. Vernon probably didn't know there had been a crew down here, and figured he would catch Tom alone. He was right. He and his buddies had been drinking. What to do? Hide? Take the flashlight and the pistol, and hide. There are more of them than you, there's no shame in that. And if they come after you? He had a very good idea of what Vernon intended. He wasn't going to put the fear of God into Tom; he was going to put the fear of Vernon into him. Vernon was going to make sure Tom learned his lesson this time. Probably, it would be expected when he was through, Tom would run from the hills and never return. 'Little chicken shit punk; he has to bring his friends with him.' Tom had a vision in his mind, so enjoyable, of him and Vernon all alone, Tommy beating Vernon's brains to a pulp. 'Be careful what you think! It might be you that gets beaten.' Tom grabbed his loaded 357 pistol and holster belt, filled to the last rung with rounds, put it on and lit his kerosene lantern, and started up the hill. The whoops and yells were still coming, even when the men saw the light.

"Hello boys, what's cooking?" He tried to make his voice sound calm.

"What's cooking? Fuck! He thinks he's a fucking comedian!" This put a dread surge through Tom's body. That sounded like John Hanes, the half Mexican, Vernon's enforcer tonight, Tom suspected. How in the hell was he going to get out of this? It didn't matter that Vernon's was being incredibly stupid, from a sober point of view. In Vernon's drunken mind, Vernon was the master of his universe.

"Oh we got something cooking, alright!" Vernon said, and John laughed arrogantly.

"Wait minute, guys!" Whose voice was that? That sounded familiar! That was someone he knew. The headlights were still on, and Tom walked up to get a better angle of view. It was Sam McCarren's car, a beat up old Plymouth. Tom knew Sam from the St. Charles, and Sam always had something positive to say to Darcy and him.

"Is that you, Sam?"

"Hello, Tom. We were all drinking at the Narrows, and we decided to bring you a six pack of beer down." Sam was drunk, too. He was lucky he hadn't gone off the mountain.

"Well, that was decent of you."

"Sam, if you can't keep your mouth shut, then get back in the car!" Vernon demanded. Suddenly, there was a door slammed violently, and the doors had all been shut. Wham, again, and even louder.

"Who the hell's car did you come down in, Vernon?" Sam was bigger that either Vernon or John, and there was plenty of anger in the man's voice as he sobered up, one hand on the door handle. "What in hell is going on here? We were going to bring Tom a few beers and put one on with him, didn't you say Vernon?"

John started to move in a flanking maneuver around Sam, and Tom said "Aaht, Aaht, that'll be enough, John. Stay in front of Sam." Just having one ally made the difference, and Tom's voice was controlled, no hint of fear.

John stopped, but Vernon demanded "take his gun, John. We need the gun."

"What in the B-Jesus did you think you were going to bring my car down here for? Huh, Vernon?" Sam was sober now.

"Don't pay any attention to him. Take the gun, John!"

"Don't do it, John! You've already got enough problems in these hills. You don't need Sheriff Ramey coming after you." Tom warned.

"You fucking little, you fucking stupid son of a ..." John was seething, slurring his words from liquor and anger together. He really wanted to hurt someone. He really wanted to. It probably didn't matter who.

"I will shoot you!" Tom knew now he would. He would and he could. The dread had turned into an enjoyable kind of control. Just one ally had made all the difference. Without that ally, Tom would have been terrified. "Ok, Sam, let's do some thinking here."

"John, take the fucking gun!" Vernon tried to dominate.

"Sam, what say we ride out, and leave these two for Sheriff Ramey?"

"God damn, Tom, we'll go plant one on at the St. Charles, and they'll all be waiting for these turkeys to walk out in the morning. No, heck, they'll be closed. No problem, we'll drink up the three six packs I brought!"

"Wait a minute, Sam. You can't leave us down here!" Vernon was sobering up too.

"We could go get Eldridge, over in Alleghany, plenty of time." Tom almost laughed.

"You son of a ..., if I ever see you alone...," John didn't sound so sure of himself now. "Vernon, we gotta get out. I'm not staying here!"

"Shut-up John. Don't panic. TAKE THE FUCKING GUN!" Tom pulled the pistol out of the holster and clicked the hammer back with his thumb, keeping it pointed down.

"Jesus Christ! Wait a minute, Tom! Hold you horses! Nothing is going on! These boys are going home!" Sam was panicking now, but Tom felt so calm.

"Are you sure that you want them in your car again? You'll be Ok?"

"I'll be Ok. We just tied one on. We're going home."

"I just want to make sure you get home Ok, Sam."

"Sam will be Ok. We're going home. Get in, John." Vernon ordered, and John got into the back seat.

"Sam, I want you to call Darcy early, please. Set your alarm. I want to tell her and Bill Rutledge to drive down here and let me know that you got home alright. Otherwise, I'm coming out and going straight to Sheriff Ramey's office. Oh, and Sam, if you need work, I need hands."

"Thank you, Tom. I will. Keep your mouth shut, Vernon!"

That late night sleep was so sound and comfy for Tom, and he decided to sleep late in the morning. Nothing could go wrong now, nothing! Darcy and Bill arrived around twelve-thirty, and they had brought sandwiches and sodas, so it was a regular picnic day, with plenty of jokes thrown in about Vernon's morning after hangover and state of mind. Bill had told his crew to make it a workday without him, but not before enlightening them of the hilarious details Sam had mentioned about Vernon's new escapade. Soon, it would be all over the hills, and it was definitely going to move Tom up a notch in the social order, but he still worried that Vernon or John might try something even more desperate.

Then Darcy had to start up again, "Tom, there's no reason for you to stay. You can come in with the next crew. Come home with me, please!"

"Yeah, Tom, you really shouldn't be here alone." Bill sympathized.

"I need to watch the equipment, in case it rains. There are a lot of things I can do down here. There'll be a crew here pretty quick. Otherwise, I might start inviting some flatlanders up!" This did not get a chuckle from either of them. Tom feared so much that if he came out, Dan might just decide to pull out. But, Darcy was so unhappy; it was hurting him to have to stick to this. "Stick with me a little longer, princess. Please. How are you guys doing?" He looked at Bill.

"Moving around a lot. I might be on the wrong ground," he had to admit. "Well, it's all a gamble. Tom might be right."

"Alright Prince Tom," she tried to smile. "I guess I can't baby you forever."

That was so hard, watching them drive up that road without him. He was probably going to be alone again tonight. Maybe several nights. 'This is ridiculous. I'm not sitting all day at these picnic tables. I'm going to get something done.' He promised Dan he wouldn't start the dredge up till a crew came down. Well, a crew had come down. Tom went to get his wetsuit, and headed for the boat, almost at the same time Bill pulled to a stop.

"As I remember, there's a triangle intersection of road here, and we can get back out the other way. I haven't been on this road for ages. Let's just take a look."

"Why?" Darcy asked, "We'll get lost."

"There used to be a cabin up here, Darcy."

TWENTY FIVE

It's funny how noises can play tricks, especially along a river. So much quiet, so much riffle of water noise, and noise travels underwater. Tom started the air compressor motor, but not the dredge, and dived to have a look around. He started by picking up all the loose rock in the work area. The basket cables that went to a dead man pulley across the river came out of the trench at an angle, not quite following the trench, but allowing the winch operator to work an empty basket back to the worksite without pulling it out of the trench. Tom wondered if the cables coming out of the water were making the strange noise he was hearing underwater. Almost like laughter. Gurgling laughter at a distance. Almost like an old woman. It was too spooky, and he came up and started the dredge just to drown out the noise.

After two hours of work, he realized the hose had lost some of its pulling power. Of all the things to happen. Nothing could go wrong, but it did. The Chevy V-8 was running rough, so Tom pulled the spark plug wires one at a time. This determined that the right hand engine head was the culprit. Probably a burnt valve or two, so it was time to let the engine cool and pull the head. There was enough light left, he had plenty of time to get it off, and he lay it on the table and started dinner. He could picture Darcy and Agnes at the supper table. 'Don't be such a weakling,' he thought. 'You could be having it a lot worse than this.' But it was a miserable dinner alone.

At four-thirty Tom was awake, and after some coffee, he headed out to Grass Valley to look for a used engine head. He could afford it out of his own pocket, and Dan could pay him back later. This would make a good impression on the boss. At the Highway 49 intersection, he stopped to consider the possibility of going back for Darcy, just to make a day trip for her, but he talked himself out of it. 'I might have to go past Grass Valley. I might have to do a lot of calling. There isn't time.' And he headed on. One of the Grass Valley junk yards called a yard in Auburn for him, and it was late in the afternoon when he finally purchased the head. So it was more practical to just drive to Downieville than to navigate that dirt road after dark.

"Why didn't you come and get me? I would have loved to have spent the day down there. We could have seen a movie."

"Awe, it was just a lot of driving around. I doubt you would have liked sitting by a junk yard for an hour at a time."

"Tom, when did you notice the motor was bad?"

"When we dredged; why?"

"You didn't say anything about it yesterday. Did you start the dredge up after we left?"

"Yes, but just to see what was wrong with the motor."

"And you didn't dive any?"

"No, of course not. I needed to get the engine working, for when the next crew comes down." This is the first serious lie he had told her. It was like a little wedge nailed in the rift between them that this project had started, but it was for good cause. It was for their future.

"Tom, why don't you just stay out for a three day weekend? You're just wasting gas for just one day."

"It's a work day, princess. Didn't I remember you telling the prince that he needed to get to work, so that bills can be paid, and bosses impressed, that second day I went to work with Ray? Of course, I won't really be working tomorrow, but just in case..." That was the perfect comeback, he thought. She would have to eat her own words, to go against that.

Friday morning down the steep section of dirt road, Tom wasn't expecting any surprises, driving slow and carefully, but the universe is always ready to deliver the unexpected. Just past a dead pine that obscured part of the view, came something big running straight down the mountain so fast he couldn't determine what it was until it got close. The adrenaline was surging as Tom hit the brakes and skidded to a bad spot, one wheel almost off the mountain road. A huge dog, bigger than either of Bill's, a Great Dane or something, jumped off the hillside and bounced like a deer to slam its paws against his door, as its fanged head came through the open window while it stood on the sideboard, and Tom ducked to the right, his feet still tight against the brake and clutch, fearing that he might go off. "Aah!" As he scrunched further down, the jaws close to his left arm. "Arouff!" The monsters head came close again, and Tom got licked on the arm.

"Get out! Get the hell out!" Funny how terror and anger can sometimes mix together, and the person experiencing these two emotions at the same time can find himself unable to control either of them. "You stupid, God damned, shit for brains, son of a bitch!" Tom killed the engine and put on the emergency brake. Had the dog actually attacked him, he probably would not have been able to muster such ferocity, he now realized. As he flung the door open, the big dog backed off, head and tail lowered way down, head moving side to side. "Look what you did to me! Look at my front wheel! I almost went off!"

"Arouff!" Half the volume of last time. "Jesus, dog!" 'What next on this mountain?' Tom thought. "I'm sorry I yelled at you, but, damn it, you…," as he walked over and petted him on the head. The dog was a pussy cat, but one that weighed well over a hundred pounds. "You're lost. Who are you looking for way down here?"

Almost as if he understood, the dog ran a ways up the road, then turned and looked at Tom with sad eyes. Is he just a stray dog, or a dog on a mission, looking for help for his master? That thought was very disconcerting, considering the way the last week had gone. "You want something to eat?" And then, "I'm talking to a dog!" He reached in the cab and pulled out the lunchbox with the two sandwiches that Darcy had fixed. Seeing that he was being offered food, the dog was right back, and wolfed one sandwich like it was a cookie. "You must be hungry, huh? So where are you going?" The dog's eyes still begged, and Tom pulled out the other sandwich. "Alright, you get this sandwich if you get up here. You can't get in my cab." It was an easy jump for the dog to get on the bed of the truck, but there was no gate to put up between the wood and the steel side rails. "You stay here. We're going to camp." Suddenly, Tom had a very positive thought concerning the dog. He would give this dog to Bill Rutledge. 'Hah, now you're thinking like Vernon. Looking for alliances, aren't you. But, four legged instead of two!' It was a humorous thought, but, it might be practical. Tom could walk to Bill's front door from now on without having to fear the wrath of Rodger Dodger. He saw this dog as an escort, a new ally. About two hundred feet down the road he heard the dog jump, and by the time he was able to stop and get out, the dog was way up the road and still running. "I can't turn around!" he yelled. The communication gap here could prove to be serious if there was a human out there in need of help, but he had no choice but to drive on to camp, as there were no turnarounds now. "Hell, he'll come back down; he knows where the food is."

At the parking landing sat an old beat up thirties model Ford truck, and Jim Sandborn was sitting at the tables. Tom had halfway expected to see Joe Randolf, since he had accidentally shorted him out of the last evening's dinner, but he was glad to see anyone. Anyone but Vernon or John. "Are you ready to go back to work?" Jim nodded a slight no, but with the expression of sympathy and concern.

"I need some money, Tom, and I thought that you might be interested in something. I'll take twenty dollars for it, and that is a good deal." Jim pulled a small pistol from his front pants, under his un-tucked in shirt, and handed it to Tom. It looked so much like Agnes' old break down five shot pistol. It was a five shot brake down of the same era, and it was loaded.

"What caliber is it? Where did you get it?"

"I don't know what caliber, Tom. I just bought it. I got it from, uh, from kinfolk, and now I need money. I thought of you first because, well, it's a good gun to keep concealed, just in case someone gets the drop on you. Everyone knows about Vernon." He grinned. "I lost my respect for that idiot. A derringer is better than this, but this works, and I need some money."

"Thank you, Jim. Twenty sounds fair, and I think I could use this. It would make me feel safer." Twenty was too much, the gun was not a name brand, but Tom knew Jim was poor, and it wasn't worth haggling over. "You want to stay for lunch?" Jim nodded no, and walked with his two tens back to the Ford.

"Thanks. I'll sure send someone down, if I run across anyone."

'That's strange!' Tom thought. 'It couldn't possibly be Agnes's.' The two peanut butter and jelly sandwiches he fixed fell far short of the turkey, ham, Swiss cheese, tomato, lettuce and mayonnaise sandwiches Darcy fixed. 'Dang it dog! You ate my sandwiches. Now get back down here!' He thought. 'Nothing is going right this week.' His stomach was still in a knot as he started up the dredge. 'One more day of work, and I'm off for the weekend.'

He was being extremely cautious of everything down under. It was inefficient, having to stop dredging and remove the rocks someone else was supposed to be removing, but it was working. He had to remember to come up at intervals to check the sluice box and make sure it wasn't loaded with rock. If he could just get some bedrock in the trench uncovered, he might see some gold. Instead, he saw something that proved to be a ghoulish ending to a strange week. Just some bones, he thought at first, of some animal. But when a human skull came into view, he had to stop. 'I feel like going to go and get Lou and Bill and going to the bar.' The skull was partially crushed from the weight of the over burden, by there was a clear bullet hole in one side. This wasn't like the movies where the cowboy get's shot and falls from his horse, and you know it's just an actor. This was saddening, and sickening.

'The Coroner isn't going to worry about it, I'm sure. It's ancient. Oh no! They'll want to give him a proper burial. That will screw up this operation for a while. Why bother. No one will ever find out who he was. Just let it ride.' That left a little tinge of guilt, but he was too exasperated with everything. 'What about the bones in the sluice? They'll just ride out and get buried, and you can pick the few pieces left out. What if a crew comes now? Then just get it done, quick.'

Tom picked up a rock and smashed the skull again and again, until it was beyond recognition. Quickly, he dredged up the remains, but now, twice the shock. Another skeleton, with fragments of clothing. He started to uncover a bigger area, panicky that someone would come down and catch him. There were four skeletons, the last a female, no doubt, with such short, thin bones, and such a female, noble looking little skull. 'Probably a pretty woman,' he theorized. 'Oh shit, I feel rough.' As if he shared in some of the guilt the perpetrators would have been glad to share. Four people, summarily executed, and then their bodies laid into the trench. Probably at some time that most of the workers would not have been aware. And what had it been over? There was no doubt in this place.

When he finally came up it was getting dim. All the bones he could see in the sluice were picked out, as well as two belt buckles. Now he would have to make some excuse for being late. He would have to lie again.

"Do you know who owns a Great Dane around here?" He asked Darcy, first off.

"Why are you late?"

"Because of a dog; I was driving out, and this huge dog was on the road, acting like it was upset, you know, like it wanted help. At least, that's what I thought." This was a lie, and it was the truth. Darcy looked at him like it was too strange to believe. "I tried to get it to come out with me, and it ran off. I hate to think it has a master somewhere who is in trouble, but it's probably just a stray. This has been one rotten week, and I can't wait to be done with this job. Gimme a kiss!" As they hugged and kissed, Tom said, "I'm so tired of this place, Darcy. I wish Bill would get into some gold. One more week like last week and I'll be ready to quit." It was really how he felt.

"Don't tease me. I'll ask around about the dog. Tom, something has happened here while you were gone this week. We're not sure when, but Agnes thinks her window was jimmied."

"Was something stolen?"

"The only thing that appears to be missing is her little pistol. She says all her valuables are safe. She thinks Vernon may have done it, because of what happened, but that is only a theory. Why would he just take that, and no jewelry or money? Well, maybe it wasn't hidden well enough. That sort of thing doesn't happen around here very often. She's not reporting it, but she is concerned."

"Thankfully they got no valuables." 'I'll bet she suspects me, and I may actually have the pistol. If that isn't strange! Should I report Jim? Oh hell, I'm just going to think on it, and make sure no one sees me with it down there.' He had hidden it under his mattress for quick retrieval. "Well, no more jokes about stealing her pistol!"

TWENTY SIX

After Sunday evening dinner, Darcy excused herself to drive over to her friend Janet's place to visit and help with a sick child. Tom was helping Agnes remove dinner dishes from the table, and she said, "I need to have a serious talk with you." When they went to sit in the living room, she continued, "I'm really very impressed with what you've been doing down there, Tom. You've managed to keep the thing going after all that's happened, and that shows you are capable of some tenacity, and we like to see that in a person. You see, I've been talking to some acquaintances of mine about you. Some very important people. I'm sorry; I forgot we have apple pie for desert. Darcy left in such a rush, and I forgot to offer it. Should we eat some while we talk?"

"Sure." Said Tom.

"Tom. I know I haven't always been as…, as courteous with you as I should have been in the past, and I'd like to take this time to say that lately, you have really impressed me. You know that my daughter's future and well being is all that is on my mind most of the time, and sometimes, I admit, I'm a little irritable."

'What an understatement!' "That's alright, Agnes."

"I'm going to tell you about an organization I belong to, one that traces back with my ancestry to Scotland."

"Like Masons or something?"

"No, just a little more secretive than the Masons. We call ourselves the Society, and we have another name that only the member's use."

"Are you talking about, like a cult? A secret society?"

"Cult is not a good word for us, but yes, a secret society. We are dedicated to the principle of success and advancement for all members of the Society, and we are considering you as a potential member. My great grandfather Dunlevy, came down this canyon in 1850, and brought with him the invitation to other members to settle this area. We have quite a few members up and down the Sierra now, some of English and some of Irish chapter ancestry. When my great grandfather saw what was going on in this canyon, he made a resolution, one that he was able to achieve. He resolved to amass a fortune off the Rush, and he was determined to never have to pick up a tool and do any manual labor to do it. He felt that sort of thing is beneath people of his carriage and breeding, and he was right. He became one of the most successful entrepreneurs in the canyon, but he did not do it without the help of the Society, and a loyalty to the principles that make it possible for the members to succeed. At times, he had to be ruthless, by that was necessary." That chilled him right to the bone. "Let me explain something about competition. Competition always goes to the advantage of those that are intelligent enough to work together as a team, and the team always works to the advantage of each individual of that team."

"Of course. That's what we were doing down there before everyone quit."

"We take things a little farther than that. You see, we are dedicated to the principle that only a few people in this world are of importance to the well being of the Society, and the advancement of these few people must be accomplished at any cost. Every society has its cream, and we like to think of ourselves as that portion of this society. Suppose someone came to town and put up a business in competition with yours. It would not be long before this non-member would be forced to pull up stakes and move on."

"Even if they sold a better product?"

"You don't seem to be envisioning the power of a secret society. Things would be done, time and again. Accidents would happen. Sooner or later the fools would move on. Of course, they could be ridiculously tenacious, but then someone would meet with an unfortunate accidental death, if that became necessary. We always win."

That sent a chill of dread through Tom. There was no way he wanted to have anything to do with these people. "Let me tell you something about what I think was the most orderly, well run society in history: the Aztec Empire. The Aztecs ran their country by the standards that we of the Society greatly admire, and we hold their principles to be those that we will someday run this country by. We all know the Aztecs had no wheels. Even the Egyptians had wheels. So to some, the Aztecs weren't so smart. Actually, they knew just how things should be run. Every man in their culture knew his place. He knew exactly what he needed to be doing to help keep that society running. And he knew that if he stepped out of line, just once, he would be put to death. The wheel was of no use to that society; it would cause the same problems that automation always causes, it would put people out of work. Therefore, I believe the Aztecs priest's in their wisdom simply forbad it. Every man worked to the benefit of the society, and every man shared in the glory of his society as a whole, the pageantry and the lavish religious ceremonies. In other words, the common man was not allowed ambition. Ambition was the sole property of the state. And, oh, what an example of the evil of letting the common man think he can be ambitious can be attributed to this country we live in. Someday, this ridiculous farce will come undone, and when it does, the Society will be ready to pick up the pieces."

Tom hated hearing this, but she was going to be his mother-in-law, so he would try and sit through this. "If you want to read an example of what ambition does to the common man, just read something about the old mining town of Bodie."

"I heard about it from Lou and others. It sounded like a rough place to be."

"I doubt that you would have survived long, not without some backing. But you must see what I am trying to say here, Tom, not to put you down, but without the help of the right people in this world, you will never really get ahead. A few, very few people, can progress their culture, but most of the common people are expendable, and tend to bring down the society a whole. I don't want you end up on that side of the equation." There was, unfortunately, a degree of logic in what she had pointed out about the mining town of Bodie. Bodie, along with other mining towns of the old west, was not a good example of the mixing of the common man and ambition. There always seemed to be too many men and too little gold, and human life often became a devalued commodity. But, to towns of the old west had eventually come the principle, at least, of law and order. The principle by which Lou, Bill, and Sheriff Ramey lived. This principle, when applied, should allow the common man some right to his own ambition, Tom believed. "Just look up in the sky some clear evening after a cold snap. Look and see how many stars you see, and then you'll see more and more, and they just don't stop appearing. Think of everyone of those stars as being some man's ambition. There isn't enough room for that much ambition. During the 'New Deal' they had a saying: 'a chicken in every pot and a car in every driveway'. What a ridiculous promotion by ignorant, foolish governmental bureaucrats. A chicken in every pot? Yes, in the Aztec society. A car in every driveway? The most absurd promise ever made! This great society is headed for a terrific fall, and these enticements to the common man will only intensify the letdown he must suffer. The best thing that can be done for the common man is to kill all ambition in him, so that he understands his true place in society. And as for gold, well, gold is not for any human. Not even the priests. In the perfect society, all gold was placed in a room ordained for the Gods. No man would dare touch that gold, not even a priest; and thus that society was made safe from the most dangerous emotion humans can experience, ambition."

"They wouldn't have thought much of your beliefs in the Gold Rush days."

"They would have simply laughed me off as a foolish old woman, and that's fine. I still would have had the power of the Society behind me. You are now going to have to do some serious thinking. If you are accepted, and you decide to join, it will be for life, Tom. You must understand that for us the highest ideal of every member is our discipline. It is the code by which we achieve our power, and the framework that holds us together. If you join, Tom, we will make sure that you succeed throughout your life. But I must warn you, I must tell you a story from the past, so that you will fully understand what our discipline is about. Bill Rutledge had, I believe, an uncle that disappeared some time before the turn of the century."

"He has a lithograph about that incident." Said Tom.

"The young man who disappeared was a member of the Society, and unfortunately, he broke with our discipline. None of the Rutledge's have been invited to join us since then. You see, he was ordered not to marry the woman he was engaged to." Tom did not like the direction of this at all. He could guess what was coming. "It was determined that she would not make a good Society member. He was given a deadline to call off the marriage, and unfortunately, he did not take that order seriously enough. He was executed."

'God Almighty!' Tom thought. 'What kind of vile, heartless people could do something like that? The same kind that put those four people in the trench, no doubt.' Agnes sat for a moment in silence, letting it sink in. Ambition was an ironic word for Agnes to use, he thought. He could visualize now the discord between her and Bob, her wanting to move to Modesto to be with her friends of a better class, probably Society members, and him just wanting to stay in his little hometown, with his far less ambitious lifestyle. It suddenly occurred to him, he saw the truth as plain as day. "He wouldn't join, would he? Bob kept you here in Downieville, and you never forgave him for that." It was true, no doubt, she could not mask her expression now, but she also gave away the hurt of how she missed him, as well. There were almost tears. "What do you think Bill would think of you if he ever learned about his uncle?"

"He would not despise me any more than he already does. That is of no concern to me. He loves my daughter, they both do. And as for that poor young man, I have to say that I would have been completely against that. I think a whipping would have been plenty sufficient. But, understand, in the end, discipline is the absolute necessity."

"Then understand me!" Tom did not himself realize how intense he had now become. The look in his eyes would have startled even himself in the mirror, as he walked up to the woman to get close eye contact. "You had better never do anything, not EVER, to come between me and your daughter. Your Society friends will not help you, I guarantee you!" For the first time since he had met her, he saw a look of fear; he had punched through that mask of confidence and made her realize that she was, among other things, just an old woman. She had to side step him as she bolted for her room. 'God, what have I done now?' he thought.

Down the dirt road Monday morning, casually, not motivated, not enthused, Tom stopped at the intersection just before the steep part down, and decided to take a detour in Dan's flatbed truck. Something to do; perhaps he would see the dog. About a quarter of a mile in he saw the other part of the triangle intersection, presumably heading back to camp. A little further on, a cabin came into view, less than a hundred feet from the road. Tom got out to search for antiques, something Darcy loved to do. The roof was still intact, with some shingles partially missing, and it seemed inside the three room house that there had been very little leakage. Two beds, a dresser drawer, and some utensils still in the kitchen. Lots of cobwebs, but perhaps, someone could come back, at some time. He drove on, and took a fork to the right. 'Don't get lost', he thought. This was getting too steep and rain damaged, and he needed to turn around.

Finally, down by a creek, a turnaround. Just beyond, a rotted tree felled across the road. The pine was small enough and rotted dry, and he walked it away from the stump, and then walked on a little further just to look. Down the hill in a boggy area full of willows and thickets, sat a Model T, almost on its side. Someone had wrecked. Or was the tree felled to keep people from getting this far? He almost went down to take a look, but decided to head to work. As he turned back, a very familiar sight to his north, at the highest ground. The Sugar Pine with the long high limb that pointed east. There was no mistaking it, and it was only half a mile or so away. Camp was very close to this spot. Maybe less than a mile. Driving out he took the new intersection, and got safely back to the main dirt road, about the same time Darcy pulled up to the cabin.

Dredging was aggravating as hell with no back up. Monotonous. 'Remember, Tom, the sand is unstable, all around. Keep twice as alert!' More and more and more sand. He checked the sluice to see if it was tilting down from overloading, but apparently it was handling it. At the head of the trench, something didn't look right. An overhead was forming; the clay and gravel layer wasn't coming down like it should. It seemed now a matter of undermining it. 'That's dangerous, Tom, with no one to watch you. Watch yourself!' It was obviously getting too steep, and he pulled the nozzle back and began to gather rock. He made several trips, closer to the wall each time, always so cautious. He did not realize that momentum a cave in was capable of. When it came for him, he could slightly hear the noise, as he pushed back and dropped rock, but it was so fast, and he was flailing as it caught up with him. Wave after wave of sand, and some rock and gravel. When it stopped, he was buried up to his waist. He was so angry. 'Hell, Tom, how could you let this happen?' Aggravation, but also something else. A little fear now? He tried flailing, pushing and jostling his legs. It was working a little. 'It's alright, keep calm, and just work yourself out of it.' And then, he saw the end of the boulder sticking out above, sitting on the ramp of sand that would deliver it to bury him. A fair sized boulder, maybe a thousand pounds, and deep blue black colored. And it was moving! Was it really moving? A trickle of sand coming out from under it. Like the rock that got Erick, it was taking its time. Tom flailed frantically. 'Don't vomit in your regulator! Oh God! Oh God! Don't vomit in your regulator!' Spasms of fear through his legs, sapping his energy, and every animal cell in his body screamed.

The thought of what he had done with those four skeletons made this horror unbearable. Darcy would be sleeping with somebody else, after the grieving. And they would be making sad comments in town about the fool who dredged alone. Now the rock was obviously starting to slide. 'Oh God! Oh God! Oh God!' Trapped, more sand coming, for what progress he had made. And then he realized he still had his weight belt on, and he could reach the buckle through the sand. Sand was coming faster, but he was jerking and pushing with adrenaline strength, his teeth tight on the regulator and his arm pit holding the air line, and he was coming out. Now his knees appeared, and whomp, the boulder was there just as he launched out and shot to the surface. "Oh good God Almighty! Oh Lord!" He pulled himself onto the dredge and shut the engine down, to sit for a time.

"Stupid! Stupid! Stupid! That's it!" He yelled to the universe in general. "I'm going home. To hell with this place!" And as he rode the boat back to the bank, still shaking, he thought simply, 'Dave would have died. I could not blame any man for running away from that.'

Tom sat for forty five minutes at the picnic tables, and then finally got out of his wetsuit. 'Go home, and lay in Darcy's arms. Just give up!' But he had to consider every angle. 'How do you tell Dan how his dredge hose got buried in the sand? Hell, just tell the truth.' He wanted to go back up the road so badly. But he remembered his accusation to Dave, calling him a deserter, and decided to sleep on it down there.

That night was a strange sleep, so deep, so peaceful, as if all the minds troubles and fears had been laid to rest. He dreamed he was falling, but in no danger. Falling into a place where there was nothing to hit, and he felt the presence of a kind female entity who sought to accompany him. In the morning, he seemed to feel completely rested and regenerated. He just had to look at the trench, and he paddled the boat out and looked over the side with his diving mask. The hose was buried in the sand, but the boulder was not on top of it. What would be necessary for Dan to retrieve his hose? 'I'll do it. I'll do him that favor.' Tom got his wetsuit on, started the air motor, and pulled a winch cable and a 15 foot of chain to the boulder. He was able to wrap the chain around the far end of the boulder by digging a little sand with his foot and hooked it, and then he came up and winched the rock about twenty feet. Diving back down, he wrapped the winch cable around part of the hose and hooked it. Back to the winch again, but it wouldn't budge. He was afraid that he would break the cable or hose, so he started up the dredge to try and pull some of the sand out of the hose. He tugged, and waited, tugged again, and it moved a little. After fifteen minutes, he had gotten the hose out, and he was exulting. "So what's your problem? Going to look for a new job?" he yelled. "Hell no; it's time to dredge!" He would never again be able to look Darcy in the face and say anything about her fear of water. It was like when Erick had caught his jay bird on the table; a sacred trust seemed to have been broken. He would never again take his life for granted. 'Hell, Tom, you're not a virgin any more!' Darcy would probably not appreciate this grim bit of humor. "About this, she must never know!" But as for this operation, the one that he was ready to walk away from yesterday? Tommy was now invincible.

Darcy and Janet spent Monday and Tuesday cleaning up the cabin, Ray and Dave Morrow worked all day

Wednesday on the roof. Thursday Darcy delivered almost all of Tom's clothing and possessions, with a suitcase of her own, a mattress and sheets, pillows, a blanket, a lantern, a Coleman stove, all utensils she needed, two ice chests stocked and a box of canned food. Friday she would drive back down to get Tom and demand that he spend nights there with her.

Tuesday afternoon Tom started the dredge up and talked himself into diving. He waited an hour past lunch time, just in case a crew came down. He would be so careful now. And if another overhang appeared, he would deal with it from above, like he should have done the first time. Right in the middle of his line of attack, a rotten tree trunk appeared, pointing straight up. Or was it a trunk? As he got it uncovered it became evident it was flat, hand hewn timber, with the bark still left on two sides, about eighteen inches in diameter. A flume leg! What if? Tom felt a little guilty about the thought. What if someone left something un-worked, on purpose, to come back to later? Could these people have died because of that? To keep them quiet? What a grim hope, he realized. Like those lost treasures that always involve some sad homicide. It took him an hour to dredge down to the base, sand slipping in all over, and there he found a two foot by two foot, six inch high wooden block, the flume leg nailed to it with huge square nails of the early era, and the block in turn actually nailed with spikes to the bedrock. With some effort, he pushed the timber off its base and laid it down in the trench. It was still early, but he would quit for the day. It might be time to go looking for Dan, Carl, Dave, Jim and Erick, if possible, to spend a night at the bar reveling in defeat. He figured he had proven the hole; proven it to be barren. As in the case of a dry well in the oilfield, it could be foolish to keep throwing money into it. It also seemed he had proven something to himself that meant so much right now, despite the failure to find gold. He had stuck it out to the end. 'Wait a minute', he thought. 'What about the other leg'. One more night on the claim, he reasoned, but he was oh, so tired of it.

After a late breakfast and slow start Wednesday, Tom resolved to uncover some higher overburden to look for the top of the other leg, and this meant walking in sand, so he had to keep his legs in almost continuous movement, to keep from sinking. It was a good two hours before he found the top of the other flume leg fifteen feet away. Another half an hour and something unexpected appeared as the leg was uncovered. Was it a board sticking out? Tom's heart was pounding now. It wasn't a board. It was another block, even bigger than the first one, and it was a good four feet higher than the bottom of the trench. Their method of fluming had involved replacing legs on one at a time with either extensions or longer legs as overburden was removed. Tom was almost yelling underwater, shaking, almost like he had done when he was pinned. 'Did you leave something? Oh hell yes, you had to leave me something.' He pulled the hose back and began working where the first leg had been. Two hours later, he hit the hard pack. Exhausted, but still excited, he was now looking at rich virgin placer gold, the way that nature had laid it in! The hard pack was gray and black, and black manganese staining left many rocks with a sooty encrustment, but there was gold visible almost everywhere. Fine gold, mostly, but there were nuggets showing up. After Tom had rolled a boulder over, of about a hundred and fifty pounds, five nuggets shown in the depression in the clay. One was easily four ounces. In the crystal clear water with the afternoon sunlight it seemed like he might be looking at some kind of museum display.

It was surrealistic the way the gold shown in the gravel and clay. Tom just gobbled, and gobbled some more. 'Jeeze, the box!' He had gone too long without checking to see that the box wasn't overloading. The dredge was obviously tilting down, and he pulled off his mask and hood, then his wetsuit top, as it was very hot above water, and began tossing rock out of the sluice, careful not to throw a quartz rock that might contain gold. Heavy material of several kinds was dropping into the box, iron rock, magnetite and hematite, and a blue rock that was exceptionally heavy. As he uncovered the build up, he saw a beautiful pattern of gold with blue and black rock laying in the riffles, nuggets by the hundreds! A sight few people have ever seen. "Hell, yeah!" He screamed. "Hell, yeah!" And the echo could be heard a quarter mile downstream.

Finally, Tom realized how foolish dredging in the dark was. He came up and let the dredge run for a while, and tossed as much rock as the light would allow. Stuck without a flashlight, he was able to navigate the boat in the twilight, landing in the wrong spot, and having to pull it back upriver. A supper of ham and cheese sandwiches proved slightly hard to digest, and it would take some time to come down from this state of emotion he was in. At two in the morning, he was still awake, his 357 pistol at the ready by his side. There were too many things to be done.

By six thirty Thursday morning, he finished breakfast, and took a camp shovel and pick with him up the mountainside past the outhouse. 'Not too far.' He reasoned. 'Gold is heavy.' Behind an old, wide live oak he started picking at the rocky ground, removing and hiding all the large rock. This would take some time, he could see, so for a diversion he dropped the tools and went to the wooden tree cabinets that some fisherman had built near the tables to retrieve four sixteen ounce coffee cans. There was a box in camp with quite a few of the cans, and that was divine providence, he thought. Out to the dredge to start picking. It might be monotonous after a while, even with gold, but right now it was so much fun! Under the jet opening, right at the front of the sluice, sat a long knurly slug of gold. He couldn't imagine how he missed it down under, and he realized that there might be one even bigger sitting somewhere in the hose. It felt like two pounds, and as for what was in the rest of the box, there seemed no end to it. Fine gold lay thick with black sand all the way to the end of the sluice. This meant that they would have to re-dredge the tailings at this spot, just to make sure.

By two in the afternoon, Tom had two of the cans half full, lying in the four by four foot pit that he'd dug, and several old plywood boards on hand to cover them. Back at the dredge, he suddenly stopped picking, looked downriver, saw nothing, and started again. Something didn't feel right. He looked again. Maybe an animal was watching him. A cold shiver, just to think how many people would kill him without hesitation for what lay in that sluice. 'God, what if Vernon came down?' Next time he would bring his pistol to the dredge.

By eight thirty, three half full cans were buried under the boards and dirt. Tom used a tree branch to smooth out the dirt as much as possible, and then tossed some leaves and twigs down. Should he go home now or sit one more night? Should he take some gold with him? He didn't need to run into the wrong people, and he decided to go early morning and take no gold. Tight lips now, that was mandatory. What a celebration to be had! Dan and Carl and their wives, Darcy and Agnes, Rene and who knows who else. Dave will want to dredge now, and so will Jim. And Tom will give Erick and Ardell a cup of nuggets. 'Fifty percent' Tom thought. 'That's the deal. Fifty percent of that is mine!' It was going to be the second most fantastic day of his life, digging those cans up while Darcy watched.

He slept badly, got off late, and headed up Friday morning at eight o'clock, way later than he had planned. At ten-ten he stopped at the Quartz to use the pay phone. "Hello, Jesse? This is Tom Hendrick. I need to speak to Dan."

"Dan is away right now, Tom. He's gone to Bakersfield on business. We own an oil well, and there was a problem. He should be back in two weeks, maybe even less."

'Unreal. He's given up on getting a crew' Tom thought. 'How can I get him back?' "Jesse, I need to speak to him about a serious problem on the claim. Can you get him to call at some specific time?"

"That takes money, Tom, long distance. I can relay a message next time he calls." Agnes was right, she really was a dip. She just wanted to know everything. "You know, Tom, you're not really supposed to be down there. Dan has more important things to attend to."

'You can go to Bill', Tom thought. 'This is ridiculous, Bill can help clean box and transport the gold. Don't waste your time with this dip. If you tell her, Dan is liable to be the last one to hear about the gold, and you'll have a stampede of nosy people down there.' "Jesse, Dan is going to be very angry that he didn't get this call." And he hung up before she could reply.

The Chevy was at the house, but when he unlocked the front door and yelled for Darcy, almost running, he found that house empty. Agnes was on her knees troweling a flower bed out back, soused already. She rarely drank before noon, but now she was hammered. "Well, Hello stranger."

"Agnes, I have to find Darcy and Bill, I have…,"

"No you don't! What you have to do is listen to me. Some things have changed around here while you were gone." Agnes was wearing a mean grin. "You're in for a big surprise."

He didn't like the tone of her voice, and he didn't want to have to deal with it, so he walked to the bedroom and fell back onto the bedspread. 'Take your time, think things through. I can wait for Darcy, or I can call Bill.' He looked up at the dresser, and something was wrong. His shaving kit was missing, but he looked in Darcy's jewelry box and everything was fine. 'A burglary, again?' He opened the first drawer of the dresser and found it empty. First and forth drawers were his, the others were Darcy's. Had he looked in the smaller dresser, he would have seen some of his clothes and underwear, but the two big drawers were empty, and Darcy's still seemed to have a fair amount of clothes. His two suitcases were gone from the closet. "Agnes, what the hell is going on?" An old woman's laughter can sometimes be downright cruel. 'What the hell is going on? I'll call Bill. Bill will know where she is, and I'll tell him about the gold.'

Bill's tone of voice didn't sound right, for some reason. "Tom, Darcy and Dave Morrow went looking down canyon for you. You should probably drive back down to meet them. She has something very important she wants to talk to you about, and the best place for her to say it is probably down there." Silence for too long. "Tom, are you with me?"

"Yes." 'Don't tell him about the gold, Tom. Find out what's going on.' "Thank you, Bill. I'll go meet them." 'I missed them on the highway, but they missed me too. I should have told Bill to come down. No, play it safe. I should call Mom.' No answer. After five minutes, still no answer. 'I should call Uncle Jack. No, he can't drive all the way out here. Hell, Tom just drive down there and meet Darcy. Just look her in the face and ask what's going on.'

Tom drove Dan's flatbed faster than he had ever driven it, running the yellow line and hitting dirt past the pavement, but he was able to remember where Dead Man's curve was. All the way down, he had to speculate, and there was only one logical conclusion: she was moving him out. Unless, Agnes had done it behind Darcy's back. No, there was something going on. That was obvious from the conversation with Bill. He had to consider the possibility that Darcy may have decided to break up with him. 'You shouldn't tell anyone up here about the gold. She would never do me this way, even if she decided to break up. She wouldn't just pack my bags. That's not her way. Man, you had better think this out! You had better think real hard on this. This could be the most serious day of your life.' That's all he could do, think about it.

TWENTY SEVEN

Dave had driven Darcy down Friday morning in his Dodge four door sedan around six, early enough to try and catch Tom at breakfast. He had spent the night at a friend's house in Downieville, partially in town for business reasons, and he had volunteered to take Darcy down that morning. He was curious to see the dredge operation, and expected a little thanks for his participation in the roof job. No one knew it someone still owned the cabin, but it was thought a little improvement wouldn't hurt anyone's feelings. They drove down the intersection to the cabin, just so Darcy could double check everything, and they just missed Tom as he drove out by five minutes. It was a severe disappointment to find him missing from the camp. She had planned it as a surprise; she wanted to get Tom to walk through the door of the cabin before telling him. Then they could spend the weekend there. There was a very serious reason for this. She had talked to Lynn and Bill about it, and also Janet. She a dread that Tom would make some excuse to not move up there with her. Perhaps he was now dredging alone. The rift that had grown between them over this project that Tom seemed obsessed with had Darcy suspicious of his every intention. She was dreading the moment, thinking how she would feel if he refused.

She asked Dave if she could drive them back out, and he reluctantly gave her permission. Just a quarter mile in the dirt road from Highway 49 was a circular turnout, and she stopped there in the shade of an oak, and they waited and speculated. About ten till two, Tom drove the flatbed up beside them and parked out of the way. It was time, Darcy thought, and her stomach was in a knot. "Thomas, please get in the car!" The tone was more stern and severe that he had ever heard her use with him.

"Darcy, I've got…,"

"Please!" The words he so wanted to say almost came to him, but it was obvious, something serious was about to be communicated. He would not mention the gold, not yet. "Not in the front seat!" Dave had started to get out to let Tom in as he walked around, and was as surprised as Tom to hear, "Dave has been working very hard with me on a project I have, and he is very tired. Please sit in the back." She had not planned it that way, but she did feel now that this might be a buffer to any arguments. Tom slowly got in the back seat of the four door car thinking, 'no hugs, no kisses, and I'm not allowed to sit by her!' "Tom, we're going to take a little drive down, and we, that is, I have some serious things I have to say to you. Some things are just going to have to change, and that's all there is to it."

'What about my clothes, and suitcases?' He thought, his stomach turning as well, a grim, almost hostile expression on his face. 'Why don't you demand an explanation? No! It's obvious an explanation is coming. Let it come in its time.'

Dave did not feel right with what was happening; he felt a tenseness here that was a far cry from the happy reunion he had expected. "Let's just head down Darcy, and we can tell him down there." That didn't come out quite right, and he was beginning to feel really strange with this situation. 'Yeah, tell me down there. Tell me all about it', Tom thought as she started the car, and he could tell she was avoiding eye contact, even in the rear view mirror.

'This isn't the way I had planned things,' Darcy thought. 'This isn't going right at all. The quicker we get to the cabin, the quicker I can make things right.' And so they drove, no casual conversation, no polite remarks, and no idea whatsoever by the two in the front seat of the new factor in this equation, the three coffee cans of gold buried by an old oak.

And now the man, the only man, he believed, that had knowledge of the gold, would have time to speculate. The rift had just gotten way bigger, and the communication necessary to close this rift had not been delivered. 'Thank God.' He thought, 'that I didn't tell anyone. That could have been a terrible mistake.' Just as in the case of Vernon's visit to the claim, the man believed he was now in need of an ally before he could make any sure moves. But who his allies were, at this point, was of question. The most trusted ally in his entire life, that is how he had perceived her. His lover, his buddy, his counsel for advice for two years, but now he was not sure. But he could speculate. Was he being run off the claim? Why would that be? Dave was a real estate man, and that would give him the expertise to handle mining claims transactions. Perhaps he was here to deliver some news. Dan was away, as if the operation wasn't that important anymore. Could he have sold it without telling Tom? Jesse said that Tom wasn't supposed to be down there. Did she mean that Darcy didn't want him down there, or did she neglect to tell Tom that the claim had been sold? Dan may have had to leave in such a rush that he didn't have time to tell Tom. And then a horrible thought came to Tom's mind. Darcy may have convinced Dan to sell to get Tom off the river. She may have such a dread for Tom's life that she was impelled to do it. 'But then why are you being moved out? If Darcy is so concerned for you, why are your suitcases packed?' Perhaps, Darcy wasn't as concerned as he would like to believe. Could she just decide to break up, sharp and quick, as some women do? Was she that kind? Was she so fed up with his obsession down there that she had decided to move on, and move him out? 'Darcy grabbed onto me in a time of desperation. Maybe she is one of those women that never seem to be able to settle down, never really learn to trust a man. Maybe what she is now doing is done out of desperation.' He had to grudgingly admit, that was a possibility. 'The man is always the last to know, Tom. You brought this on yourself, as far as she is concerned. That's how she sees it; you married this project and neglected her. That's ridiculous! In this short a time? That's not her way. Something here is deceitful. I need some real facts. Whatever has come between her and me, I can fix that. I can get that straightened out, but that will take time. As for the gold, there is no time. You should quit thinking about your relationship, and concentrate on the gold. Don't let your emotions influence you now. Understand, you will never again in your life have an opportunity like this. You had better make no mistakes here. What if you get down there and Dave tells you that you are off the claim? What are your legal rights to what you found?' He hadn't really ever expected to find that much gold; no man ever really does. Legal complications had never come into mind. 'Dan is an honest man, I believe that. He certainly wants his fifty percent of the gold. Oh God, if he sold the claim, he will have no more right to it than I will! The new owner will take possession, and I will have to fight a legal battle in court. I may have no legal right to it at all; Dan did not give me permission to dredge by myself! And if she is moving me out, I will have to move down valley to fight this. How could this have happened?' He could never have foreseen this. 'This place is cursed.'

Darcy caught a glimpse of Tom in the rear view mirror, his eyes so distraught, a stare that seemed like he could look right through anything, looking at nothing in particular. Like a man down and out sitting on a curb, with almost no motivation left, save the animal fear of death. She thought of just stopping and telling him, but no, she had planned the walk through the front door, and she must make it happen that way.

'Matt can come up with me later, and we can sneak the gold out' Tom thought. 'At least we could get it into court. What is it they say, possession is nine tenths of the law, and you don't as of this moment possess the gold. What do you think will happen if you tell the new owner, and that party forbids you to come back on the claim? They could say that there were only a few pounds of gold. You have no proof. You don't even know how much is down there right now!' The more the man thought about it, the more it seemed to box him into a corner. 'That's grand theft, if you and Matt sneak it off. You could go to jail for that. Perhaps, you should quit thinking so much in terms of legality; think in terms of only one final conclusion. The only thing that counts in the end is the legal possession of the gold. Justice and injustice are often a matter of debate, but not of practicality. In the end, when the court makes its decision, that's if it even gets to court, that will be all that really counts. You had better make the right decision this day! You will never get another chance like this!' Over and over and over again. Confusion and despair. And every thought seemed to be a negative one, there seemed no end to the logic that was stacking up against him.

Sometimes the mind works in such narrow, confined concentration that thoughts come quick and without consideration, and comments are made that make the speaker regret such un-thought out revelations. Dave had been thinking of something to help break the tension, to help get these two back to some normal conversation. "God, the expression on that woman's face, when she saw we were moving him out. I'll never forget that!" He almost laughed. It would have been perfect a moment after Tom walked in the cabin door, but it was now an extremely poorly timed remark, and it made both Darcy and Dave finally realize that Tom might have seen his clothes and suitcases were missing. Darcy gave Dave one of the most sever frowns he had ever seen on her, and he demanded, "Let's just tell him!"

"No, not yet. Not yet."

'Yeah, tell me about it down there. It doesn't matter. Tell me what you have to tell me, pencil pusher, real estate man. You don't know how mad I might get. You just don't know.' All the deep down rage, against Vernon, against the crew who deserted him, against his run of bad luck before the gold, was now welling up. And there was a new rage. The rage of a man who took the love of his woman for granted, and suddenly fears losing it. Everything she had ever done for him, every consideration, everything she gave him, he could not imagine living without. He had never really thought that he would ever lose this alliance. He did not want to go looking for another. It was outrageously unfair; he had not stopped working for their mutual success, their future. That was what this was all about. He had done it for her, as well as himself. And into his mind came an outrageous thought. 'You had better not be doing what I think you are doing, woman. And you, Dave, my so called friend. If you have helped to somehow take away my gold, you have for all practical purposes declared war on me!' And now an un-logical thought, but one that seemed to work its way into the scheme of the things. 'What if someone was watching you, the day you picked the gold out of the box?' He demanded of himself some proof, to be certain that what he buried was safe, but even that was now in question. He knew he needed to get the gold moved quickly, but he needed an ally to help him. Down the winding, rutted dirt road they drove, on the mission that was supposed to have brought Tom and Darcy closer together. And silence prevailed.

Tom was thinking of anything and everything. That trip past the cabin that day, down that old road, that was playing on his mind for some reason. And so was Connie's fathers business, and the rumors of what he had had to do to achieve success. What does it take in this world to achieve success? It takes an attitude. That's how Connie's father got to where he is at. But he was rumored to have run rough-shod over some people. Was that really what it took? It was an attitude that you would not allow anything to defeat you, and that no matter what the obstacle, you would not give up. You would never say defeat. That in itself seemed an admirable attitude, if you were running a business. That is what Tom had done to find this gold. But did that include being ruthless with some people? Was Connie's father just another Burt Dunlevy, or were rumors born of jealousy? And another thought of logic worked its way into Tom's mind, one that added immensely to his depression. A sequence of events that led him down that old road where he had seen the Model T in the creek bottom, almost hidden out of sight. He saw the three of them walking down the path to the river, to where the boat was tied, and having their little discussion. He envisioned Dave telling him to vacate the claim, the new owners having made it clear that they did not want him down there. He saw Darcy telling him he was no longer welcome with her. And he allowed a sickening thought to enter his mind. He was to shoot them both, use the dredge to dig out a spot underwater, bury them, and cover it over to appear untouched. He was to then drive Dave's car to that creek, dump it past the old Model T, and place the pine log back on the stump to look like it had never been moved. He could use a tree branch to wipe out the tracks. He could head toward the pine on the ridge with the pointing branch, and with any luck, be back at camp before dark. If not, he could bivouac in the trees, and walk down in the morning. He would dump the sluice load of black sand and gold dust back into the river, and dredge some regular gravel onto the virgin ground. Then he should walk out to retrieve Dan's flatbed truck and head to town. And of course, he would tell everyone that Dave and Darcy had left out for somewhere, and there would be no mention of the gold. With luck, the new claim owners would pull out, and he could come back months later to get his gold. It was as if logic was telling him 'you have done everything that was required to find the gold, now you must do what is required to keep it.' But Tom had another thought; 'that is the kind of thing the Burt Dunlevy's of this world would not hesitate to do!' Tom felt sick at his stomach. If someone had handed him a rifle and ordered him into the battle of war, he would have had no choice. He would have to kill to stay alive. This logic coming into his head was something Tom could never follow on, he was sure. 'How could you have let that into your mind? Can you imagine facing Bill or Lou, and telling the lie? They would see right through you.'

The intersection with the road to the cabin comes up quickly going in, just past a prominent black oak with a board nailed to it. And if you miss it, you suddenly go down a steep incline that you dare not try and back up on the one lane precarious road, nor try and turn at the other sharply angled intersection. You must go all the way down to the river to turn around. Darcy was steeped in thought, looking out over the river, and she slowed at one oak, but it was the wrong one. Then she looked right to say, "this won't take long, and then we'll come right back out. I know that you need your car back, Dave," just as she drove past the oak that both of them were circumvented from noticing.

She slammed on the brakes, but was not able to stop until she was too far down the incline to safely back up.

"I'm not worried about the time…, oh, Darcy, you missed…,"

"Oh, shit! I can't believe I did that!" She banged her hand three times on the steering wheel, the third time so painfully that it added to the tears that could not be held back. "Stupid! Stupid! Stupid!" That sounded familiar. Where had Tom heard that, recently? "Oh crap, I wasn't paying attention. Oh, No! What else? What the hell else?"

"That's alright Darcy; we'll just go down and turn around. I wanted to see the dredge anyway, remember?" He wished now that she would just tell Tom what she was up to. That's all that really needed to be done.

'What was that all about?' Tom thought. 'That makes no sense. We're going to the claim, so what difference does it make?' At this point, Tom was not inclined to try to formulate an explanation for that new turn of events. It simply didn't matter anymore. And as Darcy slowly started down the one lane road, he thought of resolving his final plan, the one he would walk out to the river with, but still, there was that vicious circle of logic. 'I could never in a million years do what a Burt Dunlevy would do. Get that off your mind. I know I'm going to be in a rage if Dave runs me off. I'll just have to watch myself. Who are we talking about here? The woman who just gave me two years of her life! The woman who gave me everything she thought she needed to give me to make me happy! I could never hurt her! I could never let her get hurt, no matter what, no matter how much it hurts me. Draw the line, in your mind,

Tom. Draw that line, that she never suffers the effects of the fight that might now take place.' The fight between Tommy and any entity in the universe that might threaten to take his gold. 'Nothing between heaven and hell is going to cheat me out of my gold.' And almost as a comeback from the universe came the thought of the laughter, the human laughter that he would have to endure, if Tommy ended up with only memories, stories about that day he pulled out the gold. "You had how much gold?" Tom could see himself an old man, sitting at a bar, reliving the story. "Tell us again, Tom, and we'll buy you another."

The most sinister thought of all came into his mind; 'this is why I met the "girl",' as Vernon had called her. 'This is why I was alone when I found the gold. I was destined to do this!' And he could almost feel again the thought that day that someone down river was watching him pick the sluice. Perhaps, some entity, and not some worldly creature. He remembered the scene from "High Noon" where Lon Chaney Jr. tells Gary Cooper, "They planned it." 'It's all been planned here,' he thought. But could he believe? Who or what would have the power to do such a thing? 'You are required to do what is necessary, if you want to keep the gold', the next thought came. 'You must play by the rules. That's how it always works. A sacrifice is required. Who is it going to be? Them or Tommy? Do you really want to keep this gold?' "No!" he said out loud, like a man talking in a dream, and it startled Darcy into staring in the mirror. The expression she now saw was one she had never seen before on this man she had been attracted to two years before. She would not have been attracted to this man.

At the landing, Darcy slowed to circle and head back up the hill, but Tom was out the door as she rolled. "Tom. Please!" She did not have the certainty of tone she had first had that day. "Tom, we want to…," but he was walking swiftly to the tents, so she stopped and cut the engine, and Dave and her both left doors open to walk after him. He dived into a tent and spent several seconds there, then came out carrying his 357 pistol in holster, belt wrapped around it, and he let the belt open to pull the gun out, laying the holster by his feet.

"I just wanted you to know", as he seemed to almost caress the pistol held in one palm. Dave and Darcy both almost missed a heartbeat, reacting much as Tom had done the day Ray fired past his head. There was a look now in his face so similar to Rays look that day; perhaps the power of suggestion transfers this state of mind from one man to another, a look of almost lifelessness as he caressed the gun again, then picked up the holster to carry the pistol back to the tent. "I just want you to know where the pistol is, in case there is any trouble down here." It was an obvious threat; it was meant as one. Dave would have a hard time delivering any arrogant dissertations now, not after that intimidation. Tom placed the pistol under his pillow, then retrieved the little five shot from under the mattress and put it down his front pants, pulling his shirt tail out to cover it. "Let's walk down to the boat and have our talk", as he waved them to walk in front of him. Dave would certainly want to see the equipment, if that was part of the deal when the claim was transferred.

Darcy and Dave walked slowly together, Darcy pulling hard the two smallest fingers of her left hand, feeling so weak in the knees. This was fear, out and out fear of a man she would never have believed would ever cause her to have fear. 'What's going on here? Just tell him. Just start telling him!' Why was it so hard to get it out? Because it was here, at this place!

'Throw the gun!' he thought as he followed. He moved closer to the river, away from the path. 'Throw the gun into the river! It doesn't matter what he has to say. Don't let yourself get to that point. The only way you could do it is to shoot while she's turned away. You could never look her in the face. You would have to shoot before they have a chance to say anything. Throw the gun in the river! This is ridiculous!' There was a noise from up the trail, and Tom turned to see the big gray dog heading down from the landing, but Tom was at such a point of emotion now that it just seemed to ignite everything in him. "YOU GOD DAMNED SON OF A BITCH! I'LL KILL YOU! I'LL KILL YOU!" There was no hint now in the man's mind of why this dog should inspire such a rage, other than it had interfered. He thought of the dog as an earthly creature of good character, and even as the echoes in the canyon died, he was feeling such a wave of regret.

Had it of been possible, Dave and Darcy would have both jumped out of their skins. An artillery explosion would not have caused more terror; they both expected to see a pistol pointed as they turned. Instead, they saw Tom waiving as he yelled, "Come Back! Please, come back!" as the dog ran past the landing and up the road. Darcy realized this might be the dog Tom had told her about, and let go her fingers and walked several steps back. It was all she could do to muster, "Tom!" It came out so soft and weak, but now she felt like the fear was beginning to drain from her body. There was nothing to fear now, she could see that, seeing the tears this man was trying to fight back; the back of his hand wiping at his nose and eyes. She turned back for a moment to say "that's the dog Tom wanted to bring home" to Dave, and turned again just in time to see the falling water from some object Tom had tossed into the river.

"He threw something, Darcy!" Dave whispered. "I think it was...,"

"Shhh. I don't want to know."

"Wait a minute. Just a minute." Tom was still wiping his nose like a little kid. "I need my shovel. Come with me."

"I'll go with him, Darcy. Why don't you wait in the car?" She nodded a yes.

With-in ten minutes, both men appeared walking down the hill, each carrying a coffee can so carefully with both hands, as if the cans exerted some unearthly force. The men both had to keep switching hands on the bottoms of the cans, especially Dave. And when the three of them stood gazing at the two cans, and Darcy picked a nugget out of one, Tom said "They're our wish cans, Darcy. They have to be!"

But Dave had to comment, "this is why...," and the expression on Darcy's face told she understood so well now.

"I have to speak with Darcy alone, Dave." Dave simply nodded and walked to the tables. "Woman, you have to tell me something. I can't keep going on like this! You have to tell me, are we ever going to get married?"

Darcy blinked her eyes, as if the sun were just a little too much, blinks that were in part the indication of the severe stress she was still coming down from. "Of course, Tommy! I've always wanted to marry you. You know that! I just wanted to make sure…, that it was the right time, and that you wouldn't change your mind, like they did."

"We should get married. Now is the time!"

"Yes, we should! We should do it this month. I do love you, Tom, even without that!" The look she gave the gold could have been reserved for a rattlesnake, a Burt Dunlevy, or a Vernon Fickett. She finally was able to walk to the man and hug and kiss him, but it was much like that which would have been given to a friend. It would take some time. For one day of her life she had seen a side of this man she had never envisioned, but she would not let that send her scurrying like a scared rabbit. She would strive instead to prove that she could show the same nerve that her mother was capable of; she was a mountain woman, and she would never forget that.

TWENTY EIGHT

Bill welcomed them that evening with, "are you two all moved in? Where's Dan's flatbed? You know, Tom, they spent a lot of time on that cabin…," but the look on Dave's face made him lose his train of thought.

"I need to be leaving, so let's get it moved."

"Alright, Dave. Bill, we have something to leave with you till Dan gets back." Darcy explained. "Dave and Tom can get it, Bill. You don't need to help. It's very heavy." When the last can had been delivered, Dave walked to his Dodge without even saying Good-Bye, and drove away. He would never again be the friend he had been, but Tom understood that, and would never try and press it.

"There's an awful lot of fine gold left in the sluice, Bill", Tom explained. "So we need to head back down tomorrow to clean up. That's if you don't mind leaving this here alone with Lynn."

"That's alright. I can get Deputy Engle to give it a drive by every once in a while. Who knows? Does Dan know?"

"No, he's out of town."

"Do you want to stay here tonight, to help guard it?"

"Sure."

Saturday morning, Darcy and Tom drove down in their Chevy, Bill followed in his old one-ton truck, with eighteen four gallon steel buckets and a fair sized wooden crate for the black sand in the sluice. Tom was able to make better time, and they arrived to find an old Ford two door at the landing. "Now how can this..., that's Elaine's mother's car..., so how did...?" Darcy said.

"Oh no! Not Vernon, not now!" They both were looking around, up and down the river, up the mountain, until finally, "who's that? I'm going to get my pistol."

"Tom, please, wait!" She could see the top of a head of black hair that seemed to move a little, and then rested in such a position that meant someone was lying face down on the other side of the dredge sluice beside the empty lawn chair. Stripping to his shorts, Tom swam to retrieve the boat that had been tied to the dredge, and paddled furiously back to get Darcy. "Nothing had better be missing!" He said as they stepped on board.

"Oh my God, no!" Darcy had almost tripped running to the other side of the dredge. "Elaine! What's wrong?" Elaine was lying on the pontoon on her stomach, head resting on folded arms.

"He wouldn't come up, so I'll just leave him there. If that's the way he wants to play it, then I just..., I'll just leave him there. It got dark out, and he just didn't care. And then the motor stopped, and I didn't know how to start it." She had been crying.

"Oh, shit no!" Tom felt sick at his stomach, and turned away, fearing he might actually puke.

"Elaine, do you mean Vernon? Elaine, get up. Talk to me, please!" Darcy was almost in tears. "What happened?"

"Elaine, get up, please!" Tom begged. Everything he had felt that day, trapped under the rock, it was all coming back. "Where is Vernon?" He knew. 'This place is cursed. It just didn't stop.'

"Elaine, did Vernon Dive?" Darcy grabbed Elaine's left arm and helped pull her up till she could sit on folded legs. Elaine just slowly moved her head from side to side. She didn't want to acknowledge anything. "Elaine, when did you come down?"

"Last evening," she said like a little girl.

"Oh hooh!" Darcy almost inhaled the last of the 'hooh'; she was breathing in little jerks. "Oh Jesus, no!" she whispered to Tom, and they walked away from Elaine. "She's been here all night. Oh dear God!" She was pulling her two fingers like she would pull them off.

"All night! I left the regulators out here, and the dredge tank was half full of gas. He ran out. He was probably using an underwater flashlight. How could he do something like this, bring her down here? I'm not going down there! He's dead! I'm not going down there ever again!"

"No one has said you have to get him. Please, Tom, help me get her back to the car. She's in shock. Don't say much of anything to her. Here comes Bill. Help me to get her off this." Tom walked over to gently grab Elaine's left arm, as Darcy said "Elaine, it's time to go home, baby. It's time to take your mother's car home."

But Elaine's eyes widened in terror. "No, what do you mean? You want to leave him?"

"No Elaine, someone will come and get Vernon." Darcy said soothingly.

"They'll be gentle with him?"

"Of course they will, honey. We have to take your mother's car home."

Tom could feel again the terror of that day under the rock. 'No one could ever imagine that, only those who have experienced it', he thought. On the trail back to camp Tom walked ahead to greet Bill and fill him in out of earshot, and the two decided to go ahead and clean the sluice and wait for the Sheriff to get down there. Tom kissed Darcy at the old Ford, but could simply think of nothing to say to Elaine. Anything that came to mind seemed like something that would just make it worse. "Drive careful!" he demanded.

At the dredge, they found new rock loading the box, and both men threw rock into the river away from the trench. There was new gold in the box, and there were some pickers, but not many. Vernon obviously hadn't been down long before it happened, and then the dredge just kept running till it died. When Deputy Engle got there about four, the men had the sluice cleaned and all the buckets loaded in the truck. Engle filled out a report and told them that Sheriff Ramey had decided to wait until the rescue divers from Sacramento got there the next day before sending down the coroner. No one that day volunteered to even take a look underwater.

As they drove both the Chevy and Bill's truck out in dimming light, Tom spotted something under a tree beside the road, perhaps a quarter of a mile in from 49, and stopped and walked to tell Bill, "could you wait a minute? I don't like what I see."

"Is that a dog?"

"Yes. I'm going to come back and bury him tomorrow when I speak to the Sheriff. I just want to take a look." He knew the dog was dead. He just knew. The dog lay on its side, eyes starting to dry out. Rigor mortis seemed to have not set in yet, he could tell as he patted the dog's side. It was much skinnier that when he had first seen it. "Why didn't you come back last week fella? I would have fed you!" Who knows how the mind of an animal works, what its motivations are. If the dog had been looking for help for someone, it could have been so obsessed with its mission it did not even think of food. That was Tom's suspicion, now more than ever. "And you scared it away!" It hurt to say these words, for so many reasons. Why did it die? There were no marks, no hint of violence. It probably was starving. Could this have been a day too long without food? Or perhaps, it had just given up the will to live. That could have happened if it had gone back and found its master dead. 'Quit thinking like that, Tom! There was nothing you could do.' This was just another of a long string of bad logic that had gone through his mind recently, and grudgingly he had to admit, 'he was just a dog.'

That did not take, something in the recess of his mind would not buy it, and the man found himself wiping a few tears with the back of his hand, but not so obviously as Darcy had done at the funeral of her kitty, Joe Joe. That was something some animals seemed to have the power to effect on some people. People who are in shock at the funeral of a loved one may sit and stare, but then cry openly at the death of a pet. "Why didn't you come back for food?" he demanded. "I would have followed you; at least I would have tried."

And now the last bit of vile logic this place had to offer came into the man's mind. The implication here was so obvious; the dog was a reminder. Darcy had again been saved from a dire fate by an unknown dog. "Ridiculous!" the man said harshly out loud, as Bill walked up behind him. Tom tried to hide the tears.

"What's ridiculous, Tom?"

"Oh, the dog could have come down to the claim, and I would have fed it. It starved to death." Tom was having trouble getting these choking words out, as if he had a severe cold. It was ridiculous; there was no way the man would ever have bought into the logic of the beast. He could never have been deceived. But the logic concerning the dog was there. It would forever be a thorn in his side. That he had tangled with "El Beastio", he had no doubt, and he would forever be wary. A sacrifice had been required; a substitution had been made, and the man would always wonder if there was some retribution waiting for him down the line. He had cheated the Beast, and it was a comfort to believe that the Beast did not have absolute power in the universe, and there were times when fate could ruin the Beast's motives. But the Beast had a power to be reckoned with, of that the man had no doubt.

The next day, Tom drove down that dirt road one more time. It took a good two hours to bury the dog, with a stack of stones for a monument. And then he headed to see Sheriff Ramey. That didn't take long, and Tom wanted to leave before he had to witness the retrieval of Vernon's body. He was at the car opening the door when he heard a yell from downriver, and then another. He would wait to give Joe Randolf a ride. Sheriff Ramey had to talk to Joe, too, but that was short, and they started up the road. "I saw something the other day, young fella." Joe was talking very casual. "I was coming up to talk to you, and I saw you doing something on the dredge." Tom looked hard at him, and the man nodded yes. "It didn't take long to figure out what you were doing, and I guess I just decided to leave you alone that day, being that you were all alone. The next day I came back up, and you were gone. I know where you buried the cans, Tom. I guess I have to admit, it was very tempting to think about hygrading you. I figured I could do so much for my niece and her kids. You probably wouldn't have noticed what I figured on taking, but I had to stop and think. I had to think about how much I personally hate a cheat, and I had to talk myself out of it." Tom glanced with a grin of relief. "Later that day I saw the three of you come down the path, just as I was coming back up canyon. I was still behind those alders down there, and I was going to yell at you. But…," Tom almost swallowed his own breath, trying to not to choke. "You yelled something, at whom, I don't know. And then I saw you throw something in the river." The old man had an inquisitive, demanding look.

"I yelled at a dog, a stray dog in camp. And I threw a pistol in the river, one that used to belong to Darcy's mother. That's the best place for it." That seemed explanation enough.

Vernon had been a cheat, no doubt, but Tom had to admit one thing to himself; Vernon had to have balls to do what he did, he granted him that. In Vernon's circle, pulling off a night's hygrading would have been considered a triumph, just as in some Indian tribes of the old west successfully stealing horses from another tribe would have brought great honor to a warrior. Life is all about survival, in the world of men, as in the world of animals, and that is always, in their minds, an excuse for those in need to do what they consider necessary to survive. There is rarely an absolute line between good and evil, and this shady area of human deeds must be considered one of the Beast's finer achievements. Had Vernon dredged more gold, picked the sluice, and then made it look like it had been before he started, no one might have been the wiser.

Five days later, Darcy asked Tom to attend the small funeral at Vernon's parents' back yard family cemetery plot near the small town of Alleghany. Tom was reluctant, but she insisted it would be all right, as Lou and Ray would be there, and it would be a show of respect for that community. There were a lot of mountain boys there, a few that were a little more prosperously attired that the rest, probably mine workers, and all seemed friendly enough to Tom, even Vernon's parents. One of the better dressed men, a cousin, gave a eulogy, and it ended with this: "We all know that we never want to hear that long mine whistle, the one that goes on for ten minutes. I heard it once at the Empire, and it seemed to go on forever. They brought up four bodies that day. Well, boys, it's time for a shift change whistle for my cousin Vernon, and this one should go on for ten minutes. Lord, forgive him his ways. He was only looking for a better life. And don't we all look for that better life?"

TWENTY NINE

Darcy Dunlevy McEarl and Thomas Riley Hendrick were married at the Downieville Baptist Church the second Saturday of July, 1959. Darcy wore a borrowed ancient wedding dress a friend lent her, and it fit a little loose, but she looked stunning in it. They had tried to keep it as low profile as possible, with invitations by phone, and a general suggestion that all who felt they would like to attend would be welcome. That was almost a mistake. The church was intimidatingly packed, many more than they had envisioned, and Tom kept thinking, 'I'm marrying one of Downieville's favorite daughters.' And outside, people were waiting in their cars just to throw rice. It was a crowd like Downieville rarely saw, quite a few Tom had recognized from Vernon's funeral, and they truly seemed to be enjoying the spirit of the moment. This was an excuse for these people to come together and literally share in the joy of the marriage, and it could actually transfer some of this joy to the well wishers and make them temporarily forget the harder side of life they must sometimes endure. And perhaps also, it was fated to serve as a partial mending of the rift between the two communities. The two towns had been cheated out of another wedding those many years before, but the pendulum of fate swings in both directions.

As they drove away in the Chevy Styleline Coupe, all shined up, dragging ten feet of cans behind them, with rice bombarding them a hundred feet down the road, Darcy suddenly looked to the side, a change of expression to disbelief. Tom looked past her and glimpsed an old man standing back from the crowd, standing so straight and unmoving, except there was an absolute direct stare into Tom's eyes. Darcy frowned and turned back, "Was that...?" Tom asked.

"That was the man that gave me my first nugget." Darcy did not look like she was feeling well. Tom looked back through the rear window, slowing way down for another look. There he was, so straight, so stiff, with eyes that looked straight into Tom's eyes, but they were kind eyes. "I heard he had died", she said in wonder.

"I'm glad he's with us still", Tom said, and then thought 'I don't believe in apparitions.'

Within the month the couple had bought a three bedroom single story brick home in Marysville, one with a chain link instead of white picket fence, and of course they paid cash for it. Dan had agreed that exactly fifty percent of the gold was Tom's, and Tom was going to be very careful with his seed money. He opened three bank accounts, one for everyday use, one for his new business, and one for a college fund. Darcy was pregnant now, and it was believed she had conceived sometime in June, and had been pregnant at the wedding. Agnes drove down twice, sometimes three times a week, thoroughly pestering Darcy and Rene, but Rene was learning to be tolerant. Both women had their opinions on so many things; diet, exercise, doctor visits, but there was a mutual understanding that they had a common cause. Tom's new business, Tom's Auto Specialist, now employed two mechanics, both older that Tom, at the used double garage building Tom has purchased reasonably with the help of a bank loan. James Atkinson was Tom's shop manager, a professional mechanic who had once worked for Allen Conrad, and quit him. James had a good reputation, and did not hesitate to correct Tom on his occasional mistakes. Allen Conrad now also ran a private garage. Tom heard that he had been asked to give up his Chevron Franchise, due to many customer complaints. Tom told his employees that neither Allen nor his workers were welcome in Tom's shop. And as he had boasted to Dave Johnston, Tom walked Darcy into the Chevy showroom, and she drove a brand new Bel-Air station wagon off the showroom floor.

But there was still residual negative feedback from that strange month of June. It all happened in one day, a Sunday in August, and then it seemed to be all over with. It started with a Sunday front page newspaper article, complete with photograph to add to the effect the story was intended to have on the reader. The editorial was a warning to the public in general, done with the cooperation of law enforcement agencies, and the photo was of a man being strapped into the gas chamber. He was being executed for murder, and the article gave the sordid details of the process of getting him ready for death. Tom unfolded the paper and began reading before he realized what it was about, and he almost choked as it hit him, tears of rage and shame forced upon him. He felt claustrophobic and quickly turned to the second section. Darcy had the good sense to not ask what was going on. Then she turned the radio on and caught part of ballad that seemed so popular at the time. Tom had heard this several times before, each time becoming a little more familiar with the intention of the ballad. "Hang down your head Tom Dooly. Hang down your head and cry…," Tom loathed this ballad. He had good reason. "Met her on the mountain. There I took her life. This time tomorrow, reckon where I'll be. Somewhere down valley, hanging from an old oak tree."

"TURN THAT CRAP OFF!" Oh, how he wished he could take those words back. They came out so quickly, so angrily, so hateful. He did not mean them for her. Darcy quickly turned the channel and caught a tune that was timed by divine providence. "I want to be …, Ba, ba, da. Ba, ba, da. Your teddy bear." Darcy leaned against the kitchen counter, hands pushing, as if she could push it all away, and sang in unison to her favorite Elvis tune. The man tried controlling his voice as he caught up with her. "I don't want to be your lion, cause lions play too rough…," They were getting back in tune, that fine tuning of their earthly partnership. When they finished with "Just let him be, your Teddy Bear. I just want to be your Teddy…, Bear." It was as if the rift had been completely healed.

But this day was not over with yet. Tom drove down to a neighborhood market to get some milk a half hour before they would leave for church, and a strange encounter took place. As Tom came out of the store, a Spanish man with very short hair approached him and said "you know Ted?" This man he had never seen before inspired all kinds of suspicions, his motives probably of bad intent, and Tom's mind quickly formulated the comeback, 'I don't know any Ted. You've got the wrong guy,' but, just as he almost produced the denial from his lips, another part of his mind caught the implication, and he said simply, "I know Ted."

"You're Tom Hendrick, right?" Tom nodded yes. "Ted wanted me to give you a message. I just got out. He's getting out early, for good behavior. He wants to see Barbara again."

"Tell Ted he is welcome to come to my garage. He will understand. I'll do my best, just tell him that." Tom reached in his wallet and handed the man what he thought was to be a ten.

The man started to walk away, and then came back. "You handed me a twenty. Did you really want to...?'

Tom intended it to be a ten, but said, "To help you get started." It was ironic an ex-con would be straight with him, but of course Tom was Ted's contact. Tom felt right in that good deed of the day.

As the couple finished prepping to look their Sunday best, the next strange occurrence came with the ring of the doorbell. Lou Montgomery and Ray Shannon were standing as if to prevent their departure. Lou had very serious business on his mind. "Tom, I have to talk to you, because I can't get anything out of Dan. Man, he's acting ridiculous. I think he's gone crazy. I know too many people who want to go to work down there, and by God, I'm going to get to the bottom of this. Dan says he wants you to be his foreman, and he won't start without you. What's this crap about?"

"Lou, please! Come and sit down," Darcy offered.

"No thank you. I know that you're getting ready for church, and this is bad timing, so I won't stay long. I just want an explanation from Tom. Couldn't you come down with us for a while, just to get started?"

"I've talked to Dan over and over again. He keeps calling here. I've got a business now, Lou. I can't leave that. I don't know what's going on with Dan, but you guys are going to have to convince him to get going. I'm not ever going back down there, and I told him that. I told him to hire you, Lou. Do you believe that?"

"I heard you did that. Thank you. What's wrong with this man? Even his wife says that he's changed. There are just too many people out of work. He can't be that greedy. I've always heard he was a fair man."

"Lou, I almost died down there, before Vernon. I'll never go back."

"Thomas! We don't have any secrets from each other!" Darcy grabbed his arm.

"You see, Lou. I can't go back. You guys are going to have to talk to him."

"Lou, let's leave them to go to church. We've had our talk." Ray grabbed the more powerful man by the arm, and Lou let out a sigh.

"I'm sorry Tom. I didn't know. God help me, I've got a crew all ready, but you were there all by yourself, that's true, and I'm sure you could have used us then."

"I called you then, remember? I sure could have used you!" Lou nodded, and the two men walked away to the car.

Tom would not have enjoyed listening to the phone conversation between a Downieville stonecutter named

Gus Harding and Darcy that afternoon. Tom had some chores in the garage that would take him half an hour and she took this time to check on a little secret project that was intended as a future monument of her admiration of a husband. It was a grim subject; it was inevitable, and she did not enjoy the idea of living past him. One of the two hard, gray Sierra granite headstones now read: 'Thomas Riley Hendrick, Born February 5, 1938. Good Husband, Good Father, Good Provider.' It would be a simple monument to a common man, perhaps inspiring one of the living to walk back and take a second look. It would be a monument of love, so different in motivation from the greed and arrogance that inspire the building of tombs to men like Napoleon.

In the garage, Tom was arranging some memorabilia from the past out of an old chest. Some keepsakes from his youth, a baseball, an old atlas, and then, what he was looking for. An old Prince Albert cigar box with a small piece of scotch tape holding it shut. He broke the tape and pulled a folded piece of paper out, something that his mother had scribbled at the eulogy of his father. She could have asked for a copy, but preferred to do it herself. Tom read the part in her writing; "and we must feel such sorrow for Brother Thomas, good father and husband, lost to that great deceit we call war. That great deceit; so many men cheated out of their future, their happiness, by this deceit. And let us not forget the prisoners of war still missing, and hope that their fate will be better. For there is no greater sorrow for man than to be delivered into the hands of the enemy by deceit. Amen." Tom pulled the tape off a brand new roll to seal the paper and other items back in the cigar box, and tears of rage and despair were coming back. He kept wrapping the box, from one angle, then another as if to seal the air out to double protect the contents. He felt like taking a steel pipe and destroying. He felt like beating all metal till dented beyond repair; all glass till broken into little pieces. He felt like throwing a fit that would make the temper tantrum of a woman look docile, but he was coming down from this rage. He knew that such a fit would only inspire terror in the woman in the other room, and he had vowed to never let that happen again. There was no reason for despair, not with her in his life. "You're a lucky man, Tom," he said to the universe in general, and any entity that might be listening.

He had won the girl, and found his fortune in gold. Tom had come to realize the incredible odds against this concerning the gold. The odds against finding it, and the odds against being able to keep it, being he was a common man. Thinking on this had made him appreciate one truth about the economic system of the country he lived in. It would have been an outrage in the minds of the tyrants of history to realize that some men of intelligence and determination had in his county amassed fortunes not by hoarding gold, but by catering to the common man. They had created a system dedicated to the mass production of inexpensive commodities that even the poor could afford. He did not see it as a perfect system, there were those who suffered and fell behind, but it seemed preferable to the systems of the past. Far preferable to the tyranny of the Aztecs. Tears all done, a good day yet to be had, the man walked up the pull down garage attic ladder to store away that sacred cigar box, forever.

EPILOGUE

Now if you take one of the dirt roads that lead west, one of the roads past the last Highway 49 bridge over the North Yuba south of Downieville, and if you know which of the intersections to take after that, you may find yourself at a fisherman's camp landing. A favorite place to for those wanting to get to where the wild trout live. You'll see one of the biggest pools on the river, and you'll be able to walk downstream to a long zone of river with no road access. Sheriff Ramey retired, and spent years trying to nail that granddaddy German Brown, but he never got it. And if you walk the river enough, you may see all kinds of antique objects in the shallow water that may have washed out. Old rusted mining picks, old lanterns, and even old mining car wheels. And perhaps, even, an old rusted five shot, break down 32 pistol. Another item you might see is a rotten mining claim post with a rusted Prince Albert can nailed to it. You might think it too old to be valid, but actually, it's been sold three times since Dan McKenzie sold it in September, 1959. It is now in the portfolio of a Canadian holding company. But other than that, it is a beautiful place to camp and fish. Nature is always patiently trying to remove the evidence of man's follies. The trench has long since filled in, that trench in the mighty North Yuba that one Thomas Hendrick pulled five hundred sixty-three troy pounds, seven troy ounces of gold out of one Wednesday afternoon in June of 1959. And you should know that unto this very day, no one has managed to re-excavate that pool.

End.

www.ingramcontent.com/pod-product-compliance
Lightning Source LLC
Chambersburg PA
CBHW051442260626
47162CB00001B/207

* 9 7 8 1 4 2 6 9 2 3 8 6 9 *